The Bet

(Indecent Intentions, Book 1)

Lily Zante

Author's Note

The Bet, (#1, Indecent Intentions), is a spin-off from the from The Billionaire's Love Story (a contemporary romance serial with 9 instalments)

This book is a STANDALONE romance, and while you don't need to have read any of The Billionaire's Love Story previously, it might enhance your reading experience if you do, since most of the characters here appeared in that series first.

LILY ZANTE

The Bet

Perfect Match Series:
The Proposal
Lost In Solo
Heart Sync
Perfect Match Boxed Set (Books 2, 3 & 4)
A Leap of Faith

Tainted Love Series:
(A spin-off from the Perfect Match Series)
Misplaced Love
Reclaiming Love
Embracing Love
Tainted Love Boxed Set (Books 1, 2 & 3)

An Ordinary Hero

Standalone books:
Love, Inc
An Unexpected Gift

Contents

Chapter 1

"**O**ne woman, for life. Hell, no."

Xavier had waited until Tobias was well out of earshot to state his observation. They were sitting outside on leather couches, on the rooftop terrace of The Oasis, the bar his friend owned.

Tobias was flying Luke and his team to his wedding on Kawaya, his three hundred acre private island in Fiji. Luke and his staff were taking care of the drinks for the four day wedding extravaganza.

"He's your brother. Be happy for him," Luke drawled.

"I am happy for him," Xavier insisted. Tobias seemed more relaxed these days, and it was all due to Savannah and Jacob. "It was about time he met someone. I could say the same about you." He glanced at his friend, but Luke kept quiet.

"Not me." Luke shook his head. "I'm too busy to be dealing with women."

Girlish laughter bubbled around the room making Xavier glance over his shoulder. Even though it was late evening and the night sky had darkened to a rich navy-blue, the soft lights from the lamps made it easy to see everyone. He raised his glass to the group of women who sat around a table scattered with jewel colored cocktails. A couple of them acknowledged him with an interested smile.

"Know them?" he asked his friend. Luke seemed to know everyone who came here.

"Lawyers and legal eagles, celebrating an engagement. That's all you need to know."

Xavier eyed them slowly, his gaze lasering in on a woman with long wavy hair and what looked like a big and beautiful pair of breasts. His mouth watered at the sight of her hard-to-miss nipples poking through her silk dress. He flashed a smile at her, appreciating the view.

Even with the slight chill in the air—a promise, in this last week of September that fall was around the corner, it wasn't that cold because of all the heaters Luke had placed around the terrace. Or maybe the woman wasn't cold and was just excited to see him.

"Quit bugging my clientele."

"I don't see them complaining." Xavier lifted his beer bottle to his lips.

"That's because they don't complain to you."

"Bullshit." Xavier looked at his friend dubiously. "Nobody's ever complained to you about me. You're making that shit up."

On second thoughts, it was probably better not to risk anything while Tobias was around. With his wedding to Savannah a week away, his brother could sometimes get easily irritated. In fact his family, especially his parents, seemed to get annoyed when it came to Xavier and his love life. He didn't understand why. He was young. Maybe not so young. But twenty-seven wasn't exactly old.

Tobias was going to celebrate his thirtieth birthday the day before he got married. Talk about hitting two major milestones one after the other.

Luke's gaze drifted to the table of women before returning to him again. "Is Xavier-The-Stud-Stone in action again? Won't your girlfriend mind?"

Xavier rolled his eyes at the mention of the nickname Luke had given him many years ago. "I'm only looking." Gisele wouldn't like him ogling other women, but she wasn't here, and he wasn't about to do anything silly. He wasn't that much of a douchebag. "You all set for the wedding? All set to show off your mixologist skills?" he asked, his fingers curling around the glass bottle.

"Don't call me a mixologist. I don't need any fancy, stupid labels."

"Okay, calm down." But Xavier guessed that his cocktail making skills behind the bar helped him pick up a lot of girls. Not that the dude needed to be behind the bar. "Think of the shit ton of publicity you're going to get from it."

"That's not why I'm doing it," Luke protested.

Xavier snorted in disbelief. "It's not as if you would have turned this opportunity down." It was Tobias Stone's wedding, for fuck's sake.

"Tobias doesn't want any press,"

It was true. Tobias was an intensely private person. "My brother's anal like that."

Luke leaned forward. His sleeves had been turned up, revealing hard, tattooed forearms that had Xavier wondering if he should get a couple of tattoos himself. Chicks loved that stuff. And that, along with the handful of bars and clubs Luke owned in and around New York, made him a babe magnet. Xavier envied him a little, and for having a thriving business which didn't seem like that much hard work.

"I don't blame him. He wants no paparazzi and nothing leaked. I respect that, and I haven't told anyone outside of my team. My staff is discreet, and they won't leak anything to the press. I'm honored that Tobias asked me."

"He's asked you based on my recommendation."

"He's been here plenty of times without you."

Xavier scratched the side of his jaw. "When?" Tobias wasn't a party-animal. "He'd rather watch the stock market than hang out in a bar."

"He's been here a few times with Savannah." Luke's eyes twinkled. He seemed to be enjoying the telling of this news. Xavier angled his head. Yeah, well, things were slightly different now that his brother had met Savannah. These days Tobias was a changed man who had gone from spending most of his time in the office, to actually having a life outside it.

Another shriek of laughter bubbled across from the table behind him, forcing him to cast another look over his shoulder. He quickly scanned around the table and zeroed in on the same woman again. His gaze settled on her a moment longer than usual, until she returned the stare, and then he turned his back on her.

Show interest, but not too much. Raise their hopes, get them excited, and then pull back.

"His fiancée seems like a nice girl," Luke said. "And he looks happy."

"He is. He never used to go out much. I had to drag him out so he could mingle and get some pussy."

Luke slanted an eyebrow. "That was considerate of you."

"I thought so, too." Xavier leaned in, eager to know, "Are you getting any?" Luke's mouth twisted as if he was trying to formulate an appropriate reply. "For a twenty-seven year old, you still talk like a teen."

"I'm being serious, dude."

"I am too. Quit the pussy talk."

Quit the pussy talk? It made him wonder. "Are you batting for the other side?"

"You idiot." Luke gave him one of his you're-a-shithead-looks. "Some of us don't like to talk about it as much as you do."

"Where were we?" Tobias rejoined them, slipping his cell phone away.

"You were about to order a glass of whiskey," Xavier replied, then raised his hand to summon a server. He should have ordered Tobias a drink while he was taking his call.

Tobias turned to Luke. "Do you have everything under control?"

"It's all taken care of," Luke assured him. "I've met with your security guys. We arrive the morning of your birthday, and I'll be there to oversee everything. You don't have to worry about a thing."

The server placed the whiskey glass down, and Xavier slid it over to Tobias. "Here you go, bro."

Tobias dismissed it with a wave of his hand. "No thanks. I'm good."

"Since when did you give up drinking?"

Tobias gave him a hard stare. "I haven't. I don't need one now. Get me a Coke, will you?"

"Coming up." He caught the server's attention again and ordered the drink before turning to Tobias. "You need to loosen up."

"I still have work to do before we fly out. We can't all work from home in our PJs."

Luke sniggered. "What is it that you do again? I've never been able to figure it out."

Tobias grinned back at him. "Let me know when you find out, because I still can't work it out myself."

"He drives a 488 Spider, though," Luke remarked casually. "He can't be doing too badly."

It ground on his nerves, the two of them talking about him like this. "I'm here, guys. I'm right here. And I'm doing fine." Xavier raised his bottle and waved it at the two of them for ganging up on him. Tobias and him were opposites. His brother was far too rigid, far too organized. But then, he was a billionaire running a hedge fund. People thought that because he was Tobias Stone's brother, that he was as successful, and as wealthy. He was nowhere near a billionaire, and never would be, and he'd almost made it to millionaire status a couple of times.

Sad thing was, a million was nothing in today's world. You had to have at least ten mill to get by. "Not all of us get Daddy's trust fund." This was aimed at Luke.

"I gave my old man the middle finger," Luke shot back. "And I'm building my empire with my own blood, sweat and tears. I haven't taken a cent from Daddy."

Tobias listened and nodded his head. He didn't need to say anything because he was a self-made billionaire who counted politicians and captains of industry as his friends. Not particularly close friends, Xavier assumed, but close enough that he could call them up if needed.

It wasn't that Xavier was jealous, but he knew he couldn't rival that. He had never been as smart, or as astute as his brother, and he was painfully aware of the fact. "Laugh all you want, but I've been creating and running businesses ever since I graduated from high-school," he said, a little too defensively. "And I can afford the Ferrari just fine." He lifted his chin in defiance.

"To confirm," said Tobias, ignoring him and turning to Luke again. "Have you got the agenda?"

Luke nodded.

"And you've signed the agreement?"

"Yes. No talking to the press, no pictures, no exclusives for any of the papers or magazines. Understood and noted."

Xavier suppressed a breath. His brother's paranoia bordered on OCD at times. He took a swig of his drink and listened to Tobias and Luke discussing the wedding details. He felt like a third party in a business meeting for two.

He was happy for Tobias. Of course he was, and it was about time things turned around for him, especially after what had happened with Ivy. But honestly, apart from that huge life-changing event, things had always gone pretty smoothly for his brother.

Unfortunately, for himself, things weren't so easy. Business had been slow lately. He didn't have the smarts and the genius to run a hedge fund, but he'd had to find his own way.

He wasn't living off of Tobias's generosity, nor did he want to. The problem with starting and running lots of small businesses, trying and failing many times over before finding a few that worked, was that it wasn't consistent. He was always looking for new business opportunities. But when he made money, and sold a business off, or made good with the stock market, he did pretty well. Well enough to afford a Ferrari and a loft conversion in Tribeca. Well enough to easily afford thousand dollar bottles of champagne when he needed to impress.

But things hadn't been as great ever since he and Petra had broken up. She had been his lucky mascot but ever since the split, at Tobias's party back in July, he hadn't seen her. A week later he'd heard she was doing the rounds with a quarterback from the Miami Dolphins.

Not that he'd been lonely for long. Shacking up with Gisele, a cute B-list actress, had relieved him of too much wrist action.

He looked up as a gorgeous woman swept past their table, then stopped and stepped back, placing her hand on Luke's shoulder and greeting him. Xavier eyed her butt as she talked to Luke, flirting with him like a nymph. Her hand slid down his arm, fingering his skin and tracing over his tattoos. "Come on over and say 'hi', when you've finished, stranger." Her pomegranate red nails squeezed his friend's bicep as a parting gesture. Xavier watched her until she was out of sight, and then turned his attention back to the conversation.

"I think we're done," said Tobias, getting up and shaking hands with Luke. "See you in Kawaya."

"Thank you, for the opportunity." Luke looked chuffed as he got off from his stool then excused himself.

"Lucky son-of-a-bitch," Xavier sniped, watching Luke and the woman talking. "I bet he has everyone's number." It seemed like a waste because for all the phone numbers Luke might have had, Xavier hadn't seen him with anyone for a long time.

Tobias gave him another one of his steely looks. "You're like a walking hard-on."

"This place is full of beautiful women, what do you expect?" The brunette on that table was giving him the come on. His mind was already in the gutter, and he could see by the way she licked her lips that hers wasn't far behind.

"You haven't confirmed if your girlfriend is coming."

"Would you mind if she did?" His mother would give him a hard time, and he would have to make sure she didn't get her claws into Gisele for too long.

"I don't care if she does or not," replied Tobias, icily. "But if her coming stops you from hitting on all my guests, then go for it."

"You have the wrong impression of me, bro."

15

"Do I?" Tobias sounded testy. "If she comes, she'd better stick to my privacy policy."

That's what he was worried about. He wasn't sure Gisele could keep her mouth shut. She was easily impressed, and a little too text-happy. Each time they went out she'd take pictures and post them to her social media accounts before they'd even had dessert.

"If she's not on Vivian's list, she's not getting in."

Tobias and his goddamn lists. Xavier didn't envy Vivian, Tobias's new PA, the task of organizing the list of attendees. This 'small' wedding was turning out to be a security nightmare, and Xavier was still none the wiser as to what had happened to Candace, Tobias's previous PA.

He'd had her once, in the supplies cupboard in The Vault, Luke's club in the basement. He'd had her up against the door with her legs wrapped around his waist, and her panties around one ankle. Maybe he shouldn't have, what with her being Tobias's PA, but the girl was a flirt, and she'd wanted it. And he had been single at the time.

It had been a simple case of supply and demand.

Maybe it was as well that she had left, or had been fired, or whatever. Even Matthias, who had been a close friend of his brother's for as long as he could remember, had gone at the same time, and Xavier was still none the wiser as to what had happened to either of them.

Tobias refused to discuss it.

Xavier ventured another try, at the risk of getting shot down, as he had on the other occasions. "Are Candace and Matthias coming?"

"No." The tone of Tobias's voice warned him against probing further.

He could take the hint. He knew that if someone pissed Tobias off, his brother would cut them off and be done with them.

"You're flying with mom and dad, right?" Tobias asked, indicating the topic was done with.

"Yup."

Fuck, yes. Xavier's insides tanked at the thought. Gisele had to come, if only to be a distraction. The seventeen-hour flight from New York to Fiji, with a stop in LA, was tough enough, and if his parents were going to be on the same flight, it was going to be hell on earth. On landing, they had to take a small plane or a boat from the main airport to Kawaya.

The thought of being stuck on the flight made his stomach churn. "Shame you decided to go a few days beforehand." Otherwise they could all have traveled on Tobias's private jet, and it would have made the journey bearable.

"It's my wedding, and I'll do whatever the hell I want." Tobias was traveling a few days earlier with Savannah and Jacob. Everyone else was coming a few days later on commercial flights, all paid for by Tobias.

With it taking almost an entire day to get there, then four days on the island and a day to get back, it was going to be nearly a whole goddamn week. He had to make sure Gisele came along because, in that heat, with his parents and god knows who else, on an island that was remote; he'd go crazy unless he had something to do. And doing Gisele would be the best way of passing the time.

Tobias gulped down his drink and announced that he was leaving.

"Already?"

He'd been hoping to hang around The Oasis for longer, and spend some increasingly rare time with his brother who he barely got to see much these days. It used to be the case that he could convince Tobias to come out every few months. Xavier used to insist on it just to get his workaholic brother out into the world of the living. But, ever since he had met and fallen in love with Savannah and her young son, Jacob, his brother no longer seemed to have much time for anyone else. Xavier missed that, a little.

"Has Savannah ordered you to be home for dinner?" The idea of domestic bliss bored the hell out of him.

"I promised Jacob I'd be home early."

Xavier's eyebrows shot north. Pretty soon Tobias Stone's household would be like The Waltons. Saccharine bliss.

Enough to make him want to puke. What the hell had happened to the man once dubbed New York's most eligible bachelor? Not that Tobias had ever been a player but, as Gisele had shown him on one of those stupid online celebrity websites, his brother still held strong on the list. It didn't seem to matter that Tobias Stone was getting married. But what irritated him was seeing that he was number seven. And what pissed him off even more was finding out that Luke was number four.

Number fucking four.

And the man didn't even seem to be interested in chicks.

As for himself, he knew why he was so far down the list. He was nowhere near as wealthy as Tobias.

He wasn't a billionaire.

Yet.

And if truth be told, he wasn't so sure he wanted to work that hard to become one. He was doing pretty well as he was.

Chapter 2

"Tobias Stone seems like a nice guy," said Cara, picking up a magazine and showing her the center pages. "See."

"Then it must obviously be true," said Izzy, running her hand through her dark hair. She flicked her bangs away from her face, but it would only take a shake of her head to have them falling back over her eyes again.

"He's not a creep, Iz. He's New York's hottest bachelor."

Izzy turned to her in consternation. "I didn't know Gideon Shoemoney was a creep either." Otherwise she would never have agreed to baby-sit for his two young children during summer.

The Shoemoneys had paid her well for covering evenings and on weekends while their au-pair had gone back home to France for the summer. Izzy's parents hadn't been too happy when she'd told them she couldn't come home for the holidays, but she had never intended to anyway. Pittsburgh didn't have the same buzz about it that New York did, and after her first year at Columbia had flown by, she was keen to stay here for the summer before entering her sophomore year.

By the end of this college year, she wanted an internship at a top firm. Even a middle one would do. But top would be better.

"You have to let that go, Iz. Shoemoney can't get to you now, and not everyone is going to be a pervert like him."

"Yeah, well ..." Just because she'd left their employment didn't mean she was over it. And just because she had fought back didn't mean she wasn't afraid of something like that happening again. He still owed her some outstanding wages, but she had written those off. With the way she had left, she had no desire to go back and ask for it, though she sometimes wondered what Shoemoney's wife had made of her abrupt departure. She had been away on business, that last time, and was often away each time her husband behaved inappropriately. She hadn't called Izzy to ask why she had left, and it sometimes made her wonder if she knew what went on.

"We're marching aren't we?" Cara reminded her. "And when we march with thousands of other women, we'll be sending out a powerful signal that men can't do this and get away with it. Not anymore."

"Maybe."

Cara flicked through the pages, and stopped. "His brother looks hot," she squealed, examining the article as if it were an exam paper. "And he's dating Gisele Steiner!"

Izzy shook her head. "Never heard of her." Nor did she care. What concerned her more was whether she was doing the right thing by accepting the job which Savannah had offered her—to babysit Jacob on weekends, as and when needed. But, before that, Savannah had asked her something that had taken her breath away.

How would you like to spend five or six days keeping Jacob company so that he doesn't get too bored at our wedding?

Izzy had had to ask Savannah to repeat the request, because she wasn't sure she heard right. Cara had nearly had a seizure when Izzy told her later.

"You're going to Fiji? To the wedding of the year?" Cara had yelled, "That isn't work, girlfriend, that is a dream!"

"It's not Fiji. It's their own—his own—private island. Kawasaki, or something." Izzy couldn't remember what it was called, even though Savannah had told her enough times.

"Staten Island is the closest I'll ever get to an island," whined Cara. "I don't care if it's Tobias Stone's private island or his shed," Cara airquoted the last few words. "If it's in Fiji, then who cares?"

And so she had decided 'yes'. Yes, she would gladly accompany Jacob to their wedding. The rest, working for them, weekends and maybe evenings, babysitting, she would have to think about.

She had to go and see Savannah now, to sign the paperwork.

"I wish you could take me with you," Cara said, yet again. "I'd ask you to put me forward for that role, but I hate kids. Can't stand the brats."

"Jacob isn't a brat," said Izzy. "But you might have been, once."

Cara swatted her butt gently. "You don't even look excited."

"I am." She was. But what if Tobias Stone was like Gideon Shoemoney?

"I couldn't tell," quipped Cara, drily. "You get to fly in his private jet!"

Izzy grinned. She hadn't told her parents yet. Flying to a billionaire's private island, on his private jet would be the last thing her parents wanted to hear. She didn't want to send her dad over the edge again. She wasn't sure what he would make of it.

"Are you going to accept her other offer?"

"I don't know," Izzy replied, bunching her hair into a ponytail. "Creeps don't have that name branded on their foreheads."

"You said Savannah's nice, down-to-earth and honest. She wouldn't be about to marry Tobias if he was an asshole, would she?"

"Some women don't know the men are assholes until it's too late." But Cara had a point. Savannah was nice, and the two of them had gotten on well when Izzy had met her for that first time at her engagement party. It had been a few weeks after that when Savannah had contacted her to ask if Izzy wouldn't mind babysitting Jacob for a few hours now and then. Savannah had told her that she didn't trust anyone with her son, and that Izzy was the exception. At that time, Izzy had been busy working for the Shoemoneys, but a month later, after what had happened in the laundry room, she'd left.

Luckily, she still had her other two jobs, one as a virtual assistant to a guy rolling out online courses, and the other taking care of ad campaigns for a mom and pop home business. It was steady money, and good money, and better than working at a fast-food place, or a bar. Plus, she could do it in her own hours, once her college work was done.

Needing to fill the gap in income, she'd called Savannah on the off chance and it turned out that luck had been in her favor.

She picked up her cell phone and handbag. "Am I doing the right thing, Cara? Do I need the money that bad?"

"You need the money that bad."

She swallowed, and let out an angry breath. Being broke was a crap state of affairs, and studying for her Media and Communications degree wasn't the thing to do, not from the small town she came from.

But federal grants, juggling the three jobs—two now that she'd left the Shoemoneys—careful spending, and eating noodles and bread more than was probably good for her, meant she had her best shot at making something of her life.

She needed to get that degree, then land a great job at a hotshot company, and she was going to do it all by herself. She wasn't going to take a cent from her parents, not that they had much in the way of financial aid to give her. Studying was her way of breaking away and going to the city, and standing a chance of getting a corporate job. She was going to dazzle New York with her smarts and her drive— the kind of drive her father had once had. Seeing him broke, and so low, with his dream in tatters was more than enough ammunition for her to pursue her dreams and make a good life for herself, and, in due course, help her family. She would make her parents proud, and show her father that it was going to be alright. The poor man had suffered enough, the family had suffered enough.

"Iz." Cara came up to her. "Don't beat yourself up about what happened. It wasn't your fault. I don't think Tobias Stone is anything like that perv."

She shrugged. "Maybe you're right."

"If you're not sure, use the week of the wedding to decide. Tell Savanah you're not sure and you're worried it might impact your studies, but personally, I don't think you need to worry much about Tobias Stone. If there's anyone you should worry about, it's his brother. He's hot stuff. A player, and ohmigod, he's a looker. Both of them are, but he's still—"

23

"Seeing someone, remember? And I'm really not interested."

"Okay. I'm just warning you. Go and sign your contract."

"That's what I've decided."

A private jet to an island in the South Pacific—she knew because she'd looked it up on the world map, and an invitation to the wedding of the year?

She would be insane not to do it.

~ ~ ~

Savannah, she had learned, was like her, a girl from a small town. Not a city girl by any means.

How had she ended up falling for a billionaire?

"Don't you find it crazy?" Izzy asked. They were sitting in the huge living room of Tobias's Upper East Side apartment, a place, Savannah had told her, they would soon be leaving because Tobias was having their new home completely refurbished, and the extensive building work was still underway.

"I find the media circus crazy. Kay keeps me grounded, tells me not to read any blogs or comments, or the papers. She says she'll have a look for me."

That cousin, Kay. Izzy had met her that one time at the party. "It's good of her to look out for you like that."

"But at times, when she can't hold back, she'll tell me some nasty piece of gossip she read about, of Tobias having an affair because he'd been photographed with someone. It's ridiculous what people can print."

"People can be nasty."

"Yes they can," Savannah agreed. "I can see why, though. Tobias was a catch, and then I turned up and caught him, so

THE BET

to speak, and now that we're getting married, I've ruined the fantasy for some of these women."

"You're a catch too," Izzy retorted.

Savannah laughed.

"You are," she insisted, hating the way some women played themselves down. "You seem down to earth, and probably nothing like the vipers he comes across."

According to Cara the man had been a workaholic, and had suffered tragedy years ago.

"Hey, Jacob." She greeted the young boy as he walked in.

"Hey, Izzy." He gave her a wide smile. "We're going to have fun, you and me," he announced.

"I know," she replied, looking at his cheeky and adorable face. So different now to that first time she had met him. "I would expect nothing less."

"Don't forget your swimming costume. I've got my Iron Man swimming trunks ready."

"I won't."

"Tobias says we've got the whole place to ourselves, and the entire sea." His eyebrows lifted as if he couldn't comprehend the enormity of the sea belonging to one man. "And there's a pool. Or was it four pools, Mommy?"

"It doesn't matter if there's one or ten you can only ever go in one pool at a time," his mother replied.

This seemed to satisfy Jacob. "Can I sit next to you on the plane?"

"I don't know." Izzy looked at Savannah. She had no idea about the travel plans. All she knew was that it was some place in Fiji.

"Honey," Savannah said, holding out her hand as Jacob came in for a cuddle. "I need to discuss a few things with Izzy. Why don't you go and play for a while?"

"Okay."

"Are you sure you're fine about taking a few days off college?" Savannah asked her. "I would hate to impact your studies, and I know that your semester has only just started."

Savannah had obviously picked up on her hesitation, and it can't have been that difficult because she hadn't exactly gushed like a prepubescent teen when Savannah had first made her the offer.

Rich men were crooks and creeps and she didn't trust them. The only reason Izzy was even considering taking those few days off, with weekend in the middle so it wasn't that much time away from her studies, was because she needed the money, and because she would be surrounded by people. Savannah wasn't going to leave her alone with Tobias, the way Cassia Shoemoney had. Still, it would be an easy few days, and Cara would never forgive her if she turned the opportunity down now.

"I'll be okay," she insisted. She would work like crazy and make sure she was all caught up as soon as she returned. "I adore Jacob. I think we'll have a lot of fun."

"Good. Jacob feels so comfortable with you, and that's important to me. I find myself trusting people less these days."

"I understand."

"It's not as if my parents wouldn't take care of Jacob, they would, but I think he would get bored. And I want them to enjoy the wedding. I want you to enjoy the wedding and your time there as well. I just feel that Jacob would have a better time with a younger person running around with him. I was hoping Rosalee would come—she used to look after Jacob before, but her daughter-in-law is about to have another baby, and she doesn't want to miss it."

"Don't worry about me, or my studies. I'm really looking forward to it. I've never been to Fiji."

"Me neither," Savannah confessed. She bunched her hair over one shoulder, and sat back, looking happy and worried at the same time. "There's so much to do. Sometimes I get so overwhelmed."

"I can imagine." She was worried about spending a few days on the island, but Savannah's whole life had changed. It was a gigantic leap. No wonder she looked slightly flushed. "But you'll be fine. I think it's normal, a new bride feeling anxious." She smiled at her, and Savannah returned the smile.

"I have some paperwork for you to sign. I'm sorry to make it so formal."

"Don't be. I understand."

"It's just that Tobias is completely paranoid about his privacy, especially when it comes to personal matters."

"It's fine with me. Where do I sign?"

"Here," said Savannah, pointing. "And you'll consider my offer to be available on weekends? I just need a little help, what with the house move, and other things …"

"I can let you have my final answer once we get back?"

"Once you get back?" Somehow she sensed that this wasn't the answer Savannah had wanted. "That's fine."

"Ummmm." Izzy cupped her chin. "Where do we get the … uh… plane?" Did she go to the airport?

"I'll get Morris to pick you up, and take you to the airfield."

"Morris?"

"He's the chauffeur," Savannah explained. "Oh, and you'll have to get used to the bodyguards."

Bodyguards?

"They'll be following you, us, everywhere. It's a bit daunting at first, but you soon forget about them."

"Cool."

Bodyguards? A chauffeur picking her up and taking her to the airfield, before she got on the private jet?

Cara was going to hyperventilate when she told her.

Chapter 3

A week later she was lying on a recliner around an aquamarine, kidney-shaped pool, with sun-loungers and cocoon pods dotted around. It was surrounded by tropical gardens, and a small walkway led to sun-kissed white sandy beaches. Tobias and Savannah were in separate hammocks under the palm trees and Jacob was further away, near the sand.

"Izzy, come and see this!" he yelled.

She got up from her recliner and held her flat hand against her forehead, like a shade from the sweltering sun. Staring at him, she couldn't help but admire the scenery. It was like a snapshot from a luxury holiday brochure.

"Izzy! Look!" Jacob held up something she couldn't make out.

"I'm coming!"

She got up and sauntered over, barefoot.

"He's not letting you have a moment's peace, is he?" Savannah, in her two-piece brilliant blue bikini, looked up from her book.

"He's excited. I'm excited!" Izzy waved at him. Kawaya was a picture perfect paradise straight out of a movie. It was a world away from her lectures and the bustle and chaos that was New York.

Even stepping foot into Tobias's private plane had her spell-bound, and no matter how much she tried not to be dazzled by such wealth, she couldn't hold back her amazement. The interior of the plane was fancier than anything she had ever seen in real life. It was luxurious, and stylish, with large cream leather seats, huge, shiny, TV screens, sleek wooden tables and vases of flowers.

Vases full of flowers on a plane?

They had arrived yesterday, and gone straight to bed, exhausted after the long flight, but this morning had been her chance to see exactly what Kawaya was like.

"Look," said Jacob, and gave her a map of the island. It was huge, with a sprawling huge main house where the immediate family stayed. Savannah had insisted that Izzy also have a room there, next to Jacob. For the rest of the guests, there were lots of small cabins dotted around, further along the beach.

The island had a waterfall and in the main, it was unspoiled, still in a state of natural beauty.

The bodyguards were discreet. Every now and then she caught sight of them in their black t-shirts and black trousers, and felt sorry for them, wondering how they kept so cool in the heat. Though a gentle wind kept the edge off.

"What have you got there, Jacob?" He was squatting, in his Iron Man swim trunks, which he had put on soon after he'd woken up.

"Seashells. Look." He fished one out with his tiny hands and put a shell to his ear. "I can't hear anything." He made a disappointed face. "Lenny says you can hear the sea but I can't hear nothing."

"Anything," she said. "You can't hear anything."

"I can't," he agreed. "You try."

She did, and couldn't hear anything either. "I think we need to find a shell that has more curvature." She looked around, until she found one. "See," she said, "This one has more of a curve." She put it to her ear and smiled. "I can hear something now."

"You try." She knelt on the soft powdery sand, like sugar, but golden, and held the shell close to Jacob's ear. "Listen," she whispered. "It's very, very, very quiet. Like a 'sssssshhhhhhhhh'. Hear it?"

He frowned, then his eyes opened wider. "Yeah … yeah, I do! I hear it!"

She let him enjoy the moment. After a while, he put it into his plastic bucket. "I'm collecting them," he explained.

"Shall we walk around the beach seeing how many we can find?"

He shook his head.

"Then what do you want to do? We could go for a swim or—"

"Let's go swim in the sea! Race you!" And he rushed off, into the water, before she could reply. She followed, and noticed that one of the bodyguards stepped forward. There were two of them—discreet, yet visible, and always around. Being here had given her a taste of what it was like, being part of Tobias Stone's world, being constantly shadowed by men who never spoke. Men who were there to guard your life.

The Shoemoneys were relatively normal compared to this.

~ ~ ~

The next day, Tobias and Savannah were still lying in their hammocks and relaxing.

31

With three days to go until the wedding, Izzy made sure to keep Jacob occupied. He was a bundle of energy, and while she didn't have a hard time keeping an eye on him, she could see why Savannah had asked her to come along.

They spent the rest of the morning building sandcastles and playing in the sea. After lunch, Tobias suggested they could explore the island.

"Alone?" asked Savannah, looking horrified.

"It's safe enough, Savannah," said Tobias, reassuring her.

"But it's so big. What if he gets lost?"

"It's an island. He's not going to go far, and it's only us here."

Izzy listened, keenly aware of Savannah's fear. She had forgotten that time, when she had found a scared looking Jacob in the shopping mall, but she realized that the fear was never going to leave Savannah.

"Can we go there?" Jacob, pointed behind in the distance.

Savannah gasped. "To the waterfall? No. No way. Unless we all go, and I'm not feeling up to it right now. Do you mind waiting, honey? We could go tomorrow?"

"I can take him," said Izzy, stepping forward. Jacob wasn't the type of child to jump up and down and throw a tantrum. He listened to his mother and went along with anything she or Tobias said. His downcast face, and his silence, had been enough to move her. "I'd like to explore the island, and the waterfall doesn't look so far away"

"They can take the jeep," Tobias offered. "But it's not far. I'll go with them, if it puts your mind at ease."

"We'll be fine," Izzy insisted, knowing that they needed time to unwind before their big day.

"They will be, Savannah." Tobias held his fiancée's hand. "One of my men will go with them." And that seemed to satisfy Savannah. "You'll need to wear sneakers, Jacob. It's rocky around the waterfall. Be careful."

They spent hours exploring the other end of the island, walking along the velvety, golden beaches fringed by palm trees and lush vegetation.

She couldn't wait to tell Cara and wished she had her cell phone with her, but one of Tobias's bodyguards had taken it from her as soon as they had arrived.

"Mommy wasn't sure that you were going to come with us," said Jacob as they walked along.

"She wasn't?" Izzy slipped her hands into the back pockets of her denim shorts.

"Didn't you want to look after me?"

"Huh? No. That's not the reason I wasn't sure about coming here, Jacob." She stopped, and turned to him, then bent down to his level, glad that they had both changed into their sneakers.

"I have college, and I didn't want to miss too many lessons, that's all."

The boy looked up at her, his expression more relaxed now, as if the news had cleared some notion he'd had. "So it wasn't because of me?"

"No! Why would you think it's because of you? You're pretty cool, and I'm super excited to be here with you."

"Yeah?"

"Yeah."

They walked along the beach, and could see, set much further inland, lush vegetation—giant ferns and huge towering trees swaying majestically in the soft breeze. Jacob announced that they were mango, coconut and breadfruit trees.

They talked about school, and his friends and his favorite Marvel movies and superheroes. Every so often, they would stop, while Jacob examined shells along the seashore, or chased after one of the tiny crabs which zig-zagged along the sand.

"It is a cool place, isn't it?" she said, looking around. "We have to make the most of it, before everyone else gets here." It was going to be painful having to share the island with everyone.

Savannah had told her that the wedding was small, around a hundred people.

Small?

Some guests would start arriving tomorrow, both of their families and a few close friends. It would mainly be the same people who had come to the engagement party. At least she knew what to expect.

"It's Tobias's birthday tomorrow." Jacob told her.

"It's his birthday?" Savannah hadn't mentioned a word of it. "I didn't know."

"Mommy said Tobias doesn't want to make a big deal of it. I don't think old people like birthdays the way we do."

She laughed. "Old people? I guess they don't. Do you think I'm old?"

"Not as old as Tobias."

"Do you think your Mom is old?"

"Mommies never get old."

She smiled.

"So they're having a celebration for Tobias's birthday?" Probably a dinner, she assumed, and some cake, and drinks, under the stars. That was the thing that had amazed her. The stars were so clear, so sharp, so easy to see, and there were so many of them. It took her breath away looking at the sky. It was beautiful. Only last night, she and Jacob had gotten into the separate hammocks and tried to count stars.

"Yeah."

"Do you know who's coming tomorrow?"

"Mommy said Grandma and Grandpa, and Tobias's mom and dad and Xavier and Kay." He counted off on his fingers.

"Kay and Xavier?" The way Jacob said it made her wonder if they were an item. Izzy had met Tobias's brother at the party and had remembered him specifically because his girlfriend had bumped into her and spilled her drink all over Izzy's jacket. And Savannah's cousin Kay was hard to miss in that blood-red dress she had worn to the party in the summer.

Izzy had been wary of going but Tobias had told her that Savannah was desperate to meet her, and that they both wanted to personally thank her for stepping in and rescuing Jacob from the clutches of that woman who was trying to take him away.

"Are they together?" she asked, wondering if Jacob had intel that Cara and her magazines weren't privy to.

He looked up at her with a puzzled frown. "You mean 'is she his girlfriend?'" He screwed up his nose as if the idea of a girlfriend was disgusting.

Izzy glanced over her shoulder, wondering if the bodyguard could hear. For some reason, she felt as if she was being nosey, sticking her nose into other people's business. She was curious. That's all.

"Dunno." Jacob shrugged. "Tobias says Xavier has a new girlfriend every week, and Millicent said it was about time he stopped making wild toast."

"What did she say?" Izzy asked.

"I dunno. Toast, or oats, or something like that."

She grinned. Sowing his wild oats, probably.

As they approached a clump of trees and shrubs, the bodyguard took charge and led the way. They followed him down a flight of rickety wooden steps, then through a clump

35

of trees and shrubs. The flowers blossoming around them had a sweet smell, like honey.

She heard the loud gushing water as they edged out into a clearing.

And there it was.

A wall of blue silk threaded with crystal, surging and thundering down the mountain. Izzy put her hands on Jacob's shoulders, not because he was in any danger of falling, but because she was cold, and thought he might be too. The temperature was cooler here.

"It's beautiful isn't it?" she said, raising her voice.

He nodded, and they watched the water swishing over the rocks and collecting into a bluish-green pool at the bottom. It was stunning. She inhaled deeply, admiring the view, feeling soothed by the sound of the water.

She wanted to be still, and to make the most of this moment. It was amazing how calm and free she felt after a few days without her cell phone. Kawaya was such a huge contrast to her daily, normal life. There were no horns blaring, no sirens screaming, or traffic growling.

The sound of nature was soothing in comparison.

She had done the right thing by coming here, and now she wished Tobias and Savannah had come a few days earlier. Tomorrow, with the guests arriving a day before the wedding, the peace and calm of paradise would be lost forever and they would not know this calm again.

Chapter 4

"Take it easy, pal. You need to stay sober for tomorrow."

"I'm getting over my jetlag." Xavier held the glass up to the midnight blue sky and the stars sparkled as a backdrop. "I'll be sober tomorrow, I swear."

"Go and spend time with your family," Luke urged. "You don't have to hang around here."

"Nothing beats the bar area." Besides, he was hiding. Tobias had glared at him when he'd stepped off the boat late. It wasn't his fault Gisele had chosen yesterday of all days to split up with him. What was he supposed to say when she told him the producer had asked her to turn up for her casting in her bikini?

"Who the fuck has an interview in a hot tub?" he'd argued. He was no prude, but even he could see that it didn't seem right.

"Why are you so jealous?" she'd screamed back. "It's no big deal!"

So they argued, and patched up, and argued some more—until he missed the plane and caught the next one out. He couldn't wait to get out of New York fast enough.

He nodded at the sky. "Kinda neat out here, isn't it?"

"I've been to many beautiful places," agreed Luke, "And I've seen a few private islands in my time, but I've never seen anything like this place."

"That's my brother for you," Xavier murmured under his breath. "Trust Tobias to get the biggest and the best fucking island he could get his hands on." He eyed Luke, again. "Come on over to this side, dude. When my brother told you to take care of the drinks, he didn't mean for you to be working all night."

Luke shook his head, then was briefly interrupted by one of the waiters who had brought over a crate of clean glasses. "I don't call this work," he said, pulling the glasses out one by one.

"Should you be doing that? Why not let your people take care of the glasses and you enjoy the party. Plenty of pussy to admire around here."

Luke finished emptying the crate. "Tobias hired me to take care of things, and I'm taking care of things." He rested his hands on the counter top. "And tone down the vulgar talk. You're not at The Oasis now, and Xavier-The-Stud-Stone doesn't need to make an entrance."

"Besides, aren't these people your close family and friends?"

"Not my friends." There were plenty of familiar faces, and a couple of guys he had met through the mastermind group that Tobias belonged to—a bunch of wealthy New York businessmen who met every other month to talk about how to make more money and play golf all day long. He had finally caved in and gone with his brother a few months ago. It hadn't been his thing. The men he met here were a mixture of mostly old money, and a few, like Tobias, who were hotshot wonder boys who had made good.

Xavier's friends were more entrepreneurial—like Luke, more fly-by-the-seat of their pants, and all new money. They were the kind of guys who bought up companies, then sold them quickly at an inflated price, guys who dabbled in cryptocurrencies, and the stock market, and who believed that if you threw enough shit at the walls, eventually some of it would stick.

Hell, no. He didn't want to end up in a boring conversation with any of Tobias's mastermind friends.

At least he had Luke for company. He'd have been lost if he wasn't here, especially now that Gisele hadn't come along.

By the time he had arrived, sometime after seven o'clock, the island was already teeming with guests.

At least he didn't have to suffer the long-ass journey with his parents. They had already cut Tobias's birthday cake by the time the boat dropped him off.

"Why aren't you spending time with your brother?" It was his mother's voice behind him, and it had the ability to freeze the blood in his veins.

"Dirty martini, please," she said to Luke.

"He looks busy," Xavier replied. No way did he want to go anywhere near Tobias.

His father sidled up on the other side. "It's his birthday, son. Go and talk to him."

Xavier groaned inwardly, his head dropping down so that his chin touched his chest. "About what?" he asked, lifting his head. This was typical of their parents. They were always walking on eggshells around Tobias—the genius, the son who became a billionaire, the apple of their mother's eye.

"About the wedding, about his feelings, and maybe even apologize for missing his birthday celebrations," his mother said. "Was Petuna? Petroleum? Petris to blame?" She held the cocktail glass to her lips, taking great joy, it seemed, from mocking him on purpose.

This was going to be a goddamn prison sentence. Four days on a remote island with his family. He couldn't even swim to safety.

"I believe her name was Petra, Milly, and they split up some months ago." At least his father kept up with the latest.

"It's not like Mother doesn't already know." Xavier took a gulp from his bottle, then eyed his mother.

"Who's your latest girlfriend?" his mother asked, pointing a long, leathery finger at him.

"Gisele." His voice sounded like an echo.

"Is she here?" His mother looked around; her head spinning round almost like an owl's.

"We split up."

"Already?" His father banged down his glass of scotch.

"Wasn't she the one you went to Miami with last month?"

"Jeez," he said, pushing off from his stool. "This is getting way too creepy."

"What's getting creepy, son?"

"This," he swung the empty bottle, using it to point to both of them, "this unhealthy interest the two of you have in my love life." He was going to go and mingle.

"Is that Oliver Rothschild?" his mother asked, staring out towards the barbeque area. "Come on, Ellery. Let's go and talk to him. I want to know how his mother got a write-up in August's issue of Vogue."

He watched his parents leave, and let out a breath he didn't even know he'd been holding. At the other end of the bar, Luke was serving a woman, and from the side profile of her, he recognized her at once. That chick had been eyeballing him ever since he'd gotten off the boat. The night was still young, and given the severe lack of hot babes on the guest list, he could do worse than end up with Savannah's cousin.

He walked over to the other end, ignored the babe and spoke to Luke. "Thanks for deserting me," he drawled, settling himself on the stool.

"Looked like your parents wanted to spend some time with you. Another bottle?" Right now, he needed one, but he was Tobias's best man, and he couldn't risk screwing up tomorrow.

"No, save it for tomorrow."

The woman sitting next to him turned to him, as he knew she would.

"Have we met before?" he asked, knowing perfectly well that they had, but curious to see how well she remembered him.

"Yes," she held out her hand. "I'm Kay, Savannah's cousin." It was always so easy to tell when a girl was interested, not because of what she said, but because of what she didn't say, or the way her sidelong glance might linger a fraction of a second longer than necessary, as Kay's did now.

As if to further confirm her interest in him, she flicked her highlighted blonde hair away from her face, drawing his attention to her glossy French Manicure and her long lashes in one fell swoop.

"Savannah's cousin," he said, slowly, as if he had only realized now.

"I didn't see you earlier." There was a hint of a question in her words. Her mouth was a giveaway, the way she started chewing on her lips.

"And here I am," he said, his gaze settling on her lips, before lifting to her eyes. "It's turning out to be a good night." He knew, as sure as he knew there was air in his lungs, that she was interested and he would bet, if he flirted with her long enough, if he gave her the usual long stare, that she would soon want to take that interest further.

"It sure is," she said, leaning forward, her elbow resting on the bar and her hand cupping her jaw.

She was flirting six ways to Sunday, and had no qualms about being so obvious about it. He liked that—a woman who knew what she was doing, and knew what she wanted—and without all the pretense that usually led up to the mating ritual.

Because after all the posturing, and preening, and flirting, and staring, it always led to that. He wondered whether he could take her to bed tonight, or wait until the wedding was over, at least.

"Only for a short while, Jacob."

He heard the voice before he noticed the legs—as someone else slowly came into view over Kay's shoulder. Tanned slim legs in shorts, not as high cut as he liked, but not bad. They had frayed bits hanging from the bottom. His gaze traveled north, and settled on the pert breasts that were encased in a lime-green colored bikini top. And before he had a chance to see her face, to see who those breasts belonged to, she had already turned her back to him.

"You're going swimming now?" Kay shouted out after her.

He leaned forward, eager to find who she was. "Great rack," he said, the words escaping his mouth before he had a chance to stop them.

She must have heard because she turned around—a pissed off expression on her face. If looks could kill, he'd be lying stone cold on the floor.

She took Jacob by the arm and sashayed away, allowing him to admire her rear until she was out of sight.

"Who the hell was that?" he asked.

"Izzy," Kay replied, in a flat voice.

Izzy? What the fuck kind of a name was that? Where had he seen her, because she seemed familiar, too.

"Someone Savannah hired to look after Jacob."

He sat back. "Jeez." She was smokin' hot. Kay threw him a hard stare, and he pulled out the pack of cards he had in his pocket as a way of changing the topic. "Want to see some tricks?" Card tricks always came in handy and helped break the ice.

His island vacation was suddenly starting to look interesting.

~ ~ ~

Nice rack?

She hated assholes like him. Xavier Stone, Tobias's asshole brother. What did he think she was? A piece of meat? The only reason she hadn't answered back was because Jacob had been by her side, otherwise she never let sexist putdowns go by without a sharp rebuke.

"Can we play tag?" Jacob asked.

"Your mom said only half an hour, Jacob."

"Aww."

"Half an hour, then a shower, then bed."

"Can't I stay up longer?"

She would have let him, but she understood Savannah's wish for Jacob to be fully rested for tomorrow. It was her big day after all.

"Maybe tomorrow night, I'll do my best to persuade your mom to let you stay up as late as you want."

He gave her a big grin, then jumped into the pool. She was thankful that most of the guests were milling around further along the beach and away from this area.

Tables, chairs and Chinese lanterns were laid out on one side of the tropical gardens, overlooking the beach, and effectively separating the pool area from the beach front.

Apparently the wedding would be held here, Savannah had preferred it as it would be easier to walk on grass, than sand. And having the aquamarine ocean as a backdrop was pretty enough.

Most of the guests hung around on the grassy area, and some spilled out onto the soft sand. She liked the privacy this afforded her. She wasn't comfortable walking around, even in her shorts and a bikini, or being ogled by guests, some of whom had had a bit too much to drink.

And while she knew Jacob needed to go to bed soon, it didn't seem fair to have him go to bed now, when so much was going on outside.

"Aren't you coming in?" Jacob asked.

She peeled off her shorts and padded into the water, watching Jacob as he scooted around with a boogie board. Poor kid. He was bored, being the only child around here. No wonder Savannah had wanted her to come along and keep an eye on him. Keep him company, more like.

She hated that they had only had the island to themselves for only two days. It wasn't nice and peaceful anymore. The place was beginning to fill up, and the majority of guests had arrived today.

Jacob's fingers skimmed her hand. "You're it," he squealed, then swam away, splashing water everywhere.

"You're a good swimmer!" she shouted. "But I'm bigger and faster." She launched after him. It was too easy, almost one-sided. Jacob giggled and squealed as she approached, and he tried desperately to wade away, his movements slow and labored as if he was like wading through a vat of treacle.

"I think we should make it fair, Jacob." She was within touching distance.

He giggled, his expression vigilant, as if he couldn't work out why she wasn't tagging him.

"I think I should only be allowed to walk and tag you."

"Okay!" He raced away, the water splashing madly around him. She walked towards him, deliberately taking her time, letting him rush this way and that way, trying to tire him out on purpose in the hope that he would want to go to bed soon.

The guests would be outside, enjoying the night for a few more hours yet. Savannah had told her to come back to the party, and to enjoy the rest of the evening once Jacob was asleep, but she wasn't so sure.

Apart from Savannah and Jacob, the only other people who seemed down to earth and on her wavelength had been a guy called Luke, and a couple of his colleagues.

The bar area was a good size, and the cocktails were flowing freely. Tobias had spared no expense, just like at the engagement party. He had the best drinks, the best food, the best decor all on his own private island paradise.

She wished Cara had been here—at least she would have someone to talk to once Jacob was asleep.

"You can't get me, you can't get me," Jacob sang, mocking her, teasing her, and giving her no choice but to wade towards him. She couldn't help but smile because his squeals were so infectious.

"It!" she shrieked, tagging him with her hand and then waded away as fast as she could. In the next second Jacob lunged towards her, a moving waterfall of splashes as he neared her, and then, tagged her in a clever underhanded move where he swam underwater and came out behind her, surprising her with his prowess.

"Gotcha!"

"Jeez, dude." A man's voice on the deck behind her made her skin bristle. She turned around.

"Xavier!" Jacob cried. "Wanna play?"

She stared at the tall, dark figure before her. With a beer bottle in his hand, he stared back at her.

She had seen that look many a time, and she didn't like it. She let out a quiet groan under her breath, and prayed that this letch wasn't about to join them.

Jacob swam up to the edge. "Wanna play tag?"

"Me?"

"Yeah."

Xavier's gaze passed to Jacob and then met hers again. "I don't know," he said, as if he was testing her resolve. "I'm not sure your friend wants me to."

Jacob looked at her. "Can he play, Izzy?"

Hell, no. "It's time to get out, Jacob."

"But we've only been here for—"

"Now, Jacob." There no negotiating this. She waded closer to Jacob and, lowering her voice, said, "It's your mom's big day tomorrow, Jacob. It's time to go to bed. I promise I'll ask her if you can stay up late tomorrow night, okay?"

"You promise to ask her?"

"You know I will."

"Okay." It wasn't a sullen, 'okay,' either. The kid was gold. Only, she now had the uncomfortable task of getting out of the water without letting the letch stand and stare at her like he'd never seen a woman in a bikini before. It made her wish she'd worn her tankini and shorts in the water.

"That's where you are!"

Her heart leapt with relief to see a woman coming towards the asshole, and command his attention.

Phew. Close call.

Chapter 5

Savannah's cousin was like a leech. Hard to shake.

"That's where you are," she said.

"You found me," he mumbled, dragging his gaze away from Lime Green Bikini, abandoning the kid's request for him to get into the pool. It wasn't for the kid that he had considered playing 'tag'. It was that babysitter of his. It wasn't often he came across someone who didn't give him the eye, and he was certain that this girl didn't know who he was.

Kay flashed him an I-want-to-get-to-know-you-better smile. It was a tell that most of the girls he met had. A lowering of the head, a looking up at him with an angled head, a smile—not too wide, and definitely not cheesy—but presumably their best impression of sultry. He knew it well.

He acknowledged her with a simple nod.

"Are you going in?" she asked, her voice lifting as if the idea of getting into a pool excited her.

Hell, no. "No." He turned to see Jacob and his babysitter coming out. The girl had her back turned to him, and was toweling herself dry.

"What are you doing here?" Kay asked, the tall stem of her champagne flute between her fingers. "The party's on the beach, and you were in the middle of a card trick."

47

"So I was." But he had no desire to finish it off. Some time back in the day, he'd learned a couple of card tricks which kept some of the girls entertained. Kay seemed particularly easy to entertain, but he'd soon lost interest and left, intending to find out where Jacob and his babysitter had gone.

"So," Kay said, fingering her necklace, and licking her lips. "Savannah says you're the best man tomorrow."

Her cleavage was on full display, and what he could see was round and luscious, and big. The visual was like a powerhouse of electricity straight to his manhood. He followed her as she walked away from the pool and over to the recliners dotted around outside the main villa.

"You didn't finish off your card trick," she said, sitting on one of the recliners. He sat on the recliner next to hers, and they both faced one another as she held out the pack of cards he'd left at the bar. He took the cards and shuffled them. Some girls were so easy to entertain. It wasn't that the card tricks were particularly interesting, they were just a hook, and even a kid would tire of them eventually. He put away half the pack, and held the rest of them out for her.

"Pick one," he said.

She giggled. Her perfectly manicured fingers hovering over the cards as she made her choice.

"Okay," he said, shuffling the pack. "Put it at the bottom."

"What if I don't want to put it at the bottom?"

Then the fucking trick wasn't going to work. "You have to."

She shrugged, the movement drawing his attention to her breasts. He felt a stirring in his loins.

"Goodnight." He turned to see Jacob walk past him, and next to him, his babysitter.

"You going to bed, kid?"

"Izzy says I have to."

"Spoilsport," he said, lifting his eyes and looking at his babysitter.

"Your mommy says you have to, Jacob."

They didn't stop to make conversation. "Goodnight!" he called out after them.

"An early night for some," said Kay.

He turned his attention back to her, and to the card game he was in the middle of. But something didn't feel right. That chase, that hunger, had disappeared. "Yeah."

She jiggled forward in her chair, and if she continued to jiggle like that, he was sure her breasts would pop out of her low-cut, flimsy dress.

The sound of distant laughter and music from further along the beach rolled gently in the background. He went through the motions of shuffling the cards, and moving them around, and a few moments later, picked out, magically, the card that was hers.

"How did you do that?" she gushed.

"If I told you, I'd have to kill you," he grinned.

"It's clever."

"Yeah."

"And predictable."

"Yeah." He shuffled the cards some more. "Want to see some more?"

And he spent the next half an hour showing her a couple of other card tricks he'd learned, and then ended up showing her how to do them.

"I'll have to remember them for the next party I go to," she said, when he finally put the cards away. "So that I can impress."

"I wouldn't have thought that someone like you had to try too hard to impress," he said, staring back at her. She looked at him as if she wasn't sure what to make of that.

It was a perfect night, warm and balmy, with the chrrrp-chrrrp of crickets all around, perfect for staying put and talking to this girl who didn't seem in any hurry to leave, perfect for getting down to business, here, under the stars with nothing but the sound of crickets and music, and laughter.

Easy times.

He would have had his tongue down her throat, on an ordinary day, and it was so predictable how the rest of the night would play out. She'd be on her knees in no time, looking up at him with a smile. He looked at her and debated what to do. Sometimes, it was almost too easy.

"It's going to be too hot to wear a suit, don't you think?" she asked, her hand settling on her neck, then sliding down, as if she were wiping the perspiration away.

"It's going to be pretty casual." Tobias wasn't wearing a suit. He would still look sharp, and crisp, and enough to make the ladies drool, but he wasn't getting married in a suit and tie.

"I'm the maid of honor, well, sort of."

"Sort of?"

She shook her head. "There's no maid of honor. Savannah wants it all to be simple, and I understand. A beach wedding isn't as formal. It's all fairly relaxed."

"That's a shame," he replied, flashing her a smile as his eyes roved over her cleavage. If she was going to have it on display like that, how could he not admire it? "Isn't there an unspoken rule about the best man and the maid of honor?"

"I don't know, is there?" Her voice was husky, tempting, teasing, and he would have a hard-on soon if he wasn't careful. He licked his lower lip. The blood from his veins gushed south, and he scrubbed his hand over his face. He had to get his shit together. The last thing he wanted was for his brother to be in a foul mood, and he would be, if he found out he'd taken Savannah's cousin to bed the night before the wedding.

After the wedding, was a different matter. But then again … the way she was playing with her necklace was so, so, so sexy. He was getting ideas just sitting there. Would Tobias even know if he took her to bed tonight? It wasn't as if he had any plans to get back with Gisele. Even when they had been dating, her hectic schedules, and the interviews she was always going for meant that they didn't see one another much anyway.

"It's kind of an unspoken rule," he murmured, leaning forward. This time, their lips were so close he could feel her hot breath. And that was all it took. His hand slipped lower barely skimming her breast as he lowered it to her arm, and his lips clamped over hers. She tasted of coconut cream, and sweet honey, and he was about to cup her face when Tobias's laughter rang out from somewhere nearby.

Xavier sprang away like a shot.

"Wh—what's wrong?" she stammered.

He jumped to his feet. "I need to get some sleep. Best man, and all. Early start."

"But we were … in the middle of something … " Mirroring his movement, she stood up.

Tobias's voice made him jump. "Did we interrupt something?" he barked.

"No, no. I was just going to go to—" Bed. But he saw Lime Green Bikini standing behind Tobias.

What the hell was she doing with him?

In a softer voice, and ignoring him, Tobias told her, "I'm going to find Savannah and then we'll come and tuck Jacob in."

"I'll let him know," she said. "And thanks for the phone."

Had she seen them kissing? Had Tobias even seen them kissing or had Xavier moved apart by then? He tried to think—because the not knowing was killing him—but the moment had been a blur of sensual heat and cold shock.

Lime Green Bikini threw him a stony look before she turned her back and left. Xavier rubbed some sand he found on his shorts, hoping that his brother would leave quietly.

"Can't you go a day without ramming your tongue down someone's throat?"

There went that wish of a silent retreat from Tobias. Not that it was any of his brother's business. For once, Xavier felt that he wasn't the one who had done all of the chasing. Savannah's cousin had made it very obvious that she was interested. But he wanted to keep his brother calm, especially since he had already pissed him off once already. "She got a little too friendly."

"Try keeping your dick out of the equation," said Tobias, his voice as steely as his gaze. "She's Savannah's cousin, for fuck's sake."

He should have known better. "Nothing happened," he replied, feeling defensive. "I know she's off limits."

"Do you even know what 'off limits' means?" growled Tobias.

"Will you calm down?" You're supposed to be relaxed. It's the night before your wedding."

"I was calm and relaxed until you arrived."

"Jeez," he muttered. Tobias could be a moody, miserable little shit at the best of times. He knew better than to say anything.

An apology seemed the only option. "I'm sorry, okay? I didn't mean to be late." And if the big bust-up with Gisele hadn't happened, he would have been here earlier.

"Then why were you?"

He didn't want to piss his brother off by telling him about Gisele, especially not given what he might or might not have seen taking place just now. "Complications. I got delayed leaving. I'm sorry. I'm really sorry. I should have been here. Happy Birthday, bro."

Tobias exhaled loudly. "Okay."

Okay?

It was as rare and it was unexpected. Tobias Stone accepting his apology. Xavier stared at his brother. The dude seemed to be softening up. "Just don't be late tomorrow."

"Hell, no. I won't." He tried to reach out. "You're nervous. I get it."

"I'm not nervous. Not about the wedding."

"Then what?"

"The usual media bullshit."

He snorted. "Don't let that crap bug you, Tobias. It's not worth it." Stuff like that never changed. He didn't get it as much as Tobias, and he was glad.

Tobias scrubbed his hands over his eyes. "I didn't expect to be putting out fires on the night before my wedding."

"No, I guess not—"

"Tobias!" They both turned at the sound of Savannah's voice, soft, yet indignant. "I hope you haven't been working."

"I haven't."

She looked at him as if she didn't believe him.

"I had to make some phone calls," he confessed, "needed to get the lawyers to take care of some media nightmare crap."

"Can't you take some time off?" she asked, walking up to him with a smile, her tone light and jovial. She exuded happiness.

"I am," replied Tobias, his voice soft, like syrup, the way it always was when he spoke to Savannah. "Izzy says Jacob's ready for you to tuck him in."

"Let's tuck him in then," she said, sliding her arm around Tobias's waist. "Goodnight, Xavier."

"Set your alarm early," Tobias told him.

"Don't worry," he replied. Bed, he thought, watching Tobias and Savannah walk into the main house with their arms around each other's waists. It would be better to go straight to bed and not make any detours.

He wondered where Lime Green Bikini had disappeared to, and it was only when he had entered his room that he remembered Kay had vanished completely.

~ ~ ~

Tobias's brother was a bigger creep than Shoemoney.

The sight of him with his lips wrapped around Savannah's cousin was more than a shock to her system. Hadn't Cara told her that he was currently dating some actress?

"Tobias has gone to find your mommy," she told Jacob when she returned. She hovered over him, tucking the duvet under his chin.

"Are you excited?"

"Soooo excited."

"Soooo excited?" she echoed.

"I can't wait for Tobias to join our family." He gave her a look that made her insides melt. Waiting for Tobias to join their family? What an endearing way to think about it, she thought.

"Goodnight, Jacob." She blew him a kiss.

"'Nite, Izzy."

She walked out just as Tobias and Savannah walked in.

"Goodnight," she said, and left them to have their own private moment.

She returned to her room next door with her cell phone. Tobias returned her cell phone , just for the night, in case she needed to speak to her parents. He didn't seem to be anything like Shoemoney. He hadn't even reminded her about his privacy policy; no texting, no emailing, no photos, no recordings. It had surprised her, that he seemed to trust her enough to hand it back to her, after all the commotion he had made of everyone giving up their phones and signing non-disclosure agreements.

Her fears about Tobias had been unfounded. He'd been the opposite of Shoemoney in every way. She'd been led to believe that he was a shit-hot negotiator, a genius, ruthless and sharp. Yet he seemed to her to be softer and more human than she had originally given him credit for.

But as for his brother?

He was exactly the type of asshole she had believed him to be.

Chapter 6

"How do I look, buddy?" Tobias bent down to Jacob's level while Xavier looked on. His brother looked the happiest he had ever seen him.

"Is this good enough for Mommy?"

The boy giggled. "You look cool."

"Cool?" Tobias frowned. "Did you hear that?" Tobias glanced back at him. Xavier shrugged. "If the kid says you look cool, I'd take it."

"I don't want to look cool. I want to be the most handsome man in the universe."

Jacob seemed to appraise him carefully. The kid was like a wise old man, sometimes. And he was what—six? Seven? Eight? Xavier wasn't sure.

"You'll pass."

"Pass?" Tobias roared. "You're too funny, buddy!"

Xavier opened the ring box to double-check that the ring was still inside, as it had been three minutes or so ago, when he had last looked.

"You make Mommy really happy."

He looked up, caught off guard by the boy's words.

"Mommy makes me really happy." Tobias tapped the kid on the nose. "And, you make me really happy. I consider myself to be a very lucky guy."

Xavier felt out of place, as if he was intruding on a tender moment. When his cell phone vibrated in his pocket, he quickly pulled it out, turning his back on his brother as he stole a quick glance at the caller id.

It was Gisele. A tight ball fisted in his gut.

What the hell was she calling him for now?

He rushed out of the room before his brother's bionic hearing picked up on the vibrating hum of the ringtone which he'd put on silent. Tobias had been so annoyed when he had turned up late yesterday, that he hadn't even remembered to confiscate his cell phone. Family—their parents and Savannah's, were allowed to keep theirs, except for him. Tobias didn't trust him, and that hurt Xavier.

"It's not you," Tobias had told him once, "It's your girlfriends that I don't trust. Maybe if you managed to hold onto the same girl for longer than a month, I'd trust you more."

He walked outside, caught between answering the call and diverting it to voicemail, when suddenly, Lime Green Bikini appeared from nowhere.

He stashed his cell phone away into the pockets of his linen trousers, his interest piquing to see her coming towards him in a knee-length black and white striped dress.

"Have you seen Jacob?" Her voice had that pissed-off-edge to it that he was accustomed to. Before he could answer, Tobias appeared with Jacob.

"Jacob, your mom wants to see you," she said, then to Tobias, "Are you guys ready? I think they're all waiting for you."

"I'm ready." Tobias sounded sure, strong, and confident.

"Savannah looks amazing," Lime Green Bikini told him.

Tobias smiled. "She always does."

"Come on, Jacob." Izzy reached for his hand and led the small boy away.

"Ready, bro?" Xavier asked, dragging his gaze away from Jacob's babysitter.

"As ready as I'll ever be."

They walked over towards the gardens, to the grassy area in the middle which had been done up in garlands of flowers. White chairs had been dressed in white silk. A wedding officiant waited patiently at the front, but looked as if he was melting under the heat of the midday sun.

Xavier wasn't a poetic man but it was too glorious for words, the setting, with the glittery sea in the distance, and the white sand before.

Everything was running according to schedule, even in the hot mid-morning sun which often slowed everyone down.

When the wedding march began, Xavier knew, even before he looked at his watch, that it was noon.

He stared at his brother's profile, at his strong jaw, and the prominent forehead, and the smile that settled on his lips as he gazed ahead. Xavier stood to the side and looked over his shoulder. Savannah walked down the pathway strewn with petals, on her father's arm. She looked pretty in her long white dress, wearing no veil and carrying a bouquet of brightly colored flowers.

Xavier placed his hand in his trouser pocket—and froze when he couldn't feel the ring box in it.

Crap. Fuck. Shit.

The ring.

The goddamn ring wasn't in his pocket.

He jerked upright, as if an ice-cold pole had jabbed him. Where the fuck had he put it?

Somewhere along the periphery of his panicked vision, he caught sight of Lime Green Bikini as she walked Jacob over to sit in the front row with Savannah's parents, and then she moved to a seat at the back.

And then he remembered.

Fuck. When Gisele had called, before he'd left the room, he'd put the ring box on the table when he'd checked the caller ID.

"I'll be back," he whispered to Tobias's chin, not daring to meet his brother's gaze. And he raced away, as discreetly as it was possible to be, knowing that there would be hell to pay for this fuckup.

~ ~ ~

Where was that idiot rushing off to?

Izzy watched Xavier turn a deathly shade of pale as he rushed away. She preferred to sit in the row at the back, observing from the sidelines, even though Jacob's grandmother had told her to sit with Jacob in the front row. She didn't want to impose or get in the way of such an intimate occasion.

At least this way she could observe everything and everyone. It took her breath away, to see how pretty everything looked—to see the garlands draped around the seating area, and to see the chairs done up so elegantly. She had kept her call to Cara last night as brief as possible, but her friend had wanted a minute-by-minute report of the wedding. She'd even had the cheek to ask for pictures.

Izzy gave nothing away.

She looked at the front, at Tobias and Savannah standing together, at the wedding official who hadn't yet started the wedding, and wondered what was causing the delay.

The answer revealed itself a moment later, when Xavier rushed back.

Her head snapped back in amazement.

He couldn't have.

Oh, goodness. Had he?

She pulled her shades down and looked over the rims, observing everything with an eagle eye.

He had forgotten the ring.

The guy was a bigger asshole than she had ever given him credit for. Not only had he messed up the one job that Tobias had given him, he was cheating on his girlfriend, and with Savannah's cousin of all people. She felt a sudden sense of solidarity for the poor actress he'd been dating. Any girl stupid enough to go out with Xavier needed her head examined.

Chapter 7

"You may now kiss the bride."

The words snapped him back to attention. In his head he had floated away to a safer place, one in which Tobias wouldn't skin him alive afterwards.

There hadn't been too much of a delay, and he had returned within minutes. He doubted anybody noticed. Tobias had, of course. That man never missed a thing, and there would be hell to pay afterwards, but for now, he was safe as long as he mingled with the guests.

As soon as the ceremony was over, he had rushed to congratulate the happy couple before they became surrounded by a sea of well-wishers. "Congratulations, bro." He shook Tobias's hand and hugged him.

He was met with Tobias's clipped tone. "I'll speak to you later." Xavier swallowed and turned to Savannah, kissing her and congratulating her.

And then he had escaped and saw Kay. "Hey," he flashed a smile at her, but she seemed not to notice him and walked past.

"How could you forget the ring?" his father asked.

His mother turned on him with a menacing stare. "One thing, you had to do one thing only." The crepey wrinkles

61

around her lips furrowed deep. "And you couldn't even get that right. How could you let him down like that?"

"I didn't let him down."

His father tried to reason with him. "It wasn't much to remember, son."

"I—" He stopped. What was the point of trying to explain? "I didn't do it on purpose."

"But still, Xavier."

He let out an angry breath. If he had known they were going to guilt trip him to an early grave, he would have super-glued the ring box to his hand. It had been a goddamn accident. "He got married, didn't he?" he muttered, then stared at his mother in shock. "Aren't you hot?"

She was wearing what looked like one of her favorite cream and black Chanel numbers.

Jeez.

Even on a tropical island, his mother had dressed as if she was attending a New York society Gala event.

"Where are you going?" his mother called out after him as he stormed away. "I haven't finished talking to you."

"To get a drink." He didn't need to stand around listening to this.

~ ~ ~

She wasn't a champagne drinker, ordinarily, but she'd had a sip of the pink champagne when Tobias's father had proposed a toast to the newly married bride and groom as everyone milled around.

Waiters skirted around with platters of seafood and canapes, and the champagne and cocktails were never-ending.

Jacob seemed especially intrigued by the trays of gargantuan prawns, lobster and crab. He fiddled about with the collar of his shirt. Like Tobias, he had worn casual clothes, beige linen trousers and a casual white shirt. "Can I get changed into my other clothes now?"

"You want to get changed now?"

He nodded.

"You can't put on your Iron Man swim trunks."

"I want to wear a t-shirt and shorts."

She looked around for Savannah. "I need to check with your mom first." She wasn't sure if Savannah wanted more photographs taken. "Have you seen her?"

"I think she went inside."

"Let's go and ask her."

They went into the main villa and towards Tobias and Savannah's bedroom which was sectioned towards a corner of the ground floor. She was about to knock on the door and stopped when she heard voices coming from inside. Her hand stilled.

"Don't give it up all at once," she heard Savannah say. "And especially when it comes to someone like Xavier. You need to be careful."

"I am careful."

It sounded like Kay.

"Why do you always need to hook up with someone?" Savannah sounded annoyed.

Jacob came up in front of her and before she could stop him, he knocked on the door. "Mommy?" He knocked again.

"Wait, Jacob." But Savannah had already opened the door.

"Hey, honey." She was still in her wedding dress, and behind her, perched on the edge of their super king-sized bed, sat Kay, looking visibly upset.

"Sorry," said Izzy. "We didn't mean to interrupt, but Jacob wants to get changed."

"I thought you might," said Savannah, ruffling Jacob's hair. "I knew you'd be uncomfortable wearing that all day, so I got you a change of clothes, honey. Over by the chaise longue. Go ahead," Savannah told Izzy.

Izzy walked in to the room and gave Kay a quick smile.

"I know my son," said Savannah. "He would have spent the entire day in his Iron man swim trunks. Honey, I'd like you to wear those in case we have any more photos taken. Do you mind?"

Jacob shook his head. "No."

"You can get him changed in the master bathroom," said Savannah.

"Come on, Jacob," Izzy beckoned, and followed him into the bathroom.

"Did anything happen?" she heard Savannah ask, but she couldn't make out Kay's reply. They were talking about last night. They had to be. She wondered if Kay had ended up being another one of Xavier's conquests.

She folded the clothes which Jacob had discarded.

"Are you listening to them?" he asked.

She looked up guiltily. "No."

He looked as if he didn't believe her.

"Why can't you enjoy being single for a while?" she heard Savannah ask. "Why do you always need to be with someone?"

"I don't! He was there, and he showed me some card tricks, and we got talking."

"You told me it was more than talking."

"Okay. So we kissed. He's a good-looking guy. I'm single, so … what's the harm?"

"How well do you know him? According to Tobias, Xavier has a girlfriend, and she was supposed to come."

"He's got a girlfriend?"

So it was true.

The dirty little rat. Izzy refolded Jacob's shirt, trying to kill time.

"I feel used."

"Serves you right."

"We're on an island, Kay. You're away from work, why not enjoy the vacation? Spend time with your mom now that you're here?"

"I have spent time with her, and with your parents. I don't know what you take me for, Sav. I'm not that bad!"

"You don't need to make out with every guy who shows you a bit of attention."

She heard a squeal of indignation from Kay.

"Can we go?" Jacob asked. Izzy blushed. He could see right through her. Could tell that she was eavesdropping.

"I was waiting for you," said Izzy, looking away and not able to face Jacob's searching eyes. He didn't believe her.

"There's my champ!" Savannah cried, her face bursting into sunshine as soon as Jacob walked into the room. "That's much better, isn't it, honey?"

"Yeah." Jacob nodded.

Izzy was reminded of what she needed to run by her. "Would it be alright for Jacob to stay up as late as he wants to tonight? He's been really good, and he went to bed early yesterday. He deserves it."

"Yes, of course." Savannah hugged Jacob tightly. "You can stay up as late as you want."

"All night?" he asked.

"All night."

Chapter 8

"I want more champagne on tables and make sure none of the bottles are less than a quarter empty." Luke's orders sent his waiters rushing off.

He turned to him again. "Your brother's still mad at you?"

"When isn't he?" Xavier replied.

"He doesn't look so angry now," commented Luke, as he looked over his shoulder. Xavier turned around. On the makeshift dancefloor laid out on the soft sand, Tobias and Savannah were dancing and with eyes only for one another. His brother looked like a different man altogether. Xavier turned his back on them. "He's dancing with his bride, of course he's going to be happy."

It seemed that the only person Tobias ever got angry with was him.

As if to confirm his thoughts, Luke winked at him and said, "I reckon it's just you, pal."

"Are you deliberately trying to piss me off?"

"Well, just look at him. I don't think I've ever seen your brother look so happy." Xavier looked again. Sure, that smile on Tobias's face was rare, but dammit, that smile had been glued to his face all day, only disappearing when he'd spoken to Xavier.

The newlyweds moved slow and close to one another, lost in their own private world under the rows of lanterns which hung above their heads. It was the kind of pretty that would have impressed Gisele if she had come along.

Xavier turned his back on them and knocked back a tequila shot.

"Are you deliberately trying to get drunk?"

"I'm celebrating my brother's wedding."

"Take it easy. You don't want to make a scene and get Tobias even more riled up."

"It's not as if I forgot the ring completely."

"True."

"And it's not as if he had to wait more than a few seconds."

"I was at the back, dude," Luke retorted. "I didn't know what had happened then, but even I could tell something was wrong."

"He didn't have to wait too long."

"Your brother is stinking rich and insanely successful, and I bet you he was never late for the important things."

"Who's fucking side are you on?" Xavier knocked back his second tequila shot. "Another one."

"Are you sure?"

"Yup."

"Coming right up."

While he waited, he shifted around on the bar stool, his gaze floating around the crowd, trying to find someone interesting. A relaxed vibe permeated the air tonight. The wedding banquet had lasted all afternoon, and there had been plenty of food and drink. Against a setting of sun, sea and sand, the only thing missing was sex.

As the afternoon darkened into evening, there was more food, more canapes, more cocktails, more champagne and more music and dancing.

Xavier lowered his head, and ran his hands through his hair, and when he looked up, Kay was at the other end of the bar. She was laughing and talking with Luke, the way she had with him yesterday.

But today, for some reason, she was deliberately avoiding him.

He turned back to his drink and wished he'd had his cell phone on him now. Tobias had remembered, and had taken it away from him just before he and Savannah were going to cut their wedding cake.

He looked across the bar again, to see Kay leaving. She hadn't so much as even glanced at him.

What the hell?

He couldn't work it out why she was behaving like this, especially after they'd gotten on so well last night. He drummed his fingers on the counter top, bummed out by the way things were unfolding. Tobias and his parents weren't too happy with him, Kay had ignored him, and Gisele wasn't here.

Things were looking dry.

Luke sauntered over to him. "No card tricks today?"

"No." He gave his friend a cold stare. "Another one."

"Steady on. You'll be falling off the stool if you're not careful."

He shrugged. "I can handle my drink."

"If you insist." Luke poured him another tequila shot and slid it over.

Another woman came up to the bar and stood waiting for Luke. Xavier eyed her up, admiring her strappy, sexy white top. His gaze trailed south at the sarong that was tied up at the waist and revealed a huge slit.

Nice legs, too.

He had a thing for a good pair of legs, and this chick had a nice pair on her. His gaze traveled back up the length of her body, and he was about to give her breasts the once over, when she turned her head and caught him leering at her. Luckily, she was wearing a flower tucked into the side of her hair.

"Nice flower," he remarked.

"Thank you." She returned the favor, making him shrink inside with her unashamed appraisal of him. She sized him up, real slow, her gaze settling on his crotch for the longest time, until he felt obliged to put a hand over his linen pants. "Can I buy you a drink?" he asked, not used to being eyed up in such an obvious manner.

"The bar's free," she said, "and I can get my own drink, but thanks."

"That's what I meant. Not buy, as in buy but—"

"I know what you meant, darling. And thanks."

Darling?

She took a sip from her cocktail glass, and smiled at him again. He was in. He was sure of it, especially with the way she was staring at him.

"Bride or groom?" he asked, not sure whose friend she was.

"Bride, and groom."

"You know them both?" He wondered if it was a work connection. Had to be, but he couldn't remember if she had been at the engagement party. It didn't matter. She had great legs, great tits—especially now that he could get a hint of their size—and a pretty enough face.

"I should have known you'd be here." A woman with short and dark-ish red hair, came up and slung her arm around the shoulders of the chick with the flower in her hair.

"I got you a Bloody Mary," her friend replied. Something about the way she was leaning up real close to her friend, something about the way her fingers caressed the soft skin on her shoulder, something about the way these two spoke and looked at one another, made him wary. His brows knit together. He didn't understand, didn't like their obvious and close display of affection.

As if she could feel him looking at her, the red head looked at him and grinned. "Xavier, isn't it?"

"Yeah." But he said it more like a question. Yeah, who the hell are you?

"I'm Briony, I work with Tobias, well, not with Tobias, but at Stone Enter—"

The lesbian.

Holy fuck.

"Jeez, yeah." He never usually blushed, but could feel the heat searing his cheeks and hoped to goodness that Luke couldn't tell. It was shameful enough him trying to hit on a woman who wasn't even into men.

Maybe he was losing his touch.

"You know Max, don't you?" Briony continued, unaware of the tsunami of confusion that swept through him.

"Max," he scrubbed his cheek, fully aware that Max had been playing him the whole time. "Yeah, yeah, I remember now." He'd been so preoccupied with trying to hit on her that he hadn't remembered.

"Nice meeting you." Max winked at him, then dropped her gaze to his crotch before lifting it back to his face. "Thanks for the ... conversation." She picked up her cocktail glass and the pair of them walked away, their hands around each other's waists.

Luke hooted with laughter. "Did you just try and chat up a lesbian and fail?"

"She was playing me." It had pissed him off. She'd treated him like a piece of meat.

"You're losing your touch, pal." The grin never left Luke's face and he ran his hands through his long floppy hair, sweeping it away from his forehead. Girls seemed to love that shit.

"She's a lesbian, dude," Xavier retorted. "That's hardly fair."

"Exactly," Luke was laughing so hard that his eyes were watering. "And Kay didn't even want to know you, and your girlfriend dumped you just a few days ago."

Xavier blinked a couple of times in quick succession. Was his friend deliberately trying to depress him? "She's an actress. They're easily bored. Nothing's forever with those kind of people."

"Forever?" Luke scoffed. "Since when were you looking for forever?"

"Fuck you." Maybe he was losing it.

"Truth hurts." Luke walked off to serve another guest, leaving him to sit by himself. As he stared at the empty shot glass, contemplating his boring evening, Lime Green Bikini edged into the periphery of his vision, only she hadn't been in that green bikini all day, but the name suited. And he wished she was wearing it now. Unfortunately, she still had on that sexy dress she'd worn earlier to the wedding. It still showed off her slim legs, and slender body, but her in a bikini would have been nicer to look at. She had the kid with her.

He brightened up, and walked over, determined to prove a point. "What have you got there, Jacob?"

"We're going to look for crabs."

"Crabs? Now?" He looked at his watch. "Kind of late for that isn't it?"

"Uh-huh," replied Jacob, solemnly. "That's what Izzy said." Xavier ventured a glance at Izzy, but she only stared back coldly. His insides prickled because he had no idea why she looked so pissed.

"If you're hungry, buddy, there are some crabs on the seafood platters." He jerked his chin in the direction of the buffet tables.

Jacob made a face, as if he had only just made the connection. "Are there crabs?" Jacob asked Izzy. She cut her eyes at Xavier. "Great answer, Einstein," she said, coldly.

"She talks," he said, returning Izzy's hard stare, and holding it, refusing to look away. If they were going to have a staring contest, he was going to win. She was going to have to look away first.

"There are crabs, Jacob," she said, looking away before he did. "Just like the salmon and the prawns."

Jacob's face contorted with pain. "I'm going to be a vegenarian like you," he said to Izzy.

Xavier couldn't help but laugh. "A vegenarian? What's that buddy?"

"Someone who likes animals."

"You mean a vegetarian," Izzy said, correcting him. She had turned her back to Xavier, effectively blocking him out of the conversation. "You won't be able to have hot dogs, then," he heard her say.

Jacob's lips pinched together tightly, as if the idea had lost its appeal. "I don't want to go looking for crabs anymore."

"Good," said Izzy. "Because I think it's too late. How about we go back to the waterfall tomorrow?"

The kid's face lit up like a firework.

"Promise?"

"Promise. There were a lot of rock pools around that area, do you remember?" The kid nodded.

"That was easy enough." Xavier tried to make conversation, but Izzy ignored him.

"Let's find something else to do now, shall we?"

"Lemme go and get Iron Man." He ran off, leaving the two of them standing awkwardly.

"Can I get you a drink?" he asked, tapping her on the back.

She turned to face him. "I don't think so."

"Have I done something to offend you?" His gaze raked over her face, but she didn't say anything. "I mean, I've barely said anything to you, I don't see how I could have pissed you off."

"No," she said, and wandered away.

No, what?

For some reason her walking away after giving him a one word answer irritated him more than if she'd said something he could at least work with, if she had at least given him a reason for her frostiness.

Defeated, he returned to the bar to find Luke eyeing him expectantly. "What happened? I thought you had the Midas touch with women." He placed his palms on the counter top and leaned over. "Seems to me you're losing your touch."

Losing his touch?

Never.

"Don't say a word," he growled, easing himself onto the stool and wondering what the hell had happened. "Do I smell?" He sniffed under his armpits.

Luke wrinkled his nose. "I can't smell anything." He leaned over, resting his forearms on the table. "Looks like you've lost your touch."

"It's a glitch," he replied, refusing to believe Luke's conclusion. He never had problems hitting on women before. One woman, he could understand, and Kay wasn't exactly his kind of woman. And if the second one was into women, it was her loss, and besides, she didn't count.

But three? Lime Green Bikini hadn't even given him the time of day.

This was definitely a glitch, or, as Gisele would have said, 'Mercury is retrograde'. Her astrobabble used to make him facepalm.

"A glitch. Sure." Luke slid a shot glass towards him.

He picked it up and downed it in one. The sharp tang of the tequila hit the back of his neck. He didn't need that salt and lime shit. He liked his tequila neat. But it was starting to hit home. "Gimme another," he demanded.

"I think you've had enough alrea—"

"Another one," he ordered. Luke reluctantly obliged, and he downed that in one as well. Wiping his mouth with the back of his hand, he looked at his friend's curious face. "I bet you I can win her over."

"Win who over?" Luke asked.

"Lime Green Bikini."

"Who?"

"Jacob's babysitter."

"Izzy?"

"You know her?" he asked, suspiciously.

"I was talking to her last night. I know everyone, pal. The bar is the social hub of any place."

"I can win her over," Xavier insisted.

Luke didn't look so sure. "What if she's not interested?"

"She will be." He hadn't lost his touch, or had a glitch. Xavier-The-Stud-Stone still had it. Besides, Jacob's babysitter seemed to hate him more than Kay did, which made her an even bigger challenge. Not that he needed to prove anything to anyone. "Bet you."

"Bet me? Are you insane?"

"No. I'm going to prove it to you."

"You don't need to place a bet, Xavier. I think you've had too much to drink. Let's see how you feel tomorrow."

"Worried you can't pay, dude?"

"Are you talking about a money bet?"

"What other kind of bet is there?" Xavier asked.

Luke seemed to be thinking it over.

"Why, are you scared?" The man had been making digs all day, telling him he'd lost his touch, and now he needed to put his money where his mouth was.

"You don't need to place a bet. I know you're a hit with the ladies, okay? No need to get so confrontational. Don't want you to go and do anything stupid, either."

"Who said anything about doing anything stupid?"

"That's the drink talking, not you."

"It's not the fucking drink." He placed the glass down with more control than he felt. "You've been saying I've lost my touch, so why don't you put your money where your mouth is?"

Luke crossed his arms. "Okay."

"Ten thousand dollars."

"What?" Luke's face exploded into surprise. "Are you crazy? Ten thousand dollars?"

"That's right. Ten thousand dollars that I can get that girl into my bed."

"I don't want you to do anything stupid."

Xavier crossed his arms. "All above board, dude. I don't ever use force to get a girl into bed. She'll want it by the time I'm finished with her."

"Ten thousand?" Luke repeated. Xavier didn't know what the big deal was. The dude had the money. He was loaded. Stinking rich. That kind of money was peanuts to him.

"You called it, dude," Xavier told him.

"No, you called it."

What the fuck did it matter? "You provoked me."

"Didn't realize your esteem was so fragile."

"It's not," he scoffed.

"Is there a time limit to this crazy bet?" Luke asked.

"A month." Xavier challenged.

Luke shrugged, as if he didn't want to be a part of this. "I don't know. What if she's already got a boyfriend."

"She hasn't. I overheard her talking to Savannah. Anyway, are you chickening out now?"

"No." Luke stopped wiping the glass he'd been wiping dry for the last few minutes. "A month doesn't seem like enough time, and I'd hate for you to do something stupid."

"I'm not going to do anything stupid. I don't know what you take me for." But the dude obviously doubted his sexual prowess. "3 months, if it makes you feel better, but I doubt I'll need that long. Watch and learn, dude. Watch and learn."

"You're an idiot."

Chapter 9

"It is you."

Izzy looked up, not recognizing the man who had come up to her.

"You used to work for the Shoemoneys, didn't you?"

She froze. The mere mention of that name temporarily paralyzed her.

"I'm sure I've seen you at one of their parties." The man clicked his fingers. "Their kids, I can't remember their names. I'm sure it was you looking after them." He still didn't look familiar, especially in his Bermuda shorts and t-shirt, but she could see that he would have been part of that crowd. He had that familiar banker look about him. Preppy specs, receding hairline and an air of entitlement about him.

"It might have been," she said, stepping back, and knowing perfectly well who he meant, but she had no desire to engage in any conversation with him. It shouldn't have come as a huge shock, but it did. Rich people all seemed to know one another. Theirs was an exclusive little club.

"Are you moonlighting?"

She was too shocked to reply.

Then, in a whispered tone, he said, "Can't say I blame you." And before she could tell them that she no longer worked for the Shoemoneys, Xavier edged into her line of sight. "Are you coming?" she asked, looking directly at Xavier, eager to find someone familiar, someone safe. His dark blue irises turned on her as if they could see right through her, like an X-ray machine at the airport, and his face went through a myriad of expressions, surprise first then puzzlement.

"Me?" he asked, and she was sure he was about to turn around and see if she was talking to someone behind him.

"Yes, you. We're going to the waterfall, remember?"

"It's really cool," Jacob chimed in.

"The waterfall? Hell, yeah." Xavier grinned a thousand-watt smile at her, making her already regret her decision to pull him in. If Shoemoney's friend hadn't accosted her, she wouldn't have.

"Hey, Xavier," the man said, and then to her, "Tell Gideon I said 'hi'," before he walked away.

"How do you know Oliver Rothschild?" Xavier asked.

"Is that his name?"

"You don't know his name?"

"I know of him, through contacts," she replied, staring at his face properly for the first time.

"Through contacts." His voice was playful, as if he was trying to make conversation, and she wasn't ready for it. "Why does that sound more mysterious than it is?"

She put her shades on. "It wasn't meant to sound mysterious, Stone." She wasn't sure why she added his surname to the end. He looked at her, his frown deepening the vertical line between his brow. "But you didn't even know who he was," then he paused. "Unless he was trying to hit on you. Was he trying to hit on you?"

She looked at him in complete amazement, and would have said how crazy he was for thinking such a thing except that her attention was drawn to the muscle twitching along his jaw. "I'm sorry if I interrupted something."

That he had reached this stupid assumption made her muscle tighten. "No, he wasn't trying to hit on me. He recognized me from a party with the last family I worked for."

"Oh." Her answer seemed to appease him.

"You don't have to come along."

"But you just asked me to," he protested.

"I must have had a temporary paralysis in brain activity."

"Or maybe," his lips quirked up at the corners, "deep down you really want me to come along."

She snorted. "You flatter yourself too much. I'm being serious. You don't need to come. It's a long walk, and," she stared down at his loafers, "you're not wearing the right shoes, and there's nothing much to see. You'll get bored. Wouldn't you prefer to sip cocktails on the beach?"

And flirt around with Kay instead?

"I would," he agreed, "but it would be rude of me not to take you up on your offer."

A gnawing feeling settled over her. "I didn't actually mean to ask you along."

"Then why did you?"

She wasn't going to tell him that she had panicked and used him to get out of the conversation with Rothschild. "I had a hangover, I wasn't thinking straight."

"You didn't drink much last night."

She turned to look at him again. "I didn't know you were policing me."

"I wasn't, but," his lips broke out into what other girls might have found to be a sexy smile, but she wasn't falling for it, "I can police you if you want."

"I want you to not waste your time with us."

"And here's me thinking you couldn't resist my charms."

She wrinkled her nose up as she looked him over. "I don't see any evidence of charm."

"That's because you're not looking hard enough."

He had an answer for everything, and dammit, he was going to stick with her no matter what.

"Please let him come," Jacob pleaded, his plastic pail in his hand, with some rashers of bacon to entice the crabs.

"Yeah, please let me come," Xavier crooned.

She ground her teeth together. "Let's go," she said to Jacob, ignoring Xavier completely.

They walked along the long stretch of beach, on velvety white sand. "So, who did you work for before?" Xavier had slipped into a stroll alongside her while Jacob led the way.

"Why are you so nosey?" She wasn't in any mood for conversation, especially not about the Shoemoneys.

"Making conversation, that's all. If you want me to quit bugging you, just tell me."

She stopped in her tracks and faced him. "Or you could just get the hint and quit bugging me all together."

"Are you two coming?" Jacob shouted. He had walked on a considerable distance ahead of them.

"Coming!" She started to speed walk towards him.

"You're stuck with me." Xavier appeared by her side once more. It was her own fault. "So," he said, "We might as well get better acquainted—"

"Is that what you were doing that night? Getting better acquainted with Kay?"

For a moment, he looked lost for words. He shrugged. "I can't help it if women find me irresistible."

She stopped and snorted loudly. This guy had a girlfriend, and this was all he could say. "Most people have a moral compass, but yours seems to have slid into your pants."

"It's not the only thing in my pants."
Unbelievable. She shivered in disgust, and marched off.

~ ~ ~

His fucking Ferragamo loafers were ruined, and she'd had the audacity to laugh at him. No. He hadn't brought a pair of sneakers with him, because he hadn't thought he would need them here.

And so he had ended up spending the next few hours traipsing along after the kid and his miserable babysitter, stopping every now and then while the kid chased a crab, or looked for shells.

Once they got to the waterfall, they walked around for about a quarter of an hour, maybe half an hour max, before heading back.

He returned having no idea why she had asked him to come along in the first place. Because clearly, she had no desire for him to be here, and it confused the hell out of him. He thought he was onto something. He thought this was going to be easy enough—this bet, when he woke up this morning and remembered what he had done.

But he could win her over. Of course he could. And having her ask him to come with them for the day had surprised him. She's come to her senses, he'd thought. But no. The whole time it had been like trying to have a conversation with a mannequin. Maybe she was jealous about Kay. Some chicks got jealous over nothing, maybe Jacob's babysitter was one of them.

She was going to be a tough one to crack, and it was something he wasn't used to—having women not be won over by his charms. It might have been different had she been friendly and had showed even an iota of interest in him.

Still, he thrived on a challenge.

And he was more eager than ever to win this one.

He recounted his woes to Luke later that evening, as he sat at the bar after the huge evening dinner that had lasted close to two hours.

It had been the last of the wedding festivities. More drink, more food, more music and dancing. Earlier in the day Tobias had arranged for the guests to go snorkeling and sailing. Later that afternoon, he had arranged for them to go parachute gliding from the air into the sea. There was enough to do to keep the guests entertained, and plenty of time for Tobias and Savannah to spend with everyone.

"It's not going to be easy," he said, contemplating the scale of the challenge that lay ahead of him.

"What's that?" Luke asked. For a change, he was on the other side of the bar, taking it easy, and mingling like a guest instead of working.

"Winning the bet."

Luke almost choked. "Are you still seriously considering that?"

"We placed a bona fide bet. Don't you remember?"

"I remember, but you'd had a few drinks by then, and I thought you were kidding."

"You don't think I can do it?"

"What's this going to prove?" Luke asked.

"That Xavier-The-Stud-Stone still has it." That he hadn't lost his touch. That he wasn't second best.

"Seriously? And this is how you're going to prove it?"

"Absa-fucking-lutely."

Luke folded his arms across his chest. "It doesn't seem right, trying to convince that girl to go out with you especially when I don't think she actually likes you. You can't force

82

someone to click with you, and you sure as hell can't force someone to fall into bed with you."

"I've never had to try too hard before." It wasn't often that women turned him down.

"That's because of your Stone name, and your good looks, and your money has helped you"

"Fuck, dude." Xavier couldn't believe what he'd heard. "I thought you were supposed to be my friend."

"I am your friend, and I'm telling you as a friend." Luke rested his beer bottle on his thigh. "You're a good looking guy, and you can have any girl you want."

"Except for that one." He nodded over in the distance, where Izzy and Jacob sat around a table with Savannah.

Luke looked over. "That's what I mean. You're probably not her type, and I don't think she's your type. You don't need to place this lousy ten thousand dollar bet to prove anything."

Oh, but he did. What Luke had said to him just now, about the Stone name and the money pissed him off. It made him want to prove it all the more. "I like a challenge."

"Don't do anything stupid," Luke warned, when he didn't reply.

"I'm not a pervert."

A short while later, he walked over to the table where Izzy was but, no sooner had he approached the table, than Izzy and Jacob left.

Annoyed more than disappointed, he sat down and casually asked Savannah what Izzy was short for.

"Isabel Laronde. She prefers Izzy."

"She's the new babysitter?"

"I'm not sure yet," Savannah replied. "She's still deciding. She's a student at Columbia, and she isn't sure she'll have the time."

A college student.

Interesting.

"She's a couple of years older. She saved up to come here."

Very interesting.

"She helped me out, and I will never be able to repay her." Savannah's voice turned quiet, and she cleared her throat. "I'd like to help her out by giving her some work."

"Jacob seems to be fond of her."

"He trusts her, and I feel comfortable knowing she's around."

The silence that followed had him wondering all sorts of things. "It's been an amazing day," he said, changing the subject.

"It's been the best."

He yawned and stretched his arms out. The sixteen hour time difference between New York and Fiji, and the long journey time had wreaked havoc with his body clock. Excessive alcohol hadn't helped.

"Bored?" Tobias tapped him gently on the side of his head as he walked past and sat down beside Savannah.

"No," he replied, defensively. "Just tired."

"Leave him alone," Savannah said, softly.

"I have left him alone." Tobias looked at him. "I haven't said anything about him forgetting the ring, have I?"

Xavier shifted in his chair. "Can't you let that go? It's beginning to get old, your joke."

Tobias ignored him and took Savannah's hand in a gesture that was so sickeningly romantic, it made him want to puke. "He's my brother," he said to Savannah, "and kid brothers are known for being pains in the butt at times."

"Thanks," said Xavier.

"Ignore him," said Savannah.

"Are you okay about Jacob?" Tobias asked her.

"What's the matter with Jacob?" Xavier wanted to know.

"Nothing," Tobias replied. "Savannah's worried about him going back tomorrow."

"He's going back?" Xavier hadn't considered that Jacob would be returning tomorrow along with most of the guests. If Jacob was returning to New York, so would Izzy. This was good news.

"We can get him to stay here, if you want." Tobias squeezed Savannah's hand. "It's up to you."

"No. He'll be fine, I know the problem isn't going to be with Jacob. It's me."

Xavier sat back in his chair, watching Tobias place a kiss on his wife's lips, and tell her, tenderly, that it would be fine, that she wouldn't have much time to worry about Jacob, that they were going to have a fabulous honeymoon.

Xavier's gaze flickered upward, and he looked away. He felt like he was watching a Hallmark movie, seeing these two gushy lovers. It was time to make his escape.

And then the brainwave of an idea came to him. "I can come over and help keep an eye on Jacob, if that helps."

Fuck, yes. That would do it.

He'd been wondering how he was going to run into Izzy in a way that wasn't so obvious. For starters, she didn't drink, so it wasn't as if he could take her out to The Oasis any time soon. Not that she would want to go anywhere with him. But this, looking after Jacob for a couple of weeks, would be enough to get him started. It would be enough time for him to win her over and show her what a catch he was.

"That's real kind of you," Savannah replied.

"We've got a whole team of people keeping an eye on him," said Tobias.

"Izzy, hopefully, and my parents, and he's at school, too, so that helps," Savannah explained.

"But I would love to spend some time with the little dude on the weekend. I'd like to get to know him better." He coughed. "We went to the waterfall earlier. It was fun." At least, Jacob had fun.

"Who's we?" Tobias asked, quirking an eyebrow at him. Xavier knew exactly what his brother was getting at. "You, Jacob and Izzy?"

"She asked me to come along." Trust Tobias to make such a comment. "You can check with her if you don't believe me."

"That's not necessary," Savannah interjected. "Izzy's nice, and friendly. And I know Jacob would have wanted you along."

It didn't go unnoticed, the way Savannah shot a glance at her husband. It was in that moment that Xavier knew, if he was to make any headway, in anything, and especially with this bet of his, he had to focus his efforts on Savannah for it was her who made the rules, especially where Jacob was concerned. Because as long as Savannah was around, she could tame Tobias. This was something to bear in mind.

"Jacob's a good kid," he replied, speaking to Savannah and avoiding eye contact with his brother. "With you guys being away, it would be nice for Jacob to have some male company, don't you think?" He didn't have any idea where Jacob's father was, but sensing that male company might have been lacking in his upbringing, he knew this was a good way to win Savannah over.

"That's so nice of you, Xavier." She turned to Tobias. "That's sweet, isn't it?"

Tobias looked at him as if there were other, more suspect reasons for Xavier wanting to spend time with Jacob. It was eerie, the way his brother could sometimes see right through him.

"Uh-huh." It was a typical Tobias response, and he took it to mean that he could.

Savannah explained how tomorrow Jacob would return to New York with her parents and Izzy, and that she would then find out what Izzy had decided to do.

Xavier hoped she would take the offer of babysitting Jacob, because, if she didn't, he'd be stuck with the kid on weekends, but if she did, his work was going to be super easy. Those college students were poor, mostly, unless they were trust fund kids, and Laronde didn't look to him like one of those.

All he had to do was to wine and dine her, show her some good times, and she'd be in his bed in no time.

Chapter 10

"So? How was it?" Cara rubbed her hands together and sat cross-legged on Izzy's bed, watching her unpack the suitcase. She was tempted to leave it until tomorrow, but the sand in some of her clothes was going to bug her if she didn't deal with it tonight.

Izzy knelt on the floor, clearing everything out, going through her suitcase which lay on the bed in front of Cara. "It wasn't so bad." She took out the clothes from her suitcase.

"Wasn't so bad?" Cara chortled. "You need to give me something, Iz. I want details."

Izzy pulled out her toiletries bag and threw a heap of dirty clothes into the laundry basket. A moment later she collapsed onto the bed, alongside Cara.

"It was okay."

"It was okay?" Cara hollered. "You went to the wedding of the year, on a private island, on a private plane—"

"Only going there," Izzy interrupted. "We came back on a normal flight."

Cara's jaw dropped open, and she turned to her side, propping herself up on one elbow.

"Just getting into a private jet would have made my year!"

"It was pretty neat." She yawned. Lying on the bed made the tiredness all rush back. It was nearing midnight, and she had lectures tomorrow which she was determined to attend. No way could she afford more time off college. "I need to get some sleep. The flight back was a bitch."

"Because you had to travel economy?"

"Because the time difference is a killer, and it's actually been an exhausting trip."

"So now you're complaining?"

Izzy yawned. "I'm not complaining at all. I'm glad I went."

"You're welcome," Cara said in a voice that indicated she was taking all the credit.

"Okay, thanks. Yes, I'm glad I went. I have to sleep, Cara. Can we talk tomorrow?"

"I'm not moving," Defiance was written all over her friend's face. "I'm not moving until you give me a run-down of the wedding."

"I can't."

"What do you mean you can't?"

"I can't talk about it. I signed an NDA with Tobias. I can't let out any details about the wedding."

"Who's going to tell?" cried Cara indignantly. "I won't."

What Tobias didn't want was for anyone to sell photos to the press. And she had none, nor would she have uploaded them or sold her story, and she knew Cara well enough to know her friend wouldn't pass on anything Izzy told her but, damn it, she had college tomorrow and a ton of notes to catch up on.

"Were there any hot guys?" Cara asked.

"I have no idea."

"What was her dress like?" Cara clearly didn't give a hoot about the NDA.

"Nice."

"And Tobias? How did he look? What did he wear?"

"He looked okay."

Cara rolled onto her back and started up at the ceiling. "Somehow, I can't see how Tobias Stone would have looked just okay on his wedding day."

Izzy sighed loudly. "He wore linen trousers, and a white shirt. It was all very casual because it was too hot to wear a suit."

"Casual?" Cara propped herself back on her elbow with a renewed interest. "How did they look together?"

"They looked good." They had. "They make a pretty nice couple."

"Is she nice?" Cara whispered.

"She's nice, and normal, like you and me."

"Lucky cow."

Izzy considered her friend's reply. Was Savannah lucky? Izzy knew her story very well by now, since Cara had drummed it into her head plenty of times, how the poor woman had made good by marrying the rich billionaire. It was the stuff of fairytales, and Izzy wasn't one for fairytales unless they were of the type where Jack vanquished the big evil giant. Those were her types of stories. Not so much the princess-being-rescued ones.

Maybe, given the circumstances, and what she had seen of Savannah and Tobias, maybe Savannah was lucky. Taking away the money, and the beautiful island, and all the trappings of wealth, when it came down to it, there was something between this couple that she hadn't seen in the Shoemoneys—a deeper sense of love and belonging. She had seen it in the way Tobias looked at Savannah, in the way the two of them held hands, automatically, in the way their hands and bodies reflected a closeness that all new lovers seemed to share.

Based on all she had seen, she had decided to accept Savannah's offer to her of babysitting Jacob on weekends. It made sense, because starting this coming weekend, while Tobias and Savannah were on their honeymoon, Jacob would be at home with his grandparents. Savannah had been thrilled when she had accepted.

She hadn't had to think about it much. Every dollar counted. She had books, bills and rent to pay. The income from babysitting would help. She could fit this in around her other jobs.

"Please, Cara," Izzy whined, yawning again, and this time raising her arms towards the headboard to have a good stretch. She'd been up for almost twenty-two hours.

"I've got to be fresh for class. I've got a ton of notes to catch up on."

Cara sat up slowly. "This wedding was wasted on you," she wailed. "If I'd have gone—"

"If you'd have gone, Tobias would have had to put a blindfold on you and gag your mouth."

"Tobias Stone can do that to me anytime."

Izzy shook her head. "That man has eyes for nobody but Savannah."

"Give it a few months. They all stray, eventually, especially these filthy rich types. Risk-takers, that's what they are, and easily bored, too."

Izzy didn't think so. "Not Tobias. He's smitten. It's not only with Savannah. He's pretty close to Jacob." She had seen him with the boy on many occasions, and it wasn't as if he was trying to be overly loving, as if he was putting on an act in front of Savannah, she had seen Tobias break away from his circle of friends and go and see what Jacob was doing, and then he would stay and spend time with him.

91

Plenty of times she'd seen him examine some of the toys he had been playing with. It went beyond being interested on the surface. The way Tobias was with Jacob was so different to the way Gideon Shoemoney had been around his kids, and even though Jacob wasn't Tobias's real son, Tobias seemed to have more love for that boy than she'd seen Gideon Shoemoney show for his own flesh and blood.

She felt sorry for the Shoemoney children. They might have been privileged, and would never worry for money or for getting by in the world, but when it came to love, to having that strong foundation that only parents could give, those children lost hands down. And Jacob, for all that his parents had split up, and he had come from a broken family, that boy seemed to be the more grounded and happier child.

"I'm not getting anything more out of you, am I?" Cara asked, sliding off the bed like a petulant five year old.

"Tomorrow." Izzy yawned. "I promise I'll reveal the details tomorrow."

"And you don't have any photos? You really don't have any?"

"No. Sorry".

Cara looked dejected. "What's his brother like?"

"A jerk". The reply came easily.

"What's Gisele Steiner like?"

"She wasn't there."

"She wasn't there?" Cara's face brightened. "Those rumors are true then."

"What rumors?"

"That they split up."

"Great." As if she cared, though it went some way towards explaining why he'd had his tongue rammed down Kay's throat that night.

"Great?" Cara repeated.

"As in 'please leave.' I need to get to bed."

Cara sauntered towards the door. "Did you get to talk to him?"

"Yes," Izzy walked towards the door and ushered her friend out.

"What's he like?"

Izzy yawned. "A jerk. He's a real jerk. He thinks he's god's gift to women."

"He's a player," Cara stuck her foot so that the door wouldn't close. "Did he try it on with you?"

"Who didn't he try it on with?"

"Really?" Cara squealed.

"You need to let me get some sleep."

"Tomorrow—you'll tell me more tomorrow?"

"Yes," she replied, letting out a harsh breath before closing the door. She thanked her lucky stars she'd never have to see Xavier Stone again.

Chapter 11

"Xavier?" Savannah's father looked at him in confusion, before opening the door wider to let him in. "Tobias and Savannah aren't back for a few weeks."

"I expect he already knows that, don't you, dear?" The woman he recognized as Savannah's mother came to the door and gave him a grandmotherly smile. "Let him in, Dale."

Her husband gave him an apologetic look. "Sorry, son. I was only following strict orders here."

"Don't worry," Xavier told him. "Tobias can be a real control freak when it comes to these things. I completely understand."

"He was very explicit in his instructions about Jacob, as you can imagine, and Savannah still worries about Jacob."

"I didn't want Jacob to get bored." He smiled sweetly at the boy's grandparents. "Not that he's getting bored with you, that's not what I meant. I'd like to take him out for the day somewhere. Catch a movie, or something. Do some kids' stuff." Only he wasn't sure, now that he was here, exactly what kids' stuff a little boy would want to do.

"He's in the pool, with Izzy."

"Is he?"

Jackpot. He had to fight hard to hold back the smile. Izzy here already, and in the pool? Hopefully wearing a bikini.

The stars were on his side.

"I'll go find them."

Tobias hadn't cared much for the pool and sauna and the other amenities situated in the basement of his condominium—he'd preferred to run alone, hitting the streets of New York in the silent hours, or spend time venting his frustrations and anger out in the boxing ring. But it didn't surprise him that Jacob would make good use of it. And he was thankful for that.

"Did you bring your swim trunks, dear?" He heard Savannah's mother call out after him, just as he closed the door behind him,

~ ~ ~

"Catch me!" Jacob shrieked, and splashed wildly as he tried to get away.

"I'm coming!" Izzy waded after him, but slowly, allowing Jacob plenty of time to get away.

The return to college after Fiji had been hard. It had been crazy of her to think she could slip back into her normal routine, her relatively boring student life, after those glorious days of walking on white, powdery sand in the heavy heat, with the aquamarine sea gently lapping at her feet.

New York in October was cold and miserable, in comparison.

The whole of last week had been like a dream compared to the harsh reality of her world.

Privately, she reveled in the knowledge that she had been to Tobias Stone's wedding, even though nobody had any idea.

It wasn't big news among her friends, apart from Cara, and it wasn't surprising given that Tobias wasn't a famous celebrity. But she had seen a couple of magazines and newspapers, none with pictures of the wedding, but older pics of Tobias and Savannah and so-called 'wedding news'. It gave her a chuckle in itself, that she had been there, had seen the wedding, had spent the time there, and was now back in the fold, and nobody but Cara knew.

Savannah had told her that Jacob's grandparents would be around to make sure Jacob was fine during the weekdays, but that she wanted him to have company during the weekends, and this she had no problem with. It was a nice and easy and fun way of earning extra cash. She had arrived early this morning, to find Jacob up and ready in his swim trunks.

"You can't catch me!" Jacob squealed.

"Yes I can!" She waded towards him easily, and then touched his shoulder. He shrieked, then waved at someone behind her. She turned around, and her face crumbled when she saw him.

God, no.

What was he doing here?

Xavier stood at the edge of the pool, thankfully still fully clothed. She swept her hair back, standing up in the water, watching, as Jacob swam to the pool edge.

"Hey, dude. How are you doing?"

"Having lots of fun."

"Hey," he said to Izzy. "How you doing, Laronde?"

She had to force herself not to narrow her eyes at him. "What does it look like, Stone?"

"I told Savannah I would keep an eye on Jacob."

"That's odd, because she didn't mention anything to me about you being here"

"That's because—" He was about to say that it was none of her business, but if he was to have any chance of getting into her good books, this wasn't the way to do it. "Because she's probably busy enjoying herself."

"Are you coming in?" Jacob asked. "We're playing tag."

No, Jacob, don't do it. Don't.

"I didn't bring my swim trunks, dude."

"Tobias has got lots."

No way. This couldn't happen. It couldn't. "I don't think Xavier wants to get wet, Jacob." She forced a smile. "We're coming out soon."

"But we just got in!"

She tried to keep her expression neutral. Thanks, Jacob. Thanks.

Xavier crouched down, but she kept her distance, a couple of meters behind Jacob who was hanging onto the pool ledge, unfortunately, still trying to convince Xavier to come in. "I'm not sure Tobias's swim trunks will fit me," he said to Jacob, and then stared directly at her. "They might be too small."

"Gross." Could he be any more big-headed? She shivered, more in disgust than fear. She didn't fear Xavier, not in the way she feared Shoemoney. Granted, they were both slime balls, but she sensed that with Xavier it was more a case of bravado.

"On second thoughts, kid, I don't want to get wet. I'll wait for you inside, buddy. How about that?"

She glanced up at him, the tension releasing across her shoulders. Thank goodness he wasn't.

"Don't you want to play with us?" Jacob's wail echoed around the pool, and she breathed easier.

"You play as long as you want, kid. It looks like you two are having fun anyways, and I've got a few calls to make. Don't worry. I'll wait for you."

~ ~ ~

"You didn't go swimming, dear?" Jean asked him when he returned. He explained that he didn't have his trunks on him. "And I have some calls to make." But instead, he hovered around in Tobias's den. Killing time.

This bet was going to be harder than he'd thought. If not altogether impossible. But the babysitter was growing on him. She had an edge to her that other girls—who were always eager to please him—didn't. He liked that. He liked that a lot. It made a change to find someone who didn't laugh at his jokes, or give in too easily.

And she looked good. It was a huge bonus. He'd had the advantage of seeing her in her bikini a few times now, and he liked what he saw.

When he won, when she gave in, she wouldn't be disappointed. He knew how to give women what they wanted, and he hadn't been joking when he'd said Tobias's swim trunks would be too small for him.

Three months was good. It would take longer than the one month he'd previously envisioned, to see this bet through. Girls like Petra or Gisele could be won over in a matter of days. He'd managed to screw Petra on the first date, in his Ferrari. She'd ridden him in the driver's seat, so impressed had she been by his car that they hadn't even made it to dinner.

And Gisele. With her he'd been in the Mile High club. They'd exchanged glances across the big ass seats in first class on a flight back to New York. He'd been on his way back from a business meeting and she'd gone for a casting in LA.

But Laronde?

Zero chance. She wasn't a model or a movie starlet, and maybe that was the problem. This college girl was giving him the runaround as if she were the prize draw in a Miss America contest.

Chapter 12

"Why don't you like Xavier?"

Jacob's comment almost made her speechless. "What do you mean? I do like him. I mean, I don't hate him." Not the way she hated Shoemoney.

"You never look happy when he's around."

"Uh, no. I'm fine. I'm happy. I'm having a good time."

"Then why didn't you tell him to come and swim with us?"

"Uh, well, because, you heard him, he didn't have his swim trunks."

"He could have borrowed Tobias's. They're brothers. Tobias wouldn't mind." Jacob wiped his hand over his face. "Just like I won't mind when my little brother wants to borrow my swim trunks."

Izzy blinked a couple of times. "A little brother?" Was Savannah already pregnant? Because, if she was, then WOW. It had to be the best kept secret of all.

"Mommy's trying to find a baby," Jacob declared.

"Trying to find a baby?" Izzy wasn't sure she understood. Was Savannah having problems conceiving? Perhaps he meant she was trying for a baby? She didn't want to question him, because she had a feeling it was the type of thing Savannah wouldn't want anyone to know about.

"That's what she said to Tobias. I wish she would hurry up about it."

"You'd like a sibling, wouldn't you?"

"Yeah." Jacob's voice was sweet, and a little doleful.

"Wouldn't you?" She asked again, because the way he'd answered, she wasn't so sure.

"I 'spose."

She placed her hand on his shoulder and bent her knees so that she was at face level. "You suppose so? Just a moment ago you sounded pretty excited."

"It's always been me and Mommy."

And that told her all she needed to know.

"I see."

He stared up at her with dewy green eyes. "I don't mind sharing her with Tobias."

"Tobias loves you as much as he loves your Mommy."

"I know."

"So why are you worried, Jacob?"

"'Cos if Mommy has a baby, I'll have to share Mommy and Tobias with the baby."

She didn't understand. "What's wrong with that, Jacob?" she asked gently.

"Tobias said that love was like elastic, and there's always enough to go around, but Mommy and Tobias are going to be busy with the new baby and they won't have any time for me."

"They will always have time for you." She splashed some water on him to try to lift his spirits. "Parents always do." She saw the flicker of disbelief skim across his face.

"How many brothers and sisters do you have?"

"I have a younger brother called Owen."

101

He seemed more interested then, as if what she said meant something because she wasn't an only child. As if she might know what she was talking about.

"And you only have one daddy?"

"Uh. Yes," she replied, not sure what he was getting to.

"I wish Tobias was my dad, but he's not. He's going to be the real daddy for the new baby. He's not going to be my real daddy."

"Uh," for the first time, she found herself with nothing to say. No comeback, and it killed her, to know she was leaving this child without some kind words of reassurance.

"I have another dad, and he's not so nice."

She could see where this was going, even if Jacob didn't know much about how children were fathered, and she wasn't sure when that was taught to kids these days. He seemed hung up on something. "But Tobias loves you like a real daddy would."

"You're just saying that because you want me to feel better."

His directness blew her away. "I'm saying that because it's true." With both hands on his tiny shoulders, she drew in a breath. "It doesn't matter who was the daddy in the house you grew up in, your real daddy, the one who's going to be there for you is the one who's there for you now."

He looked unsure. "Look at me, Jacob. I'm right, aren't I?"

He shrugged.

"Does Tobias spend time with you?"

He nodded.

"And does he tuck you in at night?"

"Yeah. And he reads to me."

"And he reads to you?" said Izzy. "And what else?"

"I don't know." He looked down and shrugged. "He takes me to the park, and he's took me on a helicopter ride."

"Taken me," she corrected.

"Yeah, he did, and he tickles me, and he makes me laugh, and we go for hotdogs and have man-to-man time."

"Man to man time?"

He shook his head proudly.

"He sounds like a real dad to me, Jacob."

His lips edged out into a tiny smile.

"So, how about we get out of the pool and shower, and maybe go to the park or something—whatever you want to do?"

~ ~ ~

"You waited for us," cried Jacob, as soon as he returned from his swim.

"Yeah, dude. I told you I would." Xavier put away his cell phone knowing that it would take a while to sift through a week's worth of backlog. He was halfway through it, that and his current goal of trying to get some investment into a new stream of business. His virtual assistant had gone AWOL on him. The normally reliable middle-aged woman who took care of his accounts and paperwork and all the other various tasks he had for her, had left to take care of her husband who'd broken his leg.

Why the fuck she couldn't work around that was beyond him. It left him in a serious bind. Coming back from the wedding to a truckload of correspondence to deal with as well as her unfinished work had been the hugest pain in the ass.

"How about we go to lunch?" he suggested. "Tobias told me you like hotdogs."

"I love hotdogs!"

"How about you?" he asked Izzy.

"I don't like hotdogs. Anyway, we've already made plans, haven't we, Jacob?"

"But I'm hungry."

"NYB," he said, trying to appeal to the babysitter. "On the Upper West Side. They do the best burgers in all of New York and you can get a huge plate of salad, and you get to pick anything you want." Jacob suddenly didn't seem too excited by that. "And you get to fill your own ice-cream bowl and put anything you want on it!" That seemed to do the trick.

"I wanna go!"

"I thought you might."

NYB was touted as a child friendly place, and had won rave reviews for its salad and ice-cream parlors. He wasn't so keen on the noise, what with it being full of families on weekends, but the burgers were amazing.

Izzy snorted. "I prefer not to pay overinflated prices."

"Lunch is on me."

"No, thank you."

"C'mon, Izzy," Jacob pleaded.

"Yeah, C'mon, Laronde," he said, easing into his usual Xavier-The-Stud-Stone smile. "A nice fat piece of meat might put a smile on that face of yours." He was fully aware of the innuendo, but he wasn't at all prepared for her answer.

"I'm a vegetarian."

How could he forget? A vegetarian. Of course, she would have to be. No alcohol, no animal products. Fuck. He hoped she wasn't one of those virgins-until-she-got-married types. "They'll do some ... some ... green stuff, I'm sure."

Jacob giggled. "Like grass, you mean?"

"Vegetarians don't eat grass, Jacob." Ouch. She sounded pissed, and pissed wasn't going to get him in her good books.

He gave her the once over, when she was glancing at her cell phone.

He didn't know what it was—a sudden change in the weather, or a lack of sexual activity, or the fact that she was so obviously not interested in him, but damn it if Laronde didn't look more attractive each time he saw her. On the flipside, she was cold, possibly frigid even, and a smile wouldn't go amiss on that pretty little face of hers either. His gaze fell to her lips, and he wondered what it would take to make her face light up.

"You want to go with Xavier?" she asked Jacob.

"Yeah. I'm staaaaar-ving. Can we go now?" Jacob asked.

"Sure, kid."

"Lemme just get my bag of toys." He raced away, leaving him and Laronde staring at one another. It was a deja-vu moment, taking him back to the party in the summer, when Petra had spilled her drink over her. Laronde was in the same jeans and leather jacket, with her nearly-dry tousled hair hanging down, and looking at him as if she wanted to scalp him.

"Have I done anything to offend you?" he asked, trying to warm the atmosphere between them.

"I had plans to take Jacob to the park this afternoon."

"We can still do that."

"My plan didn't include you."

"That was very selfish of you."

"I think it was very selfish of you to change our plans to suit you."

"Why do you have such a problem with lunch, with me coming along?" he asked, walking towards her, unable to keep that grin from spreading across his face. It was a thing with him, that hardened expression on her face was like an ultimate challenge, and he was determined to make it soft again. "And are you always going to be pissed when you see me?" he asked, ignoring the seething look on her face when she didn't say anything.

"It depends, are you always going to show up wherever I go?"

He chuckled, because she was so dangerously close to the truth and he needed to deflect it. "Don't flatter yourself, Laronde."

"Why are you here, Stone?"

"To spend time with Jacob. I didn't want him to sit around by himself and get bored."

She punched out a laugh.

"I'm ready." Jacob stood between them with a backpack on his back and Iron Man in his hands.

"Shall we go?" He flashed her an over-the-top dazzling smile, and for a fleeting second wished this chick would melt so that he could get to the fuck-like-rabbits part. She wasn't about to warm to him anytime this month, he was in for the long-haul, but once she got to know him, she would soon come begging.

He had everything on his side to win; the territory, for one. This was New York, his city and not some goddamn rock pool in Fiji which was going to ruin his Salvatore Ferragamo loafers.

All he had to do was give her the right amount of attention and he'd soon be in her panties.

Fact.

Some things were done deals, and this was one of them. "What about your grandparents, Jacob?" Izzy asked.

Grandparents? Shit. Grandparents weren't part of the deal. He knew where this was going and he opened his mouth to object, but she beat him to it.

"It wouldn't be fair to leave them at home, would it, Jacob? That would be very selfish, not to include them." She gave Xavier a self-satisfied smile.

Jacob piped up. "Can they come?"

"I'm sure they'd love to try the best burgers in New York." She exaggerated the words and flashed him a smile that was worthy of a toothpaste ad. "Go and ask them." They glowered at one another in tortured silence while Jacob disappeared.

"Burgers for lunch?" exclaimed Dale, walking into the living room. "Why, thank you, Xavier."

"Are you sure you'd like us to come along, dear?" Savannah's mother asked.

"It's supposed to be the best burger place in New York," Izzy said. "We'd love for you to join us."

He grimaced at Izzy. The conniving little thing.

"Let me fetch my bag," Jean said. "Dale, you need your jacket."

As Jacob's grandparents disappeared again, he sucked in his cheeks. This wasn't part of the plan.

"Oh," said Izzy, staring at her phone. She looked up at him. "I'm sorry. I can't come. I need to deal with an emergency."

"Aaaw." Jacob whined as if he believed her, but Xavier knew better. She had done this on purpose. "An emergency?" She'd stitched him up, and now she was pissing off and leaving him to have lunch with the kid and the golden oldies.

What the hell was he going to talk about?

"Sorry, Jacob," said Izzy, gleefully. "I'll make it up to you another time. Enjoy your lunch, guys."

"Can we still get a ride in your Ferrari?" Jacob asked.

Chapter 13

Fuck. Hard to believe how his Saturday was turning out. The kid he didn't mind so much, but Savannah's parents? What was he supposed to talk about now that they'd eaten their lunch and were sitting around waiting for the server to clear the table? They were sitting in a semi-circular booth, with big comfy leather-clad seating. He and Jacob on the ends, and Dale and Jean in the middle. He had to make conversation, and it wasn't always easy to talk to Jacob across the table.

It was all Laronde's fault. His plan had backfired magnificently. That girl had one-upped him again, and it was starting to piss him off.

"Would you like to see the dessert menu?" A server asked him. Christ. No. He didn't want to spend another second here. But then he caught sight of Jacob's face. The kid wasn't asking for anything, and he hadn't snatched the dessert menu from him. Instead, he just sat there saying and doing nothing, but, goddammit, it was clear enough to see from the look on his face. There was hope, and wanting, and something else Xavier couldn't put his finger on.

"What kind of question is that?" he replied, taking the proffered menu and handing it straight to Jacob. "We always have to have dessert. Knock yourself out, kid."

"More calories," giggled Jean.

"Now, now." Dale got out his spectacles, as did his wife, and they looked through the menu again.

"What would you like?" Xavier asked Jacob. A pair of green eyes peeked at him as the menu lowered. "You can have anything you want, don't be shy."

"Is it okay if I have a triple-chocolate sundae, please? That's what I would like."

"Isn't that too much chocolate, Jacob?" Grandma piped up.

"I think we can be a little lenient on him this weekend," Xavier winked at them.

"We could share it." The boy offered. "It looks too big, and I won't be able to eat it all."

"Eat what you can kid."

He gave the server Jacob's order, ordered nothing for himself, and watched the server take down Dale and Jean's order. And that was when he saw Izzy walk into the joint, looking around the busy, noisy floor.

What was she doing here? He looked around, anticipating who she had come to meet until, like a dart out of nowhere, he was hit by the notion that she had come back for them.

It had to be.

For a moment he indulged in the pleasure of watching her without her knowing. In her standard black leather jacket and jeans, still chewing that goddamn bubblegum, she had a didn't-give-a-shit attitude he was starting to find irresistible.

When the server led her over to their table, he sat back, and a tiny explosion went off in his chest. She had come back for him.

"Izzy!" Jacob cried. She greeted everyone, with "I changed my mind," and sat next to Jacob who moved up to make room. Now she was facing him.

"What made you change your mind?" he asked, intrigued to hear how she would explain it.

He shoved a menu in her direction, and noted the way she took the menu but pretended she hadn't heard him.

"Haven't you ordered yet?" she asked, surprised, looking at the empty table. "We've eaten, dear. We're ordering dessert," said Jean.

"Why don't you order something for yourself, Izzy?" Dale suggested. "We can wait."

"Or you could order your main dish, and sides, and we'll get our dessert," Xavier offered. He had no intention of sitting here longer than he had to. Unless by some miracle, he managed to shake Jacob's grandparents off, leaving him with Izzy and Jacob. Because now that she had come back, there was no point in wasting the day.

"I'm not actually that hungry."

"Ate something on the way before you got here?" he asked, still none the wiser as to why she had changed her mind. She ignored him again.

"I'm having a triple-chocolate sundae," Jacob told her. "You can share it with me, if you want."

"Aw, that's sweet of you to offer," she replied. "I might try a spoon of it."

The sound of a ringtone going off had them all checking for their cell phones. "Jacob," said, Dale, fishing out his phone. "Your mommy's on the line." Wildly excited, Jacob reached for the phone and started to talk, but seemed to be having problems hearing.

"I think it's too noisy for him to hear," Jean remarked, and her husband suggested they go outside where it would be quieter.

Izzy got up so that Jacob could get out, and Xavier looked for the bodyguard who followed Jacob and his grandparents outside. When she sat back again, she buried her head in the menu, probably so she wouldn't have to talk to him.

"So," he said, making another attempt to find out. "What made you come back?" He watched the way her bangs fell forward, as if she was trying to hide under them.

"I came back for Jacob."

"For Jacob?" he chortled. "Really?"

"Really," she replied, then cocked her head, as if she had realized what he was getting at. "You didn't think I came back for you, did you?" Her gaze turned from curious, to mocking. "Dude, you really should stop flattering yourself." It was the first time he'd ever heard her use his word, and his reading of body language books told him she was mirroring him.

This was a plus.

A huge plus.

She liked him, even if she didn't know it yet.

She continued, "I'd already heard you were full of yourself, and I knew what to expect from you, but how is it that you still manage to surprise me every time I see you?"

He placed his elbows on the table, leaning forwards on the large table. "I surprise you every time you see me?"

"Every single time. You're so sure of yourself, so cocky, and arrogant, and vain."

"Thank you."

"And only a complete jerk like you would take that as a compliment."

His reply sent her expression into a tail spin. Her nostrils flared, and she looked as if she was going to say more, but she held back. He grinned at her, knowing it would rile her up, because he liked getting her riled up. Because, from past experience, whenever he'd had a disagreement with a girlfriend, the make-up sex was always so much better than normal sex. He couldn't wait to see what it would be like with Izzy, on both those counts.

Her lips pressed together tightly, making him wonder what it would be like to have her mouth on him, have her on her knees. He shook himself out of the trance.

"I don't expect you to admit anytime soon that you like the idea of spending an afternoon with me … and Jacob," he added as an afterthought, "but at least have the decency to own up to it so that we can stop beating around the bush."

Her neck elongated, and her face jutted out a fraction. She looked to be in total shock or surprise, he wasn't sure which. "This is really happening," she said, talking to herself, "You really went there. Your ego is even bigger than I thought."

"It's not the only thing that's big."

She blinked rapidly a few times, her mouth opening as she shook her head. "Unbelievable. I can't wait to tell Cara," she mumbled, finally.

"Who the hell is Cara?" The idea that he was the butt of someone's joke soon sobered him up. There was fun to be had in getting her worked up, but knowing she might be talking about him to others, that they might be laughing at him, pissed him off. It was bad enough that Tobias and Luke ganged up on him at every opportunity.

"Nobody you need to know, or worry about."

Before he had a chance to say anything, dessert and Jacob and his grandparents arrived at the same time and their moment of bonding was over. She was mad though, rabid dog mad. He could see it on her face.

For some crazy ten second slot this morning at the pool, when he could see she didn't want him to get into the water with her, he'd seen something in her eyes which he hadn't been able to pinpoint. He hadn't gotten in because he could sense her unease. And even now, she had surprised him. Most girls loved this kind of subtle dirty talk, but he could see that it did nothing for Laronde. He couldn't even engage this woman into conversation without her wanting to put him down.

This wasn't about his libido, and his magic touch, or not. There was something about Laronde, something hidden, something deeper, and the more she pushed away, the more he wanted to get to know her.

~ ~ ~

He was deplorable.

She'd never met anyone who's head was stuck so far up his own ass that he couldn't see daylight if it blinded him.

The only reason she had returned was because she didn't feel right leaving Jacob with Xavier, even though his grandparents were with him.

After hearing his concerns about a sibling, about his fears that Tobias might not love him as much, it only struck her, as she got on the subway going home, that she was abandoning Jacob by leaving him with Xavier. Just because she herself wanted to avoid being around that obnoxious man, didn't mean that the poor boy had to suffer.

Izzy grit her teeth tightly together as she sat back down once Jacob and his grandparents squeezed past her and into their seats.

She couldn't wait to get home and tell Cara how insufferable Xavier Stone was.

"Here you go, Ma'am." The server placed the desserts at the table. "And here are some extra spoons for sharing."

"How was your Mommy?" she asked Jacob.

"She's having fun." He scooped out a huge spoonful of chocolate sundae and shoved it into his mouth. She took a teeny portion, seeing that he seemed to be enjoying it so much.

"But she's missing you, isn't she, dear?" his Grandma asked.

Jacob nodded. "But I told her not to worry. I told her Xavier had taken us all out to lunch, and that made her really happy."

Her gaze flew to Stone's face as she watched him take the credit for it. It made her stomach churn to see him lapping up the praise. "It was so thoughtful of you to ask everybody," she said, calling him out, and letting him know that she knew.

"I told mommy we were going to the park next, but I don't have my scooter."

"Don't worry, kid," said Xavier. "We can go back home to get it." He turned to Jacob's grandparents, and said, "I can drop you back if you're tired."

She was so embarrassed for Jacob's grandparents that she had to step in. "Or you're more than welcome to come with us." She glared at Xavier. "You're probably bored," she said. "You could take off now and enjoy the rest of your weekend. The rest of us can make our own way to Central Park."

"Are you bored?" Jacob asked.

Xavier gave them another shit-eating grin. So false, so hard to digest that it made Izzy's gut harden.

"I'm not bored, kid, and I have the whole day free."

"Wouldn't you rather hang out with your friends, or your girlfriends?" she asked, purposely making the latter plural. She wondered, at the same time, if he had hooked up with Kay ever since they had returned from the wedding. She was eager to ditch him now from the group and get back to it being only her and Jacob.

"My friends are night people," he said, staring at her intently, "and I don't have a girlfriend."

"Night people? You mean like vampires?" Jacob giggled; his lips and outer edges of his mouth were covered in runny chocolate syrup. She handed him a napkin.

"That's funny, kid," he said, messing up the boy's flopping hair.

"If you don't mind," said Dale, lifting out a piece of pecan pie that he and his wife were sharing, "We'd like to look around the Museum. What do you say, Jean? Shall we?"

"Now that we're here, I suppose we ought to do something cultural." Jean turned to her grandson. "Would you like to come with us, Jacob?"

He shook his head, and shoveled another spoonful of sundae into his mouth.

"You should definitely go to the museum," Xavier said. "And don't worry about Jacob. We'll show him a good time."

"Are you sure?" Dale asked.

"Completely." Xavier gave her a grin.

"You must be starving, dear?" Jean asked her. "You've barely eaten a thing."

She wasn't that hungry, but because she'd been checking out the menu in a bid to avoid looking at Xavier, she was starting to get hungry. The chocolate muffin she'd bought on the way here hadn't plugged as much of a hole into her ravenous belly. How she missed home cooked meals. She and Cara got by as best as they could which meant not eating out a lot, or living on home-made stew, and soups and wraps. Cara wasn't a vegetarian, so it made things a little tricky, and she was trying to convince her friend that money would last longer if they avoided eating meat.

"I had something along the way," she told Jean, hoping to placate her.

"Like what?" It was another stupid question from a stupid man. She turned her head towards him and found herself unable to give him an answer.

"What did you eat along the way?" Xavier asked.

"A—A— a muffin." Like it was any of his business. He looked as if he didn't believe her and she didn't care. But sitting here, with the warm BBQ flavored aroma wafting around everywhere, it was impossible to suppress her hunger.

Yet she didn't dare order anything here. Not now that they had all finished, and Xavier had asked for the bill. The prices in this place were ridiculous.

When they had all finished, and the bill was settled, they started to leave. She could feel people turn heads, and stare. It surprised her that anyone knew who Xavier was. But maybe with the recent wedding, she assumed that Jacob had suddenly become a person of interest.

They filed into the black SUV.

"Here," Xavier shoved a small brown package her way.

"What's this?" she asked, not taking it immediately.

"Food."

She shrank away at first, thinking he had asked for his leftovers to be boxed up. "Your left-overs?"

"No," he said, looking genuinely hurt by her accusation. "You looked hungry to me back there." He held the package up to her again. "Take it. I didn't buy the bullsh—," he cleared his throat, "the story that you weren't hungry."

Curious, she took it and opened the lip of the brown paper bag and peeked inside. Something was sealed in a foil wrapper, and it was still warm to touch.

"It's some sort of bean and halloumi mashup," he said, wrinkling his nose as if he wouldn't be caught dead sniffing something like this let alone eating it. "It was the first thing on the menu."

"You didn't have to," she said, not liking that his gesture made her feel indebted, in some way, to him.

"You had that hungry look about you," he said, his voice sexy-sweet, a come-on for most girls. But not her.

She knew what he was doing, and she wasn't about to fall for it.

"Thanks."

She was quiet as Morris drove Jacob's grandparents to the Museum of Modern Art, and then back to the apartment so that they could get Jacob's scooter. Xavier gave Morris the rest of the day off, and decided to take Tobias's Merc. There would be no point in Morris waiting around for them while they were at the park.

"Central Park?" Xavier asked her, sliding into the driver's seat. He seemed more relaxed now that Jacob's grandparents had left.

"That's where you want to go, isn't it?" she asked Jacob.

"Yeah. Can we spend six hours there?"

"Six?" Xavier laughed. "Why six? Why not seven or nine?"

Jacob giggled, and even she found herself smiling.

Chapter 14

Holy shit, it was freezing.

Maybe he should have worn his jacket. He could feel the goosebumps under his long-sleeved t-shirt.

"Aren't you cold, Jacob?" he shouted as the kid scooted past at breakneck speed.

"Nahhhhhhhhhhhh!" Jacob squealed as he raced past.

He rubbed his hands together. "How the fuck's he not feeling the cold?"

"You can't swear in front of children."

Izzy seemed to be chattier ever since he'd given her the wrap. He sensed a thawing of her once ice-cold temperament. It brought a smile to his lips to know he was going to slowly melt every piece of hardness inside her.

"He didn't hear," he shot back, defensively. "Jeez. It's cold enough to freeze my nuts off."

She looked at him in disgust.

He was going to have to try different tactics with her. A bottle of the finest champagne wasn't going to do it. "Sorry, Laronde. I didn't mean to offend you."

"You're not."

"Good, because I aim to please."

"Sick." He thought he heard her mutter under her breath. "Do you always behave like this?"

"Like what?"

"You mean you don't even know when you're being a jerk?"

"I'm not being a jerk."

"Is this how you are? Or is this a façade?"

"This is me. I don't understand what you've got a problem with. I could say you're tight-assed."

She scowled. "Tight-assed?"

"Or frigid."

"Oh, no," she said. "No. We're not going there."

"I'm not going anywhere, I'm making an observation, that's all."

They were standing face to face now. Her expression was one of pure revulsion. No woman had ever looked at him like that before, unless she was play acting and they were about to get dirty. But Laronde didn't look like she was acting. That sneer was genuine, and she looked like she hated him.

She threw her head back, tilting her chin defiantly, doing that thing she did, when she thought she had one-upped him. She stared at him with cold, flint-like eyes. "You're so different to Tobias."

What was that supposed to mean? Women who wanted serious and intense men went for Tobias, but women who wanted a good time, and lots of sexy times, went for him. They were different, and Laronde comparing them, the way he was used to people comparing his and Tobias in business, angered him. He didn't like that she seemed to know exactly which buttons to press, intentionally or not.

"You're not interested in him, are you? Because he's married and you need to be careful."

119

She threw her arms up in the air as if in total disbelief. "You asshole. How do you manage to get everything so wrong?"

"What the fuck has Tobias got to do with anything?"

His insides started to relax as it suddenly dawned on him. She was playing him like he was playing her. He riled her, and she had discovered the best way to rile him. It hadn't been enough pulling that number before lunch, this time she'd worked out what really did it.

"I'm nothing like my brother, and I thank my fucking stars for it."

"Will you stop swearing?"

He turned away, clenching his teeth. He didn't know how to win her over. She was frigid. Or a lesbian. And if that was the case, then he had no hope in hell.

He was starting to feel that the bet had been a huge mistake. A drunken proposal made in the heat of a sultry evening, after a good too many tequila shots. He had started to think that the moment he had landed back in New York and listened to the messages on his answering machine. Lots of messages, from lots of interested women. A lot of people knew he had been to his brother's wedding, and many wanted the low down, he was sure. He'd had to turn down multiple offers of lunch and brunch and drinks with gorgeous girls, for this? For a Saturday in a fucking park with a girl who had no interest in giving him the time of day.

Screw it.

Playing along with this bet was a waste of his time and frankly, he didn't have months to waste, or wait, until he got some pussy again.

As tempted as he was to tell Jacob that it was time to go home, the look on that kid's face made him wait. The boy was having a good time. But once Jacob was ready to leave, he was going to drop them home, and then hit The Oasis.

It was time to let Luke know.

He'd had enough.

~ ~ ~

She rubbed her hands together and watched Jacob whizzing down the path gleefully. He wasn't feeling the cold one bit, even though there was a chill in the air, and as the afternoon drew on, she started to feel the cold even more.

She glanced over at Xavier who looked to be freezing.

Pathetic.

He was so full of hot air she couldn't imagine him ever feeling cold, and were it not for the way he was walking around rubbing his arms, she wouldn't have been able to tell.

Okay, so, maybe she could make out the faint outline of his muscles in that fancy designer t-shirt of his. The one with the logo, the one that clung to him and showed off his lean build. They weren't huge, his biceps, but they were definitely toned, she could see, because he wore the type of t-shirt that made it impossible not to see. She looked away and swallowed. The guy could be a jerk, even if he'd been thoughtful enough to buy her something to eat.

She would have to watch what she said now because he hadn't liked the comparison she'd made to Tobias. What she had so far seen of Tobias made her see him in a different light. Tobias was a good guy, decent, honorable, and he treated women with respect.

But Xavier?

He was like the frat boys at college—only older. Too old to go to college. If Tobias had just turned thirty, she estimated that his brother was probably a few years younger. Cara had said he was around twenty-seven or twenty-eight.

There were plenty of guys like that at college. Rich ones, who wore designer clothes, albeit grungy designer clothes, ripped jeans, and vintage jackets they paid ridiculous amounts for it. She and Cara got their clothes from thrift shops. Vintage was in, and she was proud of it.

"I'm cold," said Jacob. "Can we get some hot chocolate, please?" he asked, coming to a stop in front of her.

"Hot chocolate?" She saw the kiosks in the distance. Central Park kiosks charged jacked up tourist prices. Savannah had told her to make a note of all her expenses when she was out with Jacob, and ordinarily this wouldn't have been a problem, but today she only had a few dollars on her.

Yet it wasn't often that Jacob asked for anything.

"Sure. Uh—" She looked over her shoulder. Xavier was on his cell phone and, with a pinch of anger, she wondered why he had come along with them. He should have left after lunch. Why had he insisted on coming to the park in order to spend time with Jacob, when clearly he wasn't spending any time at all with him?

"Shall we go get some now?" She had just enough to buy Jacob something. "And then maybe we should go home afterwards?" She hoped he would agree.

"Okay."

She headed for the kiosks, when Jacob, scooting beside her, asked. "What about Xavier?"

"He looks busy," she said, breezily. "He'll know to follow us."

When they reached the kiosks, she saw that she could only afford a five dollar hot chocolate, and hoped Jacob wouldn't ask for anything else.

"Aren't you having any?" Jacob asked, when she paid for it with the last of her cash.

"No." She was on a tight budget, always, and tried to pay with cash as often as she could.

"But your nose is red. You look cold."

"I'm fine."

They sat down on some benches nearby.

"Thanks for walking off without letting me know," Xavier snapped.

"You were busy on your phone," she snapped back.

"Where's mine?" he asked, looking at Jacob's hot drink.

"Do you want some?" Jacob offered his plastic cup to him.

"No, thanks, kid. You drink up. I'll go and get my own."

"Nice?" Izzy asked, rubbing her hands together and wishing she had worn her winter clothes.

"Mmmmmm," was Jacob's appreciative response. "Thanks for taking me," he said, wiping his mouth with the back of his hand.

"You're welcome."

"Mommy said you're going to be around more now, and we can do things on the weekend, even when she comes back."

"Yes. I had such a good time with you on the island, that I told your mommy I would be happy to spend more time with you."

"Cool."

"Here." Xavier appeared in front of her and shoved a cup of hot chocolate towards her. "I told them no marshmallows, on account of you being a vegetarian, and no whipped cream on account of you counting calories."

"And for you, kid." He handed Jacob a chocolate donut.

"Awesome! Thank you."

She looked up, not sure whether to be surprised or insulted. Was he being considerate, and trying too hard? Or was he just reverting back and being an asshole because it was hard-wired into his DNA?

"Who said I was counting calories?"

He seemed to pause in shock. "Okay. That was my mistake. I assumed most girls counted calories."

"Maybe the types of girls you hang around with."

He was like a chameleon, changeable, shifting. One minute she wanted to slap him, and the next she wanted to like him. And as a starving student trying to survive on a tight budget, if Xavier wanted to be her knight in shining armor, she would let him.

"Thank you," she said, taking the cup of hot chocolate and letting its warmth heat her hands.

"Move over, would you?" Xavier asked, and she scooted along the bench, deciding not to question why he couldn't sit next to Jacob because there was plenty of space on his side.

"We're going home after this," she announced.

"Aaaawwww," Jacob wailed, his lips covered in sugar.

"Are you sure you want to go home so soon, kid?" Xavier asked Jacob. "We only just got here."

"Your grandparents might be back soon." If she mentioned them, there might be less chance of Xavier inviting himself back home.

"I'll drop you guys off."

"Are you coming back with us?" Jacob asked, a hint of pleading in his voice. It made her wonder why he seemed to be so drawn to Xavier.

"I can keep you company, Jacob," she offered.

"You said you had too much homework to do."

He must have overheard her talking to Cara on the phone earlier. "It's true. But it is the weekend, and I can stay longer. I'm sure your grandparents will be tired after their day out."

"Some other time, kid."

Something was up with Xavier as he drove them back. He didn't seem as friendly, and didn't say much. And he couldn't get out of the Merc and hop into his Ferrari fast enough. He raced off, with Jacob staring at the car in awe.

Xavier and his bright red supposedly sexy babe magnet. Trust him to drive something like that. It was so him.

Chapter 15

He had to wait until the following evening to see Luke because his friend had been busy.

"Busy doing what?" he asked.

"Busy being busy," Luke drawled. They sat across one of the tables on the rooftop terrace, in a far secluded corner. The tinkle of glasses and bottles rippled in the background.

Xavier waited for his friend to elaborate, and prompted him when he got nothing. "Busy being busy with what, or whom?"

"Nothing exciting. Just looking at more premises."

"Where?" Xavier asked, directing the conversation back to his friend while he worked out how he was going to say what he needed to.

"I'm looking at some sites in Tribeca. I'm thinking it's about time I opened another bar."

"We'll be practically neighbors."

"Yeah."

"Dude, do you ever think of slowing down?" Xavier asked.

"What for? Have to keep busy."

"For what?" He didn't understand. The guy was rolling in money and didn't need to work another day for as long as he lived. But buying real estate and turning it into cash cows

126

seemed to be Luke's specialty, and, more than that, he seemed to have a real passion for it. There were times when Xavier wished he'd had the same kind of luck. Maybe luck had nothing to do with it, and it came down to good old-fashioned persistence and hard work. At times he felt like a fluke, but nobody needed to know that. It didn't matter. The gloss on the outside was what everyone saw and loved.

"So that I don't become a lazy old man floating around on my yacht like my old man."

"And instead you'll be hanging around your bars and clubs?"

Luke dismissed his comment with a nod. "When I hold the launch party, I might need you to get some of your actress and super model friends to come and create some buzz for me."

"Just say the word."

"Thanks, I will. How's that project of yours going?" Luke asked. "I'm assuming you're still batshit crazy and pursuing it?"

Xavier made a noise in his throat then reached for his beer bottle. "The project's going … fine."

"Yeah?" Luke swept his hands through his hair again, his signature move. "You getting anywhere?"

"Of course." Why the fuck couldn't he tell Luke the truth? That he wasn't even on the field yet, let alone first base.

"I don't need proof or anything. Your word's good with me."

"That's good to know." He weighed it up in his head. I want out. But instead he found himself saying. "I might need more time."

Luke grunted. "More time?" He sat forward, his cornflower blue eyes glinting under the soft light. "I always got the impression these things were a done deal with you, from the pick-up line to getting them home."

"She's complicated." And that was putting it mildly.

"Yeah?" Luke folded his arms and sat back, seemingly taking pleasure in his pained confession.

Xavier nodded. It didn't sit well with him, his manhood being challenged so blatantly. His pursuit of this woman, this girl, this college student, was turning out to be not as simple as he had once thought. Physical attraction aside—he liked the look of her, could see himself with her, and, well, what was there not to like about him?

She probably did fancy him, but was in denial about it, or she would come to, if she gave him half a chance, but, moving all the physical attraction aside, he wasn't sure they had much in common.

He hadn't dated a college student in years. He liked his women to be more experienced, and even though Savannah had said she was a couple of years older, he still wasn't sure. When it came down to it, it was now a couple of weeks since he'd met her and he still didn't know much about her. Hell, he didn't even know what she was studying. All he knew was that she was a teetotaler and a vegetarian. It hardly made for a scintillating twosome.

He just hoped that sex wasn't off her menu, either.

And now that he was here, did he really need to put himself through this? A glance around The Oasis showed him that he was surrounded by beautiful women. He only had to walk into this place, or its sister club in the basement, and he could get the number of at least five women by the time the night was over.

Why was he busting his balls over a college girl? Laronde didn't know a good thing when she saw it—but maybe that was part of the allure that stopped him from walking away completely?

"She's complicated, or she hates the sight of you?" Luke asked, digging deeper. It was spooky how spot on Luke could be at times.

"She's at college most of the day, and the only time I can see her is with Jacob. I spent yesterday having lunch with the kid's grandparents."

"There's commitment for you." Luke looked suitably impressed. "But, if you want out, pal, that's fine. Just admit it, there are some girls who you can't win."

The hell he would, especially now that Luke had given him the option to quit. To take it would be the easy way out, and Luke and Tobias already thought he always took the easy way out, in most things.

"I'm not giving up."

"It doesn't sound as if you're getting anywhere because, if you were you wouldn't be here now talking about it."

"It's only been a week since we got back."

"Does she actually like you?"

"Like is too strong a word."

"No shit."

"She hasn't fully appreciated my charms."

Luke massaged the back of his neck. "If she doesn't, you need to accept that you're not god's gift to women, and move on."

"I'm growing on her."

"You're growing on her? You mean like mold?" Luke chuckled, and it pissed Xavier off even more.

"She's interested. She just doesn't know it yet." Of that he was confident. Izzy Laronde was too bogged down in her day-to-day crap that she wouldn't know a good thing if it snuck into her bed and made her come all night.

"You're struggling to get anywhere with her, aren't you?" He hated it when Luke guessed correctly.

"No."

"I don't believe it." The wide grin on Luke's face made him want to punch him. "You've finally found a girl who's not interested in you, and you can't take it."

It might be a tiny bit true, but he was going to fix it.

It was rare that he met a girl who showed such open disdain for him. Sure, he'd been in the situation many a time, when girls were plainly interested, and he wasn't. Heck, he'd even been in the situation where more than one girl had been interested. Three had been his limit—so far—three girls all interested in him at the same time. It had been one heck of a crazy time. Two nights of debauchery in a Las Vegas hotel. Fun, pure and filthy.

But Izzy wasn't one of those virginal, sweeter than honey girls either. There was fire in her, he could sense it from her bubblegum to her ripped jeans and her attitude. He was making progress, but it was slow.

He needed more time.

"She is interested, but she doesn't know it, yet."

"Doesn't know it yet?" Luke repeated, slowly, as if he was thinking it over. "Is she allergic to your charm, or does she just find your pick-up lines offensive?"

He scratched the back of his neck. "I'm not used to dealing with college students. I barely know anything about her."

"That's never stopped you before."

He shrugged. "She doesn't drink, either." Because usually, a couple of glasses of age-worthy Cabernet Sauvignon or Pouilly-Fuissé would have lowered her steel defenses a heck of a time sooner.

"You're going to have to try some different moves," Luke suggested. "You're going to have to woo her another way."

This pursuit had left him in a precarious situation lately. He'd had no pussy in weeks, and he'd been tempted to make some booty calls last night because there was only so much of a dry spell a virile young man could take. And exactly how loyal did he have to be? He was single, and he hadn't yet paired up with Izzy.

He had even gone as far as calling someone, and then hung up before she'd picked up. Something about wanting to prove himself had made him back off, even though no one would have known if he'd been up to anything last night.

"How much time do you need?"

"Six months should do it. She has exams and shit, and Thanksgiving and Christmas is coming, and she'll probably go home."

"Take as long as you want."

"I don't need as long as I want. I've got this. Six months."

"Whatever."

Going without pussy for as long as it took to win Izzy Laronde over, meant that when he finally had her, the reward would be all the more sweeter.

Chapter 16

"Be good," Cara told her as she left to spend the weekend with her boyfriend. "And don't go getting up to anything with Xavier Stone."

"As if. I hate the guy. He's an A-star jerk, a total douchebag, a complete Neanderthal—"

Cara closed the top of her knapsack and threw it onto her shoulder. "That's a lot of hate you have for the guy, it makes me wonder ..."

"Wonder what?"

Cara threw her a searching look. "Wonder what you really think of him."

"After everything I've told you about him, you still don't get it? I don't like him, and hopefully he won't be around this weekend. I don't think he cares much about getting to know Jacob."

"Then why do you think he's spending so much time with him?"

"To get on Tobias's good side?" she explained, when Cara rolled her eyes. "Don't worry, it's complicated. You won't understand. Jacob doesn't realize it and I'm not going to tell him."

"You're onto a good thing, Iz. Karma works."

"How's that?"

"You saved that kid, and now his mom has you babysitting for her. It was a perfect fit—right after Shoemoney. And I was right, wasn't I? Tell me I'm right, about Tobias being nothing like Shoemoney?"

"You were right." Tobias Stone was a family man and he was nothing like Shoemoney.

She shivered at the memory of the first time she had experienced Shoemoney's perversion. That time, she had been on her knees picking up dried pasta shapes from the kitchen floor. She happened to look up to see Shoemoney standing a few feet away, staring at her, and she'd had no idea how long because she hadn't heard him come in. He'd been gaping down her shirt. She wasn't sure, even then, even as the hairs on the back of her neck stood to attention, warning her, and even as his stare lingered over her like a dirty stench. She had managed to stand up, somehow, but her knees had gone weak.

And still, she gave him the benefit of the doubt.

"What are you two doing today?"

"Watching a Marvel movie." Jacob couldn't get enough of his Marvel superheroes.

"Be good."

"Likewise."

Cara left and Izzy quickly washed up her lunchtime dishes, then quickly tugged on her leather jacket. She would Uber it over to the Upper East Side and check over Jacob's homework—Savannah had asked her to look over it. And then, after the movie, they would go and get something to eat.

She picked up her handbag and slipped it over her shoulder, and opened the door just as the doorbell went off.

The air from her lungs stilled.

Gideon Shoemoney stared down at her, his huge hulking frame almost as big as the doorway.

"Isabel." His smile made her want to retch. She strengthened her hold on the door, using it more like a riot shield to hide part of her body, and her jaw tightened, making speech impossible.

"Aren't you going to let me in?"

"Fuck. Off."

"Fuck …" he said slowly, using the word as a weapon. "Off?"

Creep.

She swallowed, and heard the blood pounding in her ears. You are strong, she told herself, willing for her superpower to emerge, wishing, in this moment, that she had some of Jacob's belief in the power of super-heroes.

"What are you here?

"I was in the area." He pushed his foot forward, trying to wedge it inside the door, but she held it firm, so that it only opened a fraction. There was something unhinged in the way he was looking at her. Blood coursed through her body, making her giddy from the sudden adrenaline hit. She was scared, knowing that he was a disgusting and dirty old man, and that he was here.

"What do you want?" Behind the door, with her shoulder hidden out of his sight, she slipped her hand into her handbag, to the inside pocket, and reached for her small pepper spray canister.

"Cassia's not too happy that you left so suddenly and without an explanation."

"Maybe I should call her up and tell her?"

"She says we owed you some money," he said, ignoring her veiled threat, "and she wants you to have it."

She smelled horseshit—this idea that he had suddenly developed scruples enough to come and pay her face to face. "Why didn't you pay it directly into my account?"

He wanted something. She didn't believe he'd come just to give her money.

"I wanted to see how you were, and make sure you were okay."

She didn't believe the bullshit.

"I'm fine, but I'd like you to leave." Where was Cara when she needed her? If her friend had been here now, she wouldn't have held back about telling this dirt bag exactly what she thought of him, but he was so much bigger than her, and even though she had taken self-defense classes at college, and had her Pepper spray in her hand, she didn't want to risk anything.

Gideon Shoemoney was the type of Wall Street Master who probably thought he could get away with doing whatever he wanted to her and that she would never say a word. It hit her then that it was exactly what she had done. She hadn't told a soul, apart from Cara. She had kept quiet about it, wanting nothing more than a peaceful life, not even telling her parents.

It would make her father even more depressed, and another rich and unscrupulous man had already destroyed him before.

Shoemoney held out the wad of money. The twenty dollar bills seemed to be more than the two hundred and fifty dollars she was owed.

"Here's five hundred."

Her brows pinched together. "Why the extra?" She smelled more horseshit.

"Just a little something."

"For what?" She refused to take it. Whatever his motivation, she didn't want his money.

"Take it," he ordered.

Slipping the pepper spray into the back pocket of her jeans, she quickly counted and took what he owed her, and returned the extra to him. "This is extra. I don't want it."

"It's yours."

"What for?" If he was worried she was going to tell anyone, she wasn't. Despite all these new allegations by women, against all the big bad bosses, despite everything that was starting to come out into the public arena, she couldn't find it in herself to put her hand up and confess that she too had been the victim of sexual assault, that this had happened to her, too. "Leave."

"Take the money." He ground the words out slowly.

"I don't want it. Are you afraid?" she asked, suddenly gaining strength, gaining comfort from the thought that women were beginning to speak up, and that she wasn't alone. "Are you scared of the Women's March? Are you scared that we're outing pigs like you?"

"What are you talking about?" It was clear from his face he had no idea. "Look," he said, stepping away. "I heard that you're working for the Stones now." He coughed again. "I don't want you to think we deliberately refused to pay you, especially with the way you left. People might talk."

And then she understood. He was worried she might tell the Stones what he'd done.

"You're hoping to buy my silence?" Was this compensation? Hush money? And how did he know she was working for Tobias?

He was worried. For all his tough exterior, his loud arrogance, this man didn't want anyone, least of all Tobias Stone, to know exactly what type of a creep he was. And he was worried that she might let it slip. He coughed again and shuffled back a step. "I don't want someone like Tobias Stone to think badly of me."

"You creep." She threw the money at him and tried to shut the door, but he jammed his foot in the way. "I only want to talk to you. I want to explain what happened that day—"

But she didn't want to give him the time of day. In a flash she reached for her pepper spray and pointed it directly at him.

He laughed. "You wouldn't dare."

She placed her finger over the top, her heart pumping. "Try me."

"You are a feisty little girl, aren't you?" His dirty smile did it. She pressed the top and kept her finger on it.

"You fucking bitch!" he cried, his large, fleshy hands shielding his face as he stumbled backwards.

"Get out!" she screamed, "Get out, get out, get out!" She slammed the door and bolted it in both places before securing the door chain. Closing her eyes, she leaned against the door, her insides fluttering violently, like a frightened, caged canary.

Seeing Shoemoney had brought it all back. The feeling of grime, the guilt, the hole in her stomach. She started to sweat, her throat turning drier than sandpaper.

She covered her mouth with her hands, trying to hush her loud, labored breathing, as she strained for sounds that Shoemoney might still be on the other side of the door.

She listened, trying to get her breathing to calm down, and after a while, when the thudding of her heart quietened, she heard nothing.

When her cell phone rang, she quickly silenced it, and answered the call without looking to see who it was.

"You're late, Izzy!"

"Huh?" she looked up, scowling.

"Don't worry. We're coming to pick you up." Jacob's voice shook her out of her nightmare. "Izzy? Izzy, are you there?" His sweet words made her want to cry with relief.

"I'm running late, sorry."

"'Sokay. We'll be there in…" She heard someone say it in the background first, before Jacob said, "Five minutes."

"Okay."

It was only after she had put her cell phone away, after she had waited for her breathing to still, and when she was sure there was no sound coming from the other side of the door, that she realized it had been Xavier's voice she'd heard in the background.

A short while later she heard a knock on her door. "Izzy!"

She had been sitting on the floor the entire time, slumped up against the door. She got up slowly, unbolted the locks, took off the chain, and opened the door to find Jacob's smiling eyes looking at up her. Behind him stood Xavier, not smiling. If anything, he looked uneasy.

"How many locks do you have?" he asked.

She had never been so relieved to see him before.

"We're going to the movies, remember?" Jacob said.

"Yes, we are," she replied, her voice sounding lackluster, and she couldn't instantly summon up the energy to hide her emotions.

"What's the matter?" Jacob asked.

"I was … I was studying for a test, and I got carried away," she replied. A quick glance at Xavier told her that he didn't quite believe her.

"Can I take a pee, Izzy?" Jacob asked. He still hadn't taken a step inside.

"Sorry, come in," she said, opening the door wider, then, "I don't know. Can you pee?" She smiled at Jacob, using the boy's energetic spirit to help dispel some of her shock.

"It's here," she said, showing him to the washroom, and by the time she had walked, Xavier was standing inside her apartment with the door closed.

"You were studying?" he asked. "Do you always bolt the door like that when you're studying?"

"This isn't the Upper East Side."

"No. But two deadbolts and a door chain? Who are you hiding from, Laronde?"

"No one." She clenched her mouth tightly, then forced herself to push out a smile.

"No one. Interesting that because," he opened his palm and showed her. "It's been raining money on your doorstep."

She stared at the dollar bills in his hand. The bastard had left it for her. She still didn't want it, but if she said anything now, Xavier would have questions. "Thanks." She plucked it out of his hands, and placed it in the pocket of her jeans. She would figure out what to do with it later.

She braced herself for the questions, because the way he looked at her, the way his stare reached down into her soul and held there, told her he didn't believe her.

"What's your explanation for that?"

She stared back at him. "I was wondering where my rent money had gone. It must have slipped out of my back pocket."

"Yeah?" He bent down and picked up the pepper spray can from the floor. "Then what's this?"

She struggled to swallow. "It's—uh." She was stuck. And he was more than imposing, more than nosey, more than interfering.

"Something you want to tell me, Laronde?"

She exhaled out slowly. Something about Shoemoney coming here, about him wanting to buy her off, about him getting this close to her, had made her nauseous. And she hated being in a place of weakness. Weak enough that Xavier could sense it.

"There's nothing to tell," she said, forcing a laugh.

"You don't look too good." Xavier moved so close to her she could feel the heat from his body. She gawked at him, and this time without her usual steely armor. The rising panic inside her, that he might find out her dirty little secret, made her want to implode.

"In fact," he peered at her, "you're looking paler than usual. You sure you want to go to the movies?"

"Jacob wants to go."

"We can watch something here, or we can go back to their apartment, or you could both come to mine," he said quickly.

It seemed like a better option all of a sudden, being away from the crowds in the movie theater. She was so shaken up, she wanted to withdraw into herself.

"What's going on, Laronde? I know something went down just now."

"Nothing went down," she managed to say. Her body was stiff, every muscle in her body clenched. "Nothing, Stone." She managed another grin, a tiny laugh.

"That's twice you've attempted to laugh, and you've never needed to do that before, not with me. You're always your usual defensive self."

His eyes bore down on her, the weight of his stare heavy. She tried to push everything away, his probing, his questioning, his need to discover and get down to the truth. For a moment, she wished the playboy seductor was back, the one who was so wrapped in himself, that he had no awareness of others. This new version of Xavier unnerved her, because he seemed to read her like a book.

"I'm not the pig you seem to think I am. You can tell me. I'm looking after things while Tobias is away."

"He left you in charge?" It came out as if she was being sarcastic.

He didn't seem to like that, judging by the way his brows squeezed together. She hadn't meant to say it like that, why did it come so easily to her, throwing words at him like poisoned blades, and the guy was only trying to be nice to her?

"You are looking after his step-son, and it's obvious to me that some shit went down. I'd be remiss to turn a blind eye to it." His voice was hard again, and she couldn't blame him. "We've got a change of plan, kid," he told Jacob when he returned.

The boy's face crumpled.

Wait, what? She stepped forward. "No, no. You can't just walk in and change our plans be—"

He'd turned his back to her and was addressing Jacob.

"We're going to the movies later on, or maybe even tomorrow," Xavier said, "but Izzy isn't feeling so well, so how about you both come over to my place and you can play in my media room? I've got better game consoles than Tobias."

She was about to stab him in the back with her finger when she heard Jacob's excited "Really?"

"Really."

"Cool!"

She bit her tongue. How dare Xavier change their plans? He turned around, and gave her a smile that made her want to slap him. "We're going to my place."

"Yours?" And now she really did want to slap him.

"Yay!" But an ecstatic Jacob kept that plan at bay.

Chapter 17

"Yours?" She'd said it was if it was a violation of her basic human rights.

"Yay! He's got a cool media room," Jacob cried, excitedly. Tobias had brought the kid over once a few months ago, and Jacob had declared that Xavier had better games consoles and controllers than Tobias.

"But don't you want to go to the movies, Jacob?" Izzy seemed determined not to let him have his own way, but in all seriousness, Xavier didn't feel it was the best thing to do.

Jacob shook his head. "Can't we play games at Xavier's place?"

There was her answer.

Besides, she looked shaken up. How could he turn a blind eye to what he'd seen? For fucks' sake, there had been twenty dollar bill scattered outside her door, and she had a pepper spray canister lying on the floor.

He was determined to get to the bottom of this.

"Okay, if that's what you want," she said to the boy. "It's a shame because I thought you wanted to go to the see the movie."

"Pleeeeease, Izzy?"

"Okay, fine. We'll go to Xavier's place." He wondered if she hated him that much that she was willing to be so stubborn.

He was about to say something but, seeing the sour look on her face, held back. Something had shaken her, and he didn't feel it was right to continue their verbal sparring. He'd let her have some quiet time to herself.

Once more, he had taken Tobias's Merc and left his Ferrari in his brother's underground parking lot.

He drove them all over to his apartment, mindful of the fact that Izzy had never been here before. They rode the elevator to his floor, and he let them both in to his apartment.

While most girls who came here for the first time fawned over his eight-foot tall windows that stretched across the twenty five-foot width of the living room, or looked up in awe at the high, wood-beamed ceilings, Izzy remained silent. She didn't even look around. She didn't even comment on the treadmill and punch bag in one corner. Nor was she impressed by the views overlooking Canal Street on one side and a local park on the other.

Jacob headed straight for the media room.

"No over eighteen games," Izzy warned. Then to him, "Jacob knows better than to play those games, but I can't vouch for you."

"Why don't you come in and keep an eye on him?" he asked her, as she hovered around in the living-room.

"I'm fine here, thanks. I'm not a huge game player."

"No?" Funny, he had her down as being one of those geeky girls who were into online gaming. "You don't know what you're missing."

"I'm sure I'll survive." It was an exasperated sigh, as if she had to force herself to make conversation. He still had questions, but he could tell that now wasn't the time. "Make yourself at home."

He walked through the hallway to the media room.

"Let's have some fun, kid."

He spent some time with Jacob, leaving Izzy alone. It wasn't ideal, dragging her all the way here then abandoning her, but if she didn't want to join in, he couldn't force her.

She was impossible to get close to, but now he had an extra three months and it was a saving grace. Problem was, Tobias and Savannah would be back next weekend, and then he would be fighting with them for Jacob's time—because Jacob was the link to his time with Izzy. He wasn't sure how he was going to overcome this logistical problem, but, as with most things, he would find a way or make one.

After playing a couple of games with Jacob, he left the kid to it and went back to check on Izzy.

She was on the couch, texting away on her cell phone. He wondered if she had a boyfriend now? Bummer. Because, if that was the case, it was going to be a serious problem, and one he hadn't thought of.

"You okay?" he asked.

She hastily looked up, and stopped texting. "Yes."

"Are you sure you don't want to come and play?"

"I told you, I don't like those types of games."

He walked over and stood in front of her, his hands on his waist. "What types of games do you like?"

"How is it that you turn everything into innuendo?"

"Innuendo?" He guffawed, because he hadn't meant it like that at all. Hell, he could give her some real innuendo that would make her face turn scarlet.

"Yes. Suggestive talk, hinting at something inappropriate."

"I know what it means. I'm not dumb. I was being serious."

"I can't tell with you."

"When it's innuendo, with me, you won't have to ask. It'll be pretty obvious."

Her cheeks flushed at that, and he would bet any money that she was annoyed that his words had had an effect on her.

She stared up at him through her long, curly eyelashes, her dark eyes fixing on him, her gaze searching. It was as if she could see right through his phony exterior, and reach down, and feel the real him. It was almost impossible to be brash and cocky, when the other person wasn't remotely affected by that kind of talk or behavior. Laronde had had a dampening effect on him, and in return, he'd seen through part of her armor.

He'd thought of her as cute enough, back on the island— eye candy, nice legs, average sized breasts, more a commodity, something to attain, than a person who had hopes, and fears, and feelings. He'd carried that idea all the way to New York, but now, sitting here on his couch, in his apartment, with her looking at him like that, it made him see her through a different filter.

She definitely was pretty easy on the eye—dark hair, dark eyes, and with those bangs falling over her face, tempting him to want to move them back so that he could take a good look at her face.

A thought ricocheted into his head, of what it would be like to have her eyes staring at him when she came, have her screaming his name on those full, and pretty, and delectable lips of hers. The dirty visual imprinted on his brain and stayed there a few moments until he visibly shook his head, as if to dispel it.

He straightened up, rubbed the back of his neck and looked away. Not knowing what had happened earlier, but being certain that something had, now forced him to delve deeper. To get under her skin, and find out.

"I'm sorry. I didn't mean to offend you, and I didn't mean it like that." He cleared his throat, pushing that thought away. He hadn't been hitting on her, not now at any rate, but when he resumed his tactics, once this episode was over, he'd have to try harder, do something different, woo her another way.

"Those dollar bills outside your door. How did they get there?" he asked softly. "Because I don't buy your rent money scenario."

"Is it any of your business?"

"Given that my brother and Savannah have left you to look after Jacob, definitely. I'd say it was my business."

"What has anything I do got to do with Jacob? It happened at my apartment."

"So something did happen?"

She looked away.

"Izzy," he said, sitting down and using her name on the rare occasion. It at least made her turn her attention towards him again. Tobias was a rich man, and his recent wedding had probably attracted the crazies, of that he was sure. If someone wanted to hurt Tobias, they could do it easily through Savannah, through Jacob, and through the boy's babysitter.

"I don't want to talk about it."

"I need to know."

"But I really don't want to talk about it," she said slowly, and the unsteadiness of her voice made him look closer, lean in a little closer, try, try, try to understand her and read her.

"I can be a good listener," he said, his voice so very low.

"It's something from before. I promise you." She huffed out a breath, as if it was too much. "I don't want to talk about it, Stone. Okay?"

"Can't you be nice, for once? I'm making an effort."

Her head shot back towards him. "Then stop asking me."

"People don't throw dollar bills away like that, not unless they want something. Did someone want something from you?"

She shot to her feet in outrage, her forehead creased with angry lines. "Like what? What do you think happened? Oh my god!" Her eyes widened a fraction too much. She looked at him and hesitated. "Do you think ... do you think someone paid me for something? For some favors?"

"No!"

"No?" She crossed her arms. "People don't throw dollar bills unless they want something?" She hurled his words back at him.

"I didn't mean that."

"People like you make me sick, Stone."

"People like me?" Where the hell was this coming from? "What do you mean people like me?"

He sensed that there was more going on underneath the surface than he would be able to chisel away at. He might not even get to find out what had happened, not today, and perhaps not within a week, but find out he would, one way or another. Today had been an eye-opener, that much was true.

She was on edge, and his questioning was only making things worse. "I'm sorry," he said again. It didn't even feel that strange to him that he had apologized twice already.

"You should be." She folded her arms even tighter in a defiant pose. "What you're implying is offensive," she hissed, in a barely controlled burst of anger.

"Journalists can be sneaky, and they have their ways and means of buying information. I was worried that someone had come to you trying to bribe you, with money, for information on the wedding, and with Tobias being away, and you looking after Jacob, it's easier for people to get to him."

She looked up at him as if this was new to her. "There are lots of sick people out there, Izzy. You, of all people, should know that, especially after what happened with Jacob before."

"I hadn't thought of it like that."

"That's where I was coming from."

She pressed her lips together, as if she was considering what he'd just told her. "I'm sorry I bit your head off."

His reflex action was to make a joke based on her reply, but he stopped himself in time and accepted her apology gracefully. "Don't worry about it." After a while, "Trust you to jump to that conclusion? Whatever had you thinking I might think someone was paying you for services?"

She shrugged. "I expected wild and crazy from you, doesn't everyone?"

That hurt. It hurt more than he cared to show her. So his lips spread out into a fake smile. "You know me."

She smiled too.

"For a moment I worried a new boyfriend might have crept into your life, a journalist in disguise who was after information."

"Pfffft," she made a derisive grunt. "I don't have a boyfriend, new or old." He thought he heard her mumble, 'too much hassle', but he couldn't be sure. Either way, her response warmed his heart more than a hug from her might have, and he felt proud of himself for slipping that into the conversation so easily.

"It's not the first time you've gotten something wrong, Stone."

"It isn't?"

"Just so you know, the only reason I came to that burger place last week was because of Jacob."

"Jacob?"

148

She shrugged. "We were talking in the pool, that day before you forced us all to go to that burger place—"

"I didn't force you. It was a suggestion."

"Anyway," she continued, "Jacob mentioned—he didn't actually say anything about a baby—but he seems to think that he'll soon have a sibling, and he seemed worried that when the new baby comes, Tobias won't have as much time for him."

"That's what the kid thinks?" Poor kid. He could relate to that, to wanting to please his brother, wanting his approval. Of course it was different, Tobias was his brother, and his relationship to Jacob was different, but he could so relate to what the kid was feeling.

Izzy nodded. "He thinks Tobias won't love him as much as he'll love the new baby, whenever they might have one, which," she angled her head, thinking, "might happen soon, because Jacob seems to think they're trying for a baby."

"He said that?"

"Kids pick up a lot of things. You'd be surprised."

"Wow. I'd better turn down the sound to those porn films, when he's around."

She threw him a filthy look. "You shouldn't be watching porn films when he's around."

"I was kidding."

"I wasn't."

He gave her a grin, because, possibly, this might have been the first conversation between them that hadn't been filled with hate-hate. He could see the corners of her lips lift, just a little.

"Are you trying hard not to smile?" he asked.

In answer, her lips spread out into a wide smile.

"That's better," he said, thinking how much nicer a smile looked on her face. Better than a frown. "And I thought you'd come back to the burger place because you couldn't resist my charms?" he offered, sensing no obvious animosity between them, for now, at least. Things would probably revert back to normal next time, but for now, things seemed the best they'd ever been.

"I didn't want to go, because you imposed and changed our plans, and I thought you were hitting on me. Were you hitting on me?"

"Hitting on you? Don't flatter yourself, Laronde. You're hardly my type." It was with great effort that he managed to keep his face serious.

Her face flushed the brightest shade of crimson he'd ever seen, and he could feel her embarrassment.

"That's what I thought," she said, trying to recover. "You're so not my type, either."

Chapter 18

That evening, they went out and watched a movie, then returned to the NYB burger place again where Laronde ordered the halloumi wrap thing. And, as usual, he dropped her back to her place, before returning Jacob home to his grandparents.

And then he waited another week before he could see her again.

He had decided to use his time better, to figure her out and get to know her better. He was confident that he could.

The following weekend he made his way to see Jacob again.

Except this time, it was Tobias who answered the door.

"Xavier? Didn't Savannah call you?" Tobias asked when he turned up at their door. Tobias looked relaxed, fresh, even a few years younger.

"No, she didn't. I came here to see Jacob. Didn't realize you guys would be back so early." For some reason he'd had it in his head that they were coming back Sunday evening. That was what Jean had told him.

He walked into the apartment, and at the same time looked around for Izzy and Jacob.

"Coffee?" Tobias asked.

He blinked. This was new, Tobias asking him if he wanted a drink. Marriage had changed him this much in a matter of weeks? Usually when Xavier turned up he was lucky to get a grunt out of him.

Back in the old days, Tobias's dark days, he'd find his brother surrounded by bottles of whiskey.

"Yeah, sure."

He watched Tobias and noted that the hard set of his jaw had softened and he looked different. It was as if the honeymoon, and being away from the pressures of work, had melted every worry away.

"How come you came back already? Jean said you were landing on Sunday evening."

"We got back last night. Savannah was feeling sick."

"Sick?"

"Homesick. She missed Jacob, was worried about him being alone for so long."

He followed Tobias into the kitchen where Savannah was sitting.

"Look who's turned up," Tobias said to his wife. Xavier walked over and gave her a hug while Tobias started to make coffee.

It was pure domestic bliss, this picture before him, and domestic bliss and Tobias Stone were words which had never before appeared in the same sentence.

"One sugar?" Tobias asked him.

"Three."

"Three?"

"I like my coffee sweet." Tobias pushed a coffee cup towards him.

"You not having one?" Xavier asked.

"We're taking Jacob out for lunch."

"Oh. I was hoping to spend some time with him." But the plans had obviously changed and, of course, Tobias and Savannah would want to spend time with Jacob.

"Aren't you guys jetlagged?" he asked, looking around casually for signs of Izzy. "I can take Jacob out for the day, and Izzy usually turns up by now."

"We're okay," replied Savannah, "and looking forward to spending the day with Jacob."

"I was going to take him for a helicopter ride over the city again," Tobias remarked.

"He'd love that."

"That's what I thought. Here you go," said Tobias, and handed Savannah a mug of what looked like urine-colored liquid.

"What the hell is that?" Xavier asked.

"Lemon and ginger herbal tea." Savannah placed her hands around the cup and inhaled.

"What's wrong with coffee?" He didn't understand people and their weird tastes. It was as bad as finding out that Izzy didn't eat burgers. Did she have any idea what she was missing? He'd seen the veggie alternative, and nobody could ever convince him that a halloumi and mushroom alternative was even worth biting into to.

"Jacob said you spent a lot of time with him," Savannah said, her face slightly golden.

"He's a good kid. We had fun."

"That's what he said. Thanks, Xavier. I didn't want Jacob to feel that we'd abandoned him."

"We didn't abandon him," Tobias interjected. "He was in good hands, and we FaceTimed him three times a day, at least."

"Where's he now?" Xavier asked. "And where are your parents, and Izzy?" he was aware he'd asked her about her a few times now.

"Jacob's having a shower, and my parents flew back this morning."

"So soon?"

"You know what parents are like." Savannah took a sip from her cup. "They've been away from home for weeks now. I think they wanted to get back."

"They're easy-going, your mom and dad." Compared to my parents, thought Xavier.

"They liked the burger place you took them to," Savannah told him. "Thanks for taking them."

"It was nothing." Xavier waved her comment away—part of him feeling guilty because it hadn't been his idea, and he'd been pissed off when he'd discovered that Izzy had foisted them onto him.

"I need to make a few calls," Tobias announced.

"Back to work already?" Savannah looked at him.

"Just a few calls, I promise." He squeezed her shoulder, the small act, intimate and natural, Xavier thought. He wasn't one for touchy-feely shows of emotion. Not that there was anything deliberately on show here. The love was evident between these two.

Typical for a honeymoon couple.

"Jacob's having a shower?" He hoped this would prompt Savannah into telling her more about Izzy's plans. After all, it was the main reason he'd come here.

"He'll be out soon enough," Savannah assured him.

"Was Tobias always on the phone on vacation?" Xavier asked her.

"No, he wasn't. He was as good as gold, it's probably why he's making up for it now. Catching up on everything."

"We can take Jacob out today," he suggested, sitting down next to Savannah. He was hoping that Izzy would appear, and they might be able to continue where they had left off last weekend. "Give you both a chance to recover from jetlag."

"The jetlag isn't too bad, surprisingly," Savannah replied.

"That's good," he said, then made polite small talk, asking her about the honeymoon, and, when she had finished recounting her favorite highlights, and Izzy still hadn't showed up, he looked at his watch and said, "Izzy usually comes along around about now," in a bid to prompt news of her whereabouts.

"I told her not to come today."

"You did?" His mood sank.

"I told her we wanted to spend this weekend pampering Jacob."

Damn it. No point in him sticking around here, then. He gulped down his coffee. Maybe it was a good idea for them to spend time with the kid. From what Izzy had told him, it sounded as if the kid needed his mother and Tobias more than Xavier needed to find an inroad to Izzy.

"You should do the helicopter ride," he said, taking a final gulp. Damn, that coffee was good. He was tempted to ask for another cup, but he could make it to the cafe around Tribeca for brunch, and read the morning's paper. That area was good for people-watching. Lots of models flocked to the cafe there. It was where he'd met Petra. "He would like that."

"I know he would. I just don't want him to get used to having helicopter rides the way most children get used to having ice-cream."

"He won't. He's a sensible child. Grounded. You brought him up well, Savannah. I wouldn't worry about him turning into a spoiled little brat."

"Thanks," she cupped her hands around her mug. "Izzy said everything was fine while we were away. She said Jacob didn't seem too sad or upset that we were gone for so long." She seemed to be seeking his approval, as if she felt guilty for leaving him.

"It was fine. Jacob had a ton of fun, ask him yourself. Izzy was good with him, and I would come over and we'd do stuff. Your parents were here, so I don't think the kid had any reason to feel sad at all."

"I'm glad to hear it. I was worried about him, what with me getting married and everything, it's a huge change in our lives. I felt bad that I'd left him while I was on vacation."

"He was well taken care of, Savannah. He seemed happy, and you have no reason to worry. Apart from that one small episode, I mean, I think it's a perfectly valid fear, feeling left out, and him worrying about—"

"What thing?" Savannah interjected. From her reaction it was plain to see she didn't know.

"That ... Jacob was ..." He'd assumed that Izzy would have brought Savannah up to date with everything, and now he realized she hadn't. "It's no big deal. I'm sure Izzy will fill you in when she sees you."

"What's not a big deal?"

He scratched his head wondering why he'd broached the subject at all. And so he told her what Izzy had told him, as best as he could remember, about Jacob feeling worried about a new sibling, and about Tobias not being his real dad. The more he spoke, the more worried Savannah looked. He wished he had kept his mouth shut.

"I had no idea," she said when he had finished talking. Even worse, he was now worried about the possible fall out once Izzy found out he had told Savannah before she'd had a chance to.

"I'm sure Izzy was going to tell you."

But Savannah appeared lost in thought.

"I think it's a natural reaction, Savannah. I wouldn't worry too much about it."

"Maybe it is, but it makes me feel all sad inside thinking about him." Savannah appeared to be thinking things over. "I was starting to think that I was worrying for no reason, but my fears were valid."

"What fears?"

"I think I need to focus solely on Jacob. I need to forget about the house move, and the charity work, and everything else and just concentrate on him. He obviously needs me more than I thought. The change has been too unsettling for him."

He listened, and hoped he hadn't made too many alarm bells go off. Savannah was obviously so protective of her son. "Yeah, maybe there's been a lot for him to take in."

"It's more than a young child should have to deal with. I get why Jacob feels anxious." Her voice dropped lower. "It's been mostly me and him."

"Yeah." He could see he had set something off, and hoped that Tobias wouldn't walk back into the kitchen and see that he'd unknowingly made Savannah worried.

"I want him to see he's the core of our family. Because he is."

"I'm sure you guys make him feel as if he is."

"I think it would be wrong of me to have Izzy come over on the weekends." She placed her palm flat against her forehead. "And she'd only recently agreed to come and work for me."

"You can still have Izzy come over," he said, not liking where this was going. "Jacob likes her."

"No," Savannah drew out a long breath. "No, he obviously feels worried enough to tell you and Izzy."

"He didn't tell me, he told Izzy." As if that was going to change things.

But Savannah was lost in her own thoughts. "I feel bad because I'd already promised her that she could work some hours for me, babysitting Jacob on weekends, and maybe evenings, around her college and other jobs."

"Other jobs?" What other jobs?

"She does some work on the side, to supplement her tuition," said Savannah, distractedly.

"She does?" What? Where?"

"Oh," Savannah turned her attention back to him. "She does it all online, after she's finished her college work. I get the impression she's trying to do it all by herself, and I wanted to help her, that's why I wanted to give her extra hours, apart from it helping me out, it would help her, but I see now that it would be wrong to have her continue right away. I need to postpone having her work for me."

This was the answer to his prayers—if Izzy was doing work on the side, and she needed to earn more money, he could solve that problem for her, and have her work for him a few hours a week.

He could do even better than have access to Izzy through Jacob—access which would only occur on weekends. If he made the offer attractive enough, he could have access to her all the time. And which struggling college student would say 'no' to that?

"I wouldn't worry about Izzy, Savannah." He had plenty of work and he was sure Laronde could do it. "She's a smart girl, and she's got the other jobs, as you said. She'll be fine."

But Savannah didn't seem convinced. "I've been in that situation before. I know what it's like to want work, and not have it, when you really need it the money."

"My VA left without notice, and it's left me in a bind. I have plenty of work that she could do for me, if I can convince her to."

"You?"

"Yes. I'm hopefully going to get the investment I need for another new business I'm looking to set up, and I have a lot of outstanding work that my VA left behind. Izzy could start straightaway."

"That would be a great help, Xavier." Savannah looked relieved. "I hate the idea of letting her down."

"I can definitely help give her something."

"As a temporary solution, it would help."

"But I wouldn't mention anything to her yet," he cautioned. "Or anyone else." He looked around, making sure Tobias wasn't around. His brother would be the first to reach only one conclusion about him taking Izzy on for work. "Let me reach out to her first."

"You'll speak to her?" asked Savannah.

"Leave it with me."

Chapter 19

"You're going to have to do something with the extra money. It's been lying on the kitchen table for over a week, Iz." Cara's mouth had specks of coffee-flavored cupcake icing across it.

"Don't remind me." She'd left Shoemoney's cash lying around and hadn't come to any suitable conclusion about what to do with it.

"I'm going to spend it if you don't. We're running out of toilet rolls."

Izzy groaned.

"I can't believe he had the audacity to come here and try to pay you off."

"Me neither."

Izzy shrugged. "He can't buy me off."

"No he can't. But it's not as if you were going to tell anyone. Have you told your parents yet?"

Izzy shook her head. No way. She had no intention of telling them at all.

"Why don't you mail it back to him? That way you won't have to see his ugly face again."

Izzy nodded. "Or I could slip it into one of those charity donation boxes next time I see one?"

"But you're not in a position to donate 'unwanted money' to charities. We're a charity case right now."

Cara was right. Izzy cradled her head in her hands. "I hate people like that. I hate people who think they can treat people like dirt and use them for their own sick perversion, and just walk away like nothing happened."

They sat on the couch sharing a plate of cupcakes that Cara had bought. They were a day past the best before date, but they tasted fine. It wasn't the healthiest thing to eat, but it was exactly the type of sugary lift Izzy needed.

"Xavier's on to you," said Cara, bringing the conversation back around to him again. Her friend was convinced that he was interested in Izzy, and she now regretted telling her about everything that had happened last week.

"He's not on to me," said Izzy. "He's just being nosey."

"He obviously knows that something shady's gone on. When are you going to tell him the truth?"

"I'm not."

"But he seemed so concerned." She had told Cara about his suspicions and about their subsequent row at his place when he'd gotten the wrong end of the stick about the money.

"He's a charmer, a player. I'm not falling for it."

"He might really like you."

She let out an irritated huff.

"Okay, okay. I'll stop going on about it. Here," Cara pushed the plate towards her. "Have another cupcake. You look like you could do with it."

"If you're going to shove the plate in front of my face like that I can hardly refuse."

"Go on. You know you want it. It's a lazy weekend, and you don't need to rush over and entertain that kid either."

She picked up another cupcake with half an inch of icing on top. She peeled back the paper casing on one side and took a huge bite, getting a mouthful of rich coffee flavored buttercream and soft, moist juicy sponge cake.

"But Savannah still wants to see me." She had called yesterday. The Stones had arrived back from their honeymoon a few days early, and Savannah had told Izzy there was no need for her to go over as she and Tobias wanted to spend time with Jacob. So Izzy had lain in bed this morning, having a rare weekend where she didn't have anything to do. Even her homework assignments this weekend weren't too bad.

But then she'd called again, an hour ago, asking Izzy if she could come over as there was something she wanted to discuss. "I better start making a move."

"Are you going now?"

"I'd better go and find out what it is."

"Maybe they've pampered the kid as much as they can and now need you to take over while they recover from jetlag."

"Jacob's not a spoiled child at all," Izzy replied, defensively. "And they're good parents. Jacob's really humble and really sweet. Even you would like him."

"I doubt it." Cara licked off the cream from her cupcake. "Maybe she wants to pay you?" Her lips were smudged with buttercream.

"Yay!" Payday was always good. And Savannah's rates were generous. She got paid for a few hours looking after Jacob what would easily take double the amount of time at the diner.

~ ~ ~

"Mom's back!" Jacob announced with a beaming face. "She said for you to come through." He lead her towards Savannah's bedroom.

It was only when Izzy stood at the open bedroom door, that she saw a heap of suitcases lying in one corner of the huge bedroom. It was nearly triple the size of her and Cara's entire apartment.

"Hi," said Izzy, knocking on the door.

"Hey." Savannah's smile said a thousand things. "Come in." Her skin was the color of golden honey and the reddish highlights in her hair glinted even redder.

Izzy walked in and tried not to stare at Savannah's stomach discreetly, trying to work out whether Savannah was pregnant or not, but it was hard to tell with the loose t-shirt she wore. She seemed the same as ever, only more tanned, and more glowing. Izzy couldn't tell if that was from the honeymoon or if she might be pregnant, if Jacob's words were to be believed.

"How was the honeymoon?"

Savannah closed her eyes momentarily, and smiled, as if reliving that moment. "Like a dream. It was everything I could have imagined and more."

"I can imagine." Life as the wife of a billionaire was probably a 360 degree turn from what Savannah's life had been before.

"Let's go into the living room," Savannah suggested, "this room is a mess. And, thanks for coming over at such short notice."

"It's not a problem," Izzy replied. "I wasn't doing anything." Except vegging on the couch with my friend and a plate of cupcakes.

Savannah motioned for Izzy to sit down on the couch. Already Izzy was wondering what was going on, because Savannah didn't seem her usual carefree self. She seemed more business-like, more forced, as if there was something of a serious nature she needed to discuss.

LILY ZANTE

"I could have come earlier, if you needed me to look after Jacob."

"It's not that. And, the reason I want to see you is because of Jacob." She lowered her voice, leaving Izzy with a distinctly uneasy feeling. She tried to think if she had done anything wrong, by mistake, that could be the reason for Savannah summoning her.

"Jacob?"

"I missed him so much when we were away, and coming back to him now, I think it would be wrong of me to ask you to take him out and about when I can do that, for now at least. It's nothing you've done," she rushed to reassure her. "It's me. I finally had the time and quietness to think things through and I believe I need to spend more time with my son."

Izzy clasped her hands together. She had an idea of what this was about, and she wondered if Jacob had said anything to his mother.

"I don't know how to say this," said Savannah, clasping her hands together, and looking uneasy.

"Did I do something wrong?"

"Oh my goodness," gasped Savannah. "No. Definitely not. You've been amazing, Jacob said, and Xavier said."

"Xavier?"

"Yes. He came here earlier, not knowing we were back. He was ready to go out with you and Jacob. He said you'd had a good few weekends."

Izzy forced a smile.

"This just makes it even more harder for me to say."

"Just say it, Savannah."

"Okay." She took in a deep breath. "You know that Jacob is the most precious thing in my life, along with Tobias, obviously. And, I don't want my son to feel pushed out."

"Of course not." She'd wanted to tell Savannah about the conversation with Jacob in the pool the other day, but hadn't wanted to do it over the phone.

"I hate to do this," said Savannah—and Izzy knew that a 'but' was coming—especially when Savannah couldn't look her in the eye. "But I think it would be better—for the next few months at least—if I spent as much time as possible with Jacob."

She could see that Savannah felt bad, even though she completely understood. It seemed that Jacob might have told her or hinted his worries and Savannah had picked up on something.

"I'm glad he told you," said Izzy, feeling happy that Jacob had expressed his concerns to his mother. "That's quite a mature thing for a young child to do."

"Jacob didn't tell me. Xavier did."

"Xavier?" Why would he mention something like that to Savannah?

"He mentioned it, and I'm glad he did, otherwise I would have had no idea."

"I was going to tell you," said Izzy. "But I wanted to do it face to face, because I didn't want you to worry too much, and I didn't think it was the kind of thing to tell you over the phone yesterday."

"I know you would have, but, now that I know, I have to fix it, and this is how I'm going to go about fixing it."

She recounted the conversation back to Savannah. "I tried to tell him it wouldn't be like that and that you would both continue to love him as much as you love the new baby— whenever it comes, but he seemed to worry most about Tobias not being his real dad, and not loving him as much as he would love the new baby, whenever that comes." She looked away, and it was hard not to look at Savannah's stomach, and try to guess.

"I feel bad I wasn't there to listen to him, and I'm glad you were. I knew he would open up to you. He trusts you, Izzy, as I do, and that's why this is so hard for me to do, to ask you to step away."

It was going to hit her hard, losing the easy money that came from looking after Jacob, but it wasn't Savannah's fault, and it wasn't hers. She would simply have to find a way around it. She didn't blame Savannah, and if she was in her shoes, she would have done the exact same thing. Jacob was her priority, not Izzy.

"I'm sorry, Izzy. I hate to do this to you, especially since I was the one hounding you to come and work for us. I promise you it's only temporary because I will need help in a few months' time. Just not right now. Could you give me until after the New Year?"

"Sure." She was being let go, and sweetly. While she could understand Savannah's dilemma, her own dilemma was brewing up inside her. She tried to laugh it off. "Don't feel sorry, I understand, and I have exams to cram for before Christmas. I'll be okay."

The fate of Shoemoney's extra cash had been decided. It would go to the Izzy and Cara fund.

Chapter 20

"He wants to meet," said Izzy, closing her cell phone in confusion. He had called her the day after she'd met with Savannah, and she wondered if it was some strange coincidence, or not.

"Shoemoney?"

"Xavier." After yesterday's shock news from Savannah, the last person she wanted to hear from was Stone.

Cara rolled over on her bed, propping herself up on her elbows and gave her a Cheshire Cat-worthy smile. "Xav-i-er." She stretched out his name on her lips as if it were a dirty word ripe with sexual connotations.

"Don't 'Xav-i-er', me," whined Izzy, repeating his name the way Cara had said it. "I told him I was busy studying but he said it was business related and it wouldn't take long."

"Business related? I wonder what he means?"

"I'm intrigued enough to want to find out."

Cara's brow raised slowly. "I can come with you, if you need support, or chaperoning."

"It's not what you think. I can tolerate him. If you met him you'd see what a total jerk he is."

"The offer still stands. I can come with you."

"Thanks, but I can handle Xavier Stone."

"Are you going to his apartment?"

"No."

"Where's he taking you then?"

"Nowhere."

An hour later she met him in Central Park, over by the benches near the kiosks.

"Hey," he said, getting up as she started to walk towards him. He looked sexy in navy blue. That was her first impression, seeing him the smartest she'd ever seen him, in a thick, short woollen coat and dark jeans.

"Hi."

"I won't beat around the bush."

Good, she thought. Hopefully this wouldn't take too long. "This is all very secret spy-ish."

"I was too scared to turn up at your apartment," he replied, a mischievous look danced in his eyes.

"Funny."

"You still haven't told me what happened."

"And you still haven't stopped being nosey."

"It's part of my nature, Laronde."

"I noticed, Stone. It's also very annoying."

"Glad that's out of the way," he muttered, staring straight ahead.

"You said you weren't going to beat around the bush, and it's exactly what you're doing."

"I'm making small talk. I'm trying to be polite, seeing that we don't usually have much polite conversation going on between us."

"I'm meant to be studying for tests," she lied.

"I happened to hear that Savannah doesn't need you so much, at the moment."

She stared at him in disbelief. His choice of wording was interesting. "Why did you tell Savannah?"

"I honestly thought you might have mentioned it to her."

"She only called me late on Friday, and it's not something I would have discussed on the phone."

"Are you mad at me?"

"I'm mad that you told her something that wasn't your news to tell." And she was mad that she had lost the hours, but to be fair, she would probably have lost them anyway. She was mad at him because it was easier to be mad at him than worry about where she was going to make up the shortfall in earnings.

"She told me she'd been worried about Jacob while she was away, and I tried to allay her fears. I casually mentioned the only thing the kid seemed to be down about—the stuff you told me. I never thought for a moment that she would stop you from working there."

She was silent as she tried to find something to say. Something that would be neutral. But she couldn't, and so the silence stretched uncomfortably.

It was Xavier who spoke first. "Savannah feels bad that she's left you without any work, and for taking away your income."

"So?" She had no idea what any of this had to do with him. "Did you call me so you could rub my face in it?"

"Hell, no. What kind of guy do you think I am?"

"I can never tell."

"Savannah was trying to find something for you to do so that she could still keep you on, and then I had a solution."

"You?" She flinched at his words.

"One of my virtual assistants had to take care of some personal stuff, and I have no idea when she's coming back. In fact, I don't think I want her back, but, I need someone to carry out a few administrative tasks for me, and to take care of some emails, check some of my spreadsheets, basic things."

"If they're basic things, why don't you do them yourself?"

He angled his head, as if weighing up the amount of spite in her words. "Do you want the extra work or not?"

She didn't want to say 'Yes,' because, for some reason she wasn't sure of, she didn't like the idea of letting him think he was right, or that she needed the work. "I could do with a few extra hours."

"Okay. Well, I could do with some extra help. I'm busy running the businesses," he said, "And Savannah mentioned you already did some stuff on the side. If you're not interested, just say so. There's plenty of other people I can find to fill my VA's shoes."

She jerked to attention at that, and while the last thing she wanted was to work for Xavier Stone, she didn't have a better alternative.

It was waitressing back at the fast food place, or look for some other type of babysitting—but nobody would offer her the weekend only type of work that Savannah had. And Savannah had hinted she would need her after Christmas. If she could go back to her, and look after Jacob, and get paid that much for it, she wanted back in.

"How many hours?" she asked, testing the waters.

"As many as you want."

She looked at him suspiciously. "You don't have a fixed number of hours?"

"I go through a fair number of virtual assistants. This particular one was based in the city, and I trusted her with more than the basics. She kept an eye on my sales figures, and returns for my stores. The rest of the VAs are abroad. Now, you could do her work, which is about five to ten hours' worth of work a week, or, if you want more, I can give you some work from the other VAs."

"I can only work weekends."

"You can do the work when you want, and you don't even have to turn up at my apartment, hence it being a virtual assistant."

"At your apartment?"

"I have an office at home." He eyed her suspiciously. "What did you think I did?"

"I have no idea. It never occurred to me that you did any work." She could see his jaw go hard, and knew he was grinding his teeth together, biting back on what he wanted to say. "Obviously I was wrong." She couldn't be mean to him. He wasn't Shoemoney. He was trying to help her.

"It's probably a good thing that you're not coming to my office, Laronde. You would drive me crazy, and not in a sexy way either."

She snorted. "Virtual is good."

"I'll match whatever Savannah was paying you."

"Why would you do that?"

"Because I can, and because you're local. It beats having to wait for someone to wake up in the Philippines or elsewhere. A VA in the same time zone as me, and logistically close, is better. Sometimes I need stuff done ASAP."

"Don't think I'm going to be at your beck and call."

"Are you interested in working for me or not?" He seemed irritated by her reaction, and she could hardly blame him. She'd been anything but grateful. She didn't like the idea of him being her boss, even if it was on a temporary, couple-of-hours-a-week type of arrangement, even if it was a virtual role where she didn't even need to see him. But he'd given an easy and timely solution to her money worries.

"I—" She didn't need to think about it for too long. She wouldn't see any decline in earnings, given that she'd only lost the babysitting job yesterday. What was she waiting for? "Yes. I'm interested."

"Good. Text me your email address, and I'll send you the work piecemeal."

"What about instructions?" What was it exactly? He'd been vague about the specifics of the job, and she was none the wiser as to what it would entail.

"You're a college student, you're smart, I'm sure you'll find your way around it easily. But I'll be sure to send you idiot-proof instructions, just in case."

Chapter 21

S he surprised him.

It had been easier than he had assumed, setting up work for Izzy.

Everything was done online. He'd sent her a contract which she'd signed and emailed it right back. Later, he'd sent her instructions of how to handle his documents, and she had completed the work in half the time his previous VA had.

And two weeks later, she was still surprising him. He hadn't seen her in that time, but constant contact via email and text meant that he didn't feel as if he hadn't seen her at all.

Luke had told him to woo her another way and it was exactly what he was doing, even if she didn't know she was being wooed.

Besides, he had no complaints. She was quick to pick up on things, quick to turn the work around, and she hadn't so far, made any mistakes. But there was also a slight problem: her attention to detail sometimes drove him to the edge of a cliff.

Apart from that, taking her on had been one of the best moves he'd made. She had cleared a lot of the backlog left behind by the VA who had deserted him.

"Which spreadsheets?" he asked, alarming his car as he walked towards the building that housed The Oasis.

"The ones you emailed me," Izzy replied. "I can't open them, can you resend them?"

No, he couldn't resend them. "I'm out, meeting a friend for a drink. It will have to wait."

"If you're okay with not getting the work back by tomorrow. I have a test I have to cram for—"

"It can wait."

"If you saved your spreadsheets in the old format, we wouldn't have this problem," she continued.

Wait. He stopped outside the entrance. "Are you blaming me for something that's your problem?"

"It's not my fault I don't have a Mac," she replied. "I'm a Windows girl, and yes, I know my version of Excel is old, but I get by just fine with it."

"But it's not my fault that I don't have Windows. I'm a Mac guy. And, why don't you have the latest version of Excel?" he demanded.

"Because I don't need it for my college work."

"Can't you ever own up to it when it's your fault?" If she would say the words, say sorry, it would be easier to swallow. Him using a Macbook and her using a PC was causing a slight problem.

Slight.

He always forgot to export the files so that she could read them and work in them. It was causing a problem he hadn't seen coming. Now he was not only paying for work he could have some of his other assistants do for him, but this particular assistant seemed to be causing more problems than not. He was tempted to buy her a Mac just to shut her up.

"Don't worry about it for now," he told her, getting jittery because he wanted to go to the bar, and sit and admire gorgeous women even if he couldn't take one of them home with him tonight.

Izzy distracted him again. "If you could export them before you send them to me. Please."

"I'll try to remember."

"But you wanted this back by tomorrow. You said it was urgent."

Had he? He couldn't remember half the dates he'd given her. Usually, he just reeled a date off the top of his head.

"I was hoping to get your work out of the way before I started my studying. I have to cram for a test in a few days' time."

He let out a loud sigh. "Forget the work I sent you, Laronde, and just concentrate on your test."

It came out harsher than he'd intended, but his attention was now fixed on two women who walked past him. When they entered the building, he stared through the glass windows, trying to see if they were going to take the elevator up to The Oasis or down to The Vault.

But he couldn't hit on them. This fucking bet. The pent-up frustration inside him made him feel like a bottle of fizz—he felt as if he'd explode given enough release.

"I was under the impression that it was urgent," said Izzy.

No, he thought, raking his hand through his hair. Nothing was as urgent as his need to get laid. It had been over two dry months and his manhood was at risk of shriveling up and dropping off through misuse. It might well have done, for all the action it hadn't gotten lately.

"It's not that urgent." He noticed a honey blonde coming out through the doors. They made eye contact and he flashed her a smile. Jesus Christ, some days, he was so tempted to ditch this goddamn bet and be done with it. He could feel a stirring in his boxer briefs.

"Forget the work, and concentrate on your exams. I gotta go." He hung up, suddenly recognizing the blonde in front of him.

"Kay?" he called out as she walked past.

She turned around and squinted. It had been well over a month since he'd last seen her. An awkward silence opened up between them.

He was reminded of that evening before his brother's wedding, when they'd been kissing. When he'd been tempted to jump into bed with her, but had stopped to briefly consider that it might be inappropriate.

Would he have, if Tobias hadn't found them? Kay hadn't seemed keen to stop kissing, either.

"Xavier?"

"Yeah. What are you doing here?"

"I was at the bar," she pointed up, indicating. "The Oasis. You must know it?"

"Pretty well. My friend owns the place, you know Luke, from the wedding?"

She nodded, remaining silent, not saying or moving the conversation along. He was about to ask her how she was when she said, "Nice seeing you again. I have to go."

"Wait," he said, suddenly needing to know. "Have I offended or upset you in any way?"

"If you don't know, then I wouldn't worry about it." Her words were as icy as her tone.

"I did offend you?" he asked, surprised, because he hadn't expected her to agree so readily.

"Let's just leave it."

"No. I'd like to know. If I've done something to upset you, you need to tell me."

He wondered, at the same time, how he could make it up to her, and whether she would come back to the bar with him.

She'd been a good kisser. And maybe, maybe, they could see how things progressed this evening? He was more than happy to drop the bet. Again. Izzy was working for him, and filling a need. An admin need. Not the type of need that required his immediate fixing.

"You really don't have a clue, do you?"

"About what?" If she was pissed that nothing further had happened between them, he was sorry. "Look, I didn't mean to leave the island without talking to you."

"It's not always about you, Xavier." There she went again, looking pissed as hell.

"I need to catch this cab. 'Bye." She rushed towards the curb, and put her hand out for a cab, leaving him standing there, wondering what he'd done wrong.

The hell it wasn't about him.

She was pissed. Pissed that he hadn't called her, or spoken to her after that night at the wedding. The next time he saw her, when she would have hopefully calmed down, he would remind her that she was the one who had cold-shouldered him.

Women.

They were incredibly difficult to understand.

He rode the elevator to the rooftop, and was early, just as he had planned. Luke was at the bar talking to one of his guys, and he looked super smart this evening. Black blazer, black jeans, looking like god's gift to women, as usual.

"What's this in aid of?" he asked, gesturing at his friend's attire, when Luke walked up to him.

"This?" Luke looked puzzled. They shook hands.

"You look like you made an effort." Xavier scanned around the bar. "Who are you hoping to hit on? I thought you never mixed business with pleasure."

"Nobody, and I don't." His friend's reply took a while to sink in.

"Beer?"

"Just the one," Xavier replied.

"Two beers," Luke ordered. They sat down at the usual table in the corner. Luke's table.

Xavier put his leather bound folder down. "I have a business meeting here, later," he explained.

"With who?"

"With a guy called Chad Hennessy."

"And what business scam are you going into next?"

"Fuck you." He liked the dude, but these recent put-downs were hard to stomach, and it was either that he was especially sensitive, or that some of Tobias's cynicism had rubbed off on Luke but Xavier didn't like it.

He was meeting Hennessy tonight. He didn't usually hold business meetings in The Oasis, but Chad was young, and looking to expand, and he had contacts in China, which was where Xavier had plans to manufacture snooker and pool tables with an eye to importing them to the US. Getting investment from someone who was familiar with China, and had contacts there, would give him a huge benefit. And then he could leave this small business up and running, and start something new.

"I'm kidding."

The server placed two cold beers on beermats on the table.

"Cheers," They clinked their bottles together.

"I'm sorry, pal. I didn't mean to knock you down."

"You didn't, so just let it go."

"What are you doing with Hennessy?"

"Hopefully making snooker and pool tables in China."

"And there's money in that?"

"There's serious money when you have lots of little money trees like that."

Luke nodded, looking suitably impressed.

"Of course, it's no bar in Manhattan, charging crazy prizes for drinks. Now that's what I call a serious fucking money tree."

"Hard work, though," Luke replied. "So, pal," he said, taking a swig from his beer bottle. "Do you have an update on your little project?"

"I haven't had any pussy, if that's what you're asking."

"I thought you two would have become better acquainted by now. "

"No fat fucking chance." He gulped down his beer. "But, she's coming around." He was making strides. Slow, steady strides, in the right direction.

Luke threw him a curious glance. "Why should I believe you?"

He ignored his friend's remark. "She'll be caving in soon." Though 'soon' might still be months away.

"I don't think she likes you," Luke said. "Even now."

"How the hell would you know?"

"Because I've seen you meet someone here for the first time, and then walk away with her less than thirty minutes later. I've seen you do that, here, with my own eyes." He pointed at his eyes with his fingers as if to emphasize the point. "And if you haven't even gotten to first base after what, six, maybe eight weeks, I don't think you stand any chance. I don't think she likes you. Just face it, pal. You're not her type. You might even be too old for her."

He gave Luke the middle finger. "I'm twenty-fucking-seven. I'm in my prime, and I'm making progress, and that's all you need to know."

"Fine. As long as you know what you're doing, and it isn't illegal."

"It isn't." He looked away, letting the awkwardness of the moment pass. "Savannah's cousin was here." He looked back at Luke. "You remember her, don't you? Kay?"

"Yeah, I remember her."

"I think she's pissed off with me."

"Pissed off with you?"

He finger-tapped the table. "She was standoff-ish when I ran into her downstairs. Didn't want to talk to me."

"No?"

"She's pissed I never called her." Chicks could be funny like that.

"Is that what she told you?"

"She didn't need to. I could tell."

"Were you supposed to call her?" Luke asked, leaning forward and picking up his beer bottle.

"They all expect you to, don't they?"

Luke shrugged but didn't say anything.

"Except for you, Mr. Ice-Cold and Doesn't-Give-A-Fuck." That's what Luke had always been like.

"Are you going to call her?" Luke asked.

"She's not my type," he shot back.

"Is Jacob's babysitter your type?"

He thought about it. Laronde, at first glance, wasn't his type. He probably wouldn't have noticed her in a group of women, but now that he was taking the time and getting to know her, he was discovering things about her that were intriguing. She was like a mystery he was slowly unraveling. Physically, he liked a handful of butt and breast, and she had neither in the size he preferred. And he hadn't yet been able to get his hands on either of those; he was beginning to doubt that he ever would. But there was nothing that a good push-up bra couldn't salvage, and as long as there was a mouthful, he wasn't going to complain too much. She had the sass that made up for her physical shortcomings.

"I've said it before, and I'll say it again, you don't have anything to prove."

He disagreed. "We have a love-hate thing going. It's always the prelude to better things."

"Love-hate? It's been hate-hate each time I hear from you."

"She's working for me now."

"Seriously?" Luke gave him an incredulous stare. "How the hell did you manage that? Wasn't she working for Savannah and looking after the little boy?"

"Savannah wants to spend time with the kid, and she didn't need Izzy so much yet, and what with her being a student and needing funds and all that, I came to the rescue."

"Galloping along on your big white stallion, no doubt."

"Chicks love being rescued."

"Izzy doesn't strike me as that type of girl." Luke was right. Laronde didn't seem to be the rescuing type at all.

~ ~ ~

"He's not such an idiot, after all." She hung up, thinking how strange it was that working for Xavier had been this easy. It was like doing the easiest homework assignments, only she was making money doing it.

"Who are you talking about now?"

"Xavier."

"I told you." Cara was filing her nails. "I think he's misunderstood."

"And you would know." Izzy rolled her eyes. Cara bought into the whole celebrity package, not that Xavier was a celebrity, or Tobias, for that matter, but as the brother of

New York's once most eligible bachelor—which was what Tobias had been until Savannah had snagged him—he was on her radar. "Whatever you read in the papers, is not what they're really like."

"I think you need to give him the benefit of the doubt."

Izzy stretched, dismissing her friend's sage advice with a yawn. She wasn't looking forward to the all night studying she was going to have to put in for her test. Accounting was her least favorite subject, and she had left it until the very last minute to study. If she failed, it would be her fault entirely. Not Xavier's.

"Any chance I could get to meet him?" Cara asked.

"I don't see him. He emails me the work. It's a brilliant arrangement."

"And what are you going to do when Savannah asks you to come back?"

"I'll do both." Because both jobs were easy. Looking after Jacob was fun, and working for Xavier was easy. She had no complaints.

Chapter 22

There was hope and a sense of solidarity in the air, on this surprisingly dry, yet chilly November morning.

Izzy was on a high that came from thousands of women all marching together, and she had never experienced anything like it before.

There was a harmony about the crowd which organizers had estimated to be around 100,000 strong. They had started off on the corner of Columbus Avenue and 71st Street, moving slowly down Central Park West and then turning into Columbus Circle before heading towards Bryant Park.

It was a route she knew well.

They marched with a huge group of students from the college, and Izzy hoped something like this was a sign to the Shoemoneys of this world that it wasn't acceptable to prey on women. That it wasn't acceptable to touch and grope, in the workplace, in schools, and in gymnasiums, in swim squads, or behind the scenes at movie castings and fashion shows, thinking it was normal.

Because it wasn't, and had never been, and somewhere along the line, a whole generation of men had grown up thinking it was, and a generation of women had grown up believing they were alone.

Stories such as this had been crawling out of the woodwork for months, and had given her strength, in light of what had happened to her. It gave her comfort, and made her stand straighter, to know that she was not alone.

She and Cara marched together, in unison, the collective energy building, the vibe in the air permeating each and every cell in her body.

They listened to speeches along the way, where women dreamt of a world where equal pay was possible, and not just a glass ceiling to aim for, a world in which harassment in the workplace, the smutty jokes and physical references, were a punishable offense, not just the stuff of locker room high fives, or boardroom handshakes.

For six hours they had walked and the procession had been peaceful, and friendly. It was easy to make friends surrounded by people who all shared the same values, dreamed the same dream and hoped for the same future.

It was only in the last hour of what should have been the end of a peaceful demonstration, that things turned ugly. She heard the commotion up ahead, and then what sounded like crackers going off. Women's screams filled the air as people panicked and ran.

Izzy grabbed Cara's arm and ran, as quickly as she could, fearful of being trampled on, as the crackers—someone shouted that they were gunshots—went off close by.

But just as they were about to push their way out of the thick crowd, Cara tripped and fell. "Get up!" Izzy screamed.

"I can't!" Cara's ghostly pale face stared up at her as she lay crumpled in a heap on the ground. "I can't move my foot," she groaned, her face twisting in pain.

"Get up," Izzy urged. Covering her face, as people jostled and shoved past her and Cara. They had to get away before they were trampled. She put her arm around Cara's neck then yanked her to standing. Supporting her body as best as she could, they limped to an alleyway, away from the crowd.

They cowered for what seemed like ages.

"Your face is all scratched," Cara told her.

"I'm fine." She stared down at Cara's foot. "We need to get back." But the sound of sirens suddenly filled the air and, in the next moment, police officers spilled out onto the streets like ants.

It was later, when they had been to the hospital and then returned home to watch it all on TV, that they learned how lucky they had been that Cara had only suffered a bad ankle sprain, and Izzy's face had suffered a few cuts and grazes.

They'd gotten off relatively unscathed.

They had discovered, to their horror, that an angry ex-husband had come looking for his wife with a gun. He'd shot her, and left her in a critical condition in the ICU. A hater with so much hate that he'd wanted to put a bullet through the mother of his children.

~ ~ ~

He hadn't bothered to call because he'd bought the damn thing and now he just wanted her to have it. He needed to focus on his proposal for Hennessy, not worry about fucking spreadsheets being in the wrong format.

This would fix that problem.

It had better do, or else …

He knocked a few times. Would have been here yesterday, but the goddamn streets were rammed. There had been some sort of lesbian demonstration taking place in the streets, and it had been impossible to get anywhere.

Laronde opened the door and looked slightly uneasy. "Oh," she said, when she saw him. It wasn't the usual response he was accustomed to—even if he turned up unannounced at a girl's place, but he'd always known that Laronde was never going to break out into a flirtatious smile at the sight of him.

"Nice to see you, too," he said, his tone blatantly sarcastic. It was the first time he'd seen her since that interview in the park a few weeks ago. He'd been so busy, he hadn't had time to think about the bet.

"For you," he said, handing over the thin white box.

"What is it?" she asked, staring at it, but not taking it.

"Here, have a look," he insisted, and gave it to her. "Something that will solve your problem." She had scratches on her chin and on the side of her face, making him wonder what the fuck had happened.

"What happened?" he asked, nodding at her face.

"Long story."

"Aren't you going to invite me in?"

"Sorry, come in."

She lifted the lid and peeked at the sleek shiny surface of the MacBook Pro. He hoped this would put an end to their incompatibility problems. He'd write the purchase off as a business expenses, and it would earn him bonus points. Win-win.

"For me?" Izzy asked, looking stunned. The kind of stunned girls looked like when he bought them a trinket from Tiffany. "You bought me this?"

"It's a business expense, not a personal gift."

She looked up, "I know. I get it, but … uh—you didn't need to." He followed her into the living-room.

"Shit," said a girl who was lying on one of the sofas. Her leg rested on a huge velvet green ottoman that looked like it was big enough to seat two people. She sat up with her mouth open as soon as he walked in. "Xavier Stone?" she gasped. Now, that was the kind of response he was more accustomed to. He flashed a brilliant smile at her, and saw that she wore an ankle brace. To the side of the couch lay a pair of crutches. "Hi," he said.

"This is Cara, my roommate, this is Xavier." Izzy made the introduction in a flat voice. He smiled at the roommate again. "What happened?"

"Oh, this?" her friend replied, "It's not as bad as it looks. It's nothing."

"That's not what you said when you were bawling your eyes out at the hospital," retorted Izzy.

"I wasn't bawling!" her friend protested. "I wasn't," she said, turning to him, her voice softer, as she flashed him the kind of smile he was used to.

"What's that?"

"A MacBook Pro," Izzy told her.

"You bought her a MacBook Pro?" Her friend made the kind of appreciative noises that he wished Izzy would make. "That costs almost as much as our rent."

"It makes sense, now that she's working for me," he explained, trying to be casual about it.

"But I'm not a Mac girl," said Izzy. She said it the way Gisele would have said she wasn't a Prada girl. "I'm Windows all the way."

What the fuck was she complaining about now?

"But we won't have that spreadsheet problem you keep moaning about," he replied, irked by her less-than-stellar reaction.

"I'm not used to the Mac."

For fuck's sake. What did it take to put a smile on this girl's face? "You said you have problems opening my spreadsheets. This will fix it."

"But it's a Mac."

"I know. I bought the damn thing."

"Shut up and stop whining, Iz."

"Don't you like it?" he asked, her reaction grating on his nerves like fingernails on a blackboard.

"Uh, yes. Of course I do. It's a Mac, what's not to like. It's just that I'm not used to it."

"You'll get used to it. You're a smart girl, how hard can it be?

"True," she said, running her hand over the sleek shiny top. "After all, you used it. How hard can it be?" She scratched her head. "This is an expensive machine. Do you buy these for all your VAs?"

"Most of them already have a Mac."

She looked surprised.

"You don't want it?"

"I don't need it. I mean, it's an expensive solution. All you had to do was export your spreadsheets."

There she went again. "I don't have time to do that, Laronde. Time is money and I'm a busy man."

"I bet you're really busy," gushed Cara. He let her have his signature smile, because he liked her, and she seemed to be on his side, and was a million times friendlier than Laronde. "I don't think she likes it," he said to her.

"Well, on her behalf, I'd like to thank you," Cara replied, returning the smile.

"You're welcome," he said, enjoying the banter and aware that they were deliberately blocking Izzy from the conversation.

"Sorry, sorry. I didn't mean to sound ungrateful," said Izzy. "Thank you for this. It's just that it's so … it's so … expensive."

Her constant whining about the cost was making more sense now. He was reminded of the conversation with Savannah, when she had said something about Izzy wanting to do it alone, and the other jobs she had on the side. He had assumed that everyone who went to Columbia was rich, otherwise why go there? But even though he'd known she wasn't rich, he hadn't been aware of quite how much she worried about money. Maybe she was just trying to make it, do the best she could. He looked around the small dingy apartment, and in a neighborhood that didn't scream 'safe', it confirmed his suspicions.

"Like I said, it's a business expense, and you're free to use it until you no longer need it, but I'd be grateful if you did your charts and my work on that, and not your laptop."

"Of course. Thank you. No, really. Thank you. I wasn't expecting you to go and buy me a machine. You've surprised me."

He'd surprised her, huh? Well, that had to be a first.

His work here was done, and thank fuck this was sorted.

"What happened?" he asked again, pointing to her friend's ankle brace for he was still none the wiser.

Izzy replied, "We got trampled on at the Women's March yesterday. You must have heard about it?"

He thought it was something to do with a bunch of lesbians complaining about more rights. "Women's March?" he asked, hesitating in case he said the wrong thing and they jumped down his throat.

"That's right."

He blinked. "And you went to it?"

"Yes, we went to that."

"Oh-kaay." He scratched his head, wondering why they'd gone. Who the hell went to marches and shit like that? "What was it for?"

"Taking a stand," replied Izzy, folding her arms.

"It was good fun," her friend added. "It had a party vibe to it."

He was curious now. "Taking a stand for what?"

"You don't know?" Izzy asked, looking at him as if he were a rat.

"Not really."

"We were marching for basic human rights—you know, equal pay, and standing up for women who have been victims, of sexism, and sexual harassment, and for women being underpaid, and underrepresented. Where do you want me to start?"

He cleared his throat. "I see."

"I could go on, but you get the idea." Izzy's face was hard, and she eyed him as if she was testing his reaction.

Come to think of it, he had seen a few newspaper headlines, and trending news on social media. Stuff was starting to come out, about famous people, famous women, actresses and models who had made complaints about some pretty top level people. A whole heap of scandals had come out, something to do with men and their abuse of power, mostly in the entertainment industry.

Gisele had said it was common, that everybody knew and nobody said anything. That if you wanted a role, you had to go along with it. There was a producer her friends had spoken of, it was common knowledge he was a pervert, but nobody said anything. It didn't seem to be a big deal.

He didn't fully understand. There were always two sides to a story. "No wonder the roads were a nightmare yesterday." It was all he could say for fear of saying something and getting his head bitten off.

"Sorry that you were inconvenienced," said Izzy, her tone icy. "You seem to be dismissive about the march. Do you have a problem with it?"

"No," he replied, slowly. He felt as if he was walking into a trap and worded his reply carefully. "I don't have a problem with that. Why would I have a problem with that?" He slapped a hand around his nape. "Why would you think I'd have that opinion?"

"Because of the way you asked."

"No." He cleared his throat. "I think it's a good thing."

"Standing up for something you believe in, standing up for people who've been victims, yes," she said, fire in her eyes. "It is a good thing."

"For sure," he replied. He would agree with anything she said right now, knowing he was at a disadvantage, at her place, with her friend.

"And wanting the basic things that you men have. You know, like knowing you won't get touched inappropriately by a woman at work, just because she's feeling horny and you happen to be around."

He had to fight so that his lips wouldn't spread into a smile. The idea of a woman boss trying to get it on with him suddenly appealed.

"It would make for a fairer world if women could experience the same sense of safety," said Izzy, continuing on with her rant.

"Absolutely. So how come you got trampled on?"

"A woman got shot by her crazy ex-husband who was pissed she'd gone to march. She'd probably gone because she was married to a bastard like him."

Strong words. He doubted he'd ever heard Laronde speak like that before.

"And there was panic and people ran, and I fell over and sprained my ankle but Izzy pulled me away. Except, the crowd was heaving so she didn't escape unscathed."

"Whoa, that's bad that it turned ugly."

"An angry man shot into the crowd and tried to kill his ex-wife. What do you expect?" Izzy blazed. There was a quiet anger behind her words. "I didn't realize how many men had an inability to control their dicks. He obviously felt threatened that she was empowered enough to want to rise up and make a stand."

He felt outnumbered. "That's true." He opened his mouth, tried hard to think of something to say, something which would melt the anger that was so evident on Izzy's face. "I think it's a noble cause."

"It's a necessity, in this day and age. It was about time too. Don't you think it's a sad state of affairs that so many of my friends have a story somewhere in their past, something to do with a misuse of power, something to do with a man being a pervert?"

Her anger spilled out into her eyes, and there was something about the way she said it, the way she levelled her fury at him, that made him wonder what she was so mad about. It wasn't as if he'd done anything to her.

He swallowed. Maybe Laronde wasn't the type of girl he ought to be messing around with. Already he sensed he was in way over his head. Did he need this extra headache when there was so much other shit to be dealing with? A new business to start, investment to procure.

Did he need to work his ass off just to get a taste of her pussy when all he needed to do was walk into The Oasis any day of the week and get it, guaranteed?

"It's okay, Izzy." Cara's voice drifted over, reminding him that it wasn't just him and Izzy in the room.

"I'm explaining it to him," said Izzy said, biting the words out slowly. "Because it seems as if Xavier doesn't know, or isn't aware of the protests, and why."

He let out an exasperated sigh, wondering how he had ended up being caught up in the crossfire of something that wasn't his fault, but for which he seemed to be getting the blame for. "Not all men are dirty perverts, Laronde."

"I never said they were, Stone. Just like a lot of the stuff, it needn't always be sexual, but most of the time it is."

"And sometimes, men get the blame for things they didn't do," he replied, testily. Jeez. He was starting to wonder if she wasn't one of those man-hating chicks. The kind who'd slice his dick off after they'd had sex, just to spite him. That is, if he ever got around to doing the deed with Laronde. Things looked less hopeful each time he saw her.

"And sometimes they should get the blame but they don't."

"And sometimes, men get blamed all because of a witch hunt."

"You seem to speak with authority," Izzy challenged. "Do you take a 'no' for a 'no', or does the line blur over for you?"

"I'm not an asshole." Her words offended him, as did the idea that she thought he was like those people who assaulted women.

Was that how she saw him?

Her friend coughed, making them both stop and look at her. "I'm dying here, do you mind?"

Xavier laughed. "You look as if you need some sympathy." Out of the corner of his eye, he saw the sharp turn of Izzy's head.

"Her boyfriend's coming over later," Izzy said.

"Yeah?" he replied, turning his head to face her. "And what about you?"

"She doesn't have a boyfriend," her friend chirped. He didn't miss the hard stare Izzy gave her friend.

She nodded her head towards the MacBook which she'd placed on the coffee table. "Thanks for that."

"Glad you like it."

Chapter 23

It was organized chaos, but even he had to admit—his office was a paper shitstorm. Tobias would have a heart attack if he ever saw it.

The second meeting with Chad Hennessy had been promising, but the guy wanted more figures, and detailed projections of business growth. He wanted a business plan that went far deeper than the one Xavier had presented him with. The guy must have been a few years older than him, maybe around Tobias's age, and seemed to have a better handle on the rules and regulations of doing business in overseas. Xavier needed him, more than that, he needed his investment.

He set to work, trying to put a solid plan together but, with the way his office was—what with paper everywhere and things filed out of order—he was having a hard time getting the invoices and orders from the past. He needed to do it within the next day or two, because Chad wanted to see him again a few days after Thanksgiving.

So when he set to work and then his buzzer sounded not long after, loud and angry like a bee, he ignored it at first. Hardly anyone came to his place unannounced. But when it sounded again, and kept on buzzing, he threw his pen down and pressed the intercom.

"Yes?"

He heard the sniffling first, before he heard her voice. And she sounded upset. "Xavier, it's me," she sounded upset. "Can we talk?"

Gisele?

He wiped his hand over his forehead. What did she want? He hadn't had a word from her since before Tobias's wedding, and she hadn't returned the few calls he'd made after. And now she was here. "I'm kind of busy."

She sniffled some more. His muscles tightened, and he hated that she had come to him. Obviously, without a doubt, with 100% certainty, she needed something, but he didn't have time to be there for her.

"Please, Xavier."

He straightened up and blew out a breath wondering how to deal with her quickly. High drama was not what he needed right now.

He pressed the button, giving her access to the communal door below, and waited. Quicker than he would have liked, she was at his door, banging on it, and he opened it quickly to find her standing there, her face red and splotchy.

"Why are you crying?" She was wrapped up in a bright yellow faux fur coat that looked two sizes too big on her.

"You won't believe what they did," she cried, and with drama befitting an actress of her caliber, she fell into him, dramatically, and clung to his chest. He had to pry her off him, slowly.

"What did they do?"

"They halted production on the film," she sniffled. "I was supposed to start filming in two weeks' time, but they've stopped everything until further notice."

It took him a moment to process what she was saying, primarily because he didn't give a shit. "And what do you want me to do about it?"

She looked at him with a teary face. "I didn't know who else to go to."

What did she want? Comfort? A hug? A screw? "I'm in the middle of something." He lifted his hands up in irritation. For a moment it seemed as if she was going to launch herself at him.

"You usually cheer me up," she sniffled.

"We split up, remember? Before my brother got married?"

"I'm sorry it happened like that. I'm sorry. I was excited about my casting." She sunk her fingers into the fur collars of her coat. "You don't understand. It's a huge deal for me."

"What do you want me to do about it?"

"Cheer me up! I want to talk to someone. I want to talk to you." She moved towards him, rolling into his chest with that mammoth fur ball of a coat, and burrowed her face into his chest. His arms stayed limp by his sides.

Two months of celibacy were about to be dropped to the side. He felt himself hardening, knowing how good she felt. Her mouth, her hands, her everything. His hands fisted, as he tried to forget that he hadn't had a woman's touch for weeks. He fought against the cells in his body which seemed ready to rejoice.

"Xavier," she murmured, squeezing her body against his tightly. He couldn't hold back any longer, and his arms moved around her, sinking into the soft yellow fur. Her arms encircled his waist as she stared up at him with hopeful eyes. "I've missed you."

It was tempting, feeling her warm, soft body against his, looking down into that pretty little face, full lips and those ridiculously long and very fake eye-lashes.

She tip-toed up, as if to kiss him, but he was still weighing up what to do, torn in the inferno of his dilemma. She took the split-second of hesitation as a confirmation of his approval, and her hands moved to the elasticated waist of his lounge pants. He sighed, then exhaled even louder when her hand moved over the front, feeling, and stroking and gliding over the thick, stretchy fabric. Unlike jeans, his lounge pants were flimsy, and didn't hide his tented front as well. She knew, of course she knew how excited he was.

His breathing turned faster when her fingers slipped into his briefs and she reached for him.

Her eager fingers on his naked skin drew every drop of blood south.

Fuck.

He shot to attention, felt the familiar stirring in his loins. Hungered for the kind of filthy, dirty sex he'd been dreaming about for months.

A frustrated groan caught in his throat, and it took all of his might to reach down and pull her hand away. A loud, sorry gasp left his lips, a sigh of huge disappointment.

"No," he growled, low and hoarse.

"Why not?" She reached for him again.

"No." This time more forceful. He seized her hand, preventing her from dipping further, and stepped away. What in the world was he doing? They could have had a few hours of the type of sex that left sweat-streaked bodies and a room smelling musty and stale. A good couple of hours of the best, mind-boggling, dirty, grown-up fun.

And nobody would have known.

Not Luke.

Not Izzy.

Hell, Izzy didn't even know about the bet, let alone give a shit what he was doing with Gisele.

"Xavier." It was breathless, the way her voice sounded, his name rolling off her tongue. "What's wrong with you?"

"This isn't happening."

"Why not?" She slapped her palms flat against his chest. Then, stepping back in surprise, "Who is she?"

He shook his head. "There isn't anyone."

"You liar. You liar!" her voice turned high, almost like a shriek.

"There isn't," he insisted. "This guy, the producer, is it the same guy who wanted you to wear a bikini to the interview?"

"As if you care."

"I do. Was it?"

"No. That's a different guy. And I'm on the shortlist, thanks for asking."

He swiped his hands through his hair, then intertwined them, resting the palms around the back of his head. Gisele's gaze swooped to his arms, before she ran her gaze all over him.

"You're still going ahead with it, even now, with all these scandals coming out of Hollywood?"

"Sometimes you have to do stuff to get what you want."

"How far would you go?"

"As far as I have to."

He frowned, thinking how little he knew her. "I'm busy, Gisele. I have to get something ready for an important meeting."

She stared at his body again, the way she used to, her gaze moving over him, slow and hungry. "You sure you don't want to ... ?"

"I'm sure."

She shrugged, and walked towards the door, and left.

There were days when he was sure his dick couldn't handle such a prolonged absence from sex.

Chapter 24

She hadn't heard from Xavier, and he hadn't sent her any more work.

Izzy wondered what was going on. She couldn't let too many days go by empty, and with things starting to slow down for Thanksgiving and Christmas, she was extra vigilant about her work drying up on all fronts. All of her jobs kept the wheels turning, and she couldn't afford for Xavier to slack off with his side of the deal.

It occurred to her that he was a little disorganized, that he didn't always have clear timelines in place, and she didn't like that—having fluid boundaries.

She had started to use the MacBook in earnest, because it was faster, and easier, and it now made her own laptop seem so painfully outdated in comparison. And it was loaded with the latest software. She'd even started taking it to college with her.

A few days before the Thanksgiving weekend, she sent Xavier an email, and when he didn't reply, she called him.

"Hello." He sounded gruff, short. Not like his usual self.

"You haven't sent me any work."

A sound, something like a grunt, came over the phone. "Didn't I?" he groaned again, as if it was a chore for him to find her something to do.

"Do you have anything?" She was all caught up with her studies. "I've got lots of free time right now and I can do the big stuff, if you have anything that needs doing." And she wasn't going home for Thanksgiving this year, either.

"Let me think about it."

"Something wrong? You sound stressed."

"I'm kind of busy right now. I'm not going to be able to give you anything to do until after Thanksgiving."

"Oh, really?" That didn't sound good. "I thought you had lots of paperwork for me to go through?"

"I can't do it right now."

She thought he sounded distracted, or maybe his assistant had returned and he wasn't telling her. "Has your VA come back?"

"No. Why do you say that?"

"It's just that you said before that you had lots of work for me."

"I hadn't counted on you being so fast."

"I can't help it. I'm efficient."

"I'd noticed."

"So, can you give me some more? Things have quietened down for me on all fronts."

"I'm busy, Laronde. I swear I'll sort something out for you but right now I've got papers everywhere and my office is a shitstorm. I can't even think straight."

"I could help you tidy up—if its paperwork and admin things." Anything for a few extra hours of paid work.

She needed the money and she didn't want to be in a situation where she started the New Year and had no work. Savannah might change her mind and might not want her back ever, and Xavier could say he didn't need her anymore. And where would that leave her?

He fell silent, which made her think he was thinking about it.

"In that case, hell, yeah. If you want, you can come over and tidy up my office. But I'm going to be here, because I work from home."

"Duh. I know that. You already told me."

"I'm just reminding you because earlier you seemed happy that you wouldn't have to be around me."

"I trust you now."

"You didn't trust me before?"

"I didn't know you. You had a reputation."

"There's nothing to it. It's all conjecture."

"I'm not so sure."

He let out a long breath. "Why is it never possible to have a normal conversation with you?"

"We are having a normal conversation." But she knew what he meant. It was true. They always seemed to be bickering.

"Come over when you're ready. I'm in all day."

An hour later, she buzzed up to his apartment. He was in a gray hoodie and lounge pants and had bare feet. It caught her off guard, because she was so used to seeing him dressed up, even in casual jeans and a t-shirt, they would be designer jeans and designer t-shirts. And she felt odd staring at his bare feet, as if it gave her a personal and more intimate insight into him.

"I don't wear a suit to work," he said, maybe because he caught her looking, maybe because her gaze lingered too long.

"It must be a perk of the job, being able to wear what you want."

"It is. Do you want a drink? Something warm? Coffee, tea? Something else?"

"No, thanks."

"College winding down now?"

"It's like a ghost town. People are starting to go home for the long weekend."

"When are you leaving?" he asked, his arms folded across his chest, the draw string from his hoodie hanging down over his chest.

"I'm not going home for Thanksgiving."

He looked perplexed. "You're not? I thought all starving students rushed home for Thanksgiving."

Not this one. She couldn't afford to travel home for Thanksgiving and had decided to go just the once at Christmas. It made sense with it being a longer break then. "I'll go home for Christmas." She didn't need to explain to someone like him why she could only pick one time of year to go home.

"Where's home?"

"Cleaver. It's a small town near Pittsburgh."

"It probably doesn't take too long to fly back?"

"I guess not." Not that she was flying. For her it was a nine hour train journey. "Cara's gone home."

"She has?" he asked.

She nodded. "Yes."

"So it's just you at home?"

"Yes." She smiled, letting him know she was okay about it, and that she didn't want that pitiful look from him.

"How's her ankle?"

"Fine, back to normal now."

"Good. Are you girls planning on going to any more women's marches?"

"If they have some more, then sure."

He didn't say anything to that.

"Why don't you show me this messy office of yours?" she asked.

"Follow me."

She followed him into his office and examined his workplace. "You're right." She surveyed the carpet of paper and books, and magazines all over the floor. They weren't thrown haphazardly; there seemed to be some order, but it was messy. "It is a mess."

"I've got stuff I need to get done today. It wasn't this messy a few days ago, I promise."

She cast her eyes all over it. It wasn't going to be more than a few hours work. But if she could make herself useful, she could wrangle a few more hours of work out of him.

"Show me what you want me to do."

~ ~ ~

While Izzy tidied up his office, he moved his laptop to a far corner of the kitchen and worked there.

There was much to be said for having virtual assistants take care of things, but nothing beat having someone come in and look after the paperwork the way it needed to be. He was often so busy, he didn't have time to properly do it and his businesses were suffering for it. Having her be here wasn't such a bad thing.

A couple of hours had passed, and she was still tidying up, filing away and archiving his paperwork.

He ordered a vegetarian takeout from NYB, the place he knew she'd liked food from the last time. He ordered it without asking her, because he didn't want to go through the back and forth of asking her if she was hungry, having her say no, even though he knew the chances were she probably was.

A feeling in his gut told him that she probably hadn't gone home because she probably couldn't afford it.

"I had lunch," she said, when he told her to come into the kitchen because he'd ordered some food in.

"That was hours ago." He beckoned for her to sit down.

"Aren't you having anything?"

Was that disappointment he heard in her voice? This was working—this new way of not pursuing her so doggedly. "I've got to scan some documents through," he said. "You start, and I'll be back."

He rushed into his office and saw the newly transformed neat and tidy office space.

"Nice," he mumbled to himself. She'd done a great job. He felt as if he could breathe again.

Chapter 25

He'd ordered her the halloumi and mushroom burger as well as a few other dishes. Salt and pepper edamame and crispy vegetables in tempura.

When she was halfway through the burger and Xavier still hadn't come back, she went looking for him. He was at his desk, working.

"You look harassed," she commented. And he did, compared to the flirtatious guy she had come to be wary of.

"I wouldn't say I'm harassed." He let out a sigh, short, and sharp, as if annoyed. "But I hate paperwork." He seemed a little out of his depth, as if he didn't belong in his office, in his lounge pants and hoodie, taking some papers off his desk, then shuffling them into order. His table was still a god awful mess. He'd cautioned her against tidying it up, and she'd left it, even though she was sorely tempted to make everything neat and tidy on it.

"I have stuff to get done, an important meeting to get ready for. Why don't you go and eat?"

"I was waiting for you."

"I don't want anything. I ordered it for you."

"Just for me?" She felt guilty, and happy, at the same time. "That's a lot of food for one person. Just come and have something."

"It's too healthy for me."

"Maybe you should give it a try," she suggested.

"Yeah." He seemed distracted, as he scanned a few more sheets in, and she sensed she was being a burden.

"Okay. More for me."

"Yeah." He didn't even look up.

She walked back to the kitchen. Why waste good food? It had been thoughtful of him—ordering take out from that burger place they'd gone to with Jacob's grandparents.

Sitting alone at the table, she filled her plate up and ate alone. A short while later, when she had nearly finished, Xavier joined her, taking a seat opposite.

"What?" he asked, when he caught her looking at him.

"I'm not used to seeing you looking hassled."

"Believe it or not, I work, and I have pressures like everybody else."

"I'm beginning to see that. You're always such a party animal and Tobias seems so serious. It's hard to think that you're both brothers."

"My brother's always been the moody, broody type. Miserable, is what I'd call it, but women seem to think he's intense and all that shit."

She shifted on the stool, noting that he seemed a little tense.

"I don't mean to say that you're not serious about your work. I'm sure you are."

"Thanks."

He wasn't smiling when he said it, and the air seemed to chill and turn sour. She wasn't prepared for him not to be able to take a joke especially when their relationship seemed to be built on ribbing one another.

"Are you feeling sorry for yourself today, Stone?" she asked, hoping to resurrect the type of conversation they usually had. She managed a no-hard-feelings smile because she didn't want to leave him in a miserable mood—not after he had been thoughtful enough to order her a takeout that he himself hadn't touched.

"You've caught me on a bad day, otherwise I'd match you, sarcastic word for word." He dipped his hand into the takeout box and pulled out a sweet potato chip.

"Anything I can do to help?" If she could get a few more hours of paid work from him, especially now that she was here, it would be a good thing. Besides, she'd only be returning home to an empty apartment.

"I'm putting together a report for an investor. I have all the data, and I need to resize all my charts, and shit. He needs it a few days after Thanksgiving, before he goes away for business."

"But if you're looking for funding, why don't you ask Tobias?"

"Why would I?" The tone, and the way he looked at her, told her she had crossed a line. There was something defensive in his words, subtle, but definitely there, and she pushed it to the back of her mind, to examine later when she would be home alone. "Just because he's my brother and he's loaded, doesn't mean I have to go running to him each time I need help."

"Sorry."

"I can help, if you want. I've analyzed so many case studies, and written up reports afterwards, it would be a piece of cake for me."

"Everything's a piece of cake for you," he replied, chewing. He seemed to be considering her offer. "You must be smart, being at that college. Is it a shock to the system, coming out of high school and going somewhere like that?"

"I didn't come straight from high-school. I waited a couple of years, to work and save up. Its astronomical, the fees and everything else."

"I bet." He cleared his throat. "So that makes you, what? Twenty-one?"

"Twenty-two. I'm in my second year." Why did he seem so fixated with how old she was?

She leaned forward, taking out a sweet potato wedge and dipping it into the sauce tub. "I can analyze figures and do you some pretty charts and things. I can do those things with my eyes shut."

"I'd rather you had them open."

"It would be better. Sure."

It was the first time he had smiled properly since she'd arrived.

"Have you been to any more of those women's marches?" he asked.

"There hasn't been another one, yet. Why? Are you thinking of coming along?" As if he would.

He coughed, gave her a suitably serious looking face. "Sure. Why not?"

"Why would you go?"

"Huh?"

"Why would you go?"

"To ... show my support."

"For what?"

"To ...to show that things have been kind of fucked up, lately."

"Lately?"

"Well, you know, now that it's all starting to come out."

"What is?" she asked, wondering if he actually knew, or was fumbling around, pretending to be one of the good guys.

"The—uh, the stuff that's been going on in Hollywood. The casting couch, and all that."

"That's been around for years, allegedly."

"And I find it shocking that this shit still happens."

"It's a shocking world we live in."

He nodded his head. She sensed he was being reticent, as if he was feeling his way around the conversation, mindful of what to say. She wasn't even sure if he had an opinion, or had been aware of much of what had been going on. It remained to be seen whether he was genuinely sympathetic, or merely paying lip service.

After they were done eating, he showed her what he needed doing, and she could tell already that it would be simpler than most of her homework assignments. Helping him made her feel good, as if she had a one up over him. And she liked the idea of that.

She told him she'd have his document done the day after Thanksgiving. It would give him some time to go over what she had done, and he could let her know if it needed further changes before his meeting.

He copied everything onto a memory stick and gave it to her.

Chapter 26

She called her parents on Thanksgiving, trying to gauge the mood. But things seemed not so bad. Her father even tried to crack a joke.

"And try and get Dad to go for a walk every day," she reminded her mother again.

"You know what he's like."

"You could at least ask him." Had her mother completely given up on him? It had been a tough decision to come to New York to study, not only because she knew she risked a lifetime of student debt, but she didn't want to leave her dad. Her mom and Owen weren't the most empathetic of people.

"I'll ask him." Her mother made it sound as if it was a chore, as if she had to ask him if he needed her extra kidney. It wasn't his fault that this time of the year didn't work out so well for him. The dark nights, and cold, depressing mornings made his mood slide lower into the abyss.

Izzy wondered how different life might have been for her family if things had worked out for her father, if he hadn't been screwed over, and if that slimy rich businessman had paid up and honored all of his promises. They wouldn't have had to move out of the nice house her father had bought with the profits of a thriving construction company business.

And he wouldn't have had to close down his company and declare bankruptcy. He wouldn't have felt the failure which he so clearly now felt, no matter what anybody said to make him think otherwise.

Things had plummeted for him ever since.

"You shouldn't worry so much, Isabel. He's fine, and he'll be even better when you come home for Christmas."

"I'll be home in a few weeks."

"That's not long to go."

"No, it isn't. I have to go. Love you. 'Bye."

She hung up. Money, and distance kept her from going home for Thanksgiving. Cara had promised she would bring food back for her, but for now, a grilled cheese sandwich would do.

She spent the day flitting around, reading, doing pieces of her homework, sleeping, and watching TV. And when she felt like doing some work, she added the finishing touches to the report she was working on for Xavier.

Mid-afternoon she fell asleep watching TV, then woke up at nine o'clock and watched TV again, not in the mood to do any work.

The next day, bored of being at home by herself, she went out and sat in a coffee shop, fueled by the need to be around people after the solitary confinement of the past few days.

It was unusually quiet outside, as was to be expected with most people having gone home to be with family. She reached for the MacBook Pro.

Not her MacBook.

Xavier's.

When the time came for her to return it, it was going to be hard giving it up. But one day, one day, when she had her college degree, and a good job with a company that promised excellent perks, and an excellent salary, she would be able to afford a Mac of her own. After she'd helped her parents out financially.

Getting her business degree meant she would be smarter than her dad, and it meant that ruthless, sick, greedy rich businessmen wouldn't be able to ride roughshod over her, and make promises they could not keep. Knowledge was power, as was awareness, and these two things Izzy hoped to cultivate by the bucket load.

Cara would be home in a day or two, and college classes resumed the day after. Izzy decided to call a couple of friends she knew had stayed behind in New York over the weekend, to see if any of them were up for catching a movie tonight.

She worked on Xavier's document for a few hours, making it pretty, making the charts slightly bigger, and adding some more in, for other data. He hadn't specifically asked for it, but she sometimes got carried away, and she wanted to do the best possible job she could. And it was easier to get carried away sitting in a coffee shop with a few other people, some music playing in the background, and the noise of the coffee machine in the foreground. Under these conditions, time slipped away from her.

Proud of what she had accomplished, she copied the report to the memory stick, then checked her cell phone when it pinged with a notification. One of her friends had asked if she wanted to go out that evening.

It would beat sitting at home alone. Clearing everything away, she slid her MacBook into her shoulder bag, and stepped outside into the subdued, gray afternoon. She decided to call her friend, but the call went straight to voicemail. She was about to leave a message when someone pushed past her, yanking her shoulder.

She held onto her bag even tighter, a reflex action, as the noise of the scooter temporarily confused her. It took her a few seconds to that see that the MacBook had gone.

Shock slapped her senses to alert, as the fact registered. Had it been someone on the scooter? By the time she looked up to check, the rider had sped off.

It had been fast, like lightning, the swipe into her bag and bam! Gone. She looked up and around, and everyone was going about their usual business. Nobody had even noticed, and that sense of ordinariness, of normality, seemed to numb her reaction.

Xavier.

The thought of him made her heart sink. All that work she'd done for him. And now it was gone.

No! No! No!

He would go mad.

She had meant to email it to him just now, but had become preoccupied with her cell phone messages.

She sat leaned against the wall, trying to get her breath back.

It wasn't even her laptop.

Xavier would hit the roof.

She slapped a hand to her cheek, the weight of Xavier's document and everything that rested on it, dragging her spirits to a new low. The memory stick was gone too.

He had a copy—but all her changes, everything she had worked on and fixed over the past few days, were gone. She hadn't even thought to back it up to the cloud for safety.

When she had collected herself together, she returned to the coffee shop, wanting to be somewhere warm and inside, and made the call.

"Hey, Izzy. Is it done?"

She wanted to tell him, but somehow couldn't find it in herself to say it. "Almost," she managed, swallowing and pushing down the white lie. It would soon become the whopping big mother of all lies.

He sounded happy and told her he was looking forward to seeing what she'd done.

"Are you at home?"

"I'm knee-deep in paperwork."

"I'd better let you go."

"Can you email me the final document?"

"Sure."

She hadn't had the heart, or the guts, to tell him. Instead, she turned up at his apartment block and pressed the buzzer.

~ ~ ~

Sweet Jesus.

For a second he thought he heard the sound of his buzzer.

Couldn't be.

He grunted like an animal as he released, jerking off in the bathroom. He hung his head on his chest, letting the heady sensation engulf him from head to toe. This was what happened when he wasn't getting any action. It was having a serious effect on his day to day moods.

He heard the buzzer again, but he decided to ignore it, preferring to come down slowly from his high.

But when the buzzer sounded continued, he was forced to clean up quickly, then rushed out to answer it.

"Yes?" he shouted into the intercom.

"You're in," she said. "I thought you'd gone out."

"Izzy?" Fuckity fuck. Had she mentioned that she was coming over? He was sure he'd told her to email the damn document. "What is it?"

"Uh. Could I come in?"

He rubbed his forehead, not needing this interruption, but she was here now. "Yes." He pressed the button, letting her into the building. And waited.

"Hi," she said, arriving at his door, looking a little timid, he thought. The snarkiness was gone. She seemed milder. Softer.

"You didn't have to drop it off, in person," he said. "You could have just emailed it," he said, closing the door. "You didn't have to make a special trip." On an ordinary day, if he didn't have Hennessy's meeting weighing him down, he might have been able to make good use of this unexpected appearance of hers, but today was not a good day.

"I lost my laptop."

His frown deepened. "What laptop?"

"I mean, your MacBook."

"What?" He angled his head, in case he'd misheard.

"Your MacBook. Somebody stole it from me." She looked shocked, now that he looked at her face for longer.

"Stole it from you?"

She nodded, and bit her lip. "It happened as I was leaving a coffee shop."

"What? How?" He closed his eyes, forced his breath to still, even though the anger had sparked. He'd been counting on her work so that he could finish up his report.

"I came out of a coffee shop, and some guy on a scooter grabbed it and rode off with it before I'd even realized. It happened so fast, I didn't even know."

"And my data? My report?"

She looked down. "I was going to email it to you before I left the coffee—"

"You don't have it?"

"It's gone."

"You have the USB, don't you? And you made a copy of my report?" The meeting with Chad was tomorrow.

"The USB was connected."

"You lost that, too?"

"I didn't lose it. Somebody stole it from me." She fell silent. With her face pale, and her dark eyes looking at him with an uncharacteristically sad expression, he realized he was behaving like a heartless douchebag.

He gave her the once over, trying to see if she'd been hurt, but she appeared to be fine. She was as hard as nails. "Fuck," he said, understanding the implications of this.

"I'm sorry, Xavier. I really am, and I could kick myself. I wish I'd saved a version but I didn't." Her lower lip trembled, just a little. Or maybe not. This was Laronde, after all, and he didn't think her lip was capable of trembling.

"Fuck, fuck, fuck," he said, running his hands through his hair as he paced around.

"I didn't intend to get robbed."

"Tell me you saved a copy of your changes?" The muscle in his jaw spasmed again.

She shook her head. "I'd just finished making changes. I'd worked on it all morning, adding in more charts. I know how important this meeting was for you and I wanted it to be perfect. I was going to email it to you but I got distracted. I'm sorry. I really am. It was a big mistake."

"Why didn't you email me a copy before you left?"

"Believe me, I've asked myself the same question a million times, but I was going to check it one more time and make sure it was perfect."

He inhaled sharply, closing his eyes, running through the clusterfuck scenario in front of him. He needed this deal otherwise it would be months before he had another opportunity as good as this one.

She looked awful, and he did his best not to get mad. It was just as well he'd jerked off now, otherwise he would have been frustrated beyond belief.

"Have you reported it to the police?"

"I didn't think to," she replied, calmly. "I came straight here. I was more worried about your report. I knew you were waiting on it."

"My meeting is tomorrow, first thing."

"Then you need it today."

"That was the idea." What the hell was he supposed to do now? Fuck.

"I can redo it all. You have the original files, don't you?"

"Obviously."

"I'll do it again, now. I remember most of it."

"Now? As in right now, as in here?"

She nodded.

"I had plans to go out later."

"I can do it while you're out, but I'll need access to your files." Her cheeks turned pink. "Though you probably don't trust me with your PC."

Screw going out. He couldn't leave her in his office, he didn't trust her not to mess up anything else.

"This way," he said, and headed towards his office.

Chapter 27

Xavier Stone was a pig.

He might not be quite as bad as Shoemoney, but he was a pig nonetheless. He didn't even seem remotely concerned about her, only the goddamn document. He hadn't even asked if she was ok.

He had given her access to the network, and left her at his desk, to use his computer. She could hear him in the living room, on the phone, making his calls. He seemed to be extra edgy and she sensed he was nervous about tomorrow, anyway, and she had just made things worse.

She worked hard, put her head down, and got on with it. The motivation high to prove to him that she was sorry and to do the best report she could.

Every so often he would stick his head around the door and ask her if she needed anything. And each time she would give him a curt "No, thanks," and continue with her work.

"I've got some leftovers."

She looked up. "No, thanks."

"You must be hungry now?"

"No." She wanted to be gone as soon as possible.

"Not even a washroom break?"

She eyed him with disgust. "No."

He held his hands up, as if surrendering. "Just asking. You've hardly moved."

"I'm rushing to get your work done."

"Don't rush and make a mess of it."

"I won't."

"I didn't mean that you would make a—"

"I know what you meant." She didn't even bother turning around, and hoped he would leave.

"Izzy." Oh, dear god, he was still here. He perched on the side of the desk. "I'm sorry, I didn't mean to snap at you earlier."

"I heard you. Can I get on with this? You're making me lose concentration."

His mouth started to curve into a smile. "It wouldn't be the first time."

She shook her head. "What gives, Stone?" He was making crude jokes at a time like this? And after the way he had behaved earlier?

"I'm going."

Luckily re-doing everything didn't take as long as she feared because everything was still fresh in her mind. She'd added better charts and made the whole thing much easier to understand at a glance.

She stood up and had a big stretch, feeling the muscles in her shoulder blades loosen. She moved her neck around slowly, easing out the tight knots that had formed. It was something she tried to remember to do because sometimes, as was the case now, when she sat down and concentrated too hard, she forgot that she held her breath, and often stayed in the same rigid pose for too long.

"Done?"

She jumped, as Xavier's voice startled her from behind.

"All done. Here, take a look." She bent over to pull up the report.

"Could you print it off?" He nodded at the printer.

"Sure." At least that way he wouldn't need to look over her shoulder. He walked away, leaving her to print it off. When she walked out into the living area, he was lying on the couch, with his legs up, and a TV remote in one hand. An easy life for some people.

"Here." She held it out to him, and he sat up, paused the TV, and looked it over, flicking through the pages, and making appreciative noises in his throat.

"Hey," he said, finally looking up at her. "This is impressive. You've done an amazing job."

She couldn't bring herself to say anything, but was glad he liked it. All she wanted was to go home, and she was getting antsy to leave.

"What's this?" He stared at one of the charts she'd created. When she didn't sit down on the couch to see, he stood up and pointed his finger at the chart. "This seems unnecessary."

"I can take it out if you want. I figured it showed your data off better than being in tabular form."

He nodded in agreement. "It does look better," he murmured, then turned a few more of the pages. "Would you—" he seemed to hesitate. "Would you mind doing that with the other tables? You're right. It does look so much better."

She had been thinking of it, but had only done the one. Now she wished she'd hadn't done it at all.

"Or you can show me how to do it," he offered, as if he had sensed her reluctance.

"I can do it."

"It would help."

"I said I'd do it."

"Then don't look so pissed about it."

"I'm not pissed," she retorted.

"Then at least smile, to prove it."

But a smile, for him, wasn't going to happen easily. She managed a forced grimace before turning around to leave.

"You don't have to rush to do it now."

"You need it for tomorrow."

"Just chill for a while. You've been working solidly for the past few hours."

"I don't see that I had any choice, and I'd like to go home as soon as I've finished."

"At least sit down and take a break for a while."

"And talk to you?"

"You could do worse."

Before she tried to get her head around the words, before she tried to figure out if it was innuendo, or a flirtatious response—the only types of response Xavier seemed capable of giving—he said, "I didn't mean it like that. I don't know what it is, Laronde, but you make me say things I don't mean."

"There's no point in using your pick up lines on me, Stone. They don't work."

"Who said I was using a pick-up line?"

Their gazes locked.

The way his eyes were pinned on her, soft, and searching, she couldn't make out if he was being serious, or silly.

But she knew that she couldn't stand here gawking at him all day, especially with the way her stomach suddenly felt all light and airy. "I'll get this done," she said, stepping away, hastily.

"Suit yourself."

"And get the hell out of here," she mumbled under her breath.

"We can get dinner later!" He shouted after her.

"No we won't." She shouted over her shoulder before storming into his office. She stopped cold when she saw his screensaver. Her mouth fell open. It was the picture of a woman in a bikini lying over a car that looked very much like his Ferrari. Her hand froze momentarily as she seized the mouse.

This was his screensaver?

The woman was soaked, her hair hanging around her shoulders, perched on the edge of his hood, and sitting forward, her nipples erect and staring right at her.

Gross.

She slammed the keyboard in anger. "Can you unlock your screen for me!" she shouted.

Her nostrils flared as she waited, and when, five seconds later he didn't come running in, she stormed away and rushed smack bang into him.

"Ouch!" A sharp pain tasered through her lower lip.

"Whoa," he said. His thumb on the side of her lips, his eyes all worried-looking. She caught a whiff of his cologne first, before the undercurrents of his chest close to hers, erupted. "Sorry."

She backed away, feeling her lip with her tongue.

"Your lip's bleeding."

She licked it again, the taste of blood on her tongue salty. He reached for a Kleenex and gave her one.

"You okay? Here, let me take a look."

"I'm okay. It's just a little nip."

"I'm sorry. I didn't know you were going to spring out like that.

She ignored his apology and held the Kleenex to her lip, dabbing at the blood, and she could feel, now when she licked her tongue, how quickly her lip was swelling up.

"I need the password."

"Right." He turned around and she could have sworn that he visibly flinched when he saw the screen. "I should get that picture changed."

She'd meant to keep quiet, but a noise, a derisive snort escaped from her lips.

"Sorry about that." His voice was soft. He moved away from the desk, but she waited until he had cleared a good few yards, before she sat down.

"You can go now," she told him, when he still stood there, unmoving.

He disappeared, and she got on with her work but a few moments later, he was back, and this time he had an ice-cube wrapped up a dishcloth. "This might help take the swelling down."

She reached for it, and a small 'thanks', may or may not have fallen from her lips.

Chapter 28

"I look forward to doing business with you."

"Likewise," said Xavier, smiling into the phone.

"I'll send over the contract by the end of this week. Look it over and let me know if you have any questions, otherwise we're fine to proceed."

"Thanks, Chad."

He hung up, pleased with himself. Relieved, too, to know that someone else had taken a chance on him. He would sign and return the contract as soon as possible.

He scanned through his emails on his cell phone and located the email Izzy had sent him a week ago:

I've reported the theft to the police. Will let you know if I hear back. Sorry, once again, but I didn't ask to be robbed. Hope you can claim insurance.

He was grinning like an idiot, reading through the straight-to-the-point, emotionless email, and he had no idea why. Izzy with her thorns and barbed wire response, and the obviously blatant fact that she didn't give a shit about him re-ignited his desire to conquer her.

He'd wasted a golden opportunity last week when she had come over and reworked his report. He had been so annoyed about the MacBook being stolen, so caught up in the investment he so badly needed, that he'd let that rule his behavior. He could have been softer, more understanding, more concerned about her instead of Chad's meeting. If he had been nicer to her at a time when she was so vulnerable, he might have found an easier way to connect with her.

But he'd been pissed off and she'd been eager to fix the situation and leave.

But with him and Chad almost ready to go into business together, he could use Izzy's help. He knew he needed to be mindful of her time and studies, but if she wanted more work, and he sensed she was always hungry for more, she could do more hours for him.

It was the least he could do. He owed her. He hadn't secured Hennessy's investment because of her report, but he recognized the part she'd played in putting it all together. She had produced the kind of report he wouldn't have been able to do himself. Her report had definitely helped. No doubt about it, and now it was time to make it up to her.

He called her. "I got the investment I needed."

"What?"

"The investment," he repeated, "The meeting I had, the document you put together? It worked out and I got what I needed."

"Congratulations."

"And, since you had a big part to play in it, how about I take you to dinner?"

"Dinner?" she sounded horrified.

"Dinner. You and me. No strings attached."

"Uh, no thanks."

225

"Come on, Laronde. It won't be as horrific as you're making it out to be."

"I've had dinner."

"Then come and have a celebratory drink with me."

He would take her to The Oasis, right in front of Luke, so that he could see that progress was being made.

"I don't drink."

"Then have a mocktail."

She didn't say anything. She didn't decline. He had a feeling he might have wormed his way in. She was thinking about it.

"It won't be too long and it would make me feel good to at least take you out for a drink."

"Not needed. Really. I'm pleased you got what you wanted."

"I would get what I wanted if you came out and helped me celebrate. Please."

"Why are you begging me? I didn't think you were capable of begging."

"Only when it comes to——." He was about to make a distasteful remark—was about to say 'girls-who-play-hard-to-get' but something told him he would never see her again if he said that.

Smutty replies, and conversation loaded with innuendo was his hallmark, but try as he might to dull it down when Laronde was around, he couldn't.

"Only when it comes to people who go out of their way for me," he said. "That report you did was awesome, and all I want to do is show you my appreciation."

"You're welcome."

"I behaved like a total jerk the other day, and I'm sorry." He had thought about that evening long after she'd left. And he'd felt guilty about his behavior, especially in light of the fact that she'd only just been robbed. He could have handled things differently. He'd felt like a real shit that she'd been so determined to make it up to him that she'd done nothing but work on his report.

"You don't need to take me anywhere."

"I'm not taking you anywhere, Laronde. I'm taking me for a celebratory drink, and I'm asking you to come along." He waited for her to think about it some more. There were some girls who assumed, and some girls who wouldn't have waited for him to finish asking, but Laronde needed to be persuaded. He had much to learn. And learning to woo her, fighting for it, seemed a whole heap more challenging and rewarding than anything else.

"Uh."

Hell, yes, she was thinking about it. "And if you had a virgin mocktail or two, maybe some nachos and green veggie stuff, it might feel like a celebration."

"I can't stay out for too long. I've got coursework."

"An hour, or two. Can you spare that?" He suddenly remembered what else he had for her. "Because of the new business, I'll have extra work for you, if you want it."

"A couple of hours extra?"

That was what baited her? The prospect of more money, more work, more hours? With this new line of business, he could give her exactly that.

"An extra ten, maybe twenty hours a week, if you can fit it in."

"Twenty?" she squealed, the way most girls did when he told them what sexy things he was going to do to them. "Twenty hours a week?"

"At the most, yes, if you want it."

"I want it, god, yes. Of course I want it."

Jeez. There she went again, getting her panties wet about work. He'd consider it a major advancement if he ever figured out how this girl's brain was wired. She talked about work the way most women talked about sex.

"I had a feeling you might."

"Okay, so, where are we going?"

"The Oasis rooftop bar." He gave her the address. "I can pick you up."

"I'm old enough to ride the subway, Stone. You don't have to worry about me."

He wasn't going to push it.

Chapter 29

"Y ou sure you only want one portion of each?"

"How much do you think I can eat?"

Xavier placed the order at the fancy bar he'd practically begged her to come to.

They were sitting outside on the rooftop terrace of this swanky place, she'd never heard of. It had big leather couches, and seats with soft cushions, and yellow lamps and rich red curtains. It felt as if she was in some exotic faraway place, not at the top of a bar in New York. And the people here, those rich, snobby types, not like the people she'd met at Shoemoney's house. These were young and hip and trendy.

Cara would be pea green with envy when Izzy told her.

They were both supposed to have gone out tonight, but after her mother called earlier, complaining about her father and how his 'moods were worse than ever.' Izzy had lost the heart to do anything. Cara had gone out without her and Izzy had stayed at home.

She dreaded those phone calls from home because they usually signaled bad news, or oftentimes, her mother just wanted to offload. Winter time wasn't a good time for her father. It made things worse and some days he couldn't get out of bed. But they needed him to. Her mother's job at the local supermarket only went so far. Sometimes Izzy wished she and Owen could fast forward a few years, so that they could help, in any way, so their father could stop working.

Xavier's subsequent call had been a lifebuoy in an otherwise miserable sea of an evening and here she was, an hour later, taking him up on his offer to go out and celebrate.

"So you managed to impress your investor?" she asked, trying not to notice the people around her. She felt scruffy in her coat and jeans surrounded by sharply dressed guys, and the scantily dressed women.

"Your report helped."

"You would have got it regardless."

"I'm sure I would have."

She looked at him. Cheeky, cocky, arrogant.

"But your report helped, Laronde. Maybe I couldn't have done it without you."

"Nice place, this." She said, not wanting to get sucked in by his compliments. She'd almost died when she'd seen the prices on the menu. Drinks here cost double the price of a dinner at the types of establishments she and Cara hung out at.

How the other side lived.

It was like sitting in a faraway exotic land, not in a rooftop restaurant. With three weeks to go before Christmas, New York was setting in for a cold spell. Before her, Manhattan twinkled like a thousand different colors with fairy lights.

"Recognize him?" Xavier nodded towards the tall figure of the guy, jeans, tight fitting black top. She stared at him for the longest time and it was only when he ran his hands through his hair, when he half turned so that she saw his side profile, that she remembered it was the bartender from the wedding.

He turned at the same time and looked at Xavier, and there was something complicit in their unspoken exchange, but she couldn't be certain. She wasn't sure if she was being paranoid.

He walked over to them. "Hey" he said, holding out his hand which Xavier shook firmly. The other guy touched his finger to his head, as if he was trying to remember something, then extended his hand to her.

"Izzy, isn't it?"

"Yes," she said, shaking his hand. "Hi, and yes. I remember you. It's Luke, isn't it?""

"That's right. Nice to see you again."

"Xavier says you own this place."

"I do.

"It's gorgeous."

"Thank you."

"You never let on that you owned a bar in New York. I thought you were just a bartender."

"You're not the only one."

He turned to Xavier. "Have you guys ordered?"

"Yes. We're being looked after."

"Good. This is a surprise, you turning up like this."

She wasn't sure about what he meant and pushed away her feelings of paranoia, putting it down to some strange code language between the guys. A server appeared, and set down their food and drink from a tray.

"We're celebrating. I got the funding I needed," Xavier explained.

"Cool." Luke nodded in acknowledgement.

"Izzy helped secure the deal, so we're celebrating."

Luke glanced at her. "It's about time, too," he said to Xavier, and for a moment it looked as if he was about to say something, when a passing customer tapped him on the shoulder. "Enjoy your evening," he said, then, "Excuse me," and strode away.

"What was all that about?" she asked.

"All what about?"

"Izzy helped secure the funding," she echoed. She couldn't put her finger on it right now, but something didn't feel right. She picked up on something, but couldn't define what that something was.

Or maybe, as Cara had mentioned to her recently, she needed to let go of her mistrust of wealthy men. "If he was a down-on-his-luck guitarist, or a poor student, you'd probably give him a chance."

What did Cara know?

"But your part helped," he insisted.

She picked up an asparagus in tempura and dipped it into the small pot of relish, before biting it. "Are you not having any?"

He shook his head. "You go ahead."

"Green veg not your thing?"

"Still not my thing."

"This is a cool place," she said. "Thanks for bringing me here."

"You're welcome."

"And congratulations." She lifted her virgin cocktail. "Here's to getting your investment."

He lifted his beer bottle and knocked the top of it with her glass. "And to your extra hours, hopefully."

"Hopefully?" He'd made it sound as if it was a done deal.

"I need to get the business up and running, first. It can take a while, but I'll have some hours for you, it might not be twenty straight away. And, don't get your hopes up because nothing's going to happen this month. We're looking at some time in the new year, maybe."

He'd made it sound as if she could have those hours straight away. She should have known better than to believe Xavier's bullshit.

The college would be closing next week, and then she'd be going home for Christmas. She had promises of work—the extra hours with Xavier, and maybe with Savannah, but it was all up in the air. She didn't like uncertainty.

"Just let me know, as soon as it's a sure thing."

"I don't want it to get in the way of your studies."

"As if I'd let your work get in the way of my studies," she retorted.

"I'm only trying to help you, Laronde." His expression suddenly turned somber. "Anything could change. Nothing is set in stone. This is a new guy I'm going into business with, and I don't know much about him, except that he has the resources I need. I was only trying to find a way to help you, if this contract pans out."

"Okay," she said, feeling sheepish. "I understand. I didn't mean to be so mouthy."

"I noticed you can't help it sometimes."

"You bring out the warrior in me." She shrugged. "We seem to have this hate-hate thing going, I guess."

But lately he hadn't been a total jerk most of the time. Sure, he'd been a douchebag last week when she'd turned up and told him his MacBook had been stolen, but in hindsight, she'd lost everything—the USB stick included, and she hadn't backed anything up, and his meeting had been the next day, she understood.

"I must admit, it's not a reaction I bring out in most women." His eyebrow lifted slightly, and she couldn't bring herself to look away, taking in his features, noticing how attractive his dark hair and big blue eyes were. "I don't know what I've done to deserve this."

LILY ZANTE

He was trying so hard, and it wasn't fair that her mother's phone call earlier had soured things for her, the way it always did. "It's not you," she said, slowly, letting a feeling of empathy guide her. "I'm sorry. I shouldn't have come out tonight."

"But you're out now." He peered at her closer. "Is something wrong? Have I done or said something to offend you again?"

She shook her head. "No." But the way she said it, didn't sound convincing.

"You're upset about something, Laronde. I can tell, over and above your usual disdain for me, you're got something else on your mind."

Since when had they crossed the line into this?

She couldn't think of what to say, and maybe laughing it off first would have deflected his concern. But it was too late. "It's nothing," she waved her hand dismissively.

"Maybe you should take a risk and try me."

It was embarrassing, and she didn't want to. What would this rich boy understand of her problems? "It's really nothing." She smiled at him.

"Izzy." His voice was low, and enticing, and tempting. It was enough to make her want to lose the heaviness from her chest, enough for her to be tempted to share her worries.

"It's really nothing … "

"It's really nothing?" he repeated, leaning forward on the table, as if he was all ears.

She let out a heavy, heavy breath. Stared at her fingers on the table. Didn't meet his gaze. "My mom called earlier, and," she shook her head, wondering why she was telling him. Xavier Stone would never understand.

"Your mom called and …?"

She gazed at him, tried to find something in his face—a shadow of arrogance, a veil of cockiness, something, anything, of his former self that would hinder her from spilling all. But his face was impassive, and his attention was all on her. "Is your mom okay?" he asked.

"She's fine. She's not the problem. It's my dad. He's in one of his moods."

The look on his face told her that he automatically assumed the worst.

"It's nothing like that," she said quickly, in case he thought her dad had beaten up her mom, or trashed the house or done something insane. "He's not a drinker, and he doesn't … he's not abusive. They're still sort of happily married."

"Sort of?"

"I don't really like talking about it. He gets down about things, like in a really bad can't-get-out-of-bed way."

"Is he always like that?"

She shook her head. "Just sometimes." And she was sick of carrying the burden of it all.

"Why sometimes?" he asked, gently.

She shrugged. "Sometimes he just wakes up in a bad mood."

"Why's that?"

"It's all to do with what happened years ago. I think he's angry with himself. I think he blames himself for being a failure."

"A failure?"

And so she told him, in a vague way, of how he'd once had a thriving business but everything went downhill when it failed. Their house had been foreclosed on when her father had run out of money because he'd tried to pay his employees' wages.

"Why did it fail?" he asked, his voice low.

235

She shrugged. "Just."

He was quiet for a few moments after, and looked at her as if he had many questions to ask her, but he didn't, except to say, "And so he gets down about it, from time to time?"

"Yes."

"I'm so sorry, Izzy. That can't be easy on you, especially with you being so far away."

She shrugged. "It does. It sucks big time."

"What does he do now?"

"He had to take on a normal job. He wanted to put food on the table, and keep a roof over our heads, and he did, he does. But the personal pain has been too much. He has bad days. Off days."

"And that's why you don't take anything from them?"

"That's why I promised myself I'd put myself through college, and not take a dime from them."

"I can see that about you."

"And I need to do well in my exams this year because I want to get one of those internships with a big company."

"I'm sure you'll do just fine, but if you don't, I could always put you in charge of one of my small businesses."

Her eyes opened wider. He would do that for her?

"I don't have a big corporation like Tobias does, no fancy building or management structure to speak of. I'm very entrepreneurial, and I like to outsource and make the most of this digital revolution, but hell, yes, if you ever want to get dirty and jump into a business where you have to make your own rules as you go along, I'd be happy to offer you something."

"I'll bear that in mind."

Chapter 30

Luke had given him a look as they had walked out of The Oasis, but he was careful not to reciprocate back. It suddenly felt wrong, his ulterior motive for being around Izzy. It suddenly made him feel slimy, especially now that she had told him things about her and her family.

Now that he understood her better, he preferred to look at tonight as a celebratory night out, and what he regretted was coming here, to Luke's bar. It was a reminder of the part of the equation he preferred to forget.

Xavier had insisted on driving Izzy home, refusing to let her take the subway this late at night. And though he'd been expecting a tsunami of an argument, she had agreed. Maybe things were a little changed between them.

He parked outside her apartment, on the dimly lit street, and turned the engine off. "I'm not angling to come in," he said. "I just want to make sure you get in okay."

"I'll be fine. It's not so bad around here. You're just used to your affluent areas."

"We could stay here and talk some more," he added, eager to let her know he wasn't expecting her to rush out, either. Her opening up like she did earlier had broken down some of the walls between them, in his head at least.

"Thanks for this evening. I had a great time," she said. "It was exactly what I needed."

It made a change, her saying something nice to him, but then tonight had been a night of changes. "I never thought I'd hear you of all people, say something like that after a night out with me."

"Me neither."

"Let's face it," he said, grinning, "You coming out with me. Who would have thought?"

They smiled at one another.

"You're okay, Laronde."

"You're just about bearable, Stone."

She seemed to be hesitating, as if she had something to say and, sensing this, he waited, because Izzy wasn't behaving the way she normally did around him.

"You might think I'm ungrateful and rude to you, most of the time."

He wasn't expecting this. "Sometimes," he acknowledged, shifting in his seat. "I can see why I might grate on you." What was this? Confession 101?

The pale yellow light from the street lamps was just enough to dimly light up her face, and though he couldn't see her features clearly, he could see enough to determine her expression. "It was nice of you to offer to take me out."

"It wasn't a date, or anything," he said, quickly. "I know my reputation bothers you."

"It doesn't bother me as much, these days, funnily."

"No?" he asked, grinning.

"And you were your best behavior."

"I have to be, with you." It was the truth. When he was around her, he had to lose the loose tongue and roving eye. Thinking about it, he hadn't been interested in looking at other women, This evening had been more than enlightening and he could have easily spent a few more hours with her.

"You were on your best behavior for me?" she asked, trying to do her best impression of an airhead.

He shifted his body so that more of his back rested against the door. "You're not my type, Miss Smartypants, and I get that I'm not yours, and this doesn't have to be about us needing to make it anything else, because it's not."

Because he realized, despite having seen Luke, and being reminded of that ridiculous bet, that it wasn't about getting her into bed. Hell, for the past month or so he had been so caught up in wanting the investment from Hennessy, that he hadn't stopped to think how his getting-Laronde-into-bed plan had fallen to the wayside. He was having more fun getting to know this complicated woman, than he'd had having wild sex with someone.

For him, a connection such as this was as rare as a threesome.

"I know you're probably 90% bravado, Stone, and 10% the real you."

"That's a high percentage."

"But the 10% isn't so bad."

"Glad you found something about me that isn't bad."

She eyed him for a moment longer than usual, then turned away, her face curious. "Thanks for driving me home."

"I wanted to make sure you were safe. I wasn't coming onto you or anything."

"You don't need to always say that."

"Okay."

She turned and looked out of the window. "You wanted to know about that money that my pimp threw at my door." She turned back at him, her dark eyes twinkling in the half-light.

It took him a moment to figure out what she was talking about. "I'm sorry. I jumped a mile high and reached the wrong conclusion that time." He'd already apologized for that, and assumed she was bringing it up now because they were talking more, opening up more. The notion of getting to know her, through talking and finding out more about her—as opposed to diving into foreplay—was heady stuff. Something else he wasn't used to. Hell, if he wasn't careful, he might end up falling for this girl.

She chortled. "You thought I was pushing drugs and the addicts couldn't slip the bills through the door?"

"I thought your pimp took too much of your money and had thrown the rest outside your door."

"Sick," she said, shaking her head. "You have a very active imagination."

He was about to say something inappropriate, but stopped himself. "Sorry," he said, instead.

She hadn't moved, didn't look as if she was about to leave, and if truth be told, he was more content sitting in his car, in a dodgy neighborhood, listening to Laronde, than being any place else right now.

"You were partly right," she said, her voice sounding shakier than he had ever heard it.

"Partly right?" He sat up taller. What the fuck did that mean? This was turning into a night of confessions and he was all ears.

"That money was from someone I used to work for."

He looked at her wide-eyed, and more curious than ever. "What do you mean, 'someone you used to work for?'" His mind wandered off to dark places.

"This guy I used to work for before. He came to my apartment, and he wanted to pay me off, but I took what he owed me and threw the rest of it back at him."

"Pay you off?" He tried not to sound disgusted, tried not to think of the worst alternative. And what did she mean by 'took what he owed her'?

"He wanted me to keep my mouth closed, because, earlier in the summer, when I'd been working for him and his wife, looking after their children, he abused his power. He was disgusting."

Something inside him fell, like a piece of him, something from his bones, or his ribs, or his heart. "What did he do?" he asked, slowly, a bitter taste rising in his throat. She shook her head, and he didn't push. "I left, and then luckily, or it maybe it was Karma, as Cara calls it, Savannah called and asked if I would like to come and work for her because she didn't trust anyone else to look after Jacob."

"When did you work for that guy?"

"Last summer."

He had a million questions, wanted a name, wanted to know what had happened. Felt his rage building as he flexed his knuckles instinctively.

"But the money outside your apartment?" That had only been a recent thing. "It was only a few months ago."

"Yes."

He waited for her to say more, didn't want to push her when already she had shared so much.

"I wanted to tell you, because I can see now how odd it must have looked to you."

He felt like a real idiot, for thinking what he had at that time. "I'm sorry I said what I did. If I had known … I might have been more understanding. I'm sorry for being an ass."

"Like I said, the scenario must have looked weird."

"Yes." But he could have been more understanding. Even when she'd been robbed, he'd behaved badly.

"It's not the first time I've fucked up."

"Thanks for the ride, and for dinner," she said, suddenly getting ready to leave. He wondered if she'd realized she had shared too much and now regretted it.

"It was hardly dinner. I'm glad you told me, Izzy. And again, I'm sorry for being such a douchebag." She had revealed so much about herself in the space of an evening that it had left him speechless. It had given him much to think about, so many scenarios and conversations in their short, rocky path to go back to and review.

He felt as if he had reached a place he could only have dreamed about a few months ago. He had always known there was more to her, that there were things he couldn't begin to comprehend about Isabel Laronde, and now she had unveiled those very things in the short space of an evening.

He didn't want to let her go; he wasn't ready for her to go. He wanted to hold her, and hug her, and be there for her, because the way she looked right now, a little downcast, quieter, brought out the protector in him. He wanted a name, he wanted to know what had happened, he wanted to know who the fucker was, and where the fucker was, so that he could do something.

But, the truth was, he couldn't say or do anything. He would have to be patient and wait, and be there. For her.

"Thanks for hardly dinner, then. I really needed to be with people tonight, with someone."

"Glad I could help out in that respect." He smiled. "I've ordered you another MacBook," he told her. "I've ordered it for the business," he said, correcting himself at warp-speed. "The insurance paid out."

"I'll try not to get robbed like that again."

She had a hopeless, unsure expression on her face. The kind of look he'd seen in a hundred girls before. It felt as if they were on the precipice of something.

Only this was Laronde.

It would take a kiss, some touching, and stroking of her face, saying all the right words—careful words, it being her, but he could say something. And he could get on his way to winning that prize.

Only it wasn't right.

This wasn't how he wanted it. Because maybe this was the start of Laronde getting to trust him.

Laronde. Trusting him.

He couldn't fuck that up for anything.

"I'll try not to behave like a douchebag again, if you do."

He watched her go inside, and stayed there, parked outside the street for a few moments longer than he should have. And he sat and contemplated what she had just told him.

~ ~ ~

The living room light and the TV were off when she walked back into her apartment.

But then again, it was after eleven, and she wasn't surprised that Cara had gone to bed. They had ended up at the bar for almost four hours.

Who would have thought?

Shrugging off her shoes, and her thick coat, she walked into the kitchen to make herself a cup of herbal tea. She still needed to look through some of her notes before going to bed.

"Where were you?" Cara stood in the door frame of the kitchen, wearing an oversized sweatshirt, half yawning. "You said you didn't want to come to the party, and I get back and you're not here."

"Go back to bed. There's nothing to tell."

"I was worried." Her friend walked in and leaned against one of the counter tops. "I thought Shoemoney might have come back and abducted you."

"Now you're being silly."

"Then where were you?"

"Xavier asked me to go out to this fancy bar—

"Oh, mama mia!" cried Cara, rubbing her hands together excitedly.

"Only because he got the investment he needed, and he said he wanted to celebrate."

"Yes, yes ... if that's what you want to believe, carry on."

"It is because he got the investment," she insisted. "He was in a celebratory mood."

"Tell me more," said Cara, pushing herself up onto the counter top. "Where did you go? What did you do?"

"We went some place called The Oasis."

"The Oasis?! Did you go to The Vault?" she asked, "It's the hip and trendy club in the basement."

"No, we just sat in the bar and talked."

"I think he's got a soft spot for you."

"You would."

"No, I really believe that."

"I know. You would."

Cara tut-tutted. "Is he single?"

"How should I know?" She shook her head. "And why are you asking?"

"Because I want to date him." She rolled her eyes. "Why do you think?" And then, without giving her a chance to reply, "What happened next?"

"We had snacks, caught up on stuff. He might be able to offer me extra work now."

"Yeah?" Cara didn't seem interested. Izzy didn't dare say it was twenty hours, because, despite what Xavier said, she got the feeling his business dealings were ad hoc, and she didn't want to get too excited too early.

"Did he offer you anything else?" The naughty expression on Cara's face indicated that she had non-business like dealings on her mind.

"No."

"He's single, according to Gisele Steiner's social media updates."

"What are you doing stalking Gisele Steiner?"

"Being your wing woman."

"Oh, for goodness sake," Izzy picked up her cup. "Xavier Stone and I have nothing in common. Nothing."

"That's what you think." Cara slipped off the counter top. "You'll tell me I'm right, eventually. Goodnight."

Izzy sat down on the couch, and got out her notes, and wondered how it was that she had revealed so much of herself to Xavier Stone, than she ever had to anyone else.

Chapter 31

A few days after he'd taken Izzy to The Oasis, Tobias announced that Savannah was pregnant. It broke out in the media not long after.

And on Christmas Eve, when Tobias and Savannah hosted Christmas dinner at their apartment, Xavier could tell, now that he looked closely, that Savannah was slowly filling out. She was four months pregnant, with the baby expected around May.

He didn't see Izzy again for the next few weeks, but she continued to complete the work he'd given her, and their communication during that time, mainly by email and text messages, lacked the deep connection he'd experienced that night at Luke's bar.

He was in a quandary. Wanting to see her, and feeling guilty at the same time. Wanting to come clean, and afraid of sabotaging something that was so fragile and new. Maybe her feelings for him hadn't changed, but he now saw her in a different light, and not being able to casually suggest another time for them to go out and talk, meant that he was forced to make do with only connecting to her via the work he gave her.

The main thing was, he had survived Christmas with his family. And during those days, he'd been wondering what Izzy had been doing. How she'd spent it, and with whom, and he hoped her father had been fine. A couple of times he'd almost called her, because he'd been tempted to give in and hear her voice, but somehow, he had stopped himself.

What would she think?

Because, as much as he tried not to admit to it, he cared what she thought.

With the contract with Hennessy signed and dispatched to him, he expected things to start rolling sometime at the end of January. Setting up in China, would have taken him longer, if he'd had to do it from scratch. With Hennessy and his resources, he'd be up and running much sooner, and, hopefully, with an eye to manufacturing other products out there. Not bad, given that the guy had been a recent new contact he'd acquired.

When his intercom buzzed, he answered and was surprised to hear his brother's voice. "Are you alone?" Tobias asked, in a voice that sounded uptight.

Alone? As opposed to with someone? "Yeah, I'm alone. Why are you ask—"

Tobias buzzed up impatiently, and Xavier released the lock to let him through the communal door, then opened the door to his apartment, feeling wary. He knew that voice well. And something had pissed his brother off, something he had no clue about.

A few minutes later, Tobias strode through. "How's business?" he asked, looking none too pleased.

"Going well," Xavier replied slowly. "Why?" They'd only met a few days ago, on Christmas Eve. What had changed?

"Then tell me what the fuck you're doing going into business with Matthias Rust?"

247

"What?" Shock hit him like a sledgehammer. "I'm not doing business with him."

"You're fucking lying."

"Whoa," Xavier held his hands up in a conciliatory gesture. "Calm down, will you? I'm not doing business with Matthias." He peered at his brother's red face. "What the hell is wrong with you?"

"You signed a deal with Chad Hennessy?"

"Yes."

"And did you know that Matthias is a partner in that company?"

He didn't have any goddamn idea. "I didn't know." And even if he had, even though he knew that his brother and Matthias had parted company, how the hell was he supposed to know that they had done so bitterly? "Chad never mentioned Matthias," he replied, anger swirling in his gut like bile.

"If you'd done your fucking due diligence, you would have known." Tobias's voice was brittle and hard, like glass.

"Why does it matter?" His brother could be a real ass, and Xavier hated his bullying tactics, and this, what he was doing now, barging in here like a raging bull, with his uncontrollable anger, was one of those episodes.

Tobias Stone might be a golden child in their parent's eyes, a loving father-figure to Jacob, and a knight in shining armor for Savannah, but to him, his brother had been someone to be admired, and be afraid of, at the same time.

There was a side to Tobias many didn't see. It was a side only a younger brother would know about, and Xavier was fed up with this bullshit.

"Don't come here," he warned, his voice inching up slowly. "Don't come here barking at me, when you never had the time or decency to tell me what your problem with Matthias is. I've asked you plenty of times." The silence from Tobias gave him the guts to continue. "I didn't know about Matthias, and he never came to the meetings. His name was never mentioned, but why is it such a problem for you?"

"Because the guy is a fucking moron, and the worst thing you could have done was to go into business with him."

"I don't understand why you're getting so worked up over this. I would have thought that news of a baby on the way might have calmed you down, but you're the same as ever. Who do you think you are?"

"An astute businessman, which is why I run a fucking hedge fund and you don't."

Un-fucking-believable.

"There you go again." He clasped his hands and cradled the back of his head. What more was there to say? Except, "I am going into business with Hennessy."

"And Hennessy's company is part-owned by Rust. How the fuck do you think he's got the manufacturing infrastructure in China?"

So, what? "That manufacturing infrastructure is vital for me."

"What are you making now? Butt plugs?"

Asshole.

But he didn't have the stomach to tell him about the snooker and pool tables because he would only laugh. He glared at his brother. What did Tobias expect him to do? Bail out of the deal just because he'd had a bust-up with his colleague?

"What did he do? What did Rust do to you that has you all riled up like you want to split his head open?"

"Forget it."

Xavier threw his hands into the air. "There you go again!" This was typical of Tobias. "I'm not telepathic." He'd given

249

him a chance to explain, and once again his brother had bailed out.

"If you intend to run a successful company," Tobias said, giving him a look that made him want to shrink inside, "You need to do more in-depth analysis into a company before you dive into bed with them. You need to spend more time doing better background checks on companies—more time than you'd normally spend on picking up girls at the bar."

Tobias stormed towards the door, slamming it hard behind him.

~ ~ ~

"It's not so bad, is it, Dad? Once you're out of the house. It's nice." Her father walked alongside her. "It's not so bad," he agreed, after a while.

"Whenever you feel you're not in the mood to do anything, you should at least force yourself to come out and go for a walk in the woods."

"It's better when you're around, Izzy."

"I know, Dad, I know. But I have to go back soon."

"Can't you stay another week?"

"I'll try and come back sooner next time."

He fell silent again.

Two hours. She had managed to convince her father to come out for two hours, today. It had been the longest of their daily walks. But at least she had managed to persuade him to get out.

The tricky part was convincing him to do this when she was back at college, and she was returning a few days before the New Year. Two weeks at home had been enough, but it had also sapped her. It had eaten into her reserve of energy, talking to her father, trying to bolster his spirits. Doing what her mother should have been doing. Sometimes she wondered who the parent was.

She needed the internship, and she needed good grades at the end of the summer term. Another week here would leave her too jaded to return to college, and she needed every ounce of energy to deal with the exams that would hit a few weeks after the new term started.

At least once the next few months were done with, spring would be on the way. Things always looked better in the spring.

They came out of the forest, walking silently back towards their home, when her cell phone rang. Something fluttered deep within her belly when she saw Xavier's name on the caller ID.

"It's a friend, Dad," she said, "You go ahead, and I'll catch up." She fell back, and answered the call. "Hey," she said, still walking, but at a slower pace.

"I'm not disturbing you, am I?"

"I'm out for a walk with my dad."

"How is he?"

"Sad that I'm leaving soon."

"When?"

"The day after tomorrow."

"How sad is sad?"

She sighed. "Sad enough that I feel like I should stay a few more days."

He made an empathetic noise at the back of his throat.

"But I can't stay on another week," she explained. "I have to get back into study mode. It's an important semester."

"You're back on Thursday then?"

"On Thursday." She wondered why he'd called her, and knew it wasn't to ask her about the general state of her time back home. "Did I mess up something?"

"Mess up?"

"On a report or something?" That was why he'd called, wasn't it?

"No. No. That's not why I'm calling."

"Oh." It pleased her, to hear his voice again. And it was strange because there had been times during these past few weeks when she had often thought about him, and wondered what he was up to. There had been times when she had been tempted to call him, on the pretense of asking a work-related question, but she had stopped herself. That night at the bar, she had opened up to him in a way that was unlike her. Maybe it was that he seemed, nice, for a change, and had surprised her. He seemed to be listening, and she was just plain fed up of her mother dumping on her all the time. Maybe he'd just caught her at an unguarded time.

But she had thought about that evening more times than not.

So, this was nice, him calling her.

He coughed lightly. "I—uh—wondered how things were going for you," he cleared his throat again, "being at home, and all. Just out of curiosity."

"Just out of curiosity," she repeated.

"And I—uh wanted to ask you something about how you did those charts. You know, the 3D bar charts."

"The ones I did for Hennessy's report?"

"Yeah, those."

"They're simple enough," she said, "You just need to select the rows and—"

"It can wait," he said. "It's selecting those rows and columns that's fiddly. But there's no rush."

"Are you sure?"

"I'm sure."

"I'll show you when I get back."

"Looking forward to it."

Me, too. "How was your Christmas?" she asked.

"Not as bad as I expected."

"You were expecting it to be bad?"

"You've met my mother, haven't you?"

"Briefly."

"Then you'll understand."

She giggled.

"But it wasn't so bad. We spent it at Tobias and Savannah's."

"Awww. Nice. I heard the news about Savannah being pregnant." Cara had been the one who'd told her when it broke in the press. She had called Savannah and congratulated her.

"It's exciting."

"Jacob must have been happy."

"It doesn't take much to make that kid happy."

She smiled. Jacob would make an awesome older brother.

"How was your Christmas?"

"Relaxing. Nice to be back home for a change. Nice to have lots of home-cooked food."

"I was thinking of maybe taking Jacob to the funfair, sometime next week. It's been a while since we've—I've—spent a whole day with him. And I was thinking maybe we could go out again."

"He'd like it, I'm sure."

"I meant that you could come along too. It's not a date or anything, but it's been a while since we both took him out, and it would be nice."

"Did you miss his birthday or something?"

"No. His birthday was last month. The kid's seven going on seventeen."

Izzy laughed. "He's a sensible little boy."

"Tobias was over earlier."

"At yours?"

"Yeah. He—" he paused. "He was angry."

"Angry?" She wondered why Xavier was telling her.

"Some business deal he wasn't too happy about."

"Was he angry with you?" She couldn't imagine Tobias being angry, not now that she had seen the way he'd been on the island around the time of his wedding.

"Yes, he was pretty pissed."

It sounded as if he wasn't sure about telling her, as if he'd wanted to, but now couldn't. "Was it something you did?"

"Why would you think it's something I did?"

She held her breath, surprised by his anger. "I'm just assuming, based on what you told me."

"My brother isn't an angel, and he isn't always right, and I wish people wouldn't always assume I'm the one in the wrong."

She didn't want to get into a bickering argument with him. "I'm sorry, I'm just trying to help."

"I shouldn't have said anything."

But he had, and he'd told her, and that amounted to something.

"Sibling disagreements blow over, given enough time," she said, trying to say something helpful.

"It got me thinking," he said, dismissing her advice completely, "that a trip to the fairground might be nice, get Jacob out of the house and all that. Treat him to something. I'm almost an uncle, maybe I ought to do uncle-like things."

"Uncle-like things. That's an interesting way of putting it." He didn't want to talk about it. She understood.

"Would you like to join us? I need to check with Savannah first—because that kid has a busier social life than I do—but what about next weekend?"

Next weekend would be the weekend before her exams. She could manage a couple of hours. It might do her good. "I'd like that."

Chapter 32

It was a few days into the New Year that she met Jacob and Xavier at Bryant Park, refusing Xavier's offer to pick her up along the way because she and Cara had gone into town for brunch.

"Izzy!" Jacob came running towards her as soon as he saw her. He gave her a big, tight hug—as tight and as big as his little arms would allow.

"Hey, Jacob. It's been a while."

"Xavier said he had an awesome surprise for me!"

She looked at Xavier, and nodded.

"He means you," Xavier explained. "Not the fairground."

"I'm the surprise?" she asked, laughing.

"I didn't tell him you were coming."

It had been almost a month since she'd last seen him, and it was as if she was seeing him for the first time again. She'd be lying if she said she wasn't excited to see him. She'd felt like a teenager leaving home for a date, trying on a few outfits, jeans with different tops while Cara had waited in the living room telling her to hurry the hell up because she was starving.

The quiet, gentle thrill inside her re-ignited when her eyes locked with Xavier's. All of a sudden, that feeling of irritation she often had when he was around, was no longer there.

"Are you babysitting me again?" Jacob asked as they walked towards the fairground.

She wasn't sure what to reply to that because Savannah hadn't mentioned anything.

"Izzy's having a day out," Xavier explained. "She's got exams, and this is her break. So, she's not babysitting you today, kid. I am."

"Exams?" Jacob asked her, earnestly.

"Yes. A whole week of them."

"I would hate that."

"I do," she agreed.

"That's why we're going to make sure she has a good time," said Xavier, taking her by surprise. She wondered why he was being so nice. Things seemed different between them, now. There was no more hate-hate, no quips, no sarcasm.

For the next few hours they wandered around, going on the rides Jacob wanted, sometimes the three of them, and at other times she and Xavier took turns. They bought hotdogs, and candy floss, and hot chocolate and Xavier refused to let her pay.

"My treat," he told her each time she pulled out her purse.

They followed Jacob to the fairground shooting range, and saw him staring at one of the big cuddly Monkeys that was hanging on display. It was a poor rip-off of Mickey Mouse, but he seemed in awe of it, and squealed with delight when Xavier took a shot and won it.

"Can we get that one, too?" Jacob asked, pointing to another identical toy next to it. Izzy thought it odd, on two counts. Firstly that Jacob would ask for anything, and secondly that he would ask for a toy that was identical to the one he already had.

"Another one, buddy?" Even Xavier seemed surprised.

"I've got spending money." Jacob pulled some coins out of his coat pocket.

Xavier shook his head. "I've got this, kid." He peered in her direction. "How about we let Izzy take this go?"

"Me?" She shook her head. "No. No thanks. Not me. I can't shoot to save my life." She was no good at these things, had never tried before, but knew without a doubt she would be useless.

"Relax," he said, slanting a look at her. "It's not a real gun."

Jacob chimed in. "Have a go, Izzy!"

"Oh, you guys. Can't you let it go?" She hated all things gun related, even fake guns at a fairground rifle range, even with toy targets.

"I know women don't have the hand to eye coordination for these things," Xavier remarked, casually.

"I'll do it." She moved forward, and took a hold of the gun. It would be later that night, as she lay in bed, going over the evening's events and unable to sleep, that she would realize it had been Xavier's way of prompting her. He seemed to know exactly what buttons to press.

She closed her left eye, and took aim, then pulled the trigger. And missed by a long shot.

"Try again!" Jacob's voice urged her. She still had two turns left, and aimed again, trying to laser in on the moving target. She shot, and missed widely again.

It wasn't a big deal, but Xavier was watching, and she didn't want to look like a total fool at this. Annoyed at herself, she took aim, and shot blindly, and completely missed again.

"Told you," she heard Xavier say, "Women aren't too good at this."

Fuming, because she had been so useless, she glared back at him.

"Another go?" Xavier asked, making her heart thump harder, faster. It was either anger, or something else, something that threw her and made it even harder for her to concentrate.

"She'll have another turn." Xavier slipped another bill to the man behind the kiosk.

"C'mon Izzy. You can do this!" Jacob's encouragement didn't help. She flinched; just as she raised her arm and focused her gaze at the target, she felt Xavier's arm on hers. Her body stilled, and she felt her insides beginning to heat up.

"Like this," he said, adjusting her arms. His breath tickled her ears, and her concentration flew out of the window. "Move your head like this." His chest lightly grazed her back—or was she imagining it? Her winter coat was so thick, surely she wouldn't be able to feel anything?

And yet she did.

His presence, his cologne, his warm breath. These things permeated her senses.

It's not possible, she told herself, to feel these things, not in the cold and darkness around her.

Yet she felt something.

"Try again," he said, and stepped back.

"It's only a toy gun, guys," she managed to say, managed to infuse it with a who-the-hell-cares attitude that would cover over her lapse in concentration. She turned to Xavier. "Relax, dude. It's not real."

"It feels real enough to me." His eyes were dark, darker than the blue they normally were. What did he mean? What was he talking about? The fairground? The target? Or them? Was he feeling what she was?

Jacob broke the spell. "C'mon Izzy!"

She turned her head and aimed, and this time got nearer than before. Then, because her focus was off, because she was too busy thinking of the man behind her instead of the target in front of her, she fired wildly and missed. She pulled the trigger again, and missed, and then, because she wanted this over with, she took the next shot without even focusing and totally missed it.

"Nice try."

"Not again—" she started. She wouldn't be able to concentrate. Not now, with the feel of his arms on hers. She was glad he couldn't see her face, because she could feel heat creeping along her cheeks, even though they were out in the January cold. She didn't need him to know that he was having an effect on her.

But Xavier hadn't meant for her to take the next go. He hadn't even looked her way. "Want that one, buddy?" He pointed to the large monkey, confirming with Jacob who nodded eagerly.

He shot. Three clean shots, and two of them hit the target full on.

"Yay!!" Jacob jumped up and down like he'd had a sugar rush.

"What are you going to do with two identical monkeys, buddy?" Xavier asked, handing them over to him.

"They're for the twi—" he stopped, his tiny lips suddenly going all wobbly.

She wouldn't have thought anything of it had he not pasted his hand over his mouth, in that tell-tale way that children had. The tell-tale way that had both her and Xavier exchange knowing looks.

Savannah was pregnant with twins? She waited for Xavier to say something, but he didn't.

"Here you go, buddy." Xavier was cool as a cucumber, and she, taking the cue, took a hold of the other toy. "I'll hold him for you, Jacob." She took the oversized monkey, "otherwise you're going to have problems walking around with it."

He walked in front of them, leading the way, while she and Xavier followed, each of them clutching a monkey, neither saying a word.

Later that evening, he dropped her off again at her apartment, parking outside on the street in his Ferrari.

"Don't you feel show-offy driving around in this?" she asked him. The thrill of being in this car was real. People stared when the car stopped at traffic lights, and she watched their reactions, a mixture of awe and admiration.

"No, why would I?"

"You have to be careful around here," she said. "It's not a safe neighborhood."

"Then why do you live here?"

"It's affordable." And it left enough money over so they could eat and go out a few times a month.

He didn't say anything, but she could tell by the frown on his forehead, that he was mulling things over. "Don't you have anything less... showy," she said, trying to find the right word without sounding offensive.

"I don't do less."

She stared at his huge watch. "Obviously." Then she remembered that time he'd called her at Christmas. "I can show you how to do those reports, if you want."

"Now? Are you sure?"

"I'm sure." But she didn't know why she felt a fluttering in her stomach. Why her pulse had started to race. Under her cool exterior, she was a hothouse of emotions, and she didn't like being this out of control. Worse than that, she didn't like that the reason for her insides going haywire might be the tall, hard-muscled guy walking alongside her.

In the eerie silence that clung to them like cobwebs, she considered making conversation, but what was there to say? What could she say that didn't sound trite? And so she attempted humor as she got out her house keys.

"See, no dollar bills today."

He didn't look amused. "I fucking hope not."

The way he swore, and the anger in his voice, surprised her.

"As if you'd tell me," he added.

"Tell you what?"

"Who he was."

She stared at him. "What difference would that make?"

His face had darkened; the skin around his eyes was tight as he stayed silent.

"You want to know?" They stopped outside her door. And she hung onto her key, not yet inserting it into the lock.

"Only if you're ready. When you're ready."

The thudding in her heart turned louder. Something about the simmering rage in his voice sent a shockwave through her gut. Xavier, flirting and being lewd, she could handle, she could take him down a peg or two. Xavier being intense, and angry, over a guy who had been a dick to her—made her feel special.

She opened the door and he followed her in. Stepping away, so that her gaze could better sweep over his face, and take in the seriousness of his expression, she rubbed her forehead, and wondered why she was actually considering telling him.

Cara knew. But for some reason, the way this man was looking at her, made her want to tell him.

"How's Cara doing?" he asked, suddenly interrupting her thought pattern.

"She's fine. She's at her boyfriend's place."

"She is?"

Was it her imagination or did his voice sound a little odd when he asked her? Or was she feeling odd because it was just her and him, and only the two of them at her apartment? She didn't want him to think she had asked him in because of any particular reason. Guys like Xavier went from stationary to warp speed in seconds, and she didn't want him to get the wrong idea.

But at the fairground, his body had been so close to hers, and when he had his arms around her, he'd been so close she could feel his hot breath. He'd made shivers dance along her spine. She had replayed that moment over and over on her ride home, stopping off only for a short while to take Jacob back, and even when talking to Savannah, her whole mind had been on Xavier, waiting for her in the car.

No, maybe it wasn't a good idea to show him how to do the reports now. She felt foolish, as if she'd led him on, and then backtracked. She wasn't going to ask him in. Because the more she thought about it the more she talked herself out of it. Because men like Xavier moved too fast, and girls like her weren't sure.

"You know what, Laronde? I think maybe you can show me that stuff another time."

He was backing out, too?

She shrugged. "It's no big a deal. Those charts are easy enough, once you get the hang of them."

"I'm not as clever as you."

The man who couldn't stop boasting about his accomplishments was all of a sudden feeling insecure?

"That's not true," she said, trying to bolster him. "You drive a Ferrari, and have a gorgeous place in Tribeca. You and Tobias are the epitome of success."

"Yeah, well, some people would beg to differ. Tobias mostly."

She wondered if this was about the other day, when he'd mentioned that Tobias had been angry.

"Big brothers can be a pain in the butt, sometimes."

He placed his hand on the back of his neck, then ruffled up the hair at the base. She noticed he did that sometimes.

"Do you have a big pain-in-the-ass brother?" he asked.

"No. I have a younger brother, though, and he's told me often enough that I'm a pain in the butt." But, she wasn't the one who had to live in the shadows of an older, so blatantly successful, superstar brother. She'd seen the way everyone had swarmed around Tobias at the wedding, and at his birthday party. She had a feeling that even if it hadn't been his birthday or his wedding, people still would have flocked to Tobias, somehow drawn to him. There was something magnetic about success, wealth, and power, the trifecta which many coveted, but few possessed.

It made her feel for Xavier.

"What was it about?" she asked, her voice a whisper. "The disagreement between you both?"

They were still hovering around in the hallway, neither having taken a step towards the couch or the kitchen. She didn't want to move, and was hesitant to suggest that he sit down, for fear that he might decide to leave altogether, call it a night and tell her he'd speak to her tomorrow.

She was alone, and she didn't want him to go.

"Nothing of any significance and nothing that is worth talking about."

He lifted his head, and gave her the kind of forced smile that was so fabricated it looked like it needed scaffolding to keep it in place. She always rooted for the underdog and right now, even though she didn't have all the facts, Xavier seemed like the biggest underdog of them all.

"Do you want to talk about it? Talking helps."

"Nothing much to say. He was in a foul mood when he showed up."

"Why was he mad?"

She listened while Xavier explained the exchange between the brothers, and about Tobias being angry about his former friend and confidante, someone called Matthias Rust.

"What happened with Matthias?"

"They had a falling out."

"Over what?"

"I have no idea, and each time I try to ask him, I don't get a proper answer. I've asked him plenty of times."

"That's not fair, him taking it out on you like that. If you don't know what Matthias did, it's hardly your fault."

"He's going through some major life changes, what with getting married, and the baby. I don't know about the deal with Hennessy now. It might take a while before I can get started on that deal. So I won't be able to give you extra hours."

"I've got enough to keep me busy."

"What Jacob almost let slip, I haven't been told anything, but I can guarantee that Tobias wouldn't want that news getting out."

"I can keep a secret." In that moment she saw that no matter what, this guy still looked up to his brother, would still protect him, and defend him.

"Did you tell him how you felt?"

"No. When Tobias gets that mad, I kind of let him roll with it. There's no point."

"Maybe he needs to hear that you've grown up, and that you have feelings too."

He seemed to consider her words. "I don't have the time for his drama."

She had to admit, despite her initial preconceived ideas about Tobias, he hadn't come across to her as being bad tempered. But people were complicated creatures, and this reconfirmed to her the belief that people behaved so differently with different people.

"People treat you the way you expect them to, Stone," she said, using the name that drew a line between them and that kept things at bay.

"Really, Laronde?"

"Really." She eyed him, and then said, "Thanks for today."

"Good luck with exam week," he said, stepping away from her door.

Chapter 33

He was going to confront Tobias, despite being all too aware of his brother's wrath, and his avoidance of discussing anything to do with Matthias.

Xavier stepped out of the elevator on the twenty-first floor of Stone Enterprises and found Vivian, Tobias's PA, sitting at her desk with her eyes focused on the computer screen. Not wanting to interrupt her, he waited for her to look up at him. In the past he would have usually flirted with her, but today he was checking for any messages from Izzy.

As usual, there were none. He'd emailed her once a few days ago, to let him know when she wanted more work. He understood her worry over finances, and wanted that to be one worry less for her.

But so far, she hadn't replied.

Vivian looked up. "Can I help?"

He smiled. "Is Tobias available?"

She didn't even flinch, or check a diary, or look at anything online. "He is, but he's got a meeting in twenty minutes." She seemed to know his daily schedule off by heart.

"Is he in a good mood?"

The way she opened her perfectly painted lips and said nothing, told him 'no'.

"Wish me luck."

She gave him the kind of smile that he was used to. He knocked once, and heard nothing. Impatient, he knocked again, and this time opened the door a fraction, sticking his head through the gap to find Tobias on the phone.

Ooops.

For a moment, he considered the wisdom of what Izzy had told him. What worked for one person wouldn't necessarily work for another. Maybe he could backtrack and talk about something else.

His brother lifted his face and looked at him. Angry eyes blazed into his and the tell-tale crease in the middle of his forehead signaled Tobias's already pissed off mood.

It was too late to turn around and leave.

"I'll be home early. Don't worry, babe."

Babe?

Who the hell was he talking to?

"Love you," Tobias said, in a voice what was as sweet as sugar, before slamming the phone down. "What do you want?" he asked.

Strange how much of a Jekyll and Hyde character this man could be.

"Is it safe to come in?" Xavier attempted humor, and slowly opened the door wider, but didn't step inside.

"I've got a meeting in ten. Make it quick."

Vivian had told him he had twenty minutes, but he decided not to question that. "Are you still mad at me?" he asked, walking towards Tobias's desk.

"You're so easy to pull the wool over," Tobias commented, sitting back in his leather chair.

"I don't follow."

"You do understand, don't you, that the only reason you got funding from Hennessy is because Matthias wanted a way in."

"A way into what?"

"To get to me."

Jeez. Fuck. No. "Bullshit," he spat the word out, disgusted, and annoyed by Tobias's tendency to think something was about him.

"It's the truth." Tobias replied, calmly.

"Chad injecting cash into my new venture isn't about you. For fuck's sake, Tobias, not everything is about you."

"That's because you're still not clever enough to read between the lines."

There he went again, lauding himself up. "What happened between you two? Why would Matthias need to go through me to get to you?"

And get to him for what?

Hennessy's company investing in him had been one of the few good things to happen to him for a while, and he wasn't going to sit here and let Tobias think the deal was about him.

When Tobias said nothing, his anger exploded. "I'm getting fed up of you having a go at me for something I knew nothing about," he said, slowly. "And what pisses me off even more, is that you're still being vague, and I'm still none the wiser as to what went down between you both. I'm not surprised he pissed you off. It's not difficult to piss you off, Tobias."

Tobias's mouth tightened, the usual tell that indicated he hadn't liked what he'd heard. "You're not the easiest of people to be around. You can be one of the biggest pains in the butt. People do things for you because they're scared of you. Let me guess, Matthias overstepped his mark. He went over your head and signed off on a deal you didn't approve of?"

Tobias glared at him, and still said nothing, which infuriated him further.

"If I've told you that Matthias is no longer with the company, that should have been enough for you to butt out."

"But I've signed the deal. I need his investment—or rather his company's investment, because this isn't about him or me or Hennessy, but about how we can do business together. It's not personal."

His brother's deadly gaze could have burned a hole through his skin.

"I made the mistake of thinking you had a wise head on those shoulders," said Tobias, "That despite your desire to show off and brag about what a hotshot you are, that there were some real," he tapped his head with two fingers, "brain cells up here."

"That's right, go back to being your usual condescending self, Tobias." He looked at his watch. "You think what I do is so inferior? You think because I don't have a big glass building, because I don't have a 'legitimate' business," he air-quoted the 'legitimate', "you think I'm a loser? That's your opinion, and you're entitled to it. You can think what you want. It doesn't matter."

"Go to hell."

"You're telling me to go to hell instead of explaining why Matthias has pissed you off so much?" This was typical of him. "I don't know what's going on with you but this can't go on. You're bringing a new life into the world. You should be happy. Not like this."

He stormed out.

His fingers reached for his cell phone on the elevator down, the temptation to call Izzy was strong.

He was tempted to have a cup of coffee. Tempted to talk. If there was someone right now in his life who understood more about him, it was Izzy.

But, he put his cell phone away. It was her week of exams, and he wasn't going to contact her.

Chapter 34

"Don't worry about it. Not everyone wants a math nerd." But Cara's words did nothing to comfort her. "And you kill it in all your other subjects."

She huffed out a disappointed breath, the full weight of her exam results bearing down on her. 60% wasn't enough to secure an internship with one of the bigger companies, which was exactly what she'd hoped to secure for the long summer break. Math wasn't her strong suit, but damn it, she was trying. She just couldn't afford to get extra tutoring like most of her other friends did.

Cara put her arm around her shoulders and squeezed hard. "It's only a small exam. You're allowed to have a few bad grades. It's not the end of the world."

"It's not a small exam," she muttered, looking around at the happy faces of students as they walked past her. Why were people looking so happy? "It matters. For the internships, it matters."

"Not as much as you think it does."

She knew Cara was trying to cheer her up, but nothing was going to do it. Nothing.

"Come on. Let's go to the cafeteria and get some cheesecake. Everything looks better after cheesecake."

But she didn't feel up to it. Nobody else felt this pressure, but she did. She knew too well what failure looked like, knew what it had done to her father, and she was determined never to be in that situation. Ever.

Getting 60% in math might not be a failure in Cara's eyes, but it was in hers.

"You go. I'd rather go home." She didn't want to hang around the campus any longer.

"And do what? Eat a whole tub of ice-cream all by yourself?"

"We don't have a full—"

"I know. I was joking. I was trying to make you laugh. Remember laughter? It's that thing you do, you last did it when you came back from the fairground."

She smiled. It had been a good day.

"Please let me go home." She wasn't in the mood to be around happy people. Please let me be.

"Ok." Cara gave her another bear hug. "But if you change your mind."

I won't.

But as she started to walk down the steps to the subway, she decided to make good on the thing that had been bugging her for days.

It wasn't the reason she had done so badly in her test, but seriously, something was wrong with her to have her wondering what Xavier was up to. As soon as her last exam had finished, she had caught up with the work he'd given her and had emailed it to him, but she hadn't heard back.

Since when had she started to count the days since she'd last heard from him?

273

She walked back up the subway steps, turning away from the traffic with the thought of calling him, but then she stopped, her finger pausing over his name.

Would he think it was silly—her calling him about work when she normally emailed him? What did it matter? It was work related, and she was calling him because it had been a few days since her exams had finished, and she needed to let him know she was ready for more work.

So, she called him, her gut slowly traveling to the ground, her heart beating, as she waited.

"Hi," she breathed, as soon as he picked up.

"Laronde?" He sounded cheerful, she could tell, by the way he said her name.

"I was—" she cleared her throat. "I was wondering if you uh," What the hell was wrong with her? Pull yourself together. "If the figures I sent over were OK? I didn't hear from you so I was wondering. That's all."

"I'm sure they are, you never get anything wrong, but I haven't had a chance to look through them yet. I was busy looking over Hennessy's contract."

"You're still going ahead with that?"

"No reason why not."

He sounded testy. Things were probably still tense between him and Tobias. She tried to find something to say, something neutral. "I was wondering, because you hadn't replied, and you usually do."

Needy.

That sounded needy.

Did that sound needy?

How needy?

"I did reply. I asked if you needed more work, but you didn't reply."

She'd missed one of his emails? "I must have missed it. Sorry."

"Don't be. I know you've had lots going on."

"You sound busy, too." All of a sudden she wished she hadn't called him. The conversation had hardly been as riveting as she had hoped. "I'll...uh...I'll let you go."

"I'm not busy now. It's been a lousy week."

"Lousy week?"

"A clusterfuck of a week."

She laughed, finding kinship in his misery. "Same here."

"Why, what happened with you?"

"Nothing major. Just math exam results."

"Not the end of the world stuff, then," he said, sounding a little lighter.

"No."

"I was wondering how your exams went."

He was?

"Pretty good, except for the math results."

"You should be celebrating the small victories. Exams being over counts as one of them."

"I suppose so." But everything mattered. Every exam, every result. It all mattered. Not that Xavier would ever understand. His life seemed so cushy from where she was standing. What did he know?

"What are you up to now?"

"Me?" Going home and buying a tub of ice-cream along the way. Why was he asking? "Nothing much," she replied, trying not to get excited. A shiver of goosebumps broke out along her back.

"Would you have time to show me how you did those charts? You know, those 3D bar charts?"

"Sure."

"I can come over to your place later?" he suggested.

Later? "No," she said quickly. "I was going home anyway. I'm heading for the subway. I could come to your place, if it's okay with you."

"We can commiserate together."

"Misery plus misery."

"Fun times."

She smiled, and it was the stupidest smile that stayed on her face the entire time she was on the subway.

She was there before she knew it, smoothing down her hair as she got the elevator to his apartment. She was still messing around with her hair by the time she walked to his door.

"Hey," he said, standing with the door wide open and wearing a five o'clock shadow as if it was made for him.

"Hey. You look a little rough," she remarked carefully. Sexy rough.

"It hasn't been the best of weeks," he replied, closing the door behind her.

"What's going on?" she asked. "You know about my math drama, but what's going on with you?"

"It's nothing."

The hell it was nothing. "Tobias?" she asked, hazarding a guess. He shook his head as if not wanting to talk about it. Why would he want to talk to her about matters close to his heart?

She placed her knapsack on the floor and, following his lead, walked over to the couch, sitting at one end, while he sat at the other.

"He's still pissed with me for taking that contract with Hennessy."

He was willing to talk about it. She leaned forward, eager to hear. "Because of that guy who used to be his friend?"

"Yes." Xavier ran his hand across his jaw, over the dusting of dark hairs, as if he wasn't used to it. "Something's up with him. Taking your advice, I went to his office and tried to have it out with him."

As pleased as she was that he'd listened to her, she could sense that the outcome hadn't been good. "Tried to?" she asked, then looked away when he caught her staring at his stubble, and at the beaded bracelet he wore around his wrist.

"We ended up having more words. I actually managed to say what I needed to."

"Oh," she gasped, lightly. "I was hoping you two might get to clear the air."

"No."

"Were you two ever close?"

"Honestly?" He shook his head. "I don't know. Probably not. I liked to think so, but he's got Savannah and Jacob now, and—"

"And, you think he's not bothered about you?"

"Tobias is … complicated, and competitive, and he likes to win."

"Don't you? Like to win, I mean?" she asked, aware that she was pushing at the edges of an intangible boundary. Probing deeper, and each time she pushed forward, he opened up. He seemed to want someone to talk to, and she wanted to help.

"Not as badly as he does."

He scratched above his eyebrow and gave her a look that filled her with curiosity. A feeling of empathy flowed into her, making her see, as if the curtain had been lifted, and a spotlight had exposed Xavier's deepest wound.

"At least you tried."

"Tobias can do what he likes. People always side with him. He's used to it. Nobody is ever going to correct him, because he is so wealthy and successful. The real rules and laws don't seem to apply to him."

She understood exactly. But she didn't feel that Tobias was in the same camp as those types of people, like Shoemoney, or the businessman who'd trampled on her father's dreams.

"Tobias doesn't strike me as someone who is inherently bad. I've met those types of people, and your brother isn't one of them."

He leaned forward, looking at her as if he still had unanswered questions, but didn't dare to ask them. "No, he's not a bad person. Not like that." His voice, and the way he looked at her reminded her of that night at the fairground, of his arms around her, and his body close to hers. A myriad of scenes, from that night, and others from her subsequent thoughts about that night, flooded her senses, temporarily disarming her.

"Why's your one test result bothering you?" he asked, completely changing the topic and making her think that he wasn't interested in whose side she was on. The realization made her scratch her wrist, gave her time to process this disappointment, and to think. Why would she think that being here with Xavier Stone meant anything? The guy could have any woman he liked, and he probably did. Why would he have any interest in a college girl like her?

So she explained why. Focusing on facts and talking about test results and internships; taking the emotion out of the equation was easier.

"Internships aren't a big deal. You shouldn't be so hard on yourself about it."

"Easy for you to say." A guy like him had probably been making contacts since kindergarten. "Do you want me to show you how to do those charts?"

"Good idea," he said, standing up quicker than she would have liked. Maybe he was busy, and she was in the way. "I could ask my other VAs to do it," he explained, walking towards his office area and giving her no choice but to follow, "but by the time I've explained everything to them, I might as well have done it myself."

She noted that he had changed his screensaver. Now it was the Ferrari. No woman.

"You click a row, then hold the Command key down, and then you can select non-adjacent cells," she said, feeling unsure as she tried to explain something she did automatically. Now that she had to think about it, she found herself second-guessing her actions.

"Okay."

"And then you drag it like this," she highlighted the row of figures.

"I can never get that to drag down and keep all those selected."

"And you're supposed to be the poster boy for Apple products!"

"I'm not as smart at you."

"It's not about being smart, it's just tricky. But once you get the hang of if you won't even have to think about it." She looked at him, then at his lips, then brought her gaze to his eyes again and hoped he hadn't noticed. "Try it," she suggested, and tried to move out of the way, but she was sitting down, pinned in her seat, as he gripped the mouse and tried to follow her instructions.

"Like this?" He tried to highlight the cells, but as he got to the bottom, he lost the selection.

"Like this," she said, their hands brushing as she took control of the mouse.

She could feel her heart pounding and ground down on her teeth, attempting control. She was already aware of his own familiar smell of cologne, the mix of cool and sweet that was so undeniably him. But he had a heat about him, and she could feel it, could feel something which set her on edge. It didn't make sense, this high state of alertness where she could hear every breath, see every eye blink, see the dark hairs along his jaw, and inhale his scent.

She was turning into one of those girls she detested.

"Try again." She moved her hand away, letting him take the mouse, and she watched as he tried again.

She kept her gaze on the screen, even though a strange feeling in her stomach heated up, making her not pay much attention to his attempts to highlight the correct cells.

"What keys is it again?"

"It's …" She didn't know how to explain it, like driving, or riding a bike, she only knew how to do it, but found it almost impossible to explain to someone else.

"Watch me again." She repeated her actions.

He sighed loudly. "You must think I'm thick."

She turned her head sharply towards him, their faces so close now she could taste his breath. "No. I don't."

He moved away first, raising to standing, his hands in his pockets. "This is why I don't have any of those pretty charts. I couldn't be asked to put them in. I don't have time to make things pretty in my reports. I just give people the facts."

She turned around in the swivel chair, now able to because he had taken a step back, out of her personal space. "I don't think you're thick. Tobias probably delegates a lot of his stuff to other people."

Why was she making this be about Tobias?

"I'll leave you to do those reports, Laronde. Be extra work for you—unless you have a problem?"

Extra work? No, she didn't have a problem. "That would be great."

"There might be a further delay on the extra work with the new business in China." He looked down and shifted from one foot to the other. "I wish I hadn't raised your hopes."

"You didn't." She didn't want him to feel bad about it. "I'd already dialed the hours down."

"You didn't think I'd deliver?"

Shit. It was exactly why, but she couldn't gloss over it. She wasn't one to lie easily, even though right now she would have given anything to lie like a pro. "You sounded unsure, and I didn't want to factor in the extra money. I have to budget really tightly, and I'm really conservative."

He didn't say anything, and she wasn't sure if he bought it.

"Are you going home?"

"Yes." As opposed to going where?

"I'll call you an Uber."

"What for?" she scoffed. "It's still early."

"It getting dark out there." He didn't seem to wait for her permission, and made the call.

She walked towards the couch, grabbing her knapsack, and putting on her coat.

"You're behaving like my dad."

"I have no fatherly intentions, believe me."

She looked up at him.

"That didn't come out right," he said, backtracking quickly.

She put her hat on, then pulled it down, then smiled. "Thanks."

"Thanks for coming over," he said.

"You're welcome."

"Sorry to waste your time."

She frowned. "You didn't waste my time." She touched the sleeve of his sweatshirt lightly. "That wasn't a comparison, when I said Tobias delegates stuff. I wasn't comparing you both."

"Many people do."

"I wasn't," she insisted, needing him to know. She tugged at his sweatshirt. "But people can only grow their businesses when they focus on the things they're good at, not the little tasks you can give other people to do."

"You're right, and you're the smartest VA I've ever had." He lifted his hand to her face, stroking her cheek with his thumb, making her heartbeat rocket.

"The smartest VA?" She smiled, liking the feel of his thumb on her cheek, the pressure light, the feel electric.

"For sure."

Her throat turned to sandpaper, and she swallowed, and wished, for once, that he would resort to his playboy ways. But the touch of his hand was light, so slight, she felt a pull straight through her stomach.

But he stared at her for the longest time, doing nothing, his finger resting on her chin, the look in his eyes doing more to dampen her panties than any physical move ever could.

She licked her lips, her mouth parting, because her breathing had sped up.

A vertical line ran from her head to the tips of her toes, sparks igniting and tingling all along it. Maybe it was because she hadn't had a boyfriend for going on a year, or maybe it was because Xavier Stone had the sexiest eyes and the most beautiful lips. And maybe she had thought about those lips more times than she cared to admit.

She couldn't work out if he was teasing her, or if this was a ploy, but the way her breasts tingled, the way her knees felt wobbly, she didn't care.

He moved an inch closer, as did she, and then she licked her lower lip, anticipating, waiting, wishing. And when the ringtone of his phone cut in, she let out a sharp breath.

His hand fell to his side, and he answered the call.

"Your Uber's waiting."

She blinked, it was like a fall, tripping back to reality. Hard reality. Her eyes squeezed shut for a moment longer than a normal blink.

She swallowed. "I'd better go."

"See you around, Izzy."

The whole ride home she thought about his lips, his eyes, his fingers on her skin. By the time she got home she was fully aroused, and left wanting. And what she wanted was Xavier Stone.

One look at her face in the mirror, flushed and red, told her this was real.

She felt unsatisfied, and craved his touch, his kisses, his body. She had made a complete turnaround when it came to Xavier Stone, and her dampness between her legs confirmed it. The throbbing between her breasts double confirmed it.

But Xavier? How could she? He was everything she hated in a guy. Rich, moneyed, a privileged jerk.

Only he was that and so much more.

Chapter 35

Dinner with his mother. Thank fuck it was over.

She'd wanted to grill him about the bust-up with his brother. How did she know about these things, because he hadn't said a word to her and neither had Tobias? There was an unspoken pact between the brothers not to involve their mother in any personal matters, including sibling disagreements because they both wanted an easier life.

He hadn't even ordered his first bottle of beer when she'd asked what was going on with him and Tobias.

He'd spent the rest of the evening, shoveling his food down as fast as he could, and wished he'd taken an Uber instead of driving to Lafont & Moreau in The Lancaster. That had been the first clue. His mother always picked the most expensive, most exclusive restaurant in the city when there was a 'problem' she needed to resolve. She probably assumed that in the quiet and discreet surroundings, there wouldn't be much cause for anyone to raise their voice.

He'd discovered that she had asked Tobias to come along, but "he was busy, you know how hard it is with Savannah being so tired all the time now."

The news took him by surprise, that Tobias had carried the grudge even now. Usually his brother thawed out after a few days. His temper was quick to ignite, and as fast to thaw.

"It's nothing, Mother."

"If it's nothing then why is your brother not here?"

"Ask him." And hadn't she already given an excuse as to why Tobias couldn't come?

He deserved an award for lasting the eighty five minutes it took to get through the meal. His eating time had been fifteen minutes, but it was his mother who had dragged it out minute by painful minute, taking her sweet time.

He had been contemplating the recent contract with Hennessy, and even though they had drawn up legal documents, he was now seriously starting to consider pulling out of the deal.

It would set his new business back by months, until he found a new investor, but he didn't see that he had a choice. Even though he'd mentioned it to her a few days ago, it wouldn't do much harm, would it, if he told her that he was pulling out for sure?

He called her but her cell phone went to voicemail, and he didn't bother leaving a message. Maybe he would turn up on her doorstep. He needed an excuse and this was as good an excuse as any.

When she opened the door, her look of happy surprise told him that he'd done the right thing.

"Did we have a meeting arranged?"

"No," he replied, giving her a quick once over, and trying not to hyperventilate. "I was passing through." She was wearing some kind of ripped t-shirt and tight, tight, tight leggings.

He tried to not let her body detract from his thoughts. He'd come here for a reason, dammit. What was the reason? "I had dinner with my lovely mother."

"Why are you saying it like that?" she asked, motioning for him to come inside.

"I'm just glad it was over. I should have called. Sorry. I was in a hurry to escape." He felt as if he needed to explain his sudden appearance.

"In a hurry to escape from your mom?"

"Yes. She'd asked Tobias, and he hadn't come, and she wanted to know why we had fallen out, and I wasn't in the mood to explain." It was awkward, explaining all of this without looking at her, and he was conscious of the fact that he was staring at the floor. Because staring at her in that skimpy outfit was doing things to him.

"You'll have to excuse the mess," she said, moving some books off the ottoman. He ventured a glance at her as she lifted the books, and it looked as if her clothes were painted on. No doubt it was going to give him a sleepless night getting that image out of his head.

"You don't need to tidy up," he said, folding his arms, as he watched. She was wearing what looked like a baggy tee but with two slits at the side, and joined up at the bottom. When she turned, he could see her bra top underneath, soft and seamless.

"What…" he cleared his throat again, as blood rushed straight to his manhood. He felt his breath hitch in his throat. "What are you wearing?"

"I was supposed to go to a yoga class," she explained. "But I ended up vegging in front of the TV instead."

He felt his balls tighten.

"You go to yoga dressed like that?"

"Yes, the gear has to be like a second skin so that it doesn't get in the way of the yoga poses."

Jeez. He'd get a hard-on just being in a yoga class like that.

She walked over to a door. "Could you?" she asked, turning to him.

He walked over and opened the door, staring into her bedroom. Purple bedspread, gray curtains. Books on a white wooden desk adjacent to it. She placed the books on the desk and turned around, slapping her hands together, as if getting rid of the dust.

He raised a palm to his face, heard his heartbeat thundering beneath his ribcage. He'd wanted to see her, had been wanting to see her ever since the other day when she had come over to show him how to do the 3D bar charts. He knew how to do them, more or less. Yes, they were fiddly, yes, they were a pain in the butt, and yes, he didn't include them in his reports precisely because they were fiddly and a pain in the butt.

But he'd been lying letting her think he had no clue. And now, it didn't seem right to continue the lie just because he needed to get close.

He'd jerked off to her plenty of times, because, well, he'd had to. But now, with her like this, he wasn't prepared for it. His throat dried up, and he didn't know how to start. How to begin to come clean.

"You have a great figure, Laronde." He wiped his hand over his face again, felt as if he was going to start sweating buckets if he had to stand here and stare at her any longer.

"You can come in," she said, folding her arms, and leaning against the desk. He obeyed, and stepped inside. "This is a big room," he said, scrutinizing everything slowly.

"We got lucky with this apartment, and the rent is affordable-ish, even if the neighborhood isn't that great."

His eyes met hers, in understanding.

Fuck.

She had toned triceps. He could tell by the outline of those delicate muscles. Bare arms. Like back in Fiji when he'd seen her in the pool. Shorts, and that Lime Green Bikini.

"What?" she asked, when she caught him looking.

"Nothing," he replied, looking away, wondering how he was going to begin setting the record straight.

"No," she said. "What? What was that look for?"

He took a step towards owning up. "I was thinking of you that time on the island. I had a name for you back then."

She stood up, a curious smile on her lips. "A name for me?"

"Lime Green Bikini."

"Lime Green Bikini?" she said, her hands resting on her slender hips. But she didn't sound angry. She sounded appropriately indignant, but with a smile.

"I had a name for you."

"Oh, yeah?" Now it was his turn to step nearer, put on a faux indignant tone.

"Asshole."

"Asshole," he said slowly, taking another step forward.

"Jerk," she replied, giving him an inviting smile.

"Jerk, too?"

She nodded. "And douchebag."

"And douchbag." He nodded, as if agreeing with her choice of words, and couldn't stop himself reaching out to touch her arm. When she didn't flinch, or say anything, his fingers slid down, tracing along the length. "And now?"

"Now you're just Stone."

It was an adequate description for the state of his manhood right now. She licked her lips, her eyes fixing on his lips, her head moving forward a miniscule fraction.

He was usually so confident in all the moves he made.
Usually.

But not with her.

"I have a stupid confession to make," he said, staring at her
as she stared straight back, defiant, and sexy, and driving him
wild.

"A confession?" She shifted on the desk, dropping her
arms down, making him even more aware of her body, that
neck, those shoulders. The second skin.

A hunger burned deep within him. His need for her like
nothing he had known before. "I want to kiss you, Laronde."

"Are you asking for permission?"

"I'm asking what you would do if I did."

She licked her lips again. "Why don't you try it, and see?"

And that did it. He stepped forward, and her arms went
around his neck, like in a reflex action, taking him by surprise.

His hands skirted around her slim waist and their mouths
smacked together, hard and wet and desperate, tongues
joined together like Sumo wrestlers in a ring. He couldn't
help but slide his hands along her sides, feeling, touching,
exploring, blood pumping through his body like a raging
river. His hands skimmed over that second-skin-gym-gear she
had on. She was hard, and slim, with not a roll of fat on her
body, and he'd hardened further. It would be a killer to keep
that under control because he hadn't had sex in months.

The drought was real.

She moaned, soft and low, her moan caressing every muscle
inside him, touching his body like a lightning rod, igniting
sparks all along the length where they were joined. She
walked, backwards, their lips still sealed together like hot
molten candle wax as they stumbled and staggered towards
the bed.

~ ~ ~

Jeez.

She could only think of his favorite word when he had turned up at her door; she'd only been thinking of him for the entire week.

And now he lay on top of her, on her bed, giving her long, sensual kisses, partly satisfying the need that had been tunneling through her for the past few weeks.

They pulled apart, and stared at one another. It was a strange sensation to be in this position, doing this, instead of having one of their usual verbal sparring sessions.

"I was wondering how long it would take you to make a move," she said, and watched the surprise flicker from his eyes to his lips.

"You were waiting?"

She gave a nod.

"Why didn't you say so, Laronde? If I'd known, I'd have jumped you sooner."

She rolled her head back and laughed, and felt his lips on her neck, felt his soft kisses all over.

"You didn't live up to your reputation."

He lifted his head. "And you can be scary sometimes."

"Scary? Me?"

"Daunting would be a better word."

He'd found her daunting? This sex-god, this walking, talking hard-on on legs, had found her daunting?

Incredible.

"It was after you went on the Women's March, and what you said about it, the reason you had gone. After that I was scared to open my mouth around you in case I said the wrong thing."

She was taken aback that he had actually listened to what she said and taken heed. That he'd actually had to think before he opened his mouth. "Then my work is done."

"And my work is just beginning," he rasped, and before she had a chance to work out what he meant, his mouth dipped to her shoulder and he planted a kiss there before he trailed his lips slowly up her neck, and along her jaw, a flurry of tiny kisses before his mouth settled over hers and he gave her a slow and sexy French kiss. Her toes curled, and a fire spread from her stomach downwards. She arched her back in appreciation, heat rushing through her body as she shivered at his touch. They kissed for the longest time, driven by lust and want, eager, and hungry. It reminded her of the first time she had discovered how to kiss, when the newness of it had made her want to do it over and over again.

Only, Xavier's kissing was nothing like her barely thirteen-year old boyfriend's fumbling attempts. Xavier's lips bruised, and brushed, and sucked, they teased, and ignited, and his fingers took her to blissful heights. She wanted him with a desperation that surprised her.

He paused at one point, then stood up and took his jacket off, and then smiled at her as he removed his thin fleece to reveal a t-shirt. She waited for that to come off, too, and the disappointment when he didn't, coupled with the ache between her legs, made her kiss him all the harder when he lay back down on top of her.

He ground his hips into her, and she opened her legs wider, willing for him to touch her there, with his fingers, his lips, his mouth.

But it wasn't happening.

The more he didn't stray from her face and neck, the more she felt him up, cupping his toned buttocks in her hands, brushing her fingers over his soft jeans, and hard leather belt.

He looked down at her again his lips wet, and swollen, his expression teasing. She panted, and smiled, feeling loose and giddy all over, wanting more of him. As if he sensed her longing, his hand slipped under her yoga t-shirt, to the soft bandeau top and then to her nipple. His fingers teased there, rubbed, and twisted, and tweaked, but it was his mouth she ached for, his mouth and tongue, there, in place of his hands.

When he kissed her, his hand still playing and teasing her breast, she arched her back, and pressed her hands down harder, squeezing his butt, trying to get him closer to her. His tongue was so far down her mouth, she felt as if she was part of him, felt connected, the way two people were mid-orgasm, coming together in a sea of liquid arousal.

She heard the door burst open first, before Cara's voice as she charged in. "Guess what Shelly did!" Followed by "Oh shit."

Damn you, Cara.

Xavier stilled, then moved his head, his face an inch or so away from hers, their eyes locked together in disappointment. They didn't move, didn't answer her, didn't acknowledge her.

"Sorry," and then the door closed.

But the bubble had been broken. They stared at one another, and she became aware of her panting, and the weight of his hips and hardness pressing into hers. He shifted his body, adjusting himself, his elbows propped up on either side of her.

He made to move off, but she caged him in with her legs wrapped around him.

"Where do you think you're going?" she asked, not willing to let him loose yet. He felt so good down there. If it was the closest she could get, of him, she was going to hold onto him a little longer.

"Izzy," he groaned, into her mouth.

"Kiss me again," she implored, and he did, brushing his lips gently over her neck and the sides of her face before bringing his lips close to hers. Close enough but not yet touching, he paused for a moment, and she inhaled his breath, the sensation making her dizzy. And then he kissed her, bruising her lips as he kissed her hard. He had surprised her, because the reputation that proceeded him didn't seem to be anything like the man who seemed to take everything so slowly.

With a loud sigh, he moved off her, and lay on his side, propping his head up on his hand while his free hand skated under the t-shirt top and moved over her mid-riff. She was proud of her figure. Knew instinctively that he liked the feel of her tight stomach and her well-honed body. Yoga and not always having lots to eat, did that.

"I should go."

"Already?" she said, using her best seductive voice. His hand moved from her mid-riff to her breast, and lay flat over it. She felt his heated touch, felt the throbbing reaction of her body, and the pulsating below.

"Unless you want me to stay?"

He was asking her?

"What do you think?"

His hand moved down, down, down, down, then rested just below the elastic waistband of her leggings. He was oblivious to the inferno raging a few inches below, and she prayed that he would slide his hand lower, that he would slip his fingers inside her flimsy lace panties, and she held her breath, waiting.

But he did none of those things, and looked at her, instead. A look that was sad, and quiet, devoid of all the passion and longing they had just shared.

"What?" she asked, touching his cheek. "Why do you look so somber?"

He moved his hand away, then dropped a dry kiss on her lips.

A goddamn dry kiss.

"I should go."

"With that tent pole in your jeans?" She propped herself up on her elbows, and stared at the large bulge in his jeans.

He stood between her legs, looking down at her. "That's your fault, Laronde. Almost four months," he said, letting out a breath.

"You've been counting?"

He scratched the back of his neck. "No, I was just thinking out aloud. It's taken me four months to get to kiss you."

"I'm not an easy catch, Stone," she said, slowing rising, their hands entwining automatically. "And you're not my type."

Or hadn't been.

He kissed her again, unexpectedly. "Don't keep on reminding me." Smiling, because he had lifted her mood, she kissed him back, because she liked the feel of his lips on hers, liked to feel the hardness of his muscles, liked that all of a sudden, they could.

"I'm sorry." Another kiss, his hands around her waist, her arms around his neck, tongues exploring and mating. A drawn-out kiss that had her wanting much more. She forced herself to stop, when she heard a deep guttural moan come from inside her. At this rate, she'd want him to stay the night.

"You're hot stuff, Laronde." His gaze swept over her, energizing every cell in her body.

"You're a bundle of surprises, Stone."

"You're making my balls blue."

She reached below, touching his hardness, eliciting a gasp from him. "You're right." She stroked him over the soft fabric, saw the glint in his eye, the strangled breath he pushed out of his mouth, and then his hand reached over and moved her hand away.

"I should go," he said, his eyes moist, his breath ragged.

"Why?" She couldn't understand why he was leaving. "For someone who has a reputation as a player, you're disappointing me." She grinned as she said it, but she caught something in his expression she couldn't decipher. As if he didn't like that she was calling him out on it. It surprised her because she'd assumed he'd always played that careless womanizer part so well. For a long time she had wondered why girls were stupid enough, crazy enough, desperate enough to fall for him, and here she was, doing the exact same thing herself.

"Sorry to disappoint you on this occasion, but we can continue at another time." He adjusted her yoga tee, which had slipped off one shoulder.

"Are you sure you don't want a helping hand?" she asked mischievously.

"You're killing me, Laronde."

She wasn't ready for him to go. Her evening had been gloomy, but now, after this, it wasn't just the throbbing between her legs, it was having him around. She could restrain herself but she didn't want to be alone. "We can talk, we don't have to make out."

He bent over and placed his hand around the back of her neck, tilting her head upwards. "Believe me, I want to do much more than make out with you." He dropped another kiss on her lips, leaving her breathless, and speechless, and wondering why he hadn't. "But I also don't want to rush anything."

She pressed her lips together, understanding, even though her body was a jungle of nerves, wild and unrestrained.

"I'm glad I came," he said.

"Maybe next time you actually will," she murmured, licking her lips provocatively, and surprised by her sense of letting go. It was as unnerving as it was exhilarating, the effect that Stone had on her, the way he made her throw logic out of the window, and succumb to her desire.

Chapter 36

It had been her outfit that had done it. Seeing her in those figure-hugging second skin yoga clothes had pushed him over the edge.

And it had been the right thing, to leave. This was Izzy, after all, and he couldn't do with her what he would usually have done with other girls by now. It didn't seem right.

He'd tried to tell her. At least, he'd thought about telling her, maybe not about the bet straight away. He'd have to lead into that, test the waters gently, but at least about the bar charts.

But with her dressed like that, it had been impossible. Testosterone didn't allow him to think clearly.

What was he supposed to do?

But she wasn't someone he could fuck and discard. She had more depth than the Giseles and Petras of his world. And he liked her. He liked her a lot.

But there was that fucking, stupid bet standing in the way.

Screw it.

And screw Luke, too.

Who the hell was he kidding?

He wanted Izzy. He wanted her more than he had remembered wanting anyone. Hell, if she'd been anyone else, there would have been no hesitation.

He had forced himself to leave, otherwise, a few more kisses like that, and he wouldn't have been able to tear himself away. Stepping out into the night air, he took a few long breaths, then looked around, as the sound of sirens in the distance broke the silence. Only when he got near to his car did he notice.

"Fuck." He stared at

"Fuck." This time louder. His tires had been slashed. All of them.

All.

Of.

Them. There had been no break-in, no wonder the alarm hadn't gone off. Just some petty, jealous, mindless thugs slashing all his tires before disappearing.

His two hundred thousand dollar car, trashed.

Fuck.

He tapped his phone but it wasn't working either. Looked like the battery had died completely.

"Fuck." He kicked the lamppost, then wiped his hand all over his face.

Fuck.

He looked around into the murky darkness of the deserted street. Not a soul in sight. Enraged, and totally pissed off, he turned around and headed back to Izzy's.

A moment later, he was knocking on her door again, and, not wanting to frighten her, rapped his knuckles gently. "Izzy?" he tried to raise his voice, without shouting. He knocked again. "Izzy?"

"Xavier?"

"Yeah, it's me."

She opened the door, quickly and stared back. "You changed your mind?" she asked, provocatively.

"My car," he said. "All the tires have been slashed."

She looked horrified. No," she gasped. "Your tires?"

"Yeah. Can I use your phone? My cell phone battery died."

"Sure," she said, letting him in. "We don't have a landline, but you can use my cell phone." She rushed to her bedroom and returned with her phone. "Here."

He turned his back to her, and walked around, closing his eyes, pressing down on his eyebrows, and called the police, then explained what had happened.

"Sorry to disturb you," he said, when he had finished.

"You didn't. I hadn't gone to bed yet." She reached for his hand. "What did the police say?"

"They're sending someone over to take a report."

"I told you not to bring your flashy car around in these parts," she said, her voice gentle. "I hate that this happened to you."

"It's never happened before." But he should have heeded her advice.

"Maybe you could get a battered up runaround?"

Tobias had said the same thing, or hinted at it. His brother didn't have any flashy cars, and the guy could afford anything he wanted.

"Mind if I wait?" he asked. "I don't know how long they're going to be. You can go to sleep if you want. I'll keep a look out for them."

All that time he'd been in her bedroom making out with her, and someone had been trashing his car. He didn't regret it though.

Not one iota.

She yawned. "I'll wait up with you."

"You're looking pretty sleepy. Go to bed, Izzy."

"How can I sleep when you're here?"

He shoved his hands in his pockets again. The car he would deal with.

"I'm sorry this happened to your car," she said, taking a step towards him, and touching his arm, at the elbow.

"The car doesn't matter as much." He shrugged. "I mean, it matters, and it's going to bump up my already jacked up insurance premium, but … it's still a car at the end of the day."

He swallowed. He liked her standing close like that, the defiance gone from those dark eyes. She was soft, with her defenses down, and she was so tempting. He shoved his hands further into his jean pockets. She tilted her chin up at him and he wondered what intent lay behind that curious expression.

"It's just a car," he said.

"Jacob would disagree," she said, putting her arms around him. He instinctively wrapped his arms around her, letting her sink into him. This was nice. This. He inhaled and drank in the essence of her hair, and breathed, standing still their bodies closely entwined together.

It wasn't a lustful hug, or a tight hug, or a hug that meant anything in particular, other than 'I'm sorry and are you alright?' She held onto him tightly, and they stood like that, before he thought he heard the sound of a car driving up.

"That might be them," he said, loosening his arms, and walking towards the windows. He peered out. "It's is." He turned to her. "I'd better go and tell them what happened."

"Want me to wait up for you?"

"There's no need to."

She saw him to the door anyway, and yawned again. "Go to bed, Izzy," he told her.

"Okay, but let me know if you need anything."

Chapter 37

He bought a BMW as a runaround while he waited for his beloved Ferrari to get repaired.

And in the week of all this mayhem, Izzy had had to rush home. She'd told him she would explain all when she got back, and this time, he'd made sure she caught a flight back. There was no point in spending nine hours on a train to get home when she could do it in so much less.

He had intended to see her, to try and figure out where they were headed, to gauge the depth of her feelings. But with her sudden trip home, his plans for the weekend had been thwarted.

So when Savannah asked him if he could babysit Jacob because she and Tobias had another charity fundraising event to attend, he willingly agreed.

And that was how he'd ended up spending his Saturday night looking after the kid instead of spending time with Izzy.

"Today, buddy, we're going to do whatever you want." That was what he'd told Jacob two hours ago, and the little guy had been in his media room, having fun playing on the games consoles ever since.

Luke had called him earlier, asking him to pass by the bar later on, if he was free. "I'm busy, dude. Why don't you come over to my place?" He had expected Luke to decline, but when he quickly agreed, it surprised him. Luke pretty much kept to himself, and now he found himself wondering what was going on with him.

"How come you're so busy all of a sudden?" he asked, when Luke turned up later. "I called you a couple of days ago and they said you were out of state."

"I was. Got my eye on opening up a couple of new bars. One in LA and one in Miami, next year."

"The ones in New York aren't keeping you busy enough?"

"Always got to be busy doing something," said Luke, casting his gaze around the apartment. "I haven't been here for a while."

"No, you haven't. Your friends barely see you."

"My friends come to my bar if they want to see me."

"I did come. I came last week, but you weren't there."

"I'm not always at The Oasis, pal. I have to keep an eye on the other places. In fact, why don't you call me one day when you're free? I've finally got access to the new place I bought. It's around the block from you."

"To live?"

"My next bar."

"Another bar ..." Xavier whistled in amazement at his friend's drive and ambition. Here he was, still debating whether to proceed with Hennessy or not, and Luke was sprinting ahead, buying up premium real estate and turning it into hugely successful bars and clubs.

"What are you doing these days?" Luke asked, "Or rather, who, should I say? You're running out of time with Izzy, unless you've scored and not told me."

Xavier peeked over his shoulder, and lowered his voice. "Shhh."

Luke's eyes widened. "Is she here?"

"No."

"Then why the shhhh?"

Xavier shook his head. "Because I'm babysitting."

Luke looked at him. "Babysitting? You?" He looked around the living area. "Who?"

"Savannah's son, Jacob."

"They left him with you?"

"I'm getting good at this," Xavier told him. "He's in the media room, playing on the Xbox."

"Alone? Unchaperoned? Is that wise, pal? How do you know he's not playing some eighteen plus shoot 'em ups?" Luke shook his head, as if he suddenly knew a thing or two about babysitting. "Anyway, you still haven't answered my question. Are you close to winning the bet? That's all I want to know. Is Izzy the lucky girl or not?"

"Will you shut the fuck up?" He hated Luke talking like that.

"Why are you getting so uptight? I'm not asking for proof or anything—I'm enough of a gentleman to take your word for it."

"Shhhh!" he hissed, placing his finger over his lips. He might as well have announced it on national TV.

"What's going on?" Luke asked, amusement dancing in his eyes, "Either you're on your way to winning, or I am. Just tell me how things are looking, because ten thousand dollars is still a lot of money."

"Dude. Keep it down." Jacob was playing in the media room, but he didn't want to talk about the bet right now.

"What's wrong?" Luke asked. "You look like you're about to shit a brick."

He might as well have, by the way Luke was carrying on. "Screw the bet."

"Screw the bet?" Luke scratched the side of his jaw. "Hmmm. Let me remind you that it was your idea, dude."

He drew in a long breath. This wasn't the appropriate time to be discussing this, and he wasn't the one who had summoned Luke over. Luke was the one who had come to see him.

"We can discuss this another time." He was more interested to know what had caused his friend to come over. "What's going on with you?"

"The usual, the bars, the old man."

"Yeah?" It was the same old same old with Luke.

"Nothing I can't handle."

"I know." But there was something else. He sensed that Luke hadn't come over to discuss the same old same old. Something gnawed at him below the surface, but his friend wasn't one to openly divulge information, even when he was the one who needed to.

"You seeing anyone?" Xavier asked, suddenly, wondering if that might be it.

"Are you kidding me?"

It had been worth asking. "What was it you wanted to tell me?"

"Nothing that can't wait."

"Seriously, dude. Everything okay?"

"Yeah, yeah. Everything's cool" Luke looked at his watch. "I need to shoot. We'll catch up another time."

"You sure?" Because now that he looked at him more closely, Luke didn't look all that great.

"Yeah. I'm sure. Come by the new site, it's on Canal Street. Not far from your place."

"That's handy for me."

"It's not ready yet, but I'm there most days. Place is a demolition site. We're going to strip it right back."

And watch the cash roll in. This dude was ambitious, and driven. "Will do, dude."

Chapter 38

She hated getting those kinds of calls. The ones where her dad fell to pieces and couldn't get out of bed or go to work.

They were lucky that his foreman at the local factory was good. He'd been one of the guys who'd worked for her father back when her father had a business that was thriving. But there was only so much slack the guy could cut him.

So she had gone home, hoping to help her father through another bad period. If it hadn't been for the extra money she had been making working for Xavier, she wouldn't have gone back so soon after her last trip. And, although she hadn't told him the specifics of why she'd rushed back, she'd taken Xavier's advice and got a flight over instead of taking the train.

"You didn't need to come back for him," her mother had said, the moment she had walked through the door.

"I could, so I did."

"Won't your studies suffer?"

They would, but what choice did she have? "I can't stay long," she replied. "Where is he?"

"In his room, where else?"

At least he didn't drink himself to oblivion when his bouts of depression came—they were deep, and dark, and spiraling, and alcohol would have made things worse.

Too bad she had a statistics exam to prep for, but she knew her priorities, and knew she had to step in when her mother—bless her—had run out of patience with the man she'd fallen in love with.

So she sat with her father, and hugged him, and held his hand, and tried to buoy him up. It didn't matter that he hadn't looked especially happy to see her, and hadn't asked how she was doing. He'd been a good dad, the best he could be, and sometimes the roles reversed and your parents needed you to parent them instead. Now was such a time.

She listened again, with a sinking heart, as he talked about being a failure, and how he could not provide, and what had been taken, and how different things might have been. And she did her best to counsel him, and move him out of living in the past, which was where he seemed to drift to, for it didn't serve him to revisit that part, that relentless hamster wheel of negative thoughts of what could have been.

He always refused her suggestion to get counseling because he was too proud a man to want to think about getting help. "Nothing wrong with me, Izzy. He didn't break me."

"I know, dad."

"A man can have his down days, can't he?"

"Sure, dad."

But don't be having those down days where you want to start over. He'd said it before a couple of times, that he wished he could start his life over. That he wished he could reboot. Words like that scared her to death. Words like that made her push college out of her head, and get on the next flight out.

Her coming to see him had done him good. At least, she liked to think it had. But it wasn't a quick fix. She knew that, too.

How could she get a proud man to admit to his depression? To not want to give up? She couldn't. She could only be there for him as best as she could, and it was a lot more than her brother ever was. In the few days she'd been here, she'd only seen Owen late in the evenings, usually after soccer practice. He was only living at home until he graduated high school.

A few days weren't enough. Sometimes she worried more than a girl of her years should have, and there were days when she envied Cara her easy life with two normal parents and a solid, loving family life.

"Aren't you going to fall behind in your studies being here for him?" her mother asked two days later.

"If you were here for him I wouldn't need to do your job." She'd apologized straightaway, because after spending days trying to lift his spirits, her own spirit was sagging.

Four days she stayed with him, four days before she felt she could leave. She'd needed to leave two days ago, but what could she do? Stay and help him, or run back so that she could study for another test?

So she tried to do both, and only gave half of herself to each. She wasn't even sure if it had been worth it.

There would be hell to pay at college. Too much to catch up on, a test to do, and coursework piling up on top. As well, Savannah had called her earlier to ask if she could babysit Jacob but she'd had to explain she was out of state. Savannah had also asked if she could continue doing ad hoc days on weekends, and she promised that she would come and see her about it on her return.

And then there was Xavier. Apart from a few stilted conversations, and a couple of texts, she hadn't shared much of what had gone on at home. It was better this way. It was better keeping the two parts separate—her family, and Xavier.

The Stones were from a different planet to most ordinary people.

~ ~ ~

"When did you get back?" Cara asked her the day after she returned. She'd returned late last night while Cara was sleeping.

"Last night."

"And you're not going in today?"

"I'm shattered."

"I'll go in the afternoon." She couldn't go back into lessons and catch up if she was dead tired.

"Good idea. I'll see you at the cafeteria? We can catch up then."

"I need to go into the library and catch up on all my work, first."

Cara sat down on her bed, causing Izzy to budge up. "Shouldn't you get going?" Otherwise her friend was going to be late for her lessons.

"I've got a few moments."

"And?"

"I bet lover boy must have missed you."

"Don't call him that," said Izzy, snuggling under the duvet.

"What else can I call him?" Cara asked, raising an eyebrow. "How come things changed so fast between you?"

"Can we not talk about this right now?"

"Can we talk about it later tonight?"

Izzy gave her a look that indicated otherwise.

"How's your dad?" She'd told Cara that her father had been ill. It was always better to gloss over the facts. The truth was always so much darker, so much more depressing.

"He's feeling better, thanks."

"We'll talk tonight."

But tonight she needed to cram for the test. Tests, tests, always more tests. No wonder that when she had finally slowed down enough—even though she'd gone through an emotionally draining time with her father—her body seemed to want to do nothing. She lay in bed, feeling sorry for herself, indulging herself for a change.

"We'll talk tonight," said Cara, getting up and leaving.

When she heard the front door close, she texted Xavier:

I'm back.

He texted back almost instantly:

Want to get together this evening?

She had the stats test tomorrow, and while she was contemplating what to reply back, another message from him appeared:

I've got some more work for you, if you're interested

She was interested, and replied:

I can come over on my way back from college

You know where to find me

He texted back. And then she remembered she hadn't even asked him about his car.

How's your car?

Been replaced, will show you later. Gotta go

Later that afternoon, once she had explained the reason for her absence to her college tutor, and managed to get the notes for everything she had missed, she jumped on the subway.

A part of her felt slightly on edge. She wasn't sure how to be around Xavier, not after the last time. Things might have been different if she'd seen him the next day, after that evening, but a lot had happened since then and everything between them seemed new again, at least it did for her.

It would be awkward.

"I can't stay long," was the first thing she said, when she walked in. Because as soon as she walked into his apartment, she was reminded of what Cara had told her, that the kind of place he lived in must have come with a multi-million dollar price tag.

People like Xavier had no clue about the types of pressures people like her were under. Life wasn't fair. Some had it easy, and some didn't and some, like her father, had tried to do better and had been cheated out of building a better life by someone who probably hadn't been too different to the Stones.

"Oh-kay," he said slowly. She could tell by the way he looked at her that he was puzzled by her demeanor. "How's your dad?"

"Better." A part of her wished she hadn't told him. Wished he'd been as ignorant as Cara.

"Better?" He looked at her, as if he could see through her hesitation.

He had his hands in the back pockets of his jeans. All the previous times she'd seen him he'd normally worn a hoodie and sweatpants at home. Today he was in jeans and a t-shirt, and she wondered if he was going out, because he usually didn't look so smart for working at home.

"Because you had me worried there, rushing home like that," he told her. She walked towards his huge windows and stared out.

"You shouldn't have worried. He's fine." She stared out of the windows at the views over a park. It was a stunning view. A multi-million dollar view, from a multi-million dollar apartment. It must be wonderful to wake up and have the city and its sunshine streaming in. It was a stark contrast to their windows, a fraction of the size of these, overlooking a street with broken street lamps, and the sound of police sirens which penetrated the silence at least once a day.

He was leaning against the brickwork, his shoulder resting against the wall, and with one foot over the other. He looked relaxed and casual. As if he didn't have a worry in the world.

"Are we good, Izzy?"

She looked at him, not completely understanding why she felt the way she did. Why coming back from home, from dealing with her father, had suddenly made her feel a touch of hostility towards Xavier.

She had to forcibly remind herself that he wasn't like the others. "I'm sorry. I got back late last night, I'm a little tired, and cranky, that's all."

That seemed to please him, made his mouth turn up into a smile, and then she saw the twitch in his jaw. A tiny little movement that told her that maybe she hadn't totally convinced him.

"You're not regretting what happened the other day, are you? Because I'm not."

Trust him to allude to that straight away. "The other day," she said, raising her hand to move her bangs away from her face. "That was … that was … something unexpected."

And he was putting her on the spot. She couldn't come back from that darkness with her father and step into the light with Xavier. "Your car," she said, turning to face him, and relieved to have something neutral to talk about. "Did the insurance pay out?"

He didn't seem to like it, the way she'd casually moved away from discussing them. "I bought something safe and sensible like you recommended. A runaround."

"You listened to me?"

"Believe it or not, I listen to you more than I listen to most people."

His words made her smile. "What did you get?"

"A BMW."

She almost choked in shock. "You're calling a BMW a runaround?" Their worlds couldn't be further apart.

"It's safe and sensible, you can't argue with that."

"I was thinking maybe you'd get something like a Ford."

"Can you see me in a Ford?" he asked, grinning. "I mean, that is so not me."

No, a Ford wasn't Xavier at all.

She started to melt, then. Started to ease slowly. It had been a huge switch, going home and dealing with everything there, and then to come here and be with Xavier, but he had a way of making her feel better, and that was what she needed after the draining few days she'd had back home.

Chapter 39

Had he missed something? The way they had left things the last time, made it seem like this was a different person in front of him.

He was careful not to touch her, or get close, because he could read the signs straightaway, and he'd seen how she had been careful not to look at him, how she'd looked out of the windows. And yet she was here. She could have turned him down and said no. It had to count for something.

Technically, he could have emailed the extra work to her, but he'd wanted an excuse to see her.

With Izzy, he always had to think of reasons to call her, or text her, he was never as sure as he was with other girls.

She was like a jigsaw puzzle, and he had never been good at them. He wanted instant gratification, and had never been one to take his time figuring things out. That was the difference between him and Tobias. Tobias was all about the long game, strategy, watching and observing, and analyzing. Him? Not so much.

"Are you okay?" he asked, as she gazed out again. He hadn't been expecting her to fall into his arms, but he hadn't expected her to be as distant.

"I am," she insisted, then explained it on getting home late. "So, you said you had more work for me?"

"Plenty to keep you busy. You can do the weekly figures for another one of my companies, if you want the work."

"What's the matter? One of your virtual assistants let you down?"

Her abruptness caught him off guard.

"No. I thought you might like the extra work, on account of you missing time off school and going home." He had plenty of work, and he could easily give her more hours to do, if she needed it.

He'd do whatever it took, which, right now, seemed to be the way to get through to her.

She looked tired, and aggravated, and as pissed off as hell.

He walked up to her and resisted the urge to touch her face. They'd made out a few days ago, for fuck's sake. "What's wrong? You look like the entire world just pissed you off."

"Maybe it did."

He knew it was something. "Was it going home? Seeing your folks?"

"Something like that."

"Then tell me."

"Why? Will you fix it for me?"

He moved his head back in surprise. There was a reason why he didn't talk so much to girls before he fucked them. It was easier that way. They came with less baggage when all they wanted was to come. Or to be seen with a Stone.

With Izzy he felt as if he was caught in a riptide of emotions, swirling and whirling and pulling him under, and now he was caught up in the current of their attraction. But she screwed with his mind, and it was impossible for him to hold onto the edge and stop himself from going under.

He wanted more of this girl, and sometimes he wondered if the headfuck was worth it. He didn't do emotional stuff well. It was all physical with him. And Izzy was driving him insane. He was losing control because she was so unavailable.

And yet the other night everything had changed. He'd had his first glimpse that maybe this girl wanted him. That maybe she didn't truly believe he was an asshole. But at times like now, he wanted to walk away because it would make for an easier life. He didn't care about the bet anymore. That no longer mattered, but he wanted to walk away because it would be the easy thing to do.

No mind games, no stress, no emotional baggage.

And yet, he couldn't.

It wasn't even because he'd kissed her, or wanted to touch her, or wanted to get to know her. It was because he cared about her. She was hurting about something else, this was new, this wasn't about that creep—so help him god he wanted to find the guy and kick him in—this was something to do with going home, and he wanted to know so he could make it better.

"Are you going to fix it for me?" she asked, again, in a half-jokey, half-serious voice

"I'll do what I can." He seized her arm. "If you'll let me." She was still in her thick coat and tried to pull away, but he wasn't going to let her go, as easily as that.

"Your dad's ill, and I get that you're worried. Sharing a worry is better than keeping it all to yourself."

She looked at him. "It's so easy for people like you," she said, pulling her arm away again, but he held onto it firmly. "Can I take my coat off?"

He let go, and watched as she walked over to the couch and took it off, then left it there.

"People like me?" he asked, repeating her words, and walking over.

"You and Sh—" she stopped herself. "That creep, the people who tread all over other people."

She'd almost said his name. Puzzled, he walked over and sat down beside her.

"You told me about your father. Did he have another episode?" Clearly something had happened. Maybe he'd gotten laid off. He reached for her hand. "Izzy? Or is this about that guy? The creep?"

"No," she replied, sounding weary. "I shouldn't have come here. I'm not in the right frame of mind. This isn't fair on you, me taking my bad mood out on you." She got up, as if to go.

He stood with her. "Don't go. Don't run away, Izzy. Tell me." It was taking all his might not to get angry, and if it took all day, he was going to get to the bottom of this. "That night you let me kiss you, and hold you, I didn't want to leave." She flinched when he reminded her, and her cheeks turned pink. "I wanted to stay with you, and do so many things to you."

The way her lips tightened, he knew he was getting through to her. "But I made myself leave, and you know why?"

"Why?"

"Because I want to take things slow, at least that's what I tell myself, but if I was being honest, it's because I'm scared of doing the wrong thing, and not having your approval. That's right," he said, when the expression on her face changed to one of surprise. "Your fucking approval is what I'm looking for. So don't compare me to that sleazy son of a bitch who messed around with you. You think you've got me all figured out, and I can tell you that you don't. You don't know the real me."

"What is the real you?"

"Not the womanizing asshole you seem to think I am."
"No?"

Maybe not so much now. Hell, no. He hadn't fucked a woman for months, and he could have. But that stupid bet got in the way, and now he didn't even care about it.

"I don't know what's happened to you since then, or why you're so mad, or so down, or why you hate me so much, but unless you tell me what it is, I can't help you, and for the few times in my life, I actually care about you enough to want to make things better for you."

"My dad," she said, speaking up. "Has felt like a failure for so many years now, mostly from when I was in my teens, at least, that's how I remember it. And it wasn't even his fault. People like you get away with so much."

He frowned, but knew when to keep quiet.

"Maybe not people like you." She was quiet then, as if choosing her words. "But it seems to me that the little people don't always win." She looked at him. "You don't understand, do you?"

"Then make me understand."

"You know I told you about my dad feeling like he'd failed us all?"

"When his business when downhill?"

"It wasn't his fault it failed."

"What happened?"

"He had a construction company, and it was doing well. I know that because when we were little, we lived in a big house when we were growing up, and we'd go on nice vacations. And then it all changed suddenly. Like almost overnight. And it was all because of one man."

"A competitor?"

She shook her head. "He got a big contract from this so called multi-millionaire businessman who wanted to build a

317

huge block of condos. It was going to be a new estate, and then hopefully lead to other projects, at least, that's what my mom told us, because my dad refuses to talk about that time. It was my dad's biggest and most ambitious project to date. His friends warned him not to do it, they said that the guy was an asshole, not someone to be trusted, but my dad said everyone deserved a chance, and he liked to make his own mind up about people. So he met with the guy lots of times, decided to take on this project." She stared down at her skirt, her forehead creasing. "To cut a long story short, the guy didn't pay up. My dad had paid for all the materials, because he never dreamed this guy would ever pull something like that. He trusted him. He trusted him because he looked trustworthy. He looked legitimate."

"He didn't pay a dime?"

"He came with his henchmen and paid only the bare minimum, and after my father couldn't afford to pay the mortgage on his own home, they took our house away."

"And your dad never sued him?"

She shook her head, and told him how things had deteriorated fast. And in the end, the guy had sent a bunch of heavies to a meeting with her father and his management team, and refused to pay, citing that they'd had enough publicity.

"And that was it? He never thought to sue them?"

"No. The guy was untouchable. He was rich, like really rich, and my mom was scared, she worried that he might do something if my dad went up against him. And-uh," she scratched her wrist, her forehead lining as if it was too painful to think about. "He gets down about it. It's worse in the winter, though." She looked up, her expression touching a nerve in him, and it made sense, her wariness, her hatred and contempt for people like him.

He moved closer and entwined his fingers around hers and when she didn't pull her hand away, he said, "We're not all the same people, Izzy. I'm sorry for what happened to your dad. I really am."

It would kill him slowly, inside, if something like that happened to him. He could see how failing big time, in a company you had put your heart and soul into, only to have it be ruined by an unscrupulous investor, could be so dangerous. It was obvious to see how something like that had taken a toll on her dad, and his family, even now, years later.

No wonder she seemed down, and subdued.

He lifted her hand and dropped a soft kiss on the back of it. "I can see why you're so upset."

"I'm not upset. I'm used to it. I just get sad when I think of him, but …," She drew in a breath. "It's nice to be able to offload on you."

He liked that she thought so. "Offload on me anytime."

"I haven't even told any of my friends, not even Cara."

"Cara doesn't know?" She trusted him more than she trusted her friend?

"No."

He rubbed her hand gently. "You don't need Cara, you've got me."

She smiled.

"Want something to eat?" he asked. He assumed she was probably hungry.

"No, thanks. I should go."

No, dammit. She'd only just arrived.

"Maybe I shouldn't have asked you to come over. I'm sorry. I should have emailed you the extra work. Truth is, I wanted to see you. The work was just an excuse."

She looked up at him. "An excuse?"

"I had to think of some way of getting to see you again. I've missed you."

"You did?"

He nodded. He wanted to kiss her. Had never had to think about it before. Usually, he knew within seconds what he wanted, and he claimed it, and with the types of girls he dated, it had been something he'd had to think twice about.

Izzy was barbed wire and roses.

He had to think twice about anything with her. It wasn't about the sex anymore, it wasn't about getting physical because he needed the release, it was about her. He didn't want to rush things, or move too fast, and most of the time, with Izzy, he wasn't even sure where he stood.

The sands were always shifting in these initial getting-to-know-you stages, and he was in no rush.

"I'm glad I came over," she said.

At least he'd managed to get a smile out of her.

Chapter 40

It was unfair, taking it out on him, and he was being nice. He was actually listening to her and trying to help. He wasn't Shoemoney, or that dirty businessman.

"Come on," he said, when she had told him she wasn't hungry. "It's easier if I show you the type of extra work you can do, if you want."

She followed him to his office area where he showed her the spreadsheets on his computer. "Is this something you could take on?"

"What about your VA who does this?"

"She's let me down a few times. You could do a better job of it, and you're nearby, and its similar to what you've done for me before. It's just another one of my sideline businesses."

"How many do you have?"

"Lots. Lots of little things, some work, some don't."

"Risky."

"Entrepreneurial."

Nothing like Tobias's hedge fund.

"I've realized that having someone local, as opposed to in another country, is more helpful to me. Do you want the extra work?"

She could do it, on top of the work she already did for him, on top of her other online work, and with babysitting Jacob on the weekends, depending on the hours Savannah wanted from her. She would have to make it all fit in. She exhaled slowly, remembering the stats test she had to study for. But even though she needed to go home and get to work on it, she wasn't in the mood to leave.

After being there for her father for the past few days, this was the first time someone had been there for her. It was a feeling she liked, and one she hadn't experienced in a while. "Starting when?"

"End of this week."

Her exam would be over by then. "Sure."

He grinned. "Your enthusiasm is killing me."

"Thanks," she said, perking up, breaking out into a smile, and grateful that he was here.

"That's better," he said, nodding his head in approval. "I like it better when you smile." He folded his arms, and all she wanted was for him to open them and hold her.

"I better scoot," she said, looking at her watch. Studying for stats was the last thing she wanted to do, but he seemed busy, and she needed to get back into the swing of things.

"Don't go," he said, quickly.

"Is there something you'd like me to do?" Like those charts he'd wanted her to create.

"I can think of a few things." It was the way he said it, the way his eyes smoldered with intensity, holding a promise, a thought, an intention. She swallowed as his words reminded her of that other time.

"Not those sorts of things," he drawled, slowly, dropping his hands slowly to his side, and he hooked his thumbs into the front pocket of his jeans.

"What sort of things?" she asked, taking a step closer and looking up at him. They weren't on the same page. He was being too coy, and she was not. Standing so close to him, her body felt as if it was on fire. "I didn't mean what I said earlier, about you being like the other guys. I know you're not. I know that now. I was just in a pissy mood."

"Pissy mood?" he asked, moving closer still so that they almost touched. She held her hands up to his chest as his arms snaked around her waist.

"Pretty pissy."

"Spend the day with me, and we'll do fun stuff." His head jerked back a little. "I don't mean like last time."

She worried that he was being too careful, and at a time when she wanted him to be anything but too careful. "I like doing fun stuff," she said, "Like we did last time." She caught the flicker of surprise on his face before they moved at the same time, instinctively, their lips and tongues meshed together.

Somehow they stumbled away from his desk, hands touching, lips breaking apart as they moved into the living room and made it over to the couch. She fell back onto the soft, downy cushions and he landed not on top, but to her side, his hand cupping around her neck.

"Is this what you had in mind?" he asked, his voice was thick, and raspy, and loaded with intent.

She made an agreeing noise in her throat, as she succumbed to the now familiar taste and feel of him against her. His fingers rested against the nape of her neck, while his thumb stroked her cheek. Her heartbeat raced, and her body loosened, as if it was remembering. They kissed like the last time, intense, and for a long time, and deep, as if they were in the throes of lovemaking. And she wished they were for it

323

had opened up again, that void, an emptiness inside her, an ache that needed him.

"You make it all better," she told him, when he stopped and stared at her. "Everything," she murmured, feeling his hard chest pressing into her breasts. This had been the comfort she had been searching for all along. Being away from him had made her want to come running back for more.

She reached for him, sliding her hand down between their bodies, passing over the bulge in his jeans. "Izzy," he groaned, low and hoarse.

She sighed into his mouth, and unzipped his jeans, touching the soft fabric of his boxer briefs, and feeling his hardness. His groan was a mixture of agony and joy when she moved her hand up and down, slowly, teasing, playing. With a drawn out moan, he moved her hand away, but she slipped it under his t-shirt and onto his bare skin, moaning in surprise at the feel of his abs.

Hard, hard, hard.

"Fuck, Izzy," he ground out, and pushed himself off the couch.

"What are you doing?" she asked, lifting her head.

"Making you feel better," he replied, his fingers skating around the waistband of her pantyhose. He was kneeling on the floor, facing her, as she lay, hot and sweaty on the couch, and then, without saying a word, his hand slipped under her skirt, his eyes fixed on hers, as if checking to see if she wanted this.

She did.

She shifted her body down, letting him know that she didn't object, raking her fingers through his hair as he peeled off her panty hose. Her heartbeat rocketed dangerously.

He didn't take her panties off, but moved the fabric to one side, and the sudden kiss of cold air cooled her hot, exposed skin for the briefest of seconds before his thumb moved in slow and deliberate circles. She bit her lip as ripples of pleasure circled outwards all over her body. With a hand splayed across her chest, and the other still in his hair, she arched her back as he slowly slid his finger inside her. Slow and teasing, and making her gasp.

It was gentle at first, his finger sliding, and twisting, and his thumb moving around on her most sensitive spot; two sensations, two different pressures, two sources of ecstasy. She couldn't keep it in, her low, wanton gasp as she tried not to writhe, tried not to mewl.

Her body was heat, and his touch like magic. And when he slipped in another finger and dove deeper, reaching her innermost crevices, making her legs fall apart at the knees, she opened up, completely at his mercy.

Xavier Stone was taking his sweet time pleasuring her, and all she wanted was more, more, more. Her muscles relaxed as she took all she could from him, moaning and mewling to his probing. It had never been this fast before, her getting so wet, and so hot, and so turned on, and he'd done it instantly, and when he hooked his fingers inside her, she groaned like never before.

"You feel so good, Izzy," he whispered, kissing her just above the waistband of her panties, making her shift uncomfortably at the idea that his face was so close to her most intimate part.

"You feel so good," she breathed, biting back a moan. He made her feel loose, like liquid, hazy and heady. With his fingers buried deep inside her, and moving and twisting as he pleased, he left a trail of kisses along her stomach, until he found her lips again. And then he kissed her again, teasing her lips slowly before their tongues met and swirled together in a slow dance.

Wetness above and below.

With his fingers hooked so deep inside her, and his thumb circling and teasing her mercilessly, he lifted his head up, and stared down at her. Her body jerked unashamedly, her hips bucking, short, and fast, and the whole time he watched; saw her writhe and squirm, tremble and clench as the pressure built up in her belly.

"Fuck, Izzy," he groaned, "You're so wet, I want to …" But she closed her eyes, rolled her head back and was lost in the throes of her wet explosion.

She couldn't stifle her moans, not when she came, not when she fell apart at his bidding. She had given up her sensibilities, letting him do this and watch, while he was still clothed, and as yet untouched by her.

When it was over, when he moved his hand away, she lay there, her insides still dissolving into jelly. She was breathless and drowning in pleasure when he left a short, wet kiss on her lips.

He had given her exactly what she had needed. Now she had to summon the energy to give back. She adjusted her clothing, and sat up, planting her feet on the floor, reaching forward and clamping her mouth over his, drinking deep into his kiss, needing to connect, and taste and savor him. With her other hand she reached for his boxer briefs, his thick hardness bigger than before.

His hand stilled over hers as she tried to move the zipper down

"You don't have to," he rasped.

"I want to," she murmured, her need great, to see, and touch, and to do to him what he had done to her. "Stats can wait."

"What can wait?" he asked in a hoarse whisper.

"My stats test." She tried to move her hand, but his hand held firm over hers. "You have a test tomorrow?" he asked, his face red, his breath hot. She squeezed him, gently, saw his lips part, knew he liked it, the way her hands caressed him. "Yes, but," she leaned down again, heard his disappointed groan. "You have to go and prepare for your—"

"It can wait," she insisted, the heat inside her igniting again, as she stroked him harder. He let out a short groan, and pulled her hand away. "This can wait."

"But you're so har—"

"No, Izzy." He moved her hand away, robbing her of the thrill.

"Xavier!" She needed him.

He sat up, his bulge still tenting in his boxer briefs.

"Let me—" she tried to reach out for him again, but he was quick to stand as he turned his back on her.

"You're really doing this?" she asked, her voice sounding angrier than she intended as she got to her feet. He turned around to face her. "I want to see you again, and I want to take you somewhere nice, and make it be a proper date."

"A proper date?"

"Yes."

"You don't have to take me anywhere nice."

"You want me to take you somewhere bad?"

"No, I meant, you don't have to impress me."

"I want to take you out somewhere, and have a nice time."

"I've been having a nice time with you, lately."

"Yeah?"

"Yeah."

"So we're making progress?"

"What do you think?" she grabbed his forearms and leaned up to kiss him. "Couldn't you tell?"

"You liked that, didn't you?" he asked, giving her another kiss, making her melt into him again.

"Hmmmm." She made a noise while their lips were still joined.

He pulled away, and his hand trailed down her back, cupped her butt and squeezed. "I'll drop you back."

She made a face.

Chapter 41

"Erminegard?" he asked, trying not to get too wound up. What kind of a fucked up name was that?

His mother was trying to set him up with some New York socialite princess, and it pissed him off.

"Hollister," his mother replied. "Erminegard Hollister. She's from good stock."

"Good stock?" he echoed, in disgust. "She sounds like a horse."

Savannah sniggered, and tried to cover her mouth with her hand.

"What a thing to say," his mother grumbled. "I'm only trying to help you, darling. Look at your brother, all settled and with a baby on the way."

"You'd help more if you butted out, Mother."

He was taking Izzy out later this evening, once this soiree was done with. Tobias and Savannah had invited everyone over. It wasn't dinner, thank fuck. "Just cocktails," his mother had told him.

"Tobias has an announcement to make," his father said.

Xavier assumed it was probably the news that Jacob had accidentally let slip, that he and Izzy already knew.

Tobias cleared his throat, as he and Savannah stood with their arms around one another, and Jacob stood in front, in the middle. His brother had been politely civil towards him, as was he to Tobias. Neither of them have spoken or met up since that last time when Xavier had gone to Tobias's office.

Xavier was glad it was only cocktails. A dinner to get through would have been awkward. He knew it was only a matter of time before things smoothed over between him and Tobias, but it was getting to that time that made things uncomfortable.

"You've kept us in suspense long enough, son. What is it?" Their father asked the question that was on everyone's lips. Tobias didn't often invite everyone over unless he had an announcement to make, or there was a celebration.

"The baby? Everything's fine, isn't it?" their mother asked, for once showing some concern.

Tobias looked at Savannah. "The babies are fine, yes," he replied, unable to wipe that huge grin off.

"The babies?" It took a while for their father to process the news, and their mother looked suspicious.

But Jacob was grinning from cheek to cheek.

"We're having twins," Savannah confirmed, with a proud and wide smile on her face. Her hand smoothed over her now huge baby bump.

"And what are we having, Jacob?" Tobias asked.

"We're having boys!"

A house full of boys. Xavier couldn't help but smile. It was truly the best news.

It was his parents who moved towards the happy trio, first, congratulating them, then Xavier stepped in. He hugged Savannah. "It's fantastic news, Savannah," he told her, kissing her on the cheek, before turning, with apprehension, to his brother, "Congrats, bro." He held out his hand, and waited for Tobias to shake it. Which he did, after a split-second delay.

"You're going to be an older brother to twins, dude," said Xavier, high-fiving an excited Jacob. "It's a big responsibility."

Jacob smiled, looking beyond excited. "I know!"

"We don't want the news to get out," Tobias warned. "Savannah's parents know, and that's it. Not even Kay knows."

"But it's going to be hard to hide soon," his mother countered, "Especially when she balloons up like an elephant."

"She?" Tobias asked, curtly.

"When Savannah balloons up. You're already looking bigger than usual, dear," his mother said. Xavier quaked in his shoes for his mother's sake. She could be tactless at the most inappropriate of times.

"I think she looks lovely." Their father, the diplomat as usual, stepped in.

"Shall I give Erminegard your number, darling?" his mother asked, turning to him.

"Only if you want me to talk dirty to her."

"Xavier!"

"You shouldn't make ridiculous suggestions, Mother, and I won't give you stupid answers. Shouldn't you propose a toast, dad?" he suggested, wanting to get this evening over and done with.

His father raised his glass, and proposed that everyone do the same. "Congratulations, Tobias, Savannah, and you Jacob. This is quite some news."

"And it's for your ears only, dad, remember," Tobias reminded him.

~ ~ ~

Cara had fallen back on the bed when Izzy had told her that Xavier was taking her out on their first official date.

"I knew you liked him!" she'd countered, indignantly.

"I didn't at first. But he grew on me."

"Why is it that you have all the luck?"

Izzy turned around and made a face, "If you think I've had all the luck," she said, "you haven't been listening to me."

"Have fun," Cara had called out, as she left the house.

She had thought it was sweet when he had called and told her they were going out for dinner, 'to get to know one another better.'

"But we already know one another," she'd replied.

"I want to do it properly."

That had made her laugh. "How do you normally do it?"

"Backwards."

She'd tried to second guess him, "You mean, bed, dinner, and drinks?"

"Bed, usually, and sometimes after a few drinks."

Xavier had picked her up and told her they were going to a hip new vegetarian restaurant in the city. He'd risked picking her up in his Ferrari, telling her that it didn't seem right going out on a date in his BMW.

"But you don't like vegetarian food," Izzy said.

"I'm open to trying new things."

"All because of me?" She cocked her head, pretending to be all shy, and overdoing the fluttering of her eyelashes. She didn't usually do shy, because it wasn't her, and the way Xavier was looking at her, he knew she was being facetious.

"Maybe, because of you. Maybe because veggie food doesn't taste as bad as I thought it would."

And so they had gone to a newly opened restaurant where the line had spilled out onto the street. Xavier marched up to the front and they were allowed straight in, and shown a table over in the corner, in an area that was raised slightly above the floor level. Maroon silk tablecloths dressed round tables, and black candle holders showed off mustard yellow candles. They ordered food, shared starters, and talked, and stared at one another, and he told her about the get together at Tobias's earlier.

"It was that thing that Jacob accidentally let slip," he told her, peering around discreetly, "And it can't get out." She nodded, understanding, and touched that he hadn't told her in as many words, and had honored his brother's request for the news to remain secret.

After dinner they walked around Central Park, talking and enjoying one another's company, and then he drove her home. Her heart sank when he suggested he take her back to her place, because she knew that Cara would be at home, all eyes and ears and waiting to find out.

He dropped her off, then surprised her by turning down her offer to come inside, and so they sat in the car, and talked some more.

"You're not the womanizer I imagined you to be," she said.

"You shouldn't always believe what you read in the press. That's what my brother always says, and I agree."

"It was my mistake."

"At least you've owned up to it."

"I haven't owned up to it," she cried, slapping his arm lightly. "You were quite obnoxious when we first met. You were so full of yourself." She reminded him of a few instances.

"That's because I wasn't used to being around someone who didn't think I was god's gift to women."

She roared. "You see what I mean? You were so obnoxious."

"You threw me for a loop," he protested. "I wasn't used to someone like you."

"I'm not like the girls you're used to."

"No, you're not."

After a while, when he declined her second offer to come back to her apartment, they made out for a while, light kisses at first, until they deepened into long, wet ones. They held hands, touching, and exploring one another lightly, and the thrill of being outside, in a car, not having privacy but hidden under the darkness of the night, lent a touch of risk to their intimacy.

But it wasn't comfortable, sitting with her body twisted inside the car. Sitting close and doing her best to avoid the handbrake. Making out like this wasn't the most romantic way to end the evening, but when he kissed her, making her body tingle and spark, and crave for more, she soon forgot the discomfort and lost herself in the animal heat of the moment.

"Do you want to come in?" She wished they had gone to his place instead, and part of her wondered why he hadn't. Cara would be in, and she would get talking to Xavier, and they wouldn't have the privacy they'd have had at his place.

"This is fine, for now," he said, his hand on her waist, his fingers squeezing her flesh gently. They were face-to-face, breathing in each other, lips nuzzling, and moving over one another. "I don't want you to think I'm after one thing," he said, his face somber.

"I know you're not after one thing."

"How do you know?"

She shrugged. "I just do."

He kissed her again, making her feel those same things again, turning her to liquid heat, as she arched her back anticipating good times. The very thing she had hated Xavier for, the way other girls turned into complete idiots, was the way she was behaving now. He'd touched her intimately, made her come, made her think of that moment over and over again, making her more aroused each time, until she could think of nothing but wanting him more.

"Please come on in for a while," she begged, kissing him across his jaw, inhaling his cologne, getting used to it.

"I can't."

"Can't?"

"There's no rush, is there?"

"No." She'd been wrong. So very wrong about him.

"Maybe when you have a weekend free from exams and coursework, we could go away for a couple of days."

"Like where?" Going away sounded like heaven. The only going away she ever did was to go back home, and that wasn't the most relaxing of places.

"The Hamptons. We've got a place there. I love it. It's private, but relaxing. I can't think of any place nicer where we can be alone."

Sweet.

So sweet.

Chapter 42

They went out a couple of times the following week. Proper dates. Except that unlike the dates he was accustomed to, he couldn't do anything. Or rather, he wouldn't allow her to do anything for him, but if he didn't come clean and tell her, he was going to make himself ill.

Isabel Laronde was one of the sexiest girls he had ever met, and the more he got to know her, the more he started to fall for her. Each time, whether they came back to hers, or to his, they would make out, and oh, boy was it tough on his balls, to resist her.

It had been weighing on his mind, the things he needed to say to her, and this evening, as she lay on her side in his arms, her legs entwined in his, her face resting along his chest, he was waiting for a suitable moment. They'd made out, nothing more, both fully clothed, just lying, and talking.

"You know that time I asked you about the reports?

"For Hennessy?"

"And the others, after? The bar charts I wasn't sure about?"

"The 3D ones?" she asked, her fingers moving over the ridges of his stomach. He had to keep an eye on that roving hand of hers. It wasn't fair, he knew that. He'd seen her, had touched and explored her, and yet he hadn't allowed her the same. Hadn't even let her see him naked, knowing that the day he did, he'd be unable to walk away.

"Yes, those." He cleared his throat. "I have a confession to make."

"You're a walking confessional box, Stone," she still called him that, sometimes, a reminder of where they had come from.

"I kind of knew how to do those charts."

Her fingers settled just above his navel. "You did?"

Tell her now. Tell her.

"Yeah."

"Why did you say you didn't know?" She propped herself up on her elbow, her dark eyes staring intently into his, her voice softly questioning.

"Because, at that time," he replied, clearing his throat again. "I didn't know how to get close to you, and you hated me back then." The memories of their earlier days rewound and played in front of him. He averted her gaze and focused on her hair.

"I wasn't charmed by you," she murmured, tracing her finger along the outline of his lips.

"You weren't easy to charm."

"I was allergic to it," she giggled.

"You had reason to be." He reached out and grabbed a handful of her soft hair, rubbed his thumb around the silky tresses. "So I figured that if I asked you how to do them ... it would give you the opportunity to show me. And it would give me the chance to get close to you."

"Crafty." She reprimanded him with a gentle pinch to his lower lip.

"Some girls can be won over by champagne and diamonds, but you ..." he rolled his eyes, earning a giggle from her. "You were hard work, Laronde."

337

"Any more lies I should know about?"

He heart pounded as he weighed up his answer. "It wasn't a lie, it was an excuse to see you."

"I can see why you needed an excuse, because I didn't want to have anything to do with you in the early days."

"My point exactly. I had to resort to underhanded tactics."

"I'd seen you with Savannah's cousin, as well. Meeting you in person reinforced everything I'd heard about you before."

"Yeah. You had good reason to be wary."

"I know I did."

"I considered myself a stud," he said, cringing at the reminder.

"And Savannah's cousin fell for it, but I was so determined not to. By the way, what happened with her that night?" she asked, "You can tell me. I promise not to judge."

"What happened in Kawaya, stays in Kawaya."

"Did you sleep with her?"

That's what she thought?

"Would you hate me if I did?" He was curious to see how deep her impressions of him went.

"Why would you care what I thought?" she replied, the playfulness slipping from her voice.

"I care what you think now, and I care what you would have thought then." He recalled that night, when he'd given in, and was bored, and Kay was there. And how shocked he'd been when Tobias and Izzy walked in on them.

"What happened in Kawaya, stays in Kawaya," she reminded him, not giving him an answer.

"I wasn't sure if you saw," he said, sliding his fingers out of her hair, and cupping her face.

"I saw."

"We didn't do anything. Tobias turned up and I didn't want to piss him off."

"Would you have done something if we hadn't interrupted you?"

Now she had him. "Who knows?" It was as true an answer as he could give her.

She raised an eyebrow. "You would have gone all the way with her that night even though you barely knew her? And with her being Savannah's cousin, and it being the night before your brother's wedding?"

That made him sound like a pig. He swallowed. "I'm not sure. Probably."

"Probably?"

"I was playing it by ear, and Kay seemed to want to go along."

"She did?"

"She didn't hide the fact that she liked me."

"I wasn't hiding it, either," she said, pinching his nose gently. "I really didn't like you."

"It took her three seconds to figure out what it's taken you four months to."

"And what was that?" she asked.

"That she was attracted to me."

She grinned and shook her head. "Obviously, I'm the more discerning one."

"Didn't you like me even a little bit?" he asked.

"Not even a tiny, little bit."

"You must have thought I was a real asshole, when you saw me and her kissing."

"I thought it was typical of you. Tell me what happened next."

"By the time Tobias had finished talking to me, Kay was nowhere to be found. And for the rest of the time there, she ignored me. She didn't speak to me at all. She barely even looked at me, and it was the same when I saw her a few weeks ago."

"You saw her? Where?"

"At The Oasis, she was leaving, and I was going in." He stared at her, searching her face for signs of distrust, unease.

"And?"

"And she wasn't very friendly."

"Did you think she would be after the way you treated her?"

"What did I do?" he asked, shocked.

"What you did, making out with her, and then dropping her like a hot stone, and then not speaking to her, was despicable."

He considered it. "I suppose it was."

"No, it was."

And to think he'd been under the impression that she'd liked him.

"Just because a girl pursues a guy, doesn't mean she's easy. It also doesn't mean she's going to be okay when you drop her like dirt."

"That's why I want to take my time getting to know you." He cupped the back of her neck and tried to move her face towards his, his lips eager for another one of her kisses. But she kept her head back.

"I thought you were cheating, when I first saw you. Cara had told me you were already going out with that actress."

"I don't cheat. I never have."

"But that night?"

"We had split up. The actress had dumped me. That's why she wasn't at the wedding."

"She dumped you?"

He nodded. "Over the phone. We argued about a casting she was going to. The producer wanted to interview her in the hot tub, in her bikini."

Izzy screwed her face up, looking disgusted. "Is he one of those pervs embroiled in the sex scandals?"

"I don't know, but one of the films she was due to start shooting in got delayed, because that producer was a perv."

"Sick."

"Yes, sick. She didn't see it as that, though. She seemed to think it was something that was normal, and accepted it. She believed she had to go along with it, in order to get the parts."

"Poor deluded girl."

"She came to see me."

"When?"

"Last month, she turned up on my doorstep in tears."

Izzy fell silent.

"You and I weren't together then," he said quickly.

"And? She turned up and then what?"

He tried to remember, tried to think back. "She wanted comfort."

Izzy's eyes bore into him, and he thanked his lucky stars he hadn't given in. Hadn't let Gisele tempt him into doing something. Another lie would have been too much to keep hidden. "But I told her no."

"You told her no?"

"Don't you believe me?" Because he needed her to.

"I believe you," she replied, slowly. "You've been living the life of a monk, or trying to show me that you have." Her voice turned playful, provocative. "God knows I've wanted to see your goods, Stone."

He turned his head away, grinning at the ceiling. "You won't be able to handle it, Laronde."

"No?" she asked, a challenge implicit in that one word answer.

"No." Jeez. Even having a normal conversation with her was sometimes difficult; the innuendo gave him a hard-on. The anticipation, the slow-burn of them getting to know one another was so much sexier than a quickie with a girl he barely knew.

"Why don't you let me see?" she asked, moving her hand down, trying to slide it into his lounge pants.

He placed his hand over hers, halting her, as he'd had to so many times before, wondering why he couldn't come clean and say what he needed to. Heck, he'd just tried to initiate the conversation with the bar charts and his little white lie, and here they were moments later with her hand trying to snake into his pants.

On any given day and moment, if the slate was clean, and his conscience cleaner, they'd be having full-on dirty, delicious, mind-numbing sex.

But he could not go there yet.

"Why are you being so coy?" She settled her hand on his chest again. A safer zone. "It's not like this is your first time." Her voice was hard-to-resist, and downright sexy, and he felt a twitch in his pants.

"Just," he answered, wondering if she had any idea what she was doing to him. This, being cautionary, and slowing things down was so against his nature, and yet, the pain was sweet. The anticipation of their first time together made it all seem worthwhile. "I want to get to know you properly."

She leaned over and kissed him then. Her soft lips, sweet and tender, brushing against his. "Awww, that is so sweet."

Being in close proximity to her clouded his thoughts. Lying like this on the bed was not the way to have that conversation. It had to be sitting down. Talking. In a position that wasn't conducive to touching, or kissing, or fondling.

Somewhere like in a church would do it.

"Well, since you're not going to let me strip you naked and ride you," she said, very, very slowly, so that each word dropped into his brain and lingered there, "I should get home. I have to finish off something for the online course guy. He's dropped it on me last minute, like he usually does." She slipped off the bed and smoothed down her clothes.

Focus on the online course guy, he told himself. Not on her riding you naked.

He swallowed, slowly rising to standing, both his body and his manhood.

"Do you need to do his work? You've got so many other jobs going on now."

"Only for a few months," she said. "I've told him, only until Easter. Cara wants to go away to Cancun next month, a bunch of us friends are thinking about it, and I've managed to save up a good chunk."

His ears pricked up. "You're going to Cancun? Is that for spring break?" He'd heard all sorts of stories about students on spring break.

"Not for spring break. Earlier. Cara wants to go with a couple of our friends. I'm not so keen, but I'd like to get away. I might go home and see my family."

"What about my offer to go to The Hamptons? It still stands, and you can ride me naked there, Laronde."

Her eyes sparkled. "Now there's an offer I can't resist."

Because it was her, because he could never be too careful, he wasn't sure if she was joking or being serious.

"I don't want to rush anything with you," he said, keeping his distance, before she came up to him and tempted him with her touch. "I think it's nicer to get to know one another slowly." For a change.

"I'll think about it," she promised, walking up to him.

"You've got to go home for online course guy, remember," he told her, as her hands skirted around his waist, and she pressed herself against him, soft, and sweet-smelling, and hard-to-resist. And she was giving him seriously blue balls each time he saw her.

"Hold that thought, Stone," she said, leaning up to kiss him, and taking all of his resolve with her.

Chapter 43

"And to think this was the girl who swore that Xavier Stone was the biggest of all the assholes she'd ever met."

Izzy twisted off the top to the liquid eyeliner pen. "People change," she said, drawing a thin line close to her upper eyelashes.

"I'm not sure if he changed or you did."

Izzy remained silent. She couldn't answer that question herself. She'd often wondered if she'd been the one who had had preconceived ideas about Xavier, or whether they had both changed slowly, over time.

"Where's he taking you tonight?"

"To NYB, the burger bar."

"That noisy burger place your kid Jacob likes?" Cara made a face. "That's not very romantic."

"We don't want cheesy romance."

"You guys really know how to do romance, don't you? A kids' burger place. Next you'll be telling me Jacob's coming along."

"No." She grinned at Cara's reflection in the mirror. They hadn't told anyone that they were an item. There had been no need to. "We're thinking of going away," she announced, "around the same time you go to Cancun."

"You're dropping me for him?"

"Do you blame me?"

"No way!" Cara cried in glee. "Is he whisking you away to his private island, in his private jet?"

"We're talking about going to The Hamptons. His family has a place there, and no, he doesn't have a private jet."

"Oh, sweeeet!"

She found herself looking forward to it. A few days in the Hamptons, just him and her.

"You'll come back barely able to walk," said Cara, grinning. "Don't forget your Guide to the Kama Sutra."

"I won't," she replied, giving her friend a naughty wink. Cara peered at her closely. "He's had an effect. Definitely an effect on you."

Izzy rubbed blush into her cheeks "No, he hasn't." But he had. Xavier was the sexiest man she had ever been out with. Not only was he sexy in the way he looked and carried himself, but he was sexy in the way he made her feel, and the way he was around her. He wasn't the man-whore his reputation had made him out to be, but there was no denying the way her body reacted to him. She stayed silent, not wanting to share any of her thoughts with Cara.

"You start going out with Xavier Stone," said Cara, standing with her arms folded in an I-told-you-so pose, "and you end up sounding like a hussy gagging for sex."

"That's what you think," said Izzy, doing her best to protest. She put on her barely there nude lipstick and grabbed her bag, before Cara started asking more personal questions. "Xavier's outside," she said, answering her cell phone on the first ring. "See you later."

"I've never seen you move so fast, either!" her friend shouted after her.

Izzy rushed out to find Xavier waiting in the car.

He leaned forward for a kiss as she got in. "I've just put my lipstick on," she told him, staring at his lips and holding back. "Yes. I made an effort for you," she said, in a tone what was intended to sound dismissive.

"You always look good, even without makeup."

"You charmer."

"I'm being honest."

"I'll kiss you properly, later," she promised. At least the BMW was bigger than the Ferrari, and there was more room to move around. Their kissing was more intense, more passionate, more deep. But it wasn't enough.

Soon after they arrived at NYB, the place became busy. It seemed as if it was someone's birthday party, and the noise soon soared to a crazy level. Xavier looked as if he was on edge.

"It's too noisy, isn't it?"

"Kids," he replied. "They look around Jacob's age. It's fine. So tell me, how was your day?"

"Okay. We have group projects to work on, and I hate those. I'd rather work on something myself, at least that way I know how hard I have to work to get it done."

He told her he agreed, and then the conversation drifted to how he liked being his own boss, and how he was always on the lookout for business ideas, and how to implement them. How he liked having virtual assistants helping him, as opposed to having an office full of employees, and how he preferred having lots of small ventures, as opposed to one big business.

Although she didn't say it, or probe further, she sensed he was explaining to her the different ways in which he and Tobias operated.

They talked some more, finding out about one another, and the evening was over too soon. Before she knew it, they were driving back. But, instead of taking her back to his place, as she had been looking forward to, Xavier announced that he had a day of meetings planned for tomorrow, and that he needed to get an early night.

They were parked outside her apartment by eleven o'clock.

So much for wearing the new crotchless panties she'd been hoping to surprise him with.

"Ever feel like a fake?" he asked suddenly, turning to face her. This time he had parked under a street light, and they could better make out one another's faces.

"No, never. Why? Do you?"

"Sometimes."

"Why is that?" she asked, taking his hand and wondering if this was related to the conversation back at the restaurant.

"Just sometimes," he shrugged. "I make mistakes."

"We all make mistakes."

"I can't see you making many mistakes. You're far too level-headed and sensible. You think with your head mostly, instead of letting some crazy idea guide you."

"I do, most of the time. A lot of the time, yes." The back of his hand rested on her thigh, and she stroked his open palm, wondering what it was that preyed on his mind. "But that doesn't mean I don't make mistakes."

"What mistake have you made lately?"

She tried to think. "Besides having preconceived notions about you?"

At least her answer put a smile on his face. "Sometimes I think coming here to study was a mistake. Because it costs too much, and I'll be in student debt for years."

"But it's one of the best places to study."

"And who's to say I'm going to get that dream job I've envisioned? I did this thinking I could help my dad, thinking that I would make him proud, and that it might help him get over his feeling of failure."

"You have to do it for you."

"Of course, but a part of it was that me being secure and in the corporate world might help ease the pressure off him."

"You'll land a dream job. I know you will."

"But what if I don't? What if me coming here puts my family in worse debt? What if I can't get that dream job and have to settle for less?"

"I don't see you as being the type of woman to settle for less, and I don't see you sitting around waiting for things to fall into your lap. I see you making things happen."

This time, he put a smile on her face. "It's nice to have someone believe in you."

"I believe in you, Laronde."

The smile hadn't left her lips. "So, your turn. What mistake have you made lately?" She figured that he had a lot on his mind. After all, she was always preoccupied with her studies, and her side jobs, and Xavier had the weight of his businesses, the disagreement with Tobias, and the new contract to juggle. She especially sensed that the friction between him and his brother might be a big part of it.

"Is it the argument with Tobias?" she asked.

"That hasn't helped."

"Family and work can be the worst combinations."

"The worst," he replied, agreeing. Then, "Have you thought any more about when you could go away? That is, if you still want to come to The Hamptons."

"Maybe around the end of February," she replied. She'd go sooner, if she could, but college was full on.

"End of Feb. That's a good time."

"It will be here sooner than we know it." Maybe she needed to let him know the thing he had once been curious about.

She sat back, and contemplated telling him. He'd dropped so many hints along the way, and she never gave up the name, but if they were starting something new, she wanted to get the dirt off her chest.

"That guy, the one I worked for in the summer. The creep…"

He sat up, even under the faint light of the streetlamps she could tell his face was somber.

"I want to tell you, because I don't want it to be a thing between us, getting in the way."

"Go on,"

And then she told him how it started, how that first time she'd caught her former employer staring down the front of her blouse while she had been on her hands and knees picking up pasta shapes from the floor.

"But I wasn't sure," she said, at the end.

"You weren't sure?"

"It's hard to explain. It's like I didn't want it to be true. I thought maybe I was imagining it. So I tried to push the thought away."

"Even though he'd been staring down your blouse?" Something in his tone told her he was already pissed.

"Yes. Like I said, you don't want it to be true, so you give the guy the benefit of the doubt. But then it happened again, a few weeks later." And she told him about that second occasion when her employer's wife was away, and the children were playing in their play room, and she was tidying up, and he walked by, having looked like he'd just stepped out of the shower. He had been toweling himself dry and was completely naked, his belly hanging out like an enlarged balloon.

"Son of a bitch," hissed Xavier. "What did he say?"

"He said, 'Ah, Isabel, I didn't see you there,' and he stood there, facing me, showing me everything."

"What did you do?"

"I turned around, looked the other way and I told him to leave."

It hadn't registered until much later that it was late afternoon, and the master bedroom was at the opposite end of the apartment. He had apologized, saying something about the heat being too much, but his sudden shocking nude appearance had been like a punch to her gut. She couldn't breathe, or think, or do anything until long after he had left. She'd rushed to the door, and jammed herself against it, only coming out when the children shouted out for her.

"He had a hard-on," she said, the memory filling her mind with disgust.

"Did you tell anyone?"

"It took me a few days to tell Cara."

"And that was when you left?"

"No. Not then." Telling him, hearing herself explain, it sounded ludicrous that she had stayed on, even then.

"I left a few weeks later. We came back from the park, and the children had been playing in the sand pit, so their clothes were sprinkled with sand. I showered them, and took their dirty clothes to the laundry room and again, it was at a time when Cassia, his wife, was away. And ..." She paused, uneasy with having to dredge up that memory again.

"And what?"

"And I was putting the clothes into the machine, so I didn't hear him walk in. But he came up behind me and grabbed my breast, and pressed himself into me."

"The fucker."

"And I froze, because... because you just do, I suppose. You can't believe this is happening, and I froze for a few seconds. And then his hand reached down and grabbed me between my legs. And then I told him to fuck off, but he didn't. He had me pinned against the washing machine in front and him behind. I kind of poked him in the ribs with my elbow, and he moved away. I turned around, but he came for me again, reaching out to touch me. And I lost it. I fought back. Kneed him in his balls, the moment his hand reached for my chest. He was a strong man, six-foot something, and he towered over me, and I was afraid that in that laundry room he could have done anything, and I might not have been able to defend myself. So I kicked him hard, and rushed out. I grabbed my bag, and I ran out of the house, feeling guilty that I hadn't even been able to say bye to the children."

"The fucking scumbag," he raged. Then, leaning forward and cupping her face, he said, "Hey," and thumbed her chin. "He did all that to you, and you're worried you didn't say goodbye to his kids?"

"They're just kids. They don't know why I left. They just know I left without a word."

"They don't know what their fucking father did."

Xavier pressed his forehead against hers, holding her wrist in the palm of his hand. "I wish I could do something to make it better," he said, his words caressing her soul, the way his fingers caressed her wrist.

"I am over that. I've moved on, and now you know."

"Thank you for telling me."

"You might know him, I think."

"I might know him?"

Was she imagining it? His jaw clenched, and a tiny muscle along the side of it twitched again. "He knows someone who was at Tobias's wedding."

"The fucker was at the wedding?"

"Not him," she said. Xavier wasn't listening. "A friend of his."

"Who?"

She exhaled slowly. "That day when Jacob and I were going to the waterfall, and I dragged you along. That guy I was talking to, someone Rothschild, I think."

"Oliver Rothschild?" he growled.

"He's a friend of the creep's, and he recognized me at the wedding, and he thought I still worked for them."

"Who's the creep, Izzy?"

The way he said it made her think twice about telling him. "You're not going to do anything silly, are you? Because that's not why I'm telling you."

"I'm not going to do anything."

"Gideon Shoemoney." The words fell out. "I don't know if you actually know h—"

"Gideon Fucking Shoemoney?"

Her heart missed a beat. Shit. Xavier did know him.

"Jeez." His voice tensed, and he rubbed his forehead.

"Is he a friend of yours?"

"He's no fucking friend of mine."

"Why are you so angry then?"

He leaned forward and cupped her cheek then. "Because I hate what he did you." He seemed miles away. "Rothschild and Shoemoney belong to the same mastermind group that Tobias belongs to. I've been a few times."

"Mastermind group?"

"Don't ask. Those assholes all mix in the same circles."

"They can't all be assholes."

But Xavier didn't seem to have heard her. "I hate that he did that to you. And I'm sorry."

"You don't need to apologize for anything."

"I'm sorry on behalf of all those assholes who think this stuff is okay. I'm not one of those assholes."

She wondered why he'd needed to make that point. "I know, Xavier. I know you're not."

"But you did think I was, at the beginning, didn't you?"

She had to think back, because the guy she had first met was so different to the guy who now sat in the car with her and whose kisses made her toes curl. She'd had him down for being a player, a womanizing jerk who thought women were nothing but sexual objects to be used and abused.

How wrong she had been.

They sat in the car, holding hands, saying nothing. Just like last time, when she had told him about her dad, telling him about Shoemoney had lifted a weight. She felt lighter, almost freer.

"Want me to come in with you?" he asked.

She sighed. "You have a meeting tomorrow, remember." And somehow, talking about that incident had turned her mood somber.

"Don't worry about the meeting. I want to make sure you're okay."

"I'm fine. I've got you." She leaned forward and kissed him on the lips. "And I need to sleep, and so do you."

"You're right," he said, tracing along her cheek with his finger.

"Goodnight."

Chapter 44

Gideon Fucking Shoemoney.

One of Wall Street's finest, Shoemoney and his wife were the wealthy A-list power couple who attended most of New York's society galas.

Xavier wanted to kill the man. Ever since Izzy had told him, he hadn't been able to sleep. Not just because of what she had suffered, but because he was now more conflicted than ever.

The weight of needing to confess hung like a detonator around his neck.

With Valentine's Day just over a week away, the pressure was on. Izzy didn't want to make a big deal of it. She told him she didn't want any fancy dinners, or fancy clubs. She had an accounting test and two case studies to get through in the next few weeks. Valentine's Day wasn't her focus.

And that was fine with him. Except that, as he got to know her better, he knew that she valued honesty and trust, over an expensive box of chocolates. He needed to tell her, so that they could start from a clean slate, but fear of how she would react, kept him silent.

He wrestled between confessing and keeping silent. Izzy would never find out, Luke would never tell her, and their stupid secret would be safe forever, but he didn't feel right keeping this from her. Not after everything she had already confided in him.

It had to be tonight, he decided, walking her back to her apartment. They'd gone out to dinner again, only this time she'd suggested one of her favorite student haunts, a noisy bar downtown. A night of cheap pizza and watered down fizzy drinks. The place was crammed with people, some of whom she knew. But it wasn't conducive to talking, and once again, he'd backed out of his confession.

And now that they were back at her apartment, his intention was to see her in, and tell her something.

But they were already kissing by the time they'd walked in and closed the door. God, no. Kissing her, touching her, being with her drove him to the edge of distraction. She shrugged out of her coat, and with her hands around his neck, and her breasts hard against his chest, started to lead him towards the bedroom.

He resisted the movement. "No."

Surprise filled her eyes as she looked up at him. Hell, no. His defenses were crumbling.

"No?" She bit his lower lip, then sucked it slowly.

He felt himself stiffen. It seemed to be something that happened on contact with this girl. It happened all the time, and it was going to do serious damage to his manhood, him having to jerk off as often as he did.

"Why no?" she asked, provocatively.

He pushed her back, steering her away from the couch, steering her someplace else that might be safe, places they hadn't already made out on.

"I want to talk."

She laughed, throwing her head back, forcing him to stare at her neck and try to resist planting his lips there.

"We've just been talking," she said, lowering her head and looking at him again. His heart was full of so much want for this girl, so much desire, and that, coupled with the feeling of wanting to protect her, make things be good for her, pushed him into an unfamiliar place.

He'd rushed into relationships, some just random dirty encounters with girls he'd barely known for more than a few days. This was new; strolling, not rushing, discovering, not fucking. His need for her was no longer driven by pure lust, but by the desire to know her heart and soul.

She fell back onto the ottoman, and he fell to the floor , looking up at her because he needed to see her face, needed to know what her reaction would be when he told her.

"You want to talk?" she asked, sitting back, her knees up against his chest. "Do you really want to talk, or is this another one of your moves?" With her hands on his shoulders, she leaned forwards and kissed him, and because he could never resist her, he kissed her back.

She shifted closer to him, moving her legs apart, their lips sealed hungrily as his tongue swirled around in her mouth, trying, trying, trying not to get too caught up in her.

Trying and failing miserably.

"Cara?" he said, using the word like a contraceptive.

"Isn't here," she replied, her glistening lips, red and swollen, were giving him ideas.

But his conscience was pressing on him like a giant fist.

Now.

His heart thundered.

He had to tell her, now.

"You surprise me, Stone," she said, when they paused to take a breath. "You're nothing like how I thought you would be."

His hands pressed gently against the sides of her hips. "And you're just like how I thought you would be."

Their foreheads pressed together. "I used to think you were such a hedonistic jerk," she said, in between kisses, "but now I see that I was wrong."

He swallowed, and took her hands in his, his thumbs gently massaging her wrists. "Is that so?" he asked, bracing himself.

"Yes!" Her hot breath skimmed across his cheek. "Are you sure you don't want to take this to the bedroom?"

"Izzy," he said, waiting for her to look at him.

"Yes?" she replied, lifting up her arms and taking off her sweatshirt. She had on a sleeveless t-shirt underneath, and his eyes fell to her toned, naked arms. He dragged his gaze away, making it stay on her face. "I used to be a bit of an asshole, before. You know that, right?"

She put her arms around his neck, swooped close, their faces touching. "I know."

Several times now he had run through that conversation in his head, how he would start it, what he would say. But now, now that he was kneeling on the floor, their faces level, his hands on her wrists, now her scent, and her heat, clouded his thinking. "What?" she asked, suddenly turning serious. "What is it?"

It was on the tip of his tongue. "It's…"

I have something to tell you.

But her sudden change in temperament was like a cold shower to his good intentions. If he told her and she walked, what then?

"It's what you told me, about Shoemoney. Guys like him are sick."

"Yes, they are. Why are you still thinking about him?"

Because in light of what she had told him, and the nights he'd lain in bed thinking about it, how could he now tell her what he had done? What chance did he have of her believing that he had changed his mind soon after placing that ridiculous bet?

Not a chance in hell.

Even he wouldn't believe himself.

"I can't help it. It makes me sick to my stomach, and I know this isn't about me. I'm not making it about me," he insisted, "But I can't get over how it must have been for you."

"I'm over it now. I found a way to channel my anger by going to the Women's March, and knowing I wasn't the only one."

"I remember you talking about it passionately the day after, and now I understand." He kissed her upturned wrists, first one and then the other.

"I don't allow Shoemoney to come into my thoughts, and meeting you has been one of the best things to happen to me in a long time."

Shit.

There was no way he could tell her now. He couldn't risk losing her.

He lowered his face onto her thighs, feeling more conflicted than ever. Her fingers raked through his hair, and he lifted his face. "You mean that?"

"Yes."

The zesty smell of her perfume made him heady, and his hands settled on her thighs as thoughts swirled around his head, making him contemplate, and hesitate, and want her.

Maybe later, once they were at the Hamptons, before they did anything, he would open his heart and confess. And she would see. She would understand.

His fingers snaked up towards the zipper of her jeans.

"What are you doing?" she asked, her voice low and raspy.

"Stand up," he said, looking directly up at her, holding her gaze, and when she obliged, when she stood up slowly, he undid her button, and peeled down her zipper.

Oh," she breathed, biting her lip as he tugged her jeans down a little. "This is what you had in mind."

When she still didn't object, he tugged her jeans all the way down, along with her panties. Right down to her ankles.

"You're hard to resist," he told her, pulling her back down on the ottoman, goosebumps shivering across his back as he pushed her knees apart. His mouth watered to see her glistening folds.

There would be other times for confession.

A quickening started low in her belly, rippling out, spreading like wildfire. She hesitated at first, unsure, yet tingling, her body ready to be pleasured again, like the last time.

"Closer," he said, pulling her towards him. He was seeing her naked again, making her exposed, and open, and ready for him. He wanted this, and she wanted to let him. He had been unnaturally quiet over dinner, and had seemed slightly uneasy just now, setting her on edge with worry. But then he took charge, told her to strip, and she did, because his command spoke directly to her core.

And when he sank his fingers into her wetness, he seemed to relax. He looked up at her, as if wanting to see her reaction while his fingers glided over her slickness. His touch was soft, soft, soft, and oh-so-teasing, and all she could do was fall back onto her elbows, a soft mewl escaping her lips as his fingers and thumbs slid over her soaking folds.

She should have been embarrassed, but she wasn't. He had control of her body, and made her shudder, and moan, as he played with her, pulling and teasing, and gently pinching her soft, wet flesh.

A trail of fire snaked around her, curling along her inner thighs and slowly slithering upwards. She felt herself tensing, her toes curling, and her breasts heavy with want. Until he suddenly stopped, his fingers still, halting the rising crescendo of her wave, controlling the pace of her excitement. "It's not fair," she rasped, "You never let me touch you—"

But she didn't get to finish her words, because in the next moment, he flicked his tongue, and she jerked at the change in texture, from his hard fingers, to his soft, wet mouth.

He licked her then, made her body shake and throb as he dragged his tongue, thick and flat and pressed up against her in slow, deliberate strokes. He started lower, in the heat of her center, and moved up to the tip where he lapped, and teased and sucked her, before moving back down again.

It was dirty, and intoxicating, and she writhed to his touch, clenching and releasing to his tune, in awe of his prowess, and what he could do to her. The intensity between them was raw, and animalistic, and she wanted to give him her all. Give him everything.

He kissed her below, for the longest, most delicious of moments, making her head roll back, because she had never experienced an emotion so deep, and so pure. She groaned, moving her leg to rest over his shoulders, feeling loose, and wet and shameless. He grunted appreciatively, a moan, low and guttural, coming from deep in his throat as he pulled her towards him, his tongue buried deep to the hilt, until it was all him.

She lay back, lifting her hips, pushing herself into his face, losing herself in him, then cried out, clenching her muscles and fisting her hands in his hair.

He came up for air, then, moved his face away and gave her time to breathe, and recover. But not for long. He lowered his head again and sucked her clit hard, and this time he thrust his fingers inside her at the same time. Her cries filled the air and her entire body shook, releasing a surge so powerful, it engulfed her body, mind and soul.

Chapter 45

The following weekend she was back to babysitting Jacob.

But she would never get used to having a bodyguard following her every move. It was eerie, like having a nameless, speechless shadow on her back. She was always relieved when she went home and returned to her own life, without the grandeur that was so evident in Savannah's new life. There was at least a type of freedom which she had never before realized—the freedom to live happily in her cramped little student digs in a neighborhood which turned unsavory under the cover of darkness.

This was better than to live a life shadowed by men who never spoke but would lay down their life for you.

"Do you want another hotdog?" she asked Jacob.

He considered it. Then shook his head. "No, thanks."

"Are you sure?" They'd been ice-skating for over an hour and she was cold and hungry. And she wanted to go home and finish off the big case study that the tutor had dropped on her class two days ago. It had put a halt on Xavier's Valentine's Day ideas. She had already warned him she couldn't come over tomorrow, and on matters of principle, she didn't agree with the jacked up prices at restaurants during Valentine's Day. So they'd agreed to catch a film, then have takeout at his place.

"My mom gets really hungry."

"She's having a baby, Jacob. It's to be expected."

"And," he put his fingers to his lips and glanced over at the bodyguard who was standing away from them. "Can you keep a secret?"

"Are you sure you want to tell me, if it's a secret?" She was going to pretend she didn't know.

"I trust you, and Mommy and Tobias trust you, too. They like you lots."

"That's nice to know."

"That's why mommy only lets you be the one to look after me. You and Rosalee. But Rosalee is always busy these days, and we don't get to see her much 'cos Diego's got a new baby sister now." He made a distasteful face. "Who wants a sister?"

"Sisters can be nice!"

"But brothers are better."

She cocked her head, as if debating. "I don't know. I think it's nice to have a brother or a sister. It's nice to have someone else to play with." And Jacob, she knew, was so ready for a playmate.

"Mommy isn't fat." He looked at her as if it was impossible to keep the news to himself.

"She's not," agreed Izzy, "And that's not a nice word to use, to describe anyone."

"But I didn't say she was fat."

Izzy bit her lip. "No, you didn't."

"It's the baby that's making her fat. I mean, big. And it's not one baby." He held his hand in front of his mouth, secret-spy style. "She's having two babies." He gazed at Izzy, as if waiting for her reaction.

364

"Two babies?" She whispered, looking over her shoulder to see where the bodyguard was.

"That's why she's so fat."

"Jacob! We don't use that word. It's rude."

"But she is!"

"I don't think I'm supposed to know about the babies, Jacob. Isn't this supposed to be a secret?"

"But I'm so excited, I wanted to tell you. I know you won't tell."

She wanted to hug him so tightly for being a kid, for thinking everyone else had his same sense of wonderment and honesty. "Thank you for telling me, Jacob. But you mustn't tell anyone else. Okay?"

"Okay." He bit his lip. "Can I tell you one more thing?"

She could see he was finding it difficult. "Do you need to?"

"It's boys. I'm going to have two brothers."

Her smile spread from ear to ear, not because this was news to her, but because Jacob was so overcome by emotion, his eyes glistened. He held up two little fingers. "Two brothers! We can play piggie in the middle."

"But you have friends to play with, don't you?" she asked, getting concerned.

"I've got lots of friends, but Lenny's my bestest friend, but we don't see each other when I get home from school, and that's the best time to play. So now I can play with my brothers when I come home."

She understood. "That's the best news, Jacob. But, for your own good you mustn't tell anyone else. Understood?"

He nodded.

"Can I tell you one more secret? It isn't techlickly a secret."

"Technically," she corrected him. "Why isn't it a secret?"

"Because you already know."

She tried to hide her smile. "Me?"

"His friend said you were a lucky girl."

"Which friend?"

"The one at the wedding."

She frowned. "At the wedding?" Who, and what was he talking about?

"The one who was always at the bar, at Mommy's wedding."

She had to think for a while. "Do you mean Luke?"

Jacob nodded.

"Luke was talking about me?" Surely not.

"I heard your name."

"My name?" There had to be some mistake. Jacob seemed to be doing a whole heap of eavesdropping lately.

"They said 'Izzy' and his friend called Xavier the Spud Stone."

"The what?" She shook her head as if the words were scratching her brain, as if what Jacob was telling her was crazy, and couldn't possibly make any sense. "The Spud Stone?"

And then she remembered.

Xavier-The-Stud-Stone.

She'd heard that name mentioned on the island, but couldn't remember when. It was Xavier's nickname.

"And Xavier won the bet and he's going to be rich."

"The bet?" The news was like a pick axe through her heart.

"Luke said ten thousand dollars was a lot of money. I've been saving up my birthday and Christmas money, and I've got one hundred and twenty three dollars in my money box, and that's a lot!" Jacob declared proudly.

It couldn't be. Her mind started to wander towards there—to what Xavier was like when she had first met him.

No.

No. He wouldn't do this to her.

Maybe Jacob had heard wrong, and or had misunderstood whatever snippets of conversation he had heard. "That's a lot of money, Jacob. It sounds like some sort of business deal to me." She still hoped this was the case. "Maybe you didn't hear properly."

"I was in the room when they were talking, because I was looking for Iron Man behind the couch."

"So they didn't see you?"

"Nope."

And they had no idea he had overheard.

A ten thousand dollar bet? On her? And it had been Xavier's doing?

The three questions thudded through her like poison-tipped spears, one after the other.

"Xavier's rich!" Jacob declared, happily, unaware of the tsunami of emotions he had unleashed on her unknowingly. "Are you happy I told you?"

She nodded her head weakly, and found herself sinking in the silence that followed, trying to sift through the debris of emotions. "You mustn't mention this to anyone, Jacob. Okay?" She bent down to his level, and placed her hands on his shoulders. "I mean it, Jacob. Don't tell anyone." She was breaking inside, but still aware enough to make sure he wouldn't tell anyone else.

His expression tightened. "I wanted to tell you."

"This is our secret. And you mustn't mention it to anyone, not even Xavier."

She told Jacob that it was time to go home. He wanted to play in the park for longer, but she didn't want to skate, or be here, or talk, or be around anyone.

Everything she had been looking forward to, making plans about their weekend getaway, looking forward to seeing him again—all of that happiness had been stripped away.

He'd screwed her over for a bet.

What a fool she'd been. She'd fallen for his charm, fallen for his lies, and look where it had gotten her. If only she had trusted her gut.

~ ~ ~

She had given him some dates for when they could go away.

A long weekend at the family home in the Hamptons. He would make sure that nobody would be there, and it would be all theirs. He knew she was wondering why he was taking his sweet time.

For Izzy he'd do anything. And he wanted to prove to her that he wasn't the player she had expected him to be.

For now, there was work to be done. He'd sent her an urgent email earlier, asking for the figures back on the spreadsheets he'd sent over a few days ago. Now he needed them back sooner than he had anticipated, and, because he knew she had no tests this week, he chased her up for it, but she hadn't replied to his email.

So he called her, but her phone went to voicemail.

After a second morning of not being able to contact her, he turned up at her apartment.

It was Cara who answered the door.

Something about the dirty look she flung at him, warned him that something wasn't right.

"Is Izzy okay? I can't get a hold of her."

"She's not here."

"Has she gone home?" he asked. Because something odd was going on. "I've emailed her and called her and I can't get through to her."

"She's gone home."

"Something happen to her dad?"

"Her dad?"

He could see Izzy's familiar knapsack lying on the floor. "She's here, isn't she?" he tried to walk through, but Cara stuck her foot in the way. "I need to see her."

"She doesn't want to see you."

What the fuck? "What? Why?"

"She said so."

What the hell was going on? "I need to see her. Please," he begged. "I don't even know what's wrong."

"You slime ball."

Okay. So something definitely was wrong.

"Let me through, otherwise I'm not moving, and you're going to have to stare at my face all day long."

Cara moved out of the way and he could have sworn he heard her mutter a "good luck" as he knocked on Izzy's door.

She didn't answer.

"Izzy," he raised his voice, and knocked. "What's going on?" He knocked again, tried the door handle, but she had bolted the door from inside. "We need to talk. Let me in."

"Go to hell." At least he knew she was in there.

"I will. I promise I'll leave, but you have to tell me what's wrong first. I don't have a goddamn clue."

Before he had time to knock again, the door flung open, and Izzy's angry eyes burned into his.

"What's wrong?" she cried, the rage rising in her voice. "What's wrong is that bet you placed on me. That's what's wrong."

She knew about the bet? How the fuck had she found out?

"You placed a bet on me?" The horrified look on her face hit him like a sledgehammer. "You don't deny it, then?"

His face fell, and with it, his insides. "I can explain," he said, desperate for her to hear him out. He should have told her. He should have come clean sooner. It just looked bad, real bad, and no matter what his intentions were now, they had been indecent before. "Let me explain, Izzy."

"I don't want to hear it. I already know everything I need to know."

His head was spinning in a thousand different directions. "I know it looks bad, but I can explain."

"You don't need to," she screamed. "It's easy enough to understand. You placed a bet on getting me to go out with you, and you bet ten thousand dollars to do that? What kind of an asshole are you? I thought Shoemoney was bad, but you're evil on another scale altogether."

"It's not how it sounds."

"You nasty piece of shit!" she screamed, the words emphasizing her rage more succinctly than her shriek could have. "Is that all I was to you, another pussy?"

He swallowed, knowing now exactly what she thought of him. Knowing he'd gone into the wasteland where he could never come back from. "Please let me in, Izzy. Please give me a chance."

"I don't ever want to see you again!" The whites of her eyes protruded, giving her a hysterical appearance. The devastation he had wreaked on her was written all over her face.

"You should do the decent thing and leave," Cara told him. "You've done enough damage."

"He didn't deny it," Izzy said to her friend. "You said to give him the benefit of the doubt, and I tried to, but he did it. He really did it."

Cara turned on him like an angry twin, giving him a look that could make his insides shrivel. Izzy slammed the door in his face, and he was left standing with an angry best friend to deal with .

"I need to explain," he muttered, more to himself than to anyone.

"You should go. She's hurting, and you being here isn't helping."

"It's not how it seems," he insisted, trying to find a way to explain. It wasn't going to be easy, but he was a different man now.

"I thought you were different," Cara said, pure malice dripping from her voice. "And so did she."

"The bet was off. I didn't even think about it."

Cara laughed cruelly. "The bet was off? The bet was off? You realize you just admitted you placed the bet in the first place, asshole?"

He scrubbed his stubble. No amount of pleading his case was going to make them listen.

"You animal!" Cara sneered. "How could you sink so low and play around with her feelings like that?"

"It was never meant to be like that." Only, it had been. Back then on the island in his drunken state. Hell. There was no way he could absolve himself from this, because the facts were clear cut.

He had made the bet, and had, in the beginning, intended to pursue it. He'd used her, and it didn't matter how long ago it was, or how much he had changed, the fact was he'd been a morally reprehensible shitbag and Izzy deserved better.

It didn't matter how crazy he was about her, or that he hadn't been able to sleep or let himself get close to her until he told her, the fact was, the truth was out there now, and he couldn't retell it.

"Get out," Cara ordered, as he raised his fist to bang on the door again. He contemplated trying to talk to Izzy again, but knew that the wound would be too raw. He would have to try again another time.

"I'm not giving up."

"Asshole," muttered Cara, following him to the door.

Chapter 46

She heard the sound of the front door slamming, and then Cara knocked on her door. "He's gone, Izzy. It's only me."

She opened the door.

"You okay?" Cara asked as Izzy sat back down at her desk. "You're studying?"

"I've got a lot going on."

"Hey." Cara stood behind her and placed her hands on her shoulders. "Do you want to talk about it?"

There wasn't much to talk about. She'd told Cara everything and hadn't left her room since yesterday. It had been difficult, trying to hide her grief from Jacob as Morris drove them back, trying to put on a brave face to Savannah when she returned Jacob home.

She shook her head. "I'm done going over and over it."

It was worse than she imagined. She'd been holding out for the hope that Xavier would say it was all a mistake; that maybe Jacob had gotten his facts wrong, or misheard the conversation.

She had been banking on that.

But his denial never came.

Instead, he had confirmed her worst nightmare.

The bet was real.

A ten thousand dollar bet.

Who in their right mind placed that kind of a bet?

People like these. Filthy, rich, dirty assholes. Like the man who had screwed her father over.

Never in her darkest nightmares had she imagined this would happen to her.

Never.

And what hurt more than Xavier's deception, more than his cunning, more than all those intimate words and private moments they had shared, was that he had been playing her all along.

She had opened her heart up to him and told him everything. He knew things about her family and her father that Cara had no clue about.

How stupid could she have been? How blind, and so easy to dupe?

She had become one of those vacuous airheads, the girls who lost their mind over a guy—the kinds of girls she used to feel sorry for. And now she was one of them, except that she was the main character in her own romance-gone-wrong horror movie.

A tear rolled down her cheek and she wiped it away quickly. She had tried to be brave in front of Cara yesterday when she returned. Hadn't wanted her friend to see how deep the deception had cut. How much it had broken her.

"You look rough, Iz," Cara said, leaning against the wall, facing her. "A good cry will get it all out of your system."

"I'm not going to cry over that asshole."

"That's my girl." Cara smiled.

"I never expected this from him. Even now, when I think about everything he ever said to me—"

Everything he ever did to me.

"I can't get my head around it. He was such a good actor." She would never trust another man again.

"You turned soft in the head, Iz."

Thanks.

She fell for him, and she'd let her guard down. If only she had been strong and stayed as wary of him as she had been on the island, she might not have ended up like this. Now she questioned every single thing—him coming to the apartment that first time when he'd come down to the pool in the basement, and when he'd told Savannah about Jacob's fears about Tobias not loving him. Xavier had commandeered all of that. He'd made it so that she'd lost her job, and opened the way for him to give her more work just so that he could get close to her.

He had done whatever he'd needed, to win the bet. He'd ripped out her heart, her trust, her softness, and he'd made her feel like a commodity.

In the end, there really hadn't been much difference in what Shoemoney had done, to what Xavier had done. Except that Shoemoney hadn't done it for money, he'd done it out of a sense of perversion.

Xavier had done it for fun.

"I gave him a chance."

"He must have been good in bed," Cara chuckled, then retracted. "Sorry, Iz. That was low. I was only trying to make a joke."

The situation was a joke.

Izzy looked up at her friend and confessed. "We never …"

"But that time I walked in."

"We were just kissing."

"Day-um," drawled Cara. "You guys were in such a hot cinch that time, I really thought…" Cara paused, as if she was contemplating something. "It doesn't matter what I thought.

It's probably for the best, Iz, that you didn't give him everything."

That was what their weekend away was supposed to be for. Time away from the city, somewhere nice, somewhere different, Xavier had said. 'Just you, me and a whole lot of getting to know one another.'

Now it was another thing she viewed with suspicion.

And Luke.

Now the visit to The Oasis fell into place. That night she had put it down to paranoia, the way Xavier and Luke had spoken, as if in code, she had noticed it enough to remember it. She hadn't expected Luke to be like that. The guy had seemed decent enough when she'd spoken to him at the island. But then she hadn't known he owned the bar. More than a few bars and clubs, according to Xavier. The guy was loaded.

Typical.

Two filthy rich assholes together were going to be worse than one. She lowered her head, shame burning all over her as she placed a hand over her face.

"Stop it," Cara said, getting up and putting her arms around her. "Don't keep thinking about the past and all the stuff that went on. Let it go. You're going to move on from this, and I'm going to help you."

"I can't help it. Every conversation we ever had, tells me what I so blindly failed to see. It was in my face the whole time. I thought he was changing because he was starting to feel something for me. I thought we were changing together, me giving him a chance, him confiding in me, me confiding in him." The stuff of normal relationships. She had opened up to him because she had believed that he had genuinely cared. "Now I see it for what it really was. An act. And all for the sake of money. My feelings meant nothing to him."

"You weren't to know. So you have to stop beating yourself up about it."

"You're right," she decided, drawing back her shoulders and lifting her head higher. As if she could magically harden her heart and wipe away the hurt and humiliation that now tormented her. "I'm going to stop whining, and I'm going to pick myself up and block him out of my head."

"And what about all the work you do for him?"

"He can stick that up his ass." She still had the babysitting job with Jacob, and, she hoped, more hours once Savannah's pregnancy progressed. Maybe she wouldn't need to go home for the summer, and could afford to stay on here. And if she got an internship for the summer, that would be the best news of all. It would pay well enough that she could stay in New York until the next year started. And that kind of experience would look good on her resume and possibly set her up for the future.

"I can't think about him," she said, massaging her temples. "I can't waste my time on him anymore."

"Chalk it up to experience, Iz. Guys like him are scum."

"I can usually spot scum a mile off. I don't know why I thought he would be different."

It wouldn't be a mistake she would ever make again.

Chapter 47

Valentine's Day was fucked.

Bang, bang, bang.

Workmen in safety overalls and helmets were at the far corner of the room. A handful of guys in safety gear were scattered around the dusty shell of what once used to be a memorabilia store. This was Luke's new project.

Bang, bang, bang.

The sound of a drill, filled the air.

Men shouted at one another.

"What?" Xavier shouted back.

"You shouldn't be in here," Luke shouted, directly into his ear. "It's dangerous without a helmet."

He hadn't exactly come to admire the new work in progress. He moved closer to his friend and shouted in his ear. "I can't hear you. Can we talk elsewhere?"

Luke nodded, then walked outside. Xavier followed. His friend took off his helmet. His face and hair flecked with dust.

Bang, bang, bang.

"Is it always so noisy?" Xavier asked.

"It's under construction, pal. What do you expect?"

"It's a good size," he remarked. "And you've hit the jackpot with the location".

"Yeah, I know," Luke replied, looking pretty smug.

"You're impossible to get a hold of these days, dude." Xavier cast his eye all around the dusty, dirty, demolition site. "But I can see why."

"I've been busy, and I'm going to be wrapped up in this for the next few months."

Great. Just when he needed someone to talk to, his friend was out of bounds. "Do you want to go and get a beer or something?" He needed to offload the shitstorm that was his life now.

"I could do with a couple of beers," said Luke, swiping his hands through his hair. "But I can't today. There's just too much going on." He peered closer. "Why? What brings you here?"

"She found out." His lungs squeezed each time he thought of it. "Izzy found out about the bet."

"She what?" Luke squinted in confusion. The banging continued in the distance, the shouting, the drilling. It didn't seem like the right place to get the kind of advice he was after.

"She found out. She knows, and she hates me for it."

"How the hell did she find out?"

"I have no fucking idea." Xavier let out a heavy breath. "Wasn't you, was it?" he asked, his eyes on Luke's face.

His friend looked at him in disbelief. "You're really asking me?" He shook his head. "I never said anything. You know I wouldn't, right?"

He had never doubted Luke's loyalty, but given that it had only been the two of them, and that Izzy wasn't telepathic, he was stumped.

"I don't know how the fuck she found out, then."

Luke looked confused. "You didn't seem to be getting anywhere pursuing her, and I thought you'd forgotten about it."

"I wasn't getting anywhere, and I did forget about it." Only, between then and now, he'd fallen for her, and the bet had hung over him like a dagger the entire time, something he'd needed to take care of, but had never found the right moment to do so. And now, the dagger had fallen.

"So, what's the problem?"

"Things changed."

"Things changed?"

"I like her."

"So what's the problem?"

"I meant to tell her, but she found out."

Luke's face was a mixture of many things, confusion, surprise, shock and disbelief. "Why did you need to tell her? I wasn't going to tell her. She'd never have known."

"She knows now. It's all blown up."

"I've never known you to not like pretty and sexy, and Izzy seems to be the perfect combination. What made her warm towards you?"

"Stuff," he said, "Maybe she saw my better side." Or maybe, he'd finally met someone he could the drop the façade with.

"You must have done your best to charm her?" Luke suggested, with a grin, that told him his friend knew all about him.

"I didn't play her," he answered, remembering all the times he had tried to hold back. "And what we had wasn't based on trying to get her into bed." A sad smile touched his lips. With Izzy it hadn't been about sex, because they hadn't gone that far, it wasn't about lust, and getting dirty—even though he'd loved doing the things he'd done to her.

"Why are you smiling?" Luke asked, looking confused. "Is this still a game to you?"

"No. No." Fuck, no. That's exactly why he was in this serious shit. He was starting to fall for this girl, and for once it wasn't because of the number of orgasms they'd shared.

He loved her for her heart, and mind, and soul. For her fighting spirit and all the things she believed in. For the things she'd made him see. "I'm crazy about that girl."

"How crazy, exactly?"

"The kind of crazy I've never been."

Luke whistled. "Shit."

"You see my problem? She found out, about everything. About the bet, about the money, and that it was you and me who talked about it."

"She knows I'm implicated?" Luke didn't seem to like that.

His friend's apparent unease gnawed at him. "Tell me you don't have any designs on her?" Because it jolted him, pricked him like a thorn, that it could have been Luke who told Izzy. His newfound suspicion burrowed a hole in his gut, especially when he thought back to all the conversations he'd had with Luke, lately, about who he was seeing.

"You idiot," Luke growled. "I'm not interested in your girl." Xavier looked at him as if he didn't quite believe him. He'd seen them laughing and talking a couple of times, especially early on, when he'd been trying to win Kay over with those cheesy magic tricks.

"You sure?"

"Calm your shit," Luke said, looking annoyed. "I'm not interested in your girl.

Xavier's jaw loosened. "Okay."

"The bet wasn't my idea, pal." Luke reminded him.

He knew. "It was my fucking stupid idea. So now, tell me. How do I get out of this mess?"

"You've tried to explain to her?"

"Yes, I've tried. I've texted and emailed and left long messages on her phone. She won't talk to me."

Luke covered his face with his hand. "I can see why. You were an idiot. It was a crazy thing to do."

"Who's side are you on?"

"On yours, you idiot. I'm just trying to think it through."

"I was drunk. I thought I had something to prove, and I believed she was acting all not interested, and that it was going to be easy to make her see."

"Make her see how awesome you were?"

He cringed inside, and hated his friend for stating the obvious. "I hate hearing you describe me like that."

"Luke?" One of the builders called him over.

Luke put his hand up and spread out five fingers, before turning to him again. "I can't talk. My men need me. But, look. Here's the thing, pal. You have to give her time. You have to stop pestering her. You're going to have to wait for her to come to you, but it depends."

Xavier looked up. "On what?"

"If she was really into you."

"She was."

She had been. He was certain of it. Izzy Laronde wasn't the type of girl to give any guy—no matter how interested he was in her—the time of day.

He should know.

It was what had made him place the bet in the first place. But once he got to know her, once they started to click, once he started to fall for her, she had started to feel something for him. She wasn't the type of girl to let a guy like him into her deepest and innermost places, but she had.

Something had changed between them.

"Then you have to give her time to find her way back."

One of his guys came up to him again. "We need you to take a look at this wall now."

"I'm coming." Luke turned to him. "Sorry. I need to go. Now's not a good time."

"I appreciate it."

"We'll get together, sometime."

"Yeah. You call me. I'm not as busy as you."

He walked back to his car and climbed in, pinching the bridge of his nose hard. He'd gotten himself into this mess, and he was going to get himself out of it.

It all depended on what stage of hating him Izzy was at.

Time, Luke had said.

Give her time.

Knowing how long it had taken him to get her to trust him, he was prepared for the long haul, because he understood how much he'd hurt her. With all he knew about her and her family, and the things she had been through, what he had done must have crushed her to pieces. The thought killed him, and he decided to do what it took to win her back.

His phone rang, just then, and his heart leapt, as it did each time, in case it was Izzy.

Fuck.

It was Tobias.

"Why the fuck has Matthias left me a message congratulating me on the twins? How the hell would he know?"

His first reaction was denial, quickly followed by anger. "I don't know. Why the fuck are you asking me?"

Tobias was pissed. More than pissed. He hadn't shouted. He hadn't expressed rage. He sounded normal, and that was how Xavier knew, his brother was more than pissed.

"I told you the news was a secret. It was meant to stay within the family."

383

"I haven't told anyone."

"The fuck you haven't."

"I haven't."

Tobias hung up.

Xavier punched the steering wheel. Then again, a second time.

He didn't need Tobias's shit right now.

Chapter 48

The weeks crawled by miserably, and the air of gloom that hung around her didn't lighten.

College and her studies kept her busy, as did her jobs on the side. Savannah had asked her to babysit Jacob a few times lately, which was a good thing because she no longer worked for Xavier.

It had taken one short email to let Xavier know she couldn't work for him any longer, and to her surprise he had accepted her reason and told her he understood. In the beginning, he had sent her emails and messages, had even left long, rambling voicemails for her when she refused to answer his calls. But she had purposely ignored all his attempts to get in touch.

She didn't want to hear more excuses and lies. She didn't want to be duped again.

A consequence of severing all her ties to him was that she missed the extra money, and what she had earned from him was a generous amount. His work had been simple enough to do, and she had been hoping to ditch the online courses guy whose work demands were getting ridiculous. She would go weeks without anything from him, and then he would want a heap of stuff done within a day or two. She'd had to pull all-nighters a few times in order to get his work done. It had been hard, and her studies had suffered, and the man was a pig. Demanding and rude. She'd been hoping to ditch him, but with Xavier's work gone, her choices were limited.

There were times when she now looked back and examined everything Xavier had given her, and wondered if he had ever really needed any of the reports and charts which she had put together for him. He'd owned up to his little lie about the bar charts, and now she questioned everything he'd ever told her about his VAs. It drove the knife deeper, to know how much he had conned his way into getting her to work for him.

This weekend she was taking Jacob out for the day again. A movie and some pizza, Savannah had said. She made her way to the Upper East Side once more and hoped she wouldn't run into Xavier.

Everything about looking after Jacob was linked to Xavier in some small way, and it was painful, trying to erase him from her mind when there were snippets of conversation, or reminders of him everywhere. Looking after Jacob meant having a continual link to Xavier.

She'd had a text earlier from Savannah telling her that she would be in the pool. Relieved to not have to wait in the apartment, she made her way downstairs and sat on one of the recliners by the pool.

Savannah finished swimming her length and climbed out of the water, smiling when she saw her. Izzy stared at her curvy figure, and at the baby bump which was now so noticeable.

"I must have been in the water longer than I thought," said Savannah, grabbing a towel and sitting.

"No, it's me. I'm early," Izzy explained. "I had to escape my over-excited roommate."

Savannah looked at her expectantly. "Escape?"

She explained that Cara was going away with friends to Cancun, and how she didn't want to.

"Why didn't you want to go?"

Because she was feeling miserable and preferred not to be surrounded by a group of happy people. It was the weekend she would have been free to go to The Hamptons, with Xavier, only she'd never gotten around to telling him.

"I wanted to stay behind and study," she told Savannah, instead.

"You're a bright girl, Izzy. You need to take a break sometimes, have fun, and not be cooped up inside all the time."

"I'm having a break today," she replied. "Jacob and I are going to be out all day, and we're going to have fun."

"Jacob's looking forward to it. He said there's a new Marvel movie out." She put the towel on her lap. "Is it me, or is there always a new Marvel movie coming out?"

Izzy grinned. "It's not you. There's always a Marvel movie coming out."

"At least it will keep Jacob entertained, and I need him to be busy, especially now that we are finally going to be moving."

"You're finally moving?" She'd heard Savannah talking about the new place Tobias had bought, and how he seemed to be getting carried away with its refurbishment.

"It should be done by Easter time, I hope." Savannah made a groaning sound. "I need it done by then, because..." she rubbed her swollen belly. "I'm going to have to start preparing for the birth."

"You'll have your hands doubly full." The news about the twins had broken recently in the press, angering both Savannah and Tobias in the process.

"And I thought last year was crazy."

Izzy didn't want to imagine what sort of a crazy life Savannah now led. "Don't worry about me," she said, making herself comfortable on the recliner. "You go ahead and finish off your pool lengths. I'll wait." Easier to wait down here, where there was no danger of Xavier turning up.

"I think you might be waiting longer than planned. Tobias called to say they got sidetracked. He took Jacob out on the scooter this morning, but somehow they've ended up in a Ferrari showroom.

"I can see how that might happen," replied Izzy. Knowing Tobias, it was completely understandable."

"Jacob's fascinated by Xavier's car."

Izzy nodded. Her mouth tightening at the sound of his name.

"Tobias took to heart what you and Xavier had said, about Jacob feeling left out. We've both been making a real fuss of him ever since. Has Jacob said anything else to you?" Savannah asked.

"No. He seems pretty happy to me these days."

"Tobias loves Jacob as his own, even I can see it, but I know my boy, and I know what he's been through. I know he's afraid of losing Tobias's love, and that's simply not the case, but it can be so hard trying to make a child see that."

"Yes, it is, but you've done all the right things," Izzy replied, hoping to reassure Savannah.

"Unfortunately, Tobias doesn't always get things right."

"No?"

"I mean, with Xavier."

Another jab at another mention of his name. "No, he doesn't," she replied, carefully, forcing herself to think about the topic at hand, and not what had happened between the two of them.

She thought back to the things Xavier had told her, and of the way Tobias often placed the blame on him. "I used to feel sorry for Xavier."

Savannah peered at her. "Used to?"

She brushed her bangs out of the way. "I—I ..."

She wasn't sure how much Savannah knew. Wasn't sure how much Xavier would have told them, and wasn't sure, now that she thought about it, that there had been anything worth telling in the first place. "I don't work for him anymore."

"Oh," said Savannah in a voice which indicated total surprise. "I know he was going to find you some work. I hadn't realized you were still doing it."

"I did some work for him, before," she replied. There had been nothing seedy in it, but it felt suddenly felt clandestine. "He gave me a few hours here and there, but I stopped a few weeks ago." She turned away, and coughed. She still had his MacBook Pro and had been meaning to drop it back to him.

It was a daily, constant reminder of him, lying in her bedroom, on one of her bookshelves. She no longer used it, and had reverted back to her slow and clunky laptop in the hopes of forgetting him and putting him out of her head, and her heart.

Because she had her weak moments, now that the initial burst of rage had passed, and in those moments lay the reminders of what they had once shared, of what she had started to feel for him. It went beyond the lust, and the way he made her feel, physically, and emotionally, and all the other ways in between.

She dared, in those moments, to think there might have been something between them.

"A few weeks ago?" Savannah asked, in a way that indicated there was more to the question.

Izzy nodded.

"This is news to me," confessed Savannah.

"It's old news now, and not as exciting as your news. Jacob is so excited, he can't stop talking about the twins. How are you doing?"

"Nervous, excited, ecstatic." Savannah's eyes glistened. "As for Tobias, he's been more guarded. I would even go so far as to say that's he's been more grumpy lately, and that's because there's a lot going on that I'm not always privy to. He's annoyed that the twins news broke before we were ready."

"I don't blame him." Izzy had seen firsthand how intensely private Tobias was about personal matters.

"He tries to shield me from most things," said Savannah, stroking her stomach, "but he also has an annoying tendency to go inward. And while I understand his anger over the news breaking, I think he's taking the whole argument with Xavier too far."

"They had another argument?"

Savannah looked puzzled. "Another one? I can't keep track. They're talking now, though. They argued recently about the twin's news being leaked. Xavier owned up and apologized, saying he might have—in his excitement—mentioned something to someone during a meeting, and that was how word got out."

"That's what he told you?"

"That's what he told Tobias, and he apologized and they made up. You know what men are like. They're hardly going to go out for a coffee and talk things over. I like it when things are calm, when there are no arguments. His parents do as well."

"His parents got involved?"

"Millicent, his mother, was a mess," Savannah recalled. "I knew something was wrong when she turned up here not wearing pearls, or a Chanel number."

Izzy let out a smile. That sounded like Xavier's mother, from what she remembered of her. She couldn't imagine what it would be like having someone like Millicent Stone as a mother-in-law.

From what Savannah had told her, she seemed to handle her just fine. "She turned up here because the boys were arguing?" Izzy asked.

"She wanted me to fix it."

"How?"

"You tell me. I had no idea, especially since, at that time I had no idea that Xavier had accidentally spilled the news about the twins."

Izzy jolted to attention. This didn't sound right. This wasn't what had happened. And Xavier had taken the blame for something he didn't do, and she couldn't sit by and say nothing.

"Xavier didn't tell anyone about the twins."

Savannah's eyes narrowed. "How do you know?"

"Because ..." Izzy took a deep breath, knowing that what she had were only suspicions. "He's covering up for someone he wants to protect."

Savannah let out a choked laugh. "I don't understand. We only told family, his and mine. I hadn't even told you."

"It's not me he's protecting."

Savannah blinked, and those green irises stared back at her, making her hesitate. Some mothers couldn't take the discovery that their children might have done something wrong, even by accident. Even though Izzy had a feeling that Savannah wasn't one of those women, it didn't make telling her any easier.

391

"Then who?"

"I suspect it might have been Jacob, but I don't think he would have done it intentionally."

"Jacob?"

Izzy could tell this was the last thing she'd expected to hear. "Please don't be mad at him," she urged. "I don't know what happened when Jacob was growing up, but I can tell that he gets scared easily. He doesn't like shouting and swearing, and—"

"And any kind of confrontation," Savannah finished the sentence for her, and nodded her head, agreeing. "I won't get mad at him. I hardly ever do, but, I'm surprised." And then her features relaxed. "Though I should have known better. Keeping this a secret must have been impossible, given how ecstatic he's been."

"He didn't tell us. He let it slip once when we were at the fairground."

"The fairground?" Savannah asked, "When you and Xavier took him?" She gave Izzy a peculiar look, as if she was slowly piecing things together.

"Then you'll recall he came home with those two huge plush monkeys?"

Savannah nodded.

"Jacob wanted to win them. He wanted identical cuddly toys, and we didn't understand it until he let it slip. He didn't say it outright, but he let it slip and then he stopped himself. I didn't tell anyone, and I know Xavier wouldn't have. We barely discussed it in all the time we were together. I mean, in all the time I worked for him." Heat rushed to her cheeks, and she looked down, making herself focus on her cell phone in order to avoid looking at Savannah.

"I can believe it," Savannah said, in the silence that followed. "He wouldn't be able to keep something like that in, at least not with people he felt so comfortable with."

Izzy lifted her face. "So, you see. I don't think any of this news being leaked was Xavier's doing. Xavier looks up to Tobias, he thinks the world of him, at least, that's the impression I get."

"I've seen that as well." Savannah rubbed her forehead. "Xavier's lying to protect Jacob."

Izzy nodded. "If Jacob let it slip to me and Xavier that easily, he might also have let it slip to one of his friends at school."

"Lenny," Savannah murmured, placing her hand flat on her forehead. "Julia mentioned something once, and my bump wasn't even showing that much. I think you might be right. Once it gets out in the school, I have enough school moms who wouldn't think twice about letting the news out."

"We still don't know for sure, and I would hate for Jacob to get in trouble."

"Tobias would never shout at Jacob, but maybe we expected too much, thinking he could keep the secret. I should have known the excitement of twins, and boys at that, would be too much for him to contain."

"I didn't want Xavier to get the blame for something he hadn't done."

"You still care for him." Savannah stated, not asking, or probing.

"I believe in doing the right thing."

Chapter 49

He'd waited weeks, and if he wasn't careful the coming weeks would stretch into months, and he couldn't sit around doing nothing.

He was going to have it out with her, especially since he knew exactly where she was going to be and with whom—courtesy of Savannah. He'd been surprised when his sister-in-law had called him earlier, telling him that it had been admirable, him taking the hit about the twins' news leaking out. That in itself had surprised him but he had been even more amazed to learn that Izzy had been the one who had told her.

"Leave it to me," Savannah had said, "I'll make sure that Tobias knows he owes you an apology." And right after that she'd let slip exactly how Jacob was spending the day, from the movie he was going to watch, to the new burger place he liked to go to.

It might be his only chance to get a hold of Izzy and try to apologize. He wasn't going to give up until she'd heard his side of the story. And, even as bad as it looked, she should give him a chance to explain.

Of course, knowing the right people at the burger place had its advantages, and a bodyguard walking in with a woman and a young child, were easy enough to notice.

He was at NYB about five minutes after Izzy and Jacob arrived there.

"Well, look who it isn't?" he said, trying to look surprised as he walked past their table.

"Xavier!" Jacob lifted his hand and got ready for Xavier's high-five. "You missed the movie!"

"Was it any good?" he asked.

"It was awesome!"

"I obviously need to see it."

"You should have come with us," Jacob cried.

"I didn't know you were going." His attention moved over to Izzy and he could see that his sudden appearance had left her shell-shocked. "Hey," he said softly.

"Hi."

"We're having burgers," Jacob informed him. "Can you have lunch with us?"

Xavier waited to see the reaction on Izzy's face. Stone cold. She looked uncomfortable. Perhaps this hadn't been as great an idea as he'd initially thought. Not that he had exactly decided on his plan of attack. He had simply seen it as his one opportunity to get to Izzy, and having Jacob be there seemed like a plus.

"I'm not sure, kid. I don't think it's a good idea. I don't think Izzy wants me to."

She scowled at him, understandably so, given that he'd made her out to be the bad cop.

"Don't you have other plans?" she asked. "Surely you didn't walk in here for no reason?"

"I come here for lunch sometimes." It was true, he occasionally did.

Her face seemed to harden, as she surveyed the menu.

"Izzy, can we talk?" He sat down next to her, and noted that she moved away.

"About what?" she replied, as sharply as she dared.

Out of the corner of his eye he could feel Jacob staring at him. He'd been counting on this, on having Jacob there, so that it would be difficult for her to walk away. So that she might be forced to stay put and hear him out.

"About things."

"I think we're done with all of that. Do you know what you're having, Jacob?" She smiled as she said it, but the tone of her voice didn't match her bright smile.

"I'm not sure," Jacob replied, looking slightly uneasy, as he started to look through the menu.

"Izzy, please." He was begging. It was something he never did, but he could, for her. He would beg until she listened.

She let out a breath and turned to him in irritation. "We've got nothing to say to one another," she hissed, keeping her voice low. He could see her jaw tighten, could imagine her grounding down on those molars, getting into another one of her pissy moods.

"But I've got a lot to say to you."

"I'm not interested. I'm really not."

"I know you hate me," he whispered the words quietly, and peeked at Jacob who seemed to be hiding behind a huge menu. "I would hate me too, but at least give me the chance to explain, because you might hate me less, and I'll take that over you hating me so much you can't bear to look at me."

She ground out a sigh. "It's not wise to have this conversation here. Some ears pick up everything" she said, cryptically.

She was right. He looked over at Jacob, and at the large menu covering his face, and knew of the boy's superpower to absorb information like a sponge.

"They do some excellent salad here, Jacob," he said, hoping to convince the boy. "Over there by the salad bar. Why don't you go and get some, dude?"

"I hate salad." Jacob made a face.

"But it's too good for you. Even Iron Man likes salad."

"No he doesn't!" Jacob protested. He rubbed his hand over his face, stole a glance at Izzy hoping she might help, but she didn't even look at him. She obviously wasn't going to make this easy.

"If you have some salad, maybe Izzy will let you have ice-cream later. You can make your own, remember, like last time?"

"Izzy always lets me have ice-cream, and I don't even have to have salad to get it."

"Don't you want to set a good example to your brothers?"

"That's low," he heard Izzy say.

"Don't you want to be a role model for them?"

Jacob looked thoughtful. "Okaaaaay," he said, slowly. "I'll try the salad."

"Great move." Izzy got up to go with him, but he grabbed her arm. "The bodyguard's going. Let the kid try it alone. I can see him from here."

Izzy pried her arm away from him, but didn't sit back. "This is you all over. You're despicable. You've proved that you're a manipulative asshole who thinks he can treat people like dirt. You made a seven year old go and do something, not because you care about him but because you want to speak to me."

"I care about Jacob, and I care about you. I'm in love with you Izzy. I didn't expect to fall for you, but I have." He'd said it, not out of desperation, or as a way to manipulate her, but because he was speaking the truth. He was falling for her.

The fact that her skin seemed to turn pink, gave him hope. She stayed silent, but at least he'd managed to get a reaction out of her—even if it was hate, right now.

He could work with that.

He would show her that he had changed, and that he wasn't the same loser who had made the bet. The very thing that had cost him her.

"You wouldn't know the meaning of the word," she said, sitting back stiffly. She grabbed a menu and held it up so that it half-covered her face.

"You stood up for me," he said, remembering "You told Savannah about Jacob spilling the news about the twins. Why did you do that?" It had to be because she cared about him.

"I hate lies, and mistruths, and deception."

He swallowed. "Thank you for doing that."

"There's nothing you can say to me now that will ever change the way I think about you." She turned to him with her dark, angry eyes. "I had an idea you were a jerk, way before the wedding, and I can see now that my initial impression of you was the right one."

He clasped his hands together. "I can be stupid, and I made a grave error of judgement, and I know you won't believe me, but I forgot all about that stupid bet soon after I started to get to know you. And I'll tell you when that was," he said, seeing that he had her attention now, "It was a couple of times after we started hanging out. That's all it took, Izzy. A couple of times."

"You're a liar. You even took me to your friend's bar and paraded me."

"I didn't parade you."

"You made me think you were taking me out to celebrate getting that investment."

"I was."

"I don't believe you, and I don't trust you, and I never will. Children don't lie. They tell things as they hear them, and they tell them in the context in which they hear them. They tell it like it is. You placed a bet with your friend for a stupid amount of money, and you placed it over what?" She leaned towards him, baring her teeth. "Did you collect?"

"Collect?"

"Your money. Your ten thousand dollars. Did you get it?" Her lips pressed together tightly. "What did you bet on? Was it to take me out a couple times and get to first base? Or second? Was it to get me into bed?"

He didn't know what to say, hadn't thought that she would ask him. How foolish and unprepared he'd been, to think she would quietly listen to all he had to say without asking him any hard questions.

"Was that it?" she asked, her voice lifting as if she had made that connection. She blinked fast a couple of times, her face a mirage of disappointment, her eyes seeing right through him. "I thought you might have changed, might have become the kind of man a girl like me could be with. How wrong could I have been? Under all that bling, behind that Ferrari, and your businesses, and your super-trendy apartment, you're nothing but a loser."

Her words were like heat-seeking missiles, shooting straight into his core. "You're right. What you see is a façade, most of the time. You stripped that away, and you made me see not just myself differently, but other people, and other things. You shamed me and made me hold a mirror up to my face and see the real me. I'm not proud of my actions, but I swear to you, I forgot about the bet. All I wanted was to get to know you."

"You're so full of horseshit you can't even smell it."

His brows furrowed together, as she unleashed her anger. "Do you really hate me that much?"

"Do you not feel the hate?" she blazed back, her face contorting in anger. "What must I do? How can I spell it out to you in a way that you will understand?"

He fell silent, unnerved by her venomous words.

Then she asked, "It wasn't real, was it? Any of it."

"It was real—almost all of it. Every kiss, every touch, every word."

"You liar."

"It's true. I tried to tell you. I tried to confess so many times, but I didn't know how to. Each time I tried to say something, I chickened out."

He had no way of convincing her, and he had nothing more to say, except, "Why do you think I never let us go any further? Why do you think I always left and never stayed over? I'd told myself that I had to come clean before we went away, but I couldn't, and I regret the way it happened, how you found out because I didn't have the balls to tell you myself first."

She looked at him in disbelief, but she was listening. He moved as close to her as he dared. "Why do you think I never let you do anything for me?" he asked, lowering his voice. "Do you think I never wanted to make love to you? Do you have any idea how many times I had to walk away with aching blue balls, because I couldn't let myself go further until I had told you?"

Her eyes widened, those dark, dark irises suddenly shiny. Her lips parted, slightly.

"If I was such a jerk, if the bet mattered, ask yourself why I didn't fuck you and leave?"

She let out a short, sharp breath, then swallowed, hardness creeping into her face once more. "Because this was a game to you, and you were taking your time playing it," she hissed, taking him by complete surprise. "You're the type of guy people like me hate, and you're no better than Shoemoney.

He couldn't believe his ears. "I'm nothing like Shoemoney." He wasn't. She had told him he wasn't. She'd said it before.

"I made a mistake, Izzy. I was drunk, and I made a stupid bet with Luke, and I will live to regret it, but in some ways I don't, because that stupid bet is what led me to you. I don't think you would have even noticed me if we'd met any other way."

She laughed. "You're so pathetic. Anyone else would have admitted their mistake and left it at that. You, you have to go one step further and justify it, like you did just now. Like Shoemoney did, because his wife was away and he was lonely." She shook her head, as if the idea that she had ever gotten together with him was too much to bear.

Fuck.

There was no salvaging anything from this. "Please give me a chance, and I will make you see."

"You have no regard for people, or their feelings. You treat women like objects, and the only difference between you and Shoemoney is that he hides behind his wife and family, and you hide behind the Stone family name. People only talk to you and give you the time of day because you are Tobias Stone's brother."

It was like a whip to his face. Sharp enough to draw blood.

"I'm not perfect, I'm not my brother, and I never will be. I'm me, and I make mistakes, and I've been an asshole, and an idiot for more times than I care to remember, but you make me want to reach for the stars. You make me want to be someone else, someone better."

"People like you ruin other people's lives over silly games. My life is better because you're not in it."

That hurt.

He couldn't change her mind, or make her see, and the truth of it was, if someone had done to him what he'd done to her, neither would he.

"I got salad," said Jacob, returning to the table.

Xavier forced himself to smile, even as the echoes of Izzy's words whirled around his head. "That's good, kid. That's really good. Hey," he stood up. "I have to be someplace else." He didn't even look at Izzy.

"Aww," said Jacob, looking and sounding disappointed. "Why can't you stay here?"

"I've got plans. Sorry. But you guys have fun, okay?"

He high-fived Jacob and left.

Chapter 50

He locked himself away, stayed in his apartment, and worked. Stayed busy. Hired two new virtual assistants, too. And tried to forget the things Izzy had said to him.

Weeks passed.

He ventured out one Sunday. The Stones were having lunch at The Four Seasons and his mother had told him he'd better be there, or else.

And so he had turned up, and made small talk.

But he'd almost choked when Tobias had casually mentioned that the guy sitting a few tables away was Gideon Shoemoney.

Seeing the douchebag sitting at a table with men in suits had unleashed a tidal wave of anger in him and he didn't give a shit if the guy was in a business meeting or with friends.

Rage bubbled up inside him like a hot spring. He couldn't sit by and do nothing, which was why he'd gotten up and walked over.

"Gideon?" he asked, not blinking when the guy turned to him and smiled. It was then that he threw the glass of wine at his face.

"That's for a friend you molested. You dirty, filthy, slimy piece of shit." He leaned over, until his face was barely two inches away, and the man flinched as if he was scared shitless, before expressing outrage. One, two, three expletives followed.

"Keep your dirty paws off of your au-pairs, old man," Xavier threatened, "Or else."

The mouths of the other men on the table fell open, and Shoemoney turned silent. His face had turned red, and Xavier wasn't sure if it was the wine or his outrage. Red streaks ran down his face and shirt, and two servers rushed over to him to help wipe up the spill.

He walked calmly back to his table and continued with his lunch as the commotion a few tables away raged on.

"What the fu—" Tobias had started to say, glaring at him over the table.

His mother's cocktail glass halted in mid-air. "Xavier, what on earth is wrong with you?"

"Son?" his father asked.

Jacob's mouth had remained fixed in an O.

"Son," his father said, again. "Have you lost your goddamn mind?"

"Language, dad," Tobias cautioned, his face dark, his mouth twisting. It was entertaining, seeing his brother try to resist the urge to explode.

Only Savannah eyed him silently. She had that look about her. The one where she made no judgement, but knew there was more to tell.

"Eat up, kid." Xavier told Jacob. "I won't apologize for that." He pointed his knife at Shoemoney's table. The head waiter approached. "Is everything alright, Sir?" he asked.

"Everything is perfectly fine," he replied. Nobody would ever dare tell a Stone to leave. When Xavier next turned to look, Shoemoney had left, but his guests were still digging into their meal.

"It had better be good," Tobias said, sipping his wine, and glaring at him. "Your explanation."

"You'll understand."

He knew Tobias would.

~ ~ ~

He stepped out into the busy sidewalk and decided to walk back to his apartment instead of jumping into a taxi.

Walking was good. It cleared his mind, helped him to think. Except when his cell phone rang. He pulled it out of his jacket pocket and his fingers hovered over the button when Tobias's name appeared on the caller ID.

He was surprised his brother had lasted a day. Now he wasn't sure whether to accept the call or send it to voicemail. He answered, bracing himself.

"How's it going?" Tobias asked, a simple enough question, but one which left him wondering what he was walking into.

"Good," he replied, wondering why Tobias was so calm and hadn't uttered an expletive yet. Or maybe this was the calm before the Stone eruption?

"Need to talk to you. Are you free to meet up? I can come by if you're at home."

Free to meet up? His brother hadn't yet made any accusations, or apportioned any blame, or made assumptions. This didn't sound like Tobias at all. Dare he risk it? "I can come by your office," Xavier suggested. "I've come out of a meeting, and I'm a couple of blocks away."

"Come by."

And so he did.

Tobias had a relaxed look about him, and he was actually smiling at him as Xavier walked in, so much so that he was tempted to ask him if he was feeling alright.

"Everything okay with Savannah and Jacob?" he asked, sitting down across the desk.

"Everything is fine." Tobias got up from his desk, and gazed out of his floor-to-ceiling windows. "Do you know why I like being so high up here?"

"Because you like to feel like a king?"

His brother issued a rare smile. "Because it gives me a bird's eye view of things."

"Oh-kaaaay," he said slowly, and wondered if he ought to call Savannah and ask what the hell had happened to Tobias, because clearly, something had.

His brother gave him a sidelong glance. "I need to remember that, because it's easy for me to get so caught up in the minutiae of business that I don't see the bigger picture. And that means, I don't have clarity."

What the fuck was he going on about? "What—" Xavier paused, and struggled to find the words. "are you saying?" he asked, slowly.

Tobias turned away from the window and stood facing him. "I'm sorry for blaming you. I know you didn't leak the news about the twins."

Jeez. This wasn't even about the Shoemoney incident. An apology from the almighty Tobias. He'd expected that Savannah would tell him at some point, but he'd never held out for an apology. He'd have been lucky to receive an acknowledgement via text, but this, an apology, and in person. "Savannah told you."

"You should have said something," Tobias continued

"I didn't want Jacob to get into trouble."

"I know. That's what Savannah told me. He would never have gotten into trouble." Tobias walked over to him and perched on the corner of the desk. "Do I come across as a monster?"

Xavier blinked. "Uh—" He was caught in a serious dilemma, should he tell the ugly truth or make up a pretty lie?

"The truth, Xavier. I want the truth."

"Can you handle the truth?"

His brother raised an eyebrow, and swallowed. "Yes."

"I find you intimidating at the best of times, and I'm a twenty-seven year old guy. Can you imagine how you might come across to that kid?"

"I love that boy. I've never raised my voice at him, I never would. He can't do any wrong in my eyes, not only because I'm biased, but because that's the kind of child he is, because of the way Savannah raised him."

"Sometimes you don't even have to open your mouth, Tobias. You have a look about you that could turn people to stone, if you had any supernatural powers."

"I'm working on fixing that."

"Marrying Savannah was a start."

"It was. I'm going to adopt Jacob, before the twins are born."

"You are?"

"Would have done it sooner, but his damn father was hard to track down."

"Nice."

"And," Tobias's face darkened. "I'm sorry for coming down on you like a ton of bricks, about that whole Matthias situation, about him being a partner in that company with Hennessy. I didn't tell you about what happened between us, and it was wrong of me to take it out on you."

"I've pulled out of the contract."

"You did what?"

"I pulled out."

"But you needed it. You said he had contacts and the infrastructure you needed in China."

"I can find someone else." It would take a while, and it would set back production, but it made sense. He felt it had been the right decision.

"But you'd already signed contracts."

"Doesn't matter. I told Hennessy that it wasn't the right fit for me." That was the meeting he'd come from, and he had given some vague but believable reasons for backing out of the deal.

Tobias looked surprised. "Why did you back out?"

"Because of you. Something had obviously gone down between you both, and it didn't feel right for me to proceed." He needed the investment, but did he need a pissed off brother to deal with at every turn? This had to have been big, the fall out with Matthias.

"You don't even know what happened," Tobias said.

"I didn't see the point of going into business with someone when you clearly had a problem with the guy's company. I know it had to be something serious, because you still haven't been able to tell me."

"I'll tell you," said Tobias, "I'll tell you when I'm ready to talk about it."

"For the record, I want you to know that I haven't seen Matthias for months, and he wasn't a party to any of the meetings I had with Chad."

"See that," said Tobias, pointing his finger at him, "that's what I mean. I was so wrapped up in the emotion of it all, I didn't even care to see how it affected you. I used to be better at detaching myself from emotions, that's how I built all of this." He gestured around the room. "But things are different now, with Savannah, and Jacob, and the pregnancy. I'm losing my ruthlessness."

Xavier smiled, unable to hold back. "You're becoming more human, bro."

"I think of my family, and it makes me want to tear up with joy. You ever felt that way about someone? That you would give your life for them? And if they hurt, it kills you?"

Hell, yes. He'd come the closest to feeling that depth of emotion about someone, and he'd lost her along with his heart.

"I know how he thinks," said Tobias. "And it wouldn't surprise me if Rust thought that doing a deal with you might be a way to get back in with me."

His thoughts were still wrapped up in Izzy, and Tobias had switched into business mode so fast, he had to force himself to listen. "Yeah?"

"I know how that brain of his works."

Xavier wasn't sure how he felt about that. He had believed Hennessy had invested in him. It made him feel small again, to think that Hennessy and his company would invest in him purely so that Matthias could indirectly find a lifeline to Tobias. "Do you always have to make it about you?"

"How do you mean?"

"Maybe Hennessy wanted to invest in my company," Xavier countered. "It's no corporation, but maybe he wanted to try something risky."

"Stone Enterprises does risky. Why have you never come to me for investment?"

A sharp shock ran through him. He held his brother's gaze. "Because you usually take the piss out of my business ideas."

"I get offers to fund the craziest ventures. You would be surprised."

"You would invest in me?"

"I could do worse."

"Why can't you just say, 'yes' sometimes?" Xavier asked. "Why do you always feel the need to patronize me?"

"Yes," replied his brother. "Maybe I would have said yes a long time ago, if you'd asked me properly."

Tobias was willing to invest in him? He wasn't sure how to take this news. The thought that this might be a temporary glitch in his brother's steely temperament meant he needed to take him up on the offer, and quickly. Getting Tobias to fund his ventures might not be such a crazy idea. And it would be motivation enough to try and double, or triple, his brother's investment.

"I'll consider it. I never considered Stone Enterprises in that way."

"You could do worse. You could go to Matthias Rust, but I'm grateful that you didn't."

"Does Stone Enterprises offer internships?" he asked, suddenly.

"No," Tobias replied, looking puzzled. "We already get hundreds of resumes from Ivy League students."

That was a shame. A company like Tobias's would look good on Izzy's resume. It had been over a month since their break up, and a couple of weeks since he had sought her out at NYB.

He had come away that day feeling broken, wishing he had heeded Luke's advice and had given her more time before he'd sought her out. That had been his mistake. But it didn't mean he stopped caring, and he hadn't stopped thinking about her.

She had gotten under his skin, and burrowed deep into his soul, and trying to forget her was almost impossible.

"Would you ever consider it?" Xavier asked.

"Why?"

"Why not? A lot of companies have internships. It's how they get the best people for their business."

"You have anyone in mind, for this internship?" That curious look on Tobias's face had him wondering if he knew.

"Izzy was going to start looking."

"Izzy," said Tobias, hooking his hands into his trouser pockets. "I didn't know she was looking for an internship."

"She's good. Really good, she's smart, really smart, and quick. She did some work for me a while back."

"I'd heard."

He wondered who had mentioned it to him. It was possible that Izzy might have said something to Savannah, because this thing between them had been relatively new. Only Cara had known.

"She could really do with something like that. She's driven, and she has big ambitions."

Tobias gave him a look that was part confusion, and part interest.

Non-judgmental.

"This have anything to do with the $500-a-bottle wine you threw at Gideon Shoemoney?" he asked, slowly.

"The guy is a pervert," Xavier ground out the words. "A. Sick. Fucking. Pervert."

Tobias looked at him for the longest time, then, glanced at his watch. "You can tell me over a drink, and I'll tell you about Matthias."

"You want to go out for a drink?" Wouldn't Savannah want him home? Didn't he have better things to do?

"Why do you sound so surprised?"

"Because we haven't gone out for a drink since before you got married." And even then it had been to wrap up stuff for the wedding.

"Savannah knew I was going to speak to you today. Trust me," said Tobias, turning his computer off. "This will get me extra points, if she knows we at least had a drink together."

Xavier got up. "You're doing this to score points?"

"I'm doing this because it was long overdue."

Chapter 51

She buzzed up, and when he asked who it was, she paused before answering. It had been nearly a month since she had seen or heard from him, and now she wondered if it was still too soon.

The palpitations in her chest rocketed sky-high.

"It's me. Izzy."

She imagined the look of surprise on his face. "Izzy? Uh—sure. Uh—did you want to come up?" Oh, yes. He was definitely surprised.

"I only came by to return your MacBook."

"Oh, that," he said slowly, as if he was still trying to get to grips with the fact that she was here.

"Can you come down?"

"Sure."

She smoothed down her hair, and waited outside, her heart still beating wildly. A few moments later, the door opened and he strode out, wearing not his lounge pants, but a pair of jeans, and a shirt. It made her wonder if he was busy. Maybe he was entertaining, even though it was late afternoon on a Thursday.

"I didn't mean to interrupt anything."

"You haven't. You didn't. It's just me in my office, working away." That told her how well he knew her, and how well he had anticipated her thinking.

"Here," she said, pulling his MacBook out of her knapsack. "I've been meaning to return this for a long time." She handed it to him. "I'm sorry it's taken so long, but the time never seemed right."

"You could have kept it. I didn't really need for you to return it."

"It's not mine. It belongs to your business."

"I wouldn't have minded."

"I would have."

"Okay." He held onto it with both hands, an uneasy silence prickling the air between them. "How have you been?" he asked, finally.

"Great." She nodded her head, as if to convince herself. Great.

"You look great." He gave her an appreciative nod.

She looked at him and remembered the man she had started to fall for; the one who had turned her contempt for him into mind-blowing orgasms. She tried not to think about those times, but recently, there had been times when she'd found it harder to push it away to the edges of her mind.

Their conversation was stilted, the silences freighted with something. It was strange because she had expected that he might make more of an effort to talk, and he hadn't. Now that she had been babysitting Jacob almost every weekend, she had noted that Xavier had never been there during any of these times, and she wondered if he was purposely avoiding being there because of her.

"Jacob says 'hi'. I told him I was going to see you one day this week," she said.

"Tell him I said hi back."

She had braced herself to be strong, and to not give in or fall for his smooth words—but his lack of any words came as a shock.

"You look good, Izzy," he said, finally, giving her a subdued smile.

"You don't look so bad yourself." He didn't look as if he'd been pining away for her, despite his words at the burger bar, and his pleas for her to hear him out. She wondered if he had moved on, if he had trawled The Oasis and hooked up with someone else already.

"Are you sure you don't want to come in?" he asked.

She shook her head. "Cara's dragging me out to another house party."

"Dragging you out?" A questioning expression spread across his face.

"Yes," she huffed out, thinking of how much she wanted her own time and space, how much she wanted to retreat into her room and stay there, and how much Cara wouldn't let her.

"Doesn't sound to me as if you want to go."

"House-parties are better than the double-dates she keeps forcing me into."

His eyes snapped in her direction. "You're double dating now?"

She winced, just thinking about it. The last two dates had been nothing short of slow torture. She'd been in no mood for a date, let alone going out, but Cara refused to let her mope around in the apartment.

"You?" she asked, because she couldn't help it. He was probably back on the circuit, probably hanging out at The Oasis every evening, probably getting laid frequently.

But he didn't look too happy. That spark in his eyes was gone; the mischievous, cocky smile that often hovered around his lips was gone, too. Here stood a man who seemed to be a shell of the effervescent and flirty guy she'd once known.

"No. I'm still single."

She felt lightness in her chest, the kind that made her feel warm and mushy inside. She forced her mind back to darker places, reminding herself not to forget.

Ten thousand dollars. Don't forget the ten thousand dollar bet.

"What did you do with the money?" she asked, curious to know.

"What?"

"The ten thousand dollars."

He lifted his chin and stared at her, his eyes level and unflinching. "We didn't go through with it. I told you before, I forgot about it soon after I met you."

Don't fall for his lies.

"If I could turn back time, Izzy, if I could go back to the wedding, and that stupid moment, I would."

"Placing a ten thousand dollar bet to get a girl into bed isn't something that normal guys do. I've met a lot of dickheads, but I've never met one as big as you." She hadn't intended to go there. Hadn't intended to reminisce, and jab, and get emotional, and bitter. She had intended to return the MacBook and leave.

But she couldn't help herself.

His mouth turned hard, and it was a giveaway, how the muscles flexed on either side of his jaw. She could see she'd hurt him, that what she'd said had sliced deep, and for a second, maybe two, she regretted it.

It had been like this between them for the longest time. Moments of warm softness, interspersed with searing heat passion. It had been love and hate and all the emotions in between. A shiver rolled through her skin.

Xavier Stone had made her feel. None of the guys Cara tried to pair her up with had even come close.

In the bleakest of moments, sitting in her room, she sometimes went over what he'd told her, about him wanting to confess, and how he couldn't. How he had tried to tell her and had wanted to own up before they went to The Hamptons.

And in those bleakest of moments, she had started to wonder, what if he was telling the truth?

"I'm not stupid, Izzy. I'm just a guy who's done a lot of stupid things. I've learned my lesson the hard way, and I hate that it cost me you."

Go. Leave now before you start to fall for his words.

"I've learned my lesson, too," she replied, "I should have trusted my gut, and my gut told me to stay away from you the first moment I laid eyes on you at the island."

"I have no regrets about meeting you. Most of the girls I meet are easy, but you weren't, and you were worth the chase. You're smart, and sexy, and gutsy, and I love your soul. I love everything about you."

A small rush of adrenaline spiked inside her—not enough to bring back the happiness she had experienced once-upon-a-time, but enough to lift her mood.

"That's the thing about time. You can't go back. You have to learn to live with your mistakes." It was all she could think to say, to protect herself, to push herself away, rather than lean in and risk falling for his charm all over again.

"You should go, then," he said. "You don't want to be late for your double-date."

He didn't smile, and neither did she.

She gripped the shoulder strap of her knapsack tightly. "It was cool, what you did, taking the blame for Jacob like that."

"Why did you tell Savannah?"

"It wasn't right, you taking the blame like that."

"It wasn't a big deal. Tobias gets into a rage over his privacy, and he hates the media. I couldn't have Jacob take the heat."

"Tobias wouldn't have said anything to Jacob."

"In case you hadn't noticed, he doesn't have to say anything to scare the hell out of anyone." He shrugged. "It was no biggie."

"I told Savannah because I wanted her to explain to Jacob, because he's got to be even more careful now. He's not in a normal family… being so rich, being in the limelight. He's going to have to watch what he says, more than most young kids ever will."

"You did the right thing." He smiled at her. "You always do the right thing, Izzy. That's why you were so good for me."

Don't. Don't. Don't listen.

"One more thing," he said, lifting his head, fixing her with his gaze. "I want you to know that I never intended for Savannah to take away your hours, that time after they came back from the honeymoon. I only told her what you had told me, about Jacob feeling left out, because I saw with my own eyes how much Tobias loves that kid. But I also know, because I've experienced it first hand, what my brother can be like. He's had to harden, to deal with the stuff that happened to him before, but his hardness is the thing that makes others think he doesn't care. I don't want Jacob to experience that. And, I really did think you had already told Savannah. I never intended on being the one to break that news to her."

"But it worked out so well, didn't it? Her laying me off, and you conveniently stepping in to offer me work?"

"I use a lot of virtual assistants, I told you. I didn't lie about any of that."

What did it matter. It was too late now. "I heard you threw a glass of wine at Shoemoney."

He nodded but said nothing.

"Thank you."

"You don't have to thank me for standing up for you. I met a girl once who told me that it's worth standing up for something you believe in. She told me that it was worth speaking out when something is wrong."

She was touched that he had remembered. It might have been the way his eyes turned shiny, or the way his mouth twisted before he said, "I can't get it out of my head, what he did to you."

It made her heart stop. She hadn't realized until now how much it had eaten into him. "It's done. It's over." It doesn't affect you.

"I swear I wanted to kill him."

"Please don't. I'd hate to feel responsible for his death."

They were jesting; playing with words, but neither one of them was smiling.

"It was probably childish of me to throw the wine at him. I would have gladly used my fist, but they might have thrown me out, and I didn't want to cause too big a scene, not with all my family sitting there. The press would have a field day."

She swallowed.

The more she stared into his eyes, the more she was near him, the more it made her want to believe he had changed. But she couldn't trust him again. She couldn't.

"I should go," she told him.

"Rushing for your double date?"

She looked up to find his dark blue irises pinned on her. "Something like that. 'Bye, Stone." She forced herself to forget, as she walked away. There was no need to remember what had once passed between them.

~ ~ ~

When a girl like that walked away, and it was his heart that twitched and not his dick, he knew he had let a good thing go. This had to be a monumental fuck up compared to all the other fuck ups he'd ever made in his life.

A girl like Izzy was rare.

He wouldn't have found her in a place like The Oasis.

And even though he didn't want to go looking all over again, he had to accept that she was gone.

Chapter 52

Her heart sank when she walked into the apartment and heard the radio on. Cara wandered out of her room with her hairbrush in her hand.

Izzy blinked in annoyance. A house party in Brooklyn, no thanks. She had texted Cara to say she didn't want to go, and had purposely taken her time getting back, hoping that Cara would have left without her. "What are you still doing here?" she asked, placing her knapsack on the floor. "Didn't you get my text?"

Cara ran the brush through her hair. "I did, but I ignored it. I won't have you sitting at home again, moping. I told them I was running late."

By them, Izzy assumed Cara's boyfriend and some of their friends.

"But you are going?" She was desperate to have the apartment to herself.

"Once you tell me how it went."

She wished now that she hadn't told Cara she was returning the MacBook.

"I gave him back his MacBook, and that was it."

421

"That was it?" Cara remarked, looking at her as if she didn't believe her. "And now you don't want to come out with us tonight."

"I don't feel like it."

"You were happy enough to come along before."

Izzy let out an exasperated sigh. "I didn't want to, but you always make me feel guilty, especially when you look at me like that." Izzy nodded her head at her friend.

"Like what?"

"Like you are now."

Cara folded her arms. "I'm sick of seeing you locked up in your room."

"I've had lots of homework to do."

"But you never feel like doing anything these days. You don't want to go out, unless I drag you. You don't want to meet friends. You go to college and you come back."

Izzy stared at her friend, and as much as she loved her, she didn't need this level of questioning and guilt-tripping, and concern. Not after the rollercoaster of her meeting with Xavier earlier.

At the time, she had been in the moment, hadn't had a chance to contemplate each and every thing he said. But on the way back, sitting in the clackety subway car, surrounded by a sea of disinterested people, she had been alone with her thoughts. She had dissected every single word, and sentence, and every look Xavier had given her.

The rush of that encounter had sunk deep into every pore, and even now, she could feel his presence as sharply as if he was standing next to her. She had come away with a piece of Xavier hard wired into her brain.

"I wish you'd stop breathing down my back."

"Breathing down your back? What happened? What did he say?"

She didn't reply.

Cara walked towards her, pointing the hairbrush at her. "You still have feelings for him, don't you?"

"No. No, I don't. I don't." She didn't, but she was starting to wonder about all the things he'd said to her in the past, in his defense.

"You can try and convince yourself you don't, but I can see right through you, Iz."

"I'm in shock because I haven't seen him for a while, that's all."

"You're in shock because you're not over him. I knew you were lying."

Izzy grabbed a cushion and sat down on the couch in silence.

"What happened?" Cara insisted, moving closer. "What did you guys talk about?"

Izzy hugged the cushion closer to her, and shrugged.

Cara was relentless. "Great. So you're not going to tell me. What about Shoemoney? Why did he throw the wine at him?"

She looked up. "He said it made him mad when he saw him, and he couldn't help himself."

Cara sat down beside her. "It made him mad?"

She recounted the conversation, having already gone over it in her head for what must have been the twentieth time in the past hour. Over the past few weeks, as her anger had started to die down, and was replaced by a sense of sadness, she had been left with memories pushed so far away, she had to make an effort to recall them.

"He said he wanted to kill him, and he would have punched him, but he didn't want a scene."

"Fan me down with a million feathers," said Cara, flapping the hairbrush in front of her. "I wish I had a guy who was that crazy about me."

She lifted her head. "He's not crazy about me. It's guilt that he's feeling."

"Or, you could be completely wrong," said Cara, exaggerating her words, "and he could be crazy about you."

Cara was a fool who romanticized everything. "I can't forget what he did. That would be stupid. That would be me thinking with my heart instead of my head."

"You need to do more feeling, and less thinking, Iz, because logic doesn't have the feels. Logic is cold, hard facts, and it misses what the heart instinctively knows."

"You hopeless romantic."

"You sad, miserable pragmatist."

But she had been thinking, and she'd remembered those days, those moments, those slices of time they had spent together. The times they had kissed, and he'd held her in is arms, his body hard, his face a picture of torture, as she'd run her hands over him, and he would stop her from getting carried away.

There's no rush, is there? He'd say.

She'd thought that he was quite the romantic, and so different from the womanizing asshole.

"How many times does that man have to tell you he's sorry? Sounds to me as if he knows that what he did was stupid and he's trying to get that through to you. We all make mistakes, Izzy. Why can't you get over your high morals and forgive him?"

"Once a jerk, always a jerk."

She was surrounded by jerks, it seemed. Even the guy on the last double date had tried to cop a feel at the cinema until she had 'accidentally' poured her popcorn all over him.

Xavier had never tried to cop a feel accidentally, and he'd gotten his own form of revenge back on Shoemoney, no matter how small, he had stood up for her. She tried to imagine being at the restaurant surrounded by his family, by that formidable mother of his, and Tobias, and to have had the guts to get up and do what he did.

Tobias must have hit the roof.

"I'd really like to be alone, Cara. Please. Can't you go out and leave me?"

The muscles around Cara's face tightened. "I'm not convinced you're over him."

"I am."

"I don't believe you."

"You don't have to. We weren't together for that long."

"You spent a long time in the friend zone," countered Cara.

"We spent more time in the war zone," she replied, remembering how things had been early on.

"I'm not leaving until you make a choice."

"What?" she cried. What sort of choice?

"Prove that you're over him. Come out with us tonight, or text him."

"Text him?" she shrieked, in horror. "Why?" Cara was being totally unreasonable. She shook her head. "I will not."

"Not what?"

"I will not text him."

"So you're coming to the house party? Great, because I've got the perfect guy for you. He's going to be there tonight, and I know you'll—"

"I'm not coming to the party either, and you won't hook me up with anyone."

Cara clasped her hands to her hips not unlike a Marvel super hero. "I swear to god I'm not moving from here until you make a decision either way."

"Then you can stay there all night."

"And I'll tell everyone to come over, and we'll have a party here instead," Cara threatened.

Izzy's nostrils flared in defiance. She hadn't realized that her friend could be as stubborn as she was. "You wouldn't dare."

"Try me. I will not have you sitting at your desk when you don't even have exams at the moment!"

Izzy ground her teeth together. "If I text him now, you promise to get lost?"

"Gladly."

Izzy threw her a vicious stare, before stomping over to her knapsack.

"I want to see what you write," said Cara.

Izzy pulled out her cell phone and stabbed the keypad. "There," she said, shoving her cell phone in Cara's smiling face.

Thanks

Cara's gaze flickered upwards. "It's not much, but it's something. Well done."

She spun around on her heels, rushed into her bedroom, came out seconds later with her jacket and rushed towards the door.

"Don't wait up."

~ ~ ~

Thanks

He nearly fell off his treadmill when her text came in.

Thanks

He stopped the machine, and read the message a couple of times as it slowly came to a halt.

Thanks

What did she mean by that?

Wiping his face, he got off the treadmill and walked around as the sweat trickled down his back and face, and he reread the one word.

Thanks

She might have texted him by mistake. It was a sobering thought. But then again, it might have been her reaching out.

Getting in touch.

Making contact.

Being vague, and not trying to make it mean anything.

It could be any number of a thousand fucking things.

He walked over to the windows and looked out at the park. Most days he could see kids playing, and people walking, some with dogs, some without.

Today, it had to be a couple sitting on one of the benches kissing like they didn't have a room to rent by the hour.

What he wouldn't give to be one half of that couple.

What he wouldn't give to be sitting on that bench with Izzy.

What he wouldn't give to do things right.

He turned away and looked at her message again.

Should he reply?

Or wait?

Ask her if she had texted him by mistake?

Not ask her anything at all?

Should he thank her?

Try to be funny?
Or sensible?
Or what?
He should wait. At the very least, he would wait.

He held out for twenty-three minutes before sending back a smiley face emoji. And then he felt down when she didn't send a message back.

The next morning he checked his cell phone before he even got out of bed. She still hadn't replied. So he texted back:

For what? It was great to see you again

She didn't text at all for the next few days. He checked every five minutes. Found himself getting a dopamine hit each time his cell phone pinged with a notification, and then came down from his high whenever it was a message from one of his VAs, or his friends.

It was a text message from Izzy a week later, that slowly got things rolling.

I have an interview for a summer internship at Stone Enterprises

He was smiling when he replied back:

Congrats real happy for you
You deserve it

And he was back to checking his notifications every five minutes after that, going on that emotional rollercoaster ride of hearing from her and forcing himself to wait before replying. When she didn't reply, he waited an entire day before asking the question which had been eating at him for a week, he asked, her:

How was your double date?

Her reply came back, not so instantaneously:

Not so good

Smiling, he wrote back:

There are some real jerks out there, you need to be selective

I'm extremely selective now

He asked:
You are?

She replied:
To the point of not dating at all

He liked her answer, and typed:
I hope I didn't put you off men altogether, Laronde

To which she replied:
You don't have that much of an impact in my life, Stone

His face fell at the harshness, and the finality of her words, and then, in the next moment, when she sent him a smiley face, his spirits soared. She was joking. The meaning of the written word, especially when it came to things like texting and email, was difficult to gauge at times, but in the flick of a second, she'd shown him that she had the ability to control his moods.

He tried to make sure his texts were friendly, and sensible, with no hint of anything. It was like starting over, finding out about one another, and trying not to flirt.

The light conversation continued, one liners mostly, nothing heavy, or long, but enough.

A bridge, a stepping stone, a pathway.

A way back to her, he hoped.

They continued like this for a week or so, until the texts became longer, and soon she switched to emailing him, because, she said, it was easier for her to email during study time, than texting which took longer.

It was progress of sorts.

And soon, it became a long slow month of progress, but in the right direction.

One day, as he left the Stone Enterprises building after a meeting with Tobias to discuss his investment, he stepped out into the street and saw Izzy coming out of the revolving doors, just behind him. Knowing the date she had her interview with the accounting department, a minor detail which Tobias had casually passed on to him, had helped.

They stared at one another in a combination of surprise and shock, and then she explained that she had just completed her second interview for her internship, and had just been told that she had been accepted. She would begin as soon as college ended for the summer.

"I got this thanks to you," she said.

"I had nothing to do with it. This is Tobias's company."

"That's odd," she said, giving him a pointed stare. "Because I actually called up HR months ago and asked about internship programs, and they told me they didn't run them. I even sent them my resume, asking for summer work, months ago, but they turned me down because there were stronger applicants than me."

"That's interesting."

"I thought so, especially when Tobias asked me to apply for a new internship program the company was running. What are the chances of that?"

"That is interesting."

"And they've accepted me," she said, smiling for the first time in a long, long time. Her smile reached inside him, filling him with her obvious joy.

"You must have dazzled them with your brains."

"I dazzled them with something, but something tells me this was your doing."

He looked at her, not giving anything away, but feeling good that he had done something that would help her.

"Thanks," she said, unable to stop smiling. She looked happy, and because she was happy, it made him happy.

They stood looking at one another, but smiling, for a change. It had been the longest time since they had exchanged a smile, and a look like that.

It didn't seem as if they were strangers, and it didn't seem as if they had had a falling out, because their recent communication had given them a new springboard to launch from. Things felt not-so-odd, this time. She'd grown her hair longer, and it suited her, her bangs framing her face like that.

"Had any good veggie food lately?" she asked.

"Not lately. But… " He cleared his throat. "I heard about a new place opening on a few blocks from here."

"Oh, what place?"

"I can't remember what it's called," he confessed.

"Hmm."

"If you ever want to try it, you should go."

"But you don't remember what it's called," she pointed out.

"It's uh—Benito, or Venito or something like that." He scratched the side of his face, trying to remember, but the name wouldn't come to mind.

"I'm kind of hungry now."

Her admission caught him by surprise. "You are?" It seemed the obvious question, and yet he had to think twice before he asked it. "We could try it out now, if you want." He held his breath.

"Now?"

"You said you were hungry."

And that was how it had started. A lunch, and conversation, and getting to know one another all over again.

Nothing like the old days, but good.

Good enough.

A week later, another lunch date, followed by dinner a few days after that. Nothing like the old days, though. The conversation was always light, always.

One weekend, they took Jacob to the park. As Jacob raced around on his scooter, Xavier thanked her, for letting him come with them.

"I thought about what you said," she told him, "And I want to believe you. This is me believing you, so don't ever deceive me again."

"Never," he'd told her.

A few days later they somehow ended up holding hands while he walked her back to her apartment, and Cara looked at him as if he'd won a trophy.

And then a week later, a kiss. Not the sizzling making out sessions of before, but slower, cautious, measured moves, but Izzy Laronde had a way of giving him a hard on that most girls gave him being fully naked. She could do that with something as simple as a kiss.

"I wanted to believe you, and now I do," she'd said. "I remember how you wouldn't let me touch you, and I found it odd."

"It's true," he told her. "All of it. I didn't want to go too far with you not knowing. I wanted us to start with a clean slate. But everything we did, came from here." He'd held her entwined hand to his heart.

And after that, the kissing progressed rapidly and reached scorched earth levels at warp speed.

So when, one night, as they sat in the car and kissed, and she asked him what had happened to the weekend in The Hamptons, he had to ask her a couple of times if she was sure she still wanted to go.

Because he wasn't sure what she was asking, and he didn't want to risk taking anything for granted.

"I'm willing for us to have a second chance," she'd said.

Chapter 53

The Stone mansion in the Hamptons wasn't so big as to be imposing, or impersonal.

She liked the look of it from the moment she climbed out of Xavier's Ferrari. According to him the shingle-style house with its eight bedrooms, and ten bathrooms was a five minute walk from the beach, and a short drive from the quaint town center.

"There's nice places around here," he told her. "Some nice restaurants, and bars we can go to."

Different to New York. She could already tell that the pace of life here was slow, and calmer. Exactly what they needed.

She had taken the chance on him, and things between them were almost back on track, back to how they had been before they had split. Everything about him, everything she had learned as they rediscovered one another again had made her believe they had a chance to salvage what they'd once had.

But even though they had both been looking forward to this weekend, each of them seeing it as the chance to spend much needed time away, she had noticed that Xavier had seemed quiet. He seemed more guarded, more careful with his words, and his touch.

Sometimes she missed the old Xavier. She missed his raw manliness, his assured cockiness, and the swagger that was so him.

They hadn't bothered to unpack, but he had given her a quick tour of the house, "So that you can get your bearings," and then, they had gone out for a walk along the beach. The sand here wasn't as powdery and as white as the sand on Kawaya, but darker, and dense, packed together, so that it stuck in clumps as they walked along the shore.

It was while they were walking along on the beach, that he took her hand, and, like always, she let him, then pressed her fingers in a little more, getting used to the feel of his warm flesh.

Every now and then he would turn at her and smile, as if he needed to know everything was fine, that she was okay. That they were okay.

"You don't have to look so scared," she said.

"I'm not scared."

"You seem different, sometimes."

"I'm trying to be a better version of me."

"I don't want a better version. I want you, the guy I was getting to know, once upon a time."

"You want him back?" he asked, stopping and looking at her, "The cocky, arrogant, asshole?"

She tilted her head, as if deciding. "Yes, maybe lose the arrogance and the asshole-ness, though."

She had scared him, and it had been for good reason. He'd hurt her, and at least now he seemed to understand how much.

Only, she sensed that they were going to be okay, because she trusted him, and she believed him, and because she had always believed that actions spoke louder than words. It had been the thing that made her repel his advances before, seeing him in action on the island, seeing the way he worked. No amount of his words back then could have convinced her that he was a nice guy hiding in a wolf's clothing.

But, ever since she'd started looking after Jacob, ever since she'd started working for him, it was the things he'd done for her that shone the brightest. The small things that had mattered.

And even later, after their break, he hadn't stopped doing those little things that mattered for her. And so, she knew they were going to be fine.

Because when a guy who wasn't with you, who knew you hated him, still did the smallest things to make your life better, that was a guy you couldn't let walk away so easily.

That was a guy who had earned himself a second chance.

She tugged at his hand, as her heels dug into the sand, and he pulled back, and stopped.

His eyes asked 'what', but his lips said nothing.

"I want you to know that I get it. I get what you did and why, and I believe that you're sorry. And I know we already discussed all this before, but I just want you to know one more time."

"Okay."

"Because I don't want you to be here with me and still be worried."

"Do I really look that worried?"

"You look that worried," she echoed.

"I never used to care much, how girls felt," he said, "But you mattered to me. I care about you, and I don't want to risk messing this up again."

"I know."

He opened his mouth, and she placed her finger against his lips. "I know, so let's stop it, and enjoy being here."

"Okay."

He stepped away, his eyes glistening, his shoulders relaxing down, as if a huge weight had been taken away.

They hadn't come here to play volleyball, or admire the sights, although there would be time enough to do some of those things, but she had come prepared, and ready, and knew he would not be the one to make the first move.

She'd worn her shorts today, the same frayed-at-the-edges denim shorts she'd worn on the island. His face had brightened when he'd first seen her.

She tugged his hand again. And when he moved forward a little, she tip-toed up, and kissed him, her toes digging into the sand. His mouth was soft, and luscious, and when his hands came around her waist, she slanted her mouth to the side, and deepened their kiss.

"Izzy, Izzy," he murmured, pulling away, his breath hot, and heavy against her face. He lifted her up, and she wrapped her legs around his waist, their bodies pressed together, their mouths airtight, as if nothing could pull them apart.

He set her down again, just as the gentle breeze kissed her almost-bare legs while heat started to rise and roared inside her. "Let's walk down to the end of the beach," he said, pointing to the rocks in the far distance. "I don't know about you, but my legs need a good stretch."

The three hour drive from the city had been hard enough on him, given that she had done her best to run her hands over her legs, getting pleasure in the fact that the sight of her in her shorts was turning him on.

It was refreshing to be outside, and they walked along, talking, her telling him about her and Cara and how, after this weekend, she had to put her head down and study hard. And he told her where he was with his new business, but that he already had an idea to start another business.

From the moment he had picked her up from her apartment, to now, they had spent more time together than at any one time since they had been together. Before, and after. That was how she saw their relationship, the before, being the time up until Jacob had told her of the bet. And the after, being now.

They walked to the far end, remembering Kawaya, and the walk on the beach there, and his Ferragamo loafers, and the waterfall.

"We should get supplies," he suggested, as they walked back, a taste of the salt air in her lungs, and the breeze now getting stronger, whipping her hair this way and that. She rubbed her arms, wishing she'd had the sense to ditch the shorts, and put on her jeans.

"Now?" she asked, as they stepped into the house from the back.

"It's not far," he said, leading her through the hallway and towards the main door.

"We could go into town, grab lunch and load up on a few things. It won't take long."

"Okay," she agreed, standing at the foot of the large wooden staircase while he pulled out his car keys. She rubbed her legs, hoping to wipe away the goosebumps that had sprung up all over.

"You're cold," he said, reaching down and rubbing her legs. His large hands strangely warm on her skin. He rubbed again, "Better?" he asked, stealing a glance at her.

"Better," she replied, feeling a quiver roll through her chest.

He started again, rubbing faster, heating her thighs, and making her shiver, not with cold, this time.

Putting the car keys on the side table, he reached down with his other hand and rubbed both of the legs. His hands weren't only making the goosebumps disappear, they were setting fire to her body.

An ache started, low and heavy in her breasts, as he moved his hands up, and put them around her waist pulling her closer, his mouth falling on hers, and claiming her lips. In a few seconds she was ablaze, running her hands across the tight hard ridges of his back, exploring under his sweatshirt, finding bare skin.

He took her hand and led her upstairs, her skin prickling with anticipation, as he pulled her into the master bedroom.

"Izzy," he breathed, brushing her hair away with one hand, and cupping her face with the other hand, tilting it up towards him before his lips crashed down on hers, in a bruising to-die-for kiss.

He pushed her onto the bed, and she sank into the cool silk sheets, excitement and pure animal lust mixing and coursing through her veins and pumping through her. He stood back, looking at her, his eyes hooded, and dark, standing for a moment, as if wanting to see her, as if waiting and savoring the moment. And then he lifted his arms and took off his sweatshirt, "and the tee," she urged, nodding at the white t-shirt he had on underneath.

"You first," he ordered, and she willingly obliged, sitting up and taking off her sweatshirt, to reveal the lime green bikini she'd worn on the island.

"Fuck," he moaned, his mouth falling open.

"Remember this?" she asked, teasing, as she shimmied out of her shorts, so that he could see the whole ensemble. A sexy trip down memory lane.

She heard him gasp, as she lay there, in her bikini top and matching bottoms.

"Fuck," he said, as she spread her legs, letting him sink between her, his lean body lying over hers. He was hard, and hot against her skin, against her length and everywhere they touched, his chest against her breasts, his hard stomach against her smooth one, his hardness against her hips, his muscled thighs against hers.

"Lime Green Bikini," he breathed, making a strangled noise and planting his face between her breasts, his nose in the crack of her cleavage. With one tug, he pulled down her bikini bottom, while his mouth sucked her nipple over the fabric of her bikini top.

Her brain short-circuited when his hand reached between her legs, and found her slickness. He rubbed his palm against her, making her spread her legs wider.

"Jeez," he moaned, before sliding his tongue into her mouth again, teasing, and swirling, while their hands ran rampant over each other's bodies.

How good this felt, lying, body to body on a super-sized bed, not sitting twisted in a car, trying to avoid a handbrake, no Cara in the room next door, just him and her, panting, and hot, and fully aroused. Her slickness matching his hardness. She trembled, as his kisses deepened and turned urgent, and their hands tugged, and caressed.

She pushed his head away. "Your turn," she gasped, nodding at him. "Take it off." And he did. She watched him roll his t-shirt up and off, and the throbbing between her legs deepened.

His stomach was all hard ridges, and curves and dips, and when he stood between her legs, like a shirtless beast, exuding pure lust, and hunger, she tamed him, and told him to take off the rest.

He bent over, pulling down his boxers, and when he straightened up, she gasped, almost falling back on the bed again, as her eyes fixed on his shaft.

He hadn't been lying when he'd told her he was big.

Her mouth fell open, and she dragged her gaze away to meet his dark-blue irises, their gazes locking as she bit back a moan, desperate to feel him inside her.

"No," she said, when he fell to his knees, his hands on her thighs. He looked up, his gaze questioning, his hand stilling. It wasn't his tongue she longed for this time, it was his hardness she was most desperate for.

"I need you," she moaned, arching her back, her wetness hot and sticky between her legs. She needed him hard and strong, deep inside her to counter the months of frustration. He reached over, pulling out something from his jeans, allowing her to stare at his naked body. And then she watched as he ripped the foil packet and slid on a condom, almost teasing her as he slowly rolled it over his full length. She bit back another moan, desperate to have him inside her, her nipples pebbled with anticipation. She wanted his mouth, and his hardness, and him. All of him. Now. Joined to her completely.

"I'll be gentle," he promised, lowering himself down over her, his body hot, and smooth as he connected with her. His mouth nipping and teasing, and kissing her face and neck. She was naked, now, except for the bikini top, and when she reached behind to undo it, he stopped her. "Leave it," he urged, kissing her breast, while his free hand caressed her thighs. He touched and stroked her everywhere, her breasts, her inner thighs, her stomach, her hips—everywhere except for her throbbing, heated center. Slow and determined, and taking his time, brushing feather-light fingers below her belly button, teasing her by not touching the very place that screamed out for him.

She bent her legs at the knees, her body arching upwards, as he pushed his hardness to her entrance, and stopped—just for a moment, as their gazes locked, and he could see right

441

into her. She mewled, low and desperate, when his thumb settled over her nub, touching her at last.

A thousand tiny sparks ignited and spread out all over her skin. With his eyes fixed on hers, he began to guide himself inside her, making her gasp and shudder as he filled her slowly, stretching her, as every inch of his beautiful, heated hardness pushed inside.

With his hands buried under her bottom, he pulled her towards him gently, tilting her hips so that he could bury hilt-deep, her soaking softness swallowing him completely. He was engorged to the max, rock-hard like never before, and she moaned, a long, dirty, animal moan, as he slid in.

It was sweet music to his ears.

Izzy beneath him, in that bikini. Izzy, soft, and wet, and tight, her muscles gripping him, pulling him in deeper.

"Don't stop," she rasped, when he stilled, for a moment, watching the beads of sweat above her upper lip, watching her eyes flutter open, then close, each time he slid in, then out, making her feel his length. With his thumb, he rubbed her gently, giving her double the pleasure.

He moved forward, touched her face, made her look at him, their eyes meeting, in this intimate moment. This was him, the real him, a man who wanted nothing more than to do the right thing. A man who would never, if he could help it, hurt her again. "I love you," he said, his gaze burning into hers, unblinking. She opened her mouth, and whimpered, her hips beginning to buck.

He pulled back, then thrust in hard, burying deep again, her lifted hips cradling his full length, before he pulled out, seeing the evidence of her arousal all over him. It excited him, and he thrust into her again, harder than before. In, then out, again, and again, and again, setting up a rhythm, getting faster, pounding her relentlessly as her cries matched his thrusting. It was a tune of sorts—rough and feral.

Her muscles clenched tightly around him each time he sank into her, and her pointed nipples pushed out from under the bikini top. She excited every part of him, igniting his senses with her cries, and her softness, as their lovemaking became faster and more frenetic.

They were an entanglement of legs and arms, her ankles around his waist, squeezing tight while her fingers dug deep into his back.

As her body trembled and vibrated to his touch, and her face turned pink, he could feel the pressure building up inside him. When her mouth fell open, a drop of sweat fell from his forehead onto her face, and she burst around him, tensing and jerking, her name on his lips, seductive and intimate.

He rammed into her one last time, burying deep, as he reached for her hand, entwining his and hers together, before exploding; the pent-up frustration melting as he emptied inside her, grunting out his final release.

She moaned and fluttered beneath him, and he, completely bereft of energy, squeezed her hand one final time, before falling onto his back, alongside her.

This was what happened after months of living like a monk; after months of getting to know her, months of waiting, and dreaming, and wondering.

They lay panting, and silent, with only the sound of their heavy breaths filling the air.

He reached for the box of tissues by the bedside, cleaned up then turned to look at her. Her flushed face and shiny eyes stared back.

"That was beautiful," she said, still breathless, still panting, her chest lifting and lowering. "Worth the wait."

"Was it?" He needed to know.

"Yes, oh, yes, yes yes," she murmured, arching her back lazily.

"I promise not to make you wait so long next time."

"I promise not to allow you to take so long next time."

She shuffled closer to him, forcing him to lie on his back. He opened his arms, and let her snuggle against his chest before putting his arm around her. Then, he held her close, her warm, soft body melding with his.

He could fall asleep like this, with her in his arms, and when he awoke, he could lie here happily, and be content forever.

In a world where fake happiness could be bought, where fancy cars, and overpriced watches and jewelry were temporary fixes, the real happiness, he realized, came from things which money could not buy—like creating precious moments, tender and unique, like sharing laughter and kisses with a lover, like finding a soulmate who completed you.

Izzy completed him.

And, he hoped, she felt the same way about him.

Or that she would, given time.

He had so much to tell her; so many ideas and thoughts which he had been contemplating ever since they had started their new journey. Seeds of new plans and loftier goals. Ambitious ventures he wanted to talk to Tobias about, but only once he had run his ideas by Izzy.

Delving into the past, into the circumstances surrounding her father's company going bankrupt, he had discovered the name of the unscrupulous businessman who had been involved. A man who had gone into politics a few years ago, leaving a trail of sex scandals and rumors of arms trafficking in his wake.

It had happened too long ago, for Xavier to find a way to right that wrong, but there was nothing to stop him from making things better.

He was always looking out for new business ideas and opportunities, and he liked the idea of buying premium real estate—like Luke did—but in Pittsburgh, and building luxury condos, because, why not? And if he was able to, and if Izzy's father was interested, he could come on board. The man already had the experience and the know-how.

"What are you thinking?" she asked, looking up at him through her lashes, this woman who had let him back into her life, and who now meant the world to him.

"You really want to know?"

"I really want to know."

And then he remembered what else he had to tell her. There would be a better time to discuss her father, and the future.

"They kicked Shoemoney out of the mastermind group of all those filthy rich businessmen."

Her eyes grew wider, and she propped herself up on one elbow.

"What? When?"

"A few weeks ago, at the last get together. Before they'd even started the first round of golf."

"This was your doing?"

"Tobias's."

"You told him?"

"I had to. I'm sorry."

She didn't look as annoyed as he had feared she might.

"I won't let anyone hurt you again, Izzy. And I don't think it's right for people like that fucktard to get on with their normal lives, and get away with their crimes."

"So, Tobias kicked him out? Can he?"

"Tobias commands a lot of respect in that group, even though he's one of the youngest."

"He can't have been pleased," she said, tracing a circular pattern around his chest. "Shoemoney, I mean."

"Do you care? Because I fucking don't."

"Ssshhh," she said, dropping a kiss on his chest. "You don't have to get so angry."

"I can't help it. Not when it comes to that son of a bitch." He rubbed his thumb over her skin, cupping her shoulder in the palm of his hand. "There were rumors, apparently. Tobias said a couple of the guys there said they'd heard he'd been doing things. That some of the girls had started to tell."

She let out a breath. "I wonder if the au pair ever came back from France."

"I hope for her sake she didn't."

"Maybe it's better that the truth comes out."

"If you ever want to press charges," he said, "I'll be there, by your side."

"I know." She gave him a smile that lit up her eyes.

"You just have to say 'when'."

"I know." She lowered her head and left another soft kiss on his chest.

His hand moved down slowly, sliding over her bikini top, and he rubbed his thumb over her nipple, making it peak almost instantly.

"We have a hot tub outside," he said, the blood was beginning to race through his veins.

"A hot tub?"

He watched her face, could imagine her thoughts soaring, filled with possibilities and ideas. "Or did you want to take a shower first?"

"That's a good idea," she replied, sounding dreamy, as if she was too relaxed to want to even get out of bed.

"Or we could go for a swim."

She looked at him suspiciously. "You have the energy to go swimming now?"

"Who said anything about swimming?"

Her lips spread out into a lazy smile.

"We were supposed to get supplies," he said, remembering. "Are you hungry? Maybe we should get something to eat?"

"I want to do all of those things," she said, sitting up in bed, still wearing the bikini. He reached behind her, and untied it, releasing her breasts. Throwing the flimsy garment to the floor, he sat up, lowered his head to her breast, and suckled her, moaning in appreciation as his manhood shot to attention.

"I thought we were getting out of bed," she murmured, her fingers in his hair, as he moved to the other breast, sucking that as hard, drawing the nipples out into peaks.

"We can do whatever you want." He looked up at her. "Just know that whatever you decide, I'm going to make you come."

"Again?" she breathed, her voice lifting, and unsteady, and her bedroom eyes seductive. "Then listen up," she said, breathing into his face, sending a signal directly to his excitement. "Here's what I want. I want to take a shower, first."

A groan escaped his lips. He saw an image of her standing in the shower, the water spraying onto her back while he was on his knees with his tongue buried deep inside her.

"And then I want to sit in the hot tub."

Ahhhh, the possibilities were endless.

"What about food? Aren't you hungry?" he asked.

"Food after the hot tub."

He would have her bent over the counter top or lying flat over the kitchen table.

"And then a swim."

A midnight swim. He knew how that would end.

One woman, for life.

Nobody else had ever made him feel things in his heart as deeply as this woman had. He squeezed her hand gently, feeling like the luckiest man alive.

What the hell had happened to Xavier-The-Stud-Stone?

Izzy Laronde. That's what.

THE END

I hope you enjoyed *The Bet*, and reading about Xavier and Izzy. The second book in the *Indecent Intentions Series* is *The Hookup* which is Luke's story.

About The Author

Lily Zante is the pseudonym for an author who writes contemporary romance. She lives with her husband and three children somewhere near London, England.

Connect with Me
I love hearing from you – so please don't be shy! Email me, message me on Facebook or connect with me on Twitter:

Website:
http://www.lilyzante.com

Facebook:
https://www.facebook.com/LilyZanteRomanceAuthor

Twitter:
http://twitter.com/lilyzantebooks

Newsletter sign-up:
www.lilyzante.com/newsletter

Email:
lily@lilyzante.com

40214552R00277

Made in the USA
Lexington, KY
27 May 2019